Lies That Bind

Lies That Bind
Copyright ©2006 by Thomas Domenici
Published by Arbor Books

All rights reserved. No part of this book may be reproduced (except for inclusion in reviews), disseminated or utilized in any form or by any means, electronic or mechanical, including photocopying, recording, or in any information storage and retrieval system, or the Internet/World Wide Web without written permission from the author or publisher.

This is a work of fiction. Names, characters, places, and incidents either are the product of the author's imagination or are used fictitiously, and any resemblance to actual persons, living or dead, business establishments, events, or locales is entirely coincidental.

Book design by
Arbor Books, Inc.
19 Spear Road, Suite 202
Ramsey, NJ 07446
www.arborbooks.com

For more information, please contact:
info@arborbooks.com
or
1-877-822-2500

Printed in the United States of America

Lies That Bind
Copyright ©2006 by Thomas Domenici
LCCN: 2005933431
ISBN: 0-9771870-3-9

LIES THAT BIND

by Thomas Domenici

"In three words I can sum up everything I've learned about life: It goes on…" - Robert Frost

"I'm scared that even if I let you in my head you still won't understand me."

Arbor Books, Inc

Acknowledgements

FOR MY MOTHER, ANGELINA, with love and appreciation for all her gracious support, love and understanding.

And for my daughters Jacqueline and Anne Marie, and my grandchildren Jessica, Josephine and Alexander, who bring joy to my life.

And to the memory of my beloved and much missed grandparents, Thomas and Josephine.

I am deeply grateful to several people who have supported me and this book in exceptional ways: Mathew Fagan, my son-in-law and much valued friend, and my daughter Jackie, who suffered through the first and second drafts of this book; Dennis Morrison, Nancy Faranda and Joan Petty who read through the final draft; Robert Singer, Tyler Molinari, and Michael Kasten for their friendship, and for helping me remain physically sound through a long and arduous process; William Righter, for his belief and insistence that I can achieve goals I had thought beyond me, and for a new found friendship. I especially want to thank Kate Gilpin, my editor, for her expertise.

Prologue

EARLIER IN THE DAY he noticed an occasional lightheadedness coupled with shallow breathing and a tingling at the tips of his fingers; anxiety mixed with excitement; the tension of unspoken expectations. He enjoyed a flush that occasionally washed over his body; the throb of secret passions; forbidden desires fueled by vengeance. He spent the daylong drive to their mountain campsite envisioning what he hoped would be yet another success, with his prey sitting innocently in the van beside him. He savored the accompanying feelings of arousal.

He recalled the afternoon he and his marine buddies had left Camp Pendleton to find girls and "score." Although he would not admit it to them, it was the first time he had had intercourse. He called to mind the evening of his wedding. As devout Catholics, he and his wife had vowed chastity until that night. However, neither rivaled the exquisite pangs of anxiety that now were wed to the fictions he created while anticipating what was about to occur.

He welcomed the passage of time; the setting of the sun, the rise of the moon. The day ended, the night was upon them; everyone else was asleep.

He lay there, quietly staring at Chris.

The beauty of innocence.

He was sure Chris must be in a deep sleep. It had been at least an hour since the boy's breathing grew steady. He rolled to his side. His fingers cautiously searched for the zipper on Chris's sleeping bag. Finding the tab, he slowly pulled it down. He again lay back. His breath was quick and shallow; his erection was becoming almost painful.

Timing, it's all in the timing.

Again he rolled to his side, reached over, and carefully uncovered Chris. He was sleeping in the nude.

How often can this work? It's almost too easy.

Adrenaline coursed through his body, making the moment surreal. He had wondered if his excitement was tied to the risks he took, the breaking of a taboo. Or, perhaps, it grew from the anger that was always present. Regardless, these questions no longer troubled him. He had long ago become comfortable thinking of himself as a predator.

The tent provided privacy from the others. He reached for his flashlight, covered its face with his hand, and turned it on. The glow was just enough light for him to gaze upon his soon-to-be thirty-seventh trophy; yes, he was counting. Chris's body was more beautiful than he remembered: tight, smooth, not muscular, but defined: a boy's body newly re-formed by puberty.

Lying back he became aware of his heart pounding in his chest, his clammy hands, and the dryness of his mouth. He turned and stared at Chris's face; his lust turned to rage.

How innocent you look.

The thought of smashing the head of the flashlight into Chris's skull gave him a rush.

How pure your body is, he thought as he glanced at Chris's naked torso. *And how troubled your mind is. But I helped free you from your loneliness. I gave you what you wanted.*

He turned off the flashlight and put it at his side.

Now I take what I want.

He waited and listened to make sure Chris was still sleeping soundly. He reached over, gripped the top of the boy's sleeping bag. and pulled. so that Chris rolled onto his side and faced him. He stirred, but soon relaxed into a deep sleep.

Each move he made was followed by the flush of building excitement. Slowly, but with purpose, he took Chris's hand by the wrist, moved it toward him, and gently laid it upon his throbbing erection. The touch of the boy's hand sent a wave of energy through his body. He sighed. His eyes rolled back in his head as his back arched, he thought he might climax. Again, he waited. Again, Chris did not rouse. After gently manipulating the boy's fingers around his penis, he covered himself with his sleeping bag. Placing his hand on top of Chris's hand to hold it in place, he jostled his victim.

Let the fun begin.

He could feel Chris waking; he felt the tension in Chris's hand as the awareness of what was happening penetrated the boy's waking mind. Chris remained still at first. He could feel the hand gripping his penis, and he knew the boy's mind was struggling to grasp what was happening. Again, stillness. Slowly, the pressure on his erection lessened as Chris began to open his fingers, trying to slip his hand free.

"What the fuck are you doing?" he whispered to Chris, as if he had just awakened.

Chris froze.

Part One: Friday

Chapter One

MOVERS HAD SPENT THE morning unloading my belongings into Adam's house. By afternoon "my stuff"—Adam's words—was put away. While I tied together the collapsed brown cardboard boxes that I stacked according to size, Adam showered, and then primped for the gym. I soon realized he did this almost every day. Eventually, ready to leave, Adam entered the garage, catching me struggling as I pushed a bundle of boxes into the rafters. "Why are you saving boxes?" he asked.

Was it his question, or the way he looked that produced the emotional pulse that set that memory indelibly?

I glanced up at the boxes and wondered why I *was* saving boxes. I returned my gaze to Adam. Did he always dress like this to work out? I took a deep breath; an immediate roiling in my guts accompanied a weakness in my legs. "Just habit," I said.

Adam stood six feet to my five feet ten, and weighed 185 pounds to my 150. He wore a tight black tank top against his tanned, toned torso, and a pair of black Nike spandex workout shorts. He had shaved his face clean and labored every blond hair on his head into place. As he approached me, he opened his arms, and we embraced. How I loved being in his arms. My hands moved across the strength of his back and came to rest on the roundness of his buttocks; his form was sculpted. His hand, which sat at the small of my back, pressed me against him. A haunting, wistful fragrance of summer lime mixed with his own masculine scent filled me as I deeply breathed him in. I knew this was what it felt like to melt into someone's arms. Scents are a powerful aphrodisiac for me, and I felt a stirring. When he pulled away, he said, "Catch ya later, hon."

He looked hot and hungry, but for the first time it occurred to me that the look I was seduced by was not just for me. As he drove away in his black Jeep Laredo, equipped with ski and bicycle racks, I again wondered why I was saving boxes. I glanced up. "Mercury Moving Co." was embossed in large black letters on the side of each box, along with the naked torso of the winged Mercury.

Lies That Bind

Now, two years later and I was waiting for an elevator with two of those same collapsed boxes under my arm. Seldom did a day pass that some memory of Adam did not steal its way into my consciousness. But this moment, this specific memory, the template upon which other memories came to be organized, foretold the rest of our year-long relationship. So, a year later, those same brown cardboard boxes carried my stuff from Adam's house in the Hollywood hills to an apartment in Santa Monica where, for the last year, I had lived alone. And now I was about to make another move, winged Mercury and me.

"Good morning, Dr. Mitchell," Nurse Greene said, as I entered the elevator. "Late breakfast," he added, pointing to his poppyseed bagel. The nursing staff started their day shift at seven in the morning.

"Good morning, Nurse Greene." Ronald Greene was the head nurse on the adolescent psychiatric ward on the sixth floor. We smiled. These formalities between friends, although appropriate and probably necessary at the hospital, always felt awkward to me. Ron and I had developed a friendship over the past year; he helped me piece together my heart after my breakup with Adam.

"You going to the sixth floor?" he asked.

"Yes."

"Boxes," Ron said. He noticed the naked silhouetted torso of Mercury stenciled on the boxes. Raised eyebrows; he smiled. I nodded and returned his smile. I had mixed feelings about leaving, but I knew my decision to move back to New York was the right one.

"Let me get the lock," he said, as we exited the elevator.

"Thank you, Nurse Greene," I answered with a shared smile. Ron is the type of person whose presence always demands notice. This is partially due to his size, but more than that, to his demeanor. Ron was a six foot two 220-pound attractive intelligent gay African-American man who dressed in nurse whites. His strengths, those needed to run an adolescent psychiatric ward, emerged from the tension created between his lighthearted sense of humor and his personal power, clarity, and vigor.

"Do you need help with those boxes?" he asked.

"No, but is there someplace I can store them until I'm ready to pack up my office?"

"Sure," he said, pointing as we walked toward a locked storage closet. "Next Friday's your last day, right?"

"Yeah."

Thomas Domenici

As we entered the nurses' station I asked Ron, "How is Carl this morning?" Carl was a fourteen-year-old patient assigned to me two weeks before, after his failed attempt at hanging himself.

"Just finished breakfast," Ron answered. "I'd say his depression is lifting. He took on three attendants last night," he added, glancing up from one of the charts he was reading. "You certainly lit a fire under his ass. They had to put him in restraints." His gaze returned to the chart. I glanced through the window into the dayroom and noticed Carl staring back. He waved. I wondered if I was doing him any good. "He's not taking your leaving very well," Ron added.

"I'm sure you're right. Did they medicate him?" I asked. I had earned a reputation on the ward as the psychologist who refused to medicate his patients. It was not that I would never use medication with a patient, but if I thought I could get the same result without medication, especially with an adolescent, I preferred to put in the extra time and make the effort. Most of these kids self-medicated anyway.

"No meds, they know he's yours. But I was just looking at his chart. Torrel wrote up orders to start him on anti-depressants today." Dr. Karen Torrel, a psychiatrist, is the ward chief. Typically, she allowed me a week to show progress with a kid, after which we talked about medication; two weeks was exceptional.

"I know. Hold off on the meds, okay? I want to ask her to give him another day and see if he continues to improve," I explained, as I read through the mail in my box. "I'll see him this afternoon."

"She wants to see you," Ron said, pointing to the chart he had been reading. "You've got a new kid, Christopher Bellesano. He came in last night. Torrel tagged him for you," he said, looking at me.

My teeth clenched. I stared at Ron for seconds and then said in a sigh, "Damn it. She must be on glue. I am not going to do it. No, I am not," I said, shaking my head. "I'm just not going to take another patient five days before leaving here. It's not good for the patient, and it's not good for me." I just could not listen to how another kid was abused. I wanted to get away from all this pain and turmoil. I had visions of a warm, sun-drenched beach, twelve-foot breakers and a cool ocean breeze. And me? I would be sitting at the hotel pool, sipping something out of a pineapple and eyeing a lifeguard in his Speedos.

"My, my, the doctor has attitude today," Ron said, doing his very bad imitation of RuPaul. "You know you love this work."

Lies That Bind

"I need a break, a long break."

Ron rolled in his chair across the office toward me. "No, what you need is a good man," he said in a whisper.

"Yeah, and where are all these good men?"

"Robert," he said as we huddled, "I told you there are two very hot psychiatric residents asking about you. 'What's his story?' they ask. One word from me and you'd have more dates than a nut bread." We both laughed.

"Don't start with that again. Anyway, my mind is made up. I'm New York bound."

"Okay, okay," he said, moving back to his desk. "Are you sure you aren't going to do hospital work in New York?"

"I don't think so. Not for a while. I need to take some time off from hospital work. I'm looking forward to teaching again." I had a new position at John Jay College waiting for me. Two years ago, when I had moved from New York I had quit my job at Mount Sinai Hospital, my job teaching at City College in Manhattan, and my small private practice. Adam and I had met a year before at a psychoanalytic conference in New York. After a year of trying to negotiate a long-distance relationship, I had decided to make the move. Why not, I thought. Here was my chance to put physical distance between my parents and me. We had not spoken in nearly eight years. And, in Los Angeles, I could make a new start: a new job, a new city, and best of all, a new love.

"You're too good at this to quit," Ron said. "Except for the fact that no one can read your charting, and the fact that your kids are not to be drugged, and then there's the fact that sometimes you can be a real pain in the ass,' he added and smiled. "Just teasing. The nursing staff loves you."

"Except for all of that," I said, as the phone rang. As I turned to leave, Ron held up his hand. "Yes, Dr. Torrel, he's here now. I'll send him in." Ron glanced at me and smiled as he hung up the phone. "She wants to see you *now*, and she told me to get Mr. Bellesano ready to see you," he said.

I stood there staring into the dayroom, then at Ron. "I don't get her sometimes."

He looked at me and smiled and said, mimicking me, "She must be on glue." He laughed and gave me another RuPaul nod.

We both laughed, "Let's have lunch before I leave. My treat, okay?"

"Casa Rosa?" he suggested.

"Sure." One thing I knew I would miss about Los Angeles was good, spicy, fresh Mexican food. I would also miss some of the staff at Saint Charles Hospital.

Torrel's office was at the other end of the ward. As I made my way there, I rehearsed my refusal. But I knew there was no way that I would not be seeing my new patient. Her door was open, "Dr. Torrel," I called out as I walked into her office.

"Come in, Dr. Mitchell, and close the door behind you," she answered, casting a friendly glance my way. Karen Torrel was a handsome woman of about sixty; a younger version of Nancy Reagan, with warmth and compassion. The contradictory qualities were part of Torrel's charm. She was stylish, sophisticated, and articulate, but down to earth. She was a senior training analyst at a California psychoanalytic institute, and well published in dozens of professional psychoanalytic journals. She had written several seminal books regarding child and adolescent psychology and had an excellent reputation as a therapist. She was also a lesbian.

Karen was reading through an intake report. "My, my, you *are* dressed to impress today," I said, as I closed the door behind me. Even I could hear the edgy tone to my voice.

"Sit down, Bobby. Yes, I'm having lunch with the hospital trustees today," she said, putting down her pen.

"Nurse Greene tells me that you've assigned me a new patient." I anxiously forced a smile. "Karen, I just can't do it."

"Yes, I have, and yes, you can," she said as she glanced up. "I want you on this." She motioned me to be seated. "Bobby, I wouldn't ask if it weren't essential."

Yes, you would, I thought to myself. "I don't think it's a good idea." I hated myself for not just saying no. I had a great deal of respect for Karen. My role as a psychologist on a psychiatric ward had its own set of dynamics. The price for Karen's support was that she never hesitated to ask a favor and she did not expect me to refuse.

"I want this boy off the ward by Monday, absolutely no later than Tuesday. My guess is that he shouldn't have been admitted, but he's here now."

"Kendrell?" Dr. Kendrell was a child and adolescent psychiatrist who worked both on the wards and in admitting. As I took a deep breath, I noticed a subtle fragrance.

"Yes, Kendrell."

"So let Kendrell work with him," I said, feeling my anger intensifying.

Lies That Bind

"Karen, Dr. Torrel, I'm out of here on Friday. I am leaving Los Angeles in three weeks. I need time to close out charts, I have meetings today, I'm on call this weekend and probably will have to come in, and I have packing to do at home. I just don't have the time."

"I want you to work with this boy," she said, removing her glasses and giving me a smile. I knew I was in trouble. She was pulling her warm and caring routine on me. "Bobby, I don't usually have to justify my assignments, but if that's what it will take, I will."

Bobby. She and my sister Janet are the only people who get away with calling me Bobby. "Make it good, Karen," I said tersely.

"This patient is originally from New York and has plans to return soon. He is going to attend Columbia University in September."

He must be bright, I thought. "Oh, and that's supposed to give me some special insight into him?" I said, sounding annoyed, but feeling interested. I knew I was being seduced into doing what she wanted, but I had to admit I did like being her favorite. Karen could be a formidable adversary, as Kendrell was finding out, and she was a powerful friend. I was sure it had been her connections that had facilitated my job as a tenure-track professor at John Jay College of Criminal Justice; that and my research.

Karen said, "I do not want him leaving here medicated. Kendrell will see him today, again on Monday, and then send him home with a script for anti-depressants."

"Wait a minute," Now I was getting it. Kendrell never came in on the weekends. "You want me to see him tomorrow and Sunday?" There it was again. What is she wearing, I wondered? It was something familiar.

"You're on call this weekend, and I thought you might be coming in tomorrow to see Carl. He's been making progress. You've really done a great job with him, Bobby. I'd hate to see him medicated over the weekend. But that isn't the real reason."

"Oh! There's more?" I asked. I couldn't decide if my frustration was with Kendrell or Karen, or perhaps both.

"Bobby, Kendrell crosses his legs and tightens his sphincter each time you enter the room."

"You've noticed." I smiled and shook my head. "You think he's gay?"

"Kendrell?" she asked, shaking her head. "Not so that it would ever occur to him."

"No, no, not Kendrell," I said laughing. "He's so rigid he's got to be straight." I grimaced. "No, I meant the kid."

She didn't answer, which was not unusual. Karen expected you to hold onto and fully grasp the meaning of everything she said. "His family, his mother and her mother and father, will be here soon. They were at the hospital until midnight last night, and said that they would be back first thing this morning."

"Christopher Bellesano," I said knowingly.

"What?"

"New York Italians."

"Does that mean something to you?"

"What families sit in the lobby of a hospital, day and night, while their kid is on a ward? New York Italians," I asked and answered. *I know that fragrance. It is remarkably elusive. Leave it to Karen to be restrained in her use of perfume.*

"Thank you, Bobby. I knew you were the right person. Give Nurse Greene your schedule for the morning. He said he would be happy to take care of it." She put her glasses on and thumbed through the intake report and added, "Christopher signed a waiver so you can talk to his family after you see him. I freed an hour at one; I'll see you then. I want to know what is going on with him."

"You were that sure I would take him?" I asked. Again, she didn't answer. Karen was done with me and now it was back to business.

She picked up her phone, punched four numbers and said, "Ron, is Christopher Bellesano ready for Dr. Mitchell?" She looked up at me and nodded. "Thank you, Ron." She smiled at me, "He is waiting for you in treatment room four."

"What's the urgency with this kid?" I asked as I stood up. "I haven't had my coffee yet."

"Get your coffee and take it in with you. I want you in with him before Kendrell arrives. Now, go," she said waving her hand at me.

As I opened the door to leave her office, I stopped. I had to ask. "What perfume are you wearing?"

"It's called "*Je Reviens.*" Do you know it?"

"Oh sure, by Worth. It's a perfume my mother wore. You wear it well."

She smiled, "Thank you. And thank you for the favor. I am going to miss you." I nodded, feeling annoyed, but I knew I would miss her also.

I entered the doctor's lounge and grabbed my cup from inside the cupboard. It was a twelve-ounce driving cup with a stainless steel finish that had "Porsche" on it. I did own a Porsche; a black-on-black 911 Targa.

Lies That Bind

Adam had said a Porsche suited me perfectly; a lean machine that responds to a soft touch and has a nice tight chassis. I enjoyed the 'soft touch with a tight chassis' part, but I always bristled at 'lean'. I knew he had been attracted to muscular men. But, as he had pointed out, it did not bother me enough to motivate me into joining the gym. Nothing did.

I filled my cup with black coffee and started for treatment room four. Whenever I interviewed a kid for the first time I got butterflies in my stomach. It took me at least twenty minutes to get my bearings and relax. I peeked into the room through a small window in the door. All I could see was a mop of straight dark hair sitting atop the head of an athletic-looking young man.

"Good morning, Mr. Bellesano. I am Dr. Mitchell," I said as I opened the door. He quickly unfolded his hands, wiped them on his pants and began to stand up. "Don't get up, that's okay." He reached out to shake my hand and then noticed that mine were full. I stepped farther into the room and let the door close. I put my coffee, notebook, and pens on the desk. We shook hands. His hand was clammy, and seemed to be trembling. His grip was strong, but his handshake was gentle. As I thought about how best to start our time together, I took a long look at my new patient. His sadness seemed to fill both the room and me. I felt my mouth being pulled into a frown. I decided to take a moment and allow the silence for both of us. Simultaneously, we took a deep breath; he turned his head toward me and smiled, but still did not make eye contact. He glanced around the room as if he had just entered it. Other than a couple of chairs, a gray metal desk and bookshelves, and an Ansel Adams poster of Yosemite, the room was empty. I found myself following his gaze.

"Why am I here?" he asked, looking down at his feet.

"I really don't know. I was hoping you would tell me."

He nodded. "I was giving my speech at graduation. I got really confused and stuff. I said things I guess I didn't want to say. I started shaking and I couldn't stop." He paused, his mouth twisted as if he was about to cry, but he did not. Again he only half looked toward me. "And then . . ."

"And then?"

"It's happened before, but never so that anyone knew. I guess it's kind of gross." He looked frightened. He wiped his hands on his pant legs and sighed. "My mouth makes all this saliva. I mean, so much that I can't swallow it all. It just pours out of my mouth." His eyelids closed and remained closed. He looked as if he might fall asleep. Slowly, his eyelids opened. He slid his fingers through his hair, lifting it from his face. "Am I going crazy?"

"I know you went through an initial interview with Dr. Kendrell. However, I prefer not to read intakes. I would rather hear what is going on with you from you." He nodded. "I very much doubt that you are, to use your words, going crazy. But I can do a much better job of answering your questions after we've spent time talking." I opened my notebook. "I am going to take notes while we speak. It will help me later when I have to write my report." He shrugged. I jotted down that I was beginning to feel at ease, and noted the time. I thought that was a good sign. I had found that the more disturbed a patient is, the longer it took for me to feel comfortable.

"What do I talk about? I mean, what do you want to know? Where do I start?"

I nodded. "I glanced in through the window there," I said pointing toward the door, "before I entered." He glanced around and noticed the small window in the door. "You looked to be deep in thought." He again turned his attention to his lap. "Why don't you start with what you were thinking about then, and we'll go from there." I found that the fewer questions I asked, the less I intruded upon a patient's thought process, and the more I learned.

"I was thinking about *Alien* and *Jaws*. You know. The movies," he said, again pushing his hair out of his eyes. "They're on my list of favorite movies."

"What about those movies?" I asked with raised eyebrows.

"Actually, the beginning of *Jaws*, you know where that girl gets eaten by the shark. And the end of *Alien*, when Ripley escapes in her shuttle." He sat silently, stared down at his hands and took a deep breath, swallowing hard.

"Powerful images," I said, hoping he would continue. The pallor of his face was remarkable for such an obviously athletic boy, whom I imagined spent hours in the sun. I noticed the armpits of his tee shirt were wet with sweat; the hospital was air-conditioned. Again, he wiped his hands on his pant legs. He crossed his arms over his chest, tucking his hands into his armpits. He began to rock in his chair. I decided to break the silence. "Can you tell me what you are thinking about now?" He turned his head and stared at the wall behind me, then looked away. His presence was both powerful and gentle, much like his handshake. I wrote down the words, "Alien" and "Jaws" on my notepad and then added, "He fills the room, but in no way intrudes upon my space, he looks to be in a state of agitated depression" He glanced toward me. I looked up and we made eye contact for the first time. His eyes, which were partially covered by his hair, were a luminous blue-green. However, they were pained and hopeless. He was strikingly handsome for a boy of seventeen.

"I was thinking about another time like this."

"This is not your first time in a hospital?" I asked, surprised.

"Oh, well, I've been in a hospital before, but not for being . . ." he hesitated.

"You are not crazy. What was the other time?"

"Confession. I had to go to confession," he said as he sat up in his chair, continuing to stare at the floor. His chest quivered as he drew in a deep breath.

My first impulse was to explain to him that I wanted to know about his previous hospitalization. But I decided I could get to that later. I had to trust that he knew what we needed to talk about. If I didn't trust his process, how could I expect him to trust me? "Please go on."

* * * * *

North Hollywood, California is one of scores of small communities that make up the San Fernando Valley, along with large independent cities, such as Burbank and Glendale. The San Fernando Valley lies at the northwesternmost corner of Los Angeles. It is mountain-girt with the rolling, lush Santa Monica Mountains, which separate it from the coastal area.

During the depression motion picture studios moved from Hollywood to the Valley; people followed. In the 1940s industrial expansion started in Burbank and Glendale. After World War II housing tracts were developed, varying from modest dwellings, such as those in North Hollywood, to luxurious hillside homes in Sherman Oaks. The population of the San Fernando Valley had grown to over one million by 1960, when only six of the nation's largest cities exceeded its population. However, with growth came major changes. Where there was once clean air, fields of onions, corn, and strawberries, and orange, plum, and fig orchards, there was now urban sprawl, smog and freeways. What currently is known as the greater Los Angeles Basin. And North Hollywood sits at its center.

This Sunday would not be the first time Christopher Bellesano had served mass, but it was the first Sunday he would serve mass in Saint Patrick's Church; not the one in Manhattan, but in North Hollywood. This church was not cathedral-like, with vaulted ceilings, large stained glass windows, or painted statues towering over wealthy penitent women, wriggling children, and hushed tourists shuffling through the maze of pews. Rather, it was a small, box-like, red brick church with only its requisite statues of the Blessed Virgin Mary on one side of the church and the risen Christ on the other. It had the obligatory statue of the near-naked crucified Christ above the altar and the statue of Saint Patrick to its right. Of course, it had stained glass windows, but they were small and unremarkable. The red-velvet-draped confessionals stood at the rear of this unexceptional church situated in the middle of a very conventional community.

Chris squirmed as he remembered his favorite movie, *Alien*, while kneeling in a church pew. Ripley, fully armed and filled with terror, courageously makes her way through the starship *Nostromo* to the escape shuttle. After successfully breaking free from the starship, Ripley readies herself to enter her cryo-sleep capsule. But the alien has secretly stowed away aboard the shuttle. In their final battle, Ripley blows the alien out of the airlock.

Chris's green blazer weighed heavily on his shoulders on this mid-October day. He slid his index finger between his starched collar and his neck and gave a tug; suddenly, his tie seemed to be too tight. After wiping the sweat from his upper lip, he clasped his hands and bowed his head—but not in prayer. Chris was stalling as he considered his options. Making a false confession was a sin. He considered skipping confession and receiving communion on Sunday, but he knew that to be even worse. What had worked all summer, refusing to confess and not receiving communion, was no longer an option. The nuns insisted that all the altar boys make a confession before serving mass. Feeling he had no choice in the matter, he remained kneeling in his pew, waiting for divine intervention.

Without raising his head, he glanced up and scanned the church, looking for Sister Bernadette.

"Chris, don't dally," she ordered from the end of the pew where he was kneeling. "I want you back in class in fifteen minutes."

Chris nodded, but remained on his knees. He watched as she walked up to the front of the church and genuflected before the altar. After rising to her feet, she approached the gate at the altar railing, opened and walked through it, and then turned to close the gates behind her. When she glanced back at Chris she pointed him toward the confessionals and silently mouthed, "Now." Then she disappeared into the sacristy.

Chris sighed audibly. He sat back on the edge of the seat and relaxed. At least she was no longer lurking somewhere out of sight. He had a fifteen-minute reprieve. He was convinced that she had a particular dislike for him, which showed in her silent glares and an impatient tone in her voice.

Chris hesitantly glanced around and counted his schoolmates who were still in line waiting to make their confession to Father O'Brien, the pastor. Chris closed his eyes and thought about how angry he was with his mother. She insisted that he once again be an altar boy. If it weren't for her, he decided, he wouldn't be in this mess. He blamed her for everything that had happened to him since their recent move to Los Angeles.

Diane Bellesano had moved from New York to Los Angeles last May immediately following her marriage to Richard Patrona. She wanted Chris to accompany her when she moved, but Chris and her father had convinced her to allow him to finish the seventh grade in New York.

Diane had divorced Chris's father when Chris was seven years old. After her divorce Diane had returned to work, leaving Chris during the day with her parents, Anthony and Josephine Dinato. Chris's relationship with his father had deteriorated from a once-a-month Saturday afternoon meeting, and he had not seen his father for almost a year. After spending most of his days with his grandparents for the last five years, Chris was having difficulty separating from them, especially his grandfather. It was his grandfather, the owner of two Italian grocery stores, who had done the work of fathering Chris after the divorce. At twelve years of age, Chris resented having to move across the country just to accommodate Richard and his new job. He pleaded with his mother to allow him to remain in New York with his grandparents for one more year so that he could finish middle school at Saint Dominic's, but she refused. Diane feared that if Chris remained behind with his grandparents he would fight again to remain in New York to attend high school. She finally insisted he leave New York. Chris arrived in Los Angeles a week before eighth grade began.

Chris glanced at his watch and realized he could not delay much longer. His fifteen minutes' respite was nearly at an end. He knew Sister Bernadette would soon emerge from the darkness of the sacristy.

Before moving to Los Angeles, Chris had attended Catholic school in the Bronx. The Catholic Church had always been a place of solace for Chris, an island in the sea of confusion called his childhood. The church's rituals provided a shield against chaos, and its rules provided structure. And in school, Chris had been in the boys' choir until a year ago, when his voice had begun to change; he then became an altar boy. During the summers he played little league baseball, much to his grandfather's pleasure. He played first base and had the best batting average in his league.

But, six weeks ago Chris had arrived in Sherman Oaks to live with his mother and Richard. Diane made every effort to enroll Chris in the eighth grade at the nearby Sacred Heart Middle School in Sherman Oaks, but she was unsuccessful. The school had a strict limit on class size, and the eighth-grade was filled to capacity. It was one of the best schools in the area, and was where all the Catholic children who lived in the neighborhood attended school. A Catholic education was important to Diane. She believed the structure and discipline provided the cover of safety she wanted for Chris in a new city, with new friends. Chris, therefore, would attend Saint Patrick's school in North Hollywood and then, most likely, attend Sacred Heart High School starting with the ninth grade.

Chris heard the door of the sacristy open. He glanced up toward the altar to see Sister Bernadette glaring at him. He decided he could no longer avoid what was inevitable. He felt like a trapped animal, helpless and scared. Before she could make her way to where he was kneeling, he stood and slowly walked out of the pew. He stepped into the center aisle, genuflected, bowed his head, and crossed himself. Under his breath, he made his last plea for strength to Saint Anthony, the patron saint of lost causes and the saint for whom his grandfather was named. He stood and slowly walked to the rear of the church. He tried to remember Ripley's first name; he thought he might pray to her too.

Chris had been successful in avoiding confession all summer, ever since he had masturbated with Larry, his best friend. Since sex of any kind was never discussed in his family, all he knew about what had happened was that it was considered a sin, one he would have to confess in order to serve mass and receive communion. At the age of twelve, the idea of admitting to anyone, especially a priest, that he was masturbating, let alone with a friend, was more than he could bear. However, today his anxiety about confessing was not about masturbation.

He wanted to be the last in line to confess, but people from the neighborhood were congregating in the church. The adults had to wait for all the students to finish their confessions so they could return to class. But, once the students were finished, the parishioners could begin gathering in line. Chris watched as the line began to dwindle down to just a few of his schoolmates. Soon it would be his turn to enter the confessional.

Chris had always been an attractive boy. He had straight dark brown hair, a square jaw, a straight nose, and full lips that opened to a generous

Lies That Bind

smile that brightened his entire face. People often said that Chris's most striking feature was his eyes. He had long, dark eyelashes and dark, full eyebrows that framed his large blue-greenish-gray eyes. They seemed translucent. There was both an intensity and softness to them. The softness was most obvious when he smiled; the intensity when he was in a bad mood. Chris thought his most attractive feature was his hair. His mother had always had it cut short and combed with a part on the left side of his head, much the same as his father. When he turned twelve, he began combing his hair as his grandfather combed his, straight back and without a part. But, unlike his grandfather's, Chris's hair was now long, so long and thick that he was able to comb it back over his ears.

Chris had entered puberty well before other boys his age. He had grown several inches in height, lost the little baby fat he had, but gained weight. He started putting on lean upper-body muscle, and developed underarm and pubic hair. However, as a young boy, Chris, much to his father's disappointment, had always been thin and small in stature. Some people had referred to him as delicate; his father referred to him as a sissy. Now, at almost thirteen years of age, there was nothing delicate or sissified about him.

As Chris knelt on both knees inside the confessional, he took a breath that reverberated through his chest. He realized he was trembling. Kneeling there, he waited for what he knew would happen. At some point, under this kind of stress, he would experience what he referred to as "breaking free;" a skill he had developed as a child. Although he had no control over this skill, he thought of it as an ability to separate himself from his body and not experience emotion. Emotions were his curse. They were the driving force behind everything that troubled him. He longed to be their master, and to Chris that meant living apart from them.

Chris again tugged at his shirt collar; his breath was shallow and quick. He silently hummed a song he had been trying to compose on his guitar. It was something that had calmed him in the past. A sweet aroma filled his nostrils and turned his stomach. The smell was from the beeswax candles that burned at the feet of a statue of some unidentifiable saint standing at the rear of the church. It was an aroma he had always enjoyed, but now it seemed to be overwhelming his senses. Chris clasped his hands and readied himself for confession. As he heard the mumbled voice of Father O'Brien just beyond the curtained screen, Chris's anxiety continued to grow. *All of this isn't my mother's fault. I made this all happen. I deserve whatever happens to me.*

This pattern of feeling anxiety and dread followed by guilt, self-accusation, and finally numbness was familiar to Chris. So familiar it had become ordinary.

On a hot August evening when Chris was five years old, while sitting on the front steps of the apartment building where he lived in Manhattan, a stray dog had bitten him. Frank, his father, who was supposed to be watching him, stood nearby, but his attention was with his friends; several of whom were Vietnam veterans. Although they never talked about their time in the service, there was a deep bond between them. They shared in a communal misery, a coincident rage, and a habitual need to self-medicate. The street corner had become their refuge from the demands of work and family.

As usual, Frank held a lit cigarette in his left hand and a bottle of beer, wrapped in a brown bag, in his right. It was his third. When Frank bought his third beer from the corner store he bought Chris a lollipop. As Frank joked with friends, his back toward Chris, a large black stray dog slowly approached and became fixated on Chris's candy. Chris, who loved dogs, called to the stray, waving his lollipop as he did. Hearing him, Frank looked over his shoulder to see what was happening. Frank noticed the dog, and was content to afford Chris any distraction. Anything to keep him off my back, Frank thought. As Chris moved the lollipop back into his mouth the dog lunged for it, leaving Chris with a torn lip. Chris screamed out in pain as the dog fled with the stolen candy. Hearing Chris scream, Frank ran to him as his friends unsuccessfully tried to apprehend the dog.

"Daddy!" Chris screamed out in between long breaths and loud sobs.

Frank pulled off his tee shirt and wiped the blood from Chris mouth. "Stop crying, it's nothing," Frank insisted, feeling his frustration rise as he tried to see where all the blood was coming from. Frank could feel his anger growing. All he wanted was an evening of peace. He felt his grip tightening on Chris's shoulder. He thought if Chris did not stop screaming, he might hit him. "Shut up, Chris," he whispered tersely. "God damn it. Shut up!" He looked into Chris's mouth, but all he could see was blood covering his teeth and tongue. Then he noticed a large gash across the inside of Chris's lower lip.

"Daddy," Chris cried out again, trying to reach up to him.

Frank held Chris down by putting one hand on his shoulder as he tried to wipe the blood from his mouth. He battled his anger as his friends gathered around them. He glared at Chris and insisted, "Chris, stop screaming, you're making it worse." Frank kept wiping blood, but

Lies That Bind

the blood kept flowing. Chris continued crying as he tried desperately to push himself into his father's arms. "Damn it, Chris," Frank yelled more forcefully, "you stop this right now!" Sit still," Frank insisted, shaking Chris by his shoulders. Frank moved closer to Chris and growled through his teeth. "You sound like a girl. Do you hear me?"

"Frank," one of his friends called out, "it looks bad. You'd better get him to a hospital."

"He doesn't need to go to any hospital." Frank picked Chris up and carried him under one arm like a sack of potatoes, up the stairs and into their apartment as blood continued to stream from Chris's mouth, leaving a trail behind them.

"Mommy!" Chris cried out, as he heard Diane's voice.

"Oh God, oh my God!" Diane shouted as Chris threw himself into his mother's arms. "What happened? Frank, what happened?" Frank could barely contain his anger as he explained to Diane that he had seen it all happen, but as if it were happening in slow motion.

"You were supposed to be watching him."

"I *was* watching him," Frank insisted. "I was sitting right next to him on the stoop when this dog came out of nowhere."

Diane carried Chris into the bathroom and carefully wiped blood from his mouth with a towel. "How could a dog come out of nowhere? We live in the middle of a city." Frank moved into the bathroom and held Chris's head still while Diane tried to stop the bleeding. Frank could feel his anger in the grip he had on Chris's skull. Diane searched Chris's mouth until she was finally able to see the extent of the gash that would not stop bleeding. "Damn it, Frank, you stink of beer," Diane hissed.

"Chris waved his candy at the dog," Frank explained. "He was teasing him, and before I could grab the dog, he lunged at him."

"You were bullshitting with your friends. I know you. You weren't watching him."

"God damn it, Diane. He should know better," Frank shouted, violently letting go of Chris's head, "and he shouldn't have been teasing that fuckin' dog." Frank searched his pockets for his pack of cigarettes. "And make him stop crying now. I can't fuckin' stand his crying. He cries like a girl."

"And how do I do that, Frank?"

"I don't know, Diane, just fuckin' do it."

"Frank, he's badly hurt. We've got to take him to a doctor," Diane pleaded.

"Forget it. He'll be fine." Frank inhaled deeply. "He's a boy. Just ice it or something."

"He's bleeding a lot, Frank," Diane said calmly. She decided that if she calmed herself Frank might calm down. "Frank, please get the car." Diane grabbed a clean washcloth and applied pressure to Chris's lip. "I don't understand why you didn't stop him from teasing the dog." Chris continued to sob.

"He's got to learn somehow," Frank said, filling his lungs with smoke. "I bet he won't be teasing dogs again," Frank chortled.

Diane, holding Chris in her arms, walked into the living room where Frank sat smoking. "Frank, I asked you to please get the car. I'm going to call Dr. Sherman. He has to see a doctor."

"I said no doctor."

"You know, Frank, you're dangerous," Diane shouted. "And do you want to know why?" Her voice was quaking with anger. "Because you're a sadistic bastard and you don't have the sense you were born with. Now go and get the god-damn car, or I'll get a cab," Diane shouted.

After cleaning the wound and sending the Bellesanos home, Doctor Sherman decided that he should report the bite to the health department. Later that evening the hospital called to tell Diane that since the dog could not be located and quarantined, Chris would have to undergo a two-week series of anti-rabies injections. They informed Diane that if the dog was rabid and Chris began to show symptoms, since the bite was to the mouth, it would be too late to start the anti-rabies treatment. Therefore, the series of fourteen shots, given one each day, would have to start immediately.

Diane called Dr. Sherman, who told her they would have to meet him at Lenox Hill Hospital. When they arrived, he asked Diane to wait in the outer office and asked Frank to join him with Chris. The doctor explained to Frank that he would have to use a rather large syringe and long needle so he could penetrate to the inner lining of the stomach. He preferred that Chris not see it. When the syringe was assembled, the doctor attached a four-inch sterile needle and then filled the syringe with the appropriate amount of serum. After Frank helped Chris undress, he laid him down on the doctor's examining table. Chris was wearing his Scooby Doo jockey shorts. They were white with a blue band of elastic around the waist and each leg. The image of Scooby Doo sat squarely in the front.

Mary, Dr. Sherman's nurse, said, "Wow, Chris, cool underwear you have there," as she began to wash the skin of his stomach with iodine.

Lies That Bind

"Scooby Doo," Chris said smiling nervously, his eyes darting from person to person. Where was his mother, he wondered. The smell of iodine cut through his nostrils, flooding his senses, already overwhelmed by the bright lights, the coldness of the sterile room, and the lingering taste of his own blood. Every sound brought a reflexive shudder that passed through his gut. "My cookie grandma bought them for me."

Frank stood over Chris and insisted that he be brave and not cry. Dr. Sherman explained to Frank that Chris would have to be held down. "Frank, I want you to stand over his head, rest your elbows on his shoulders and then use your hands to hold his arms and hands still. Mary, I want you to stand beside him and hold down his legs." The doctor was shielding the syringe from Chris's view.

Chris looked at his father in terror and began to cry. "Daddy, it's going to hurt. Daddy, please Daddy, don't let him do it, Daddy. I promise I won't cry anymore."

"Hold still, and you'd better not cry," Frank ordered in a stern voice as he stared down into Chris's pleading eyes. As the doctor again washed the skin of Chris's stomach with iodine, Chris began to scream in anticipation. "Chris, you stop that," Frank snarled though his teeth, this time pushing Chris's shoulder into the table. Chris's eyes grew wider as he stared up at his father. The strength of Frank's grip drew Chris's attention to his father's face. Desperately trying to obey Frank, Chris began to hold his breath.

"You have to hold him still, I don't want the needle to break," the doctor said in a very low voice. "I will say 'okay' as I insert the needle, and then I will count to five. On the count of five, I will remove the needle. You must hold him still until then." Dr. Sherman took a deep breath and bent over Chris. "Get ready."

Mary took a deep breath and used all her weight to hold Chris's legs still. Chris could not hold his breath any longer and again started to plead with his father, and again, Frank warned him not to move. As the doctor said, "okay," and the needle entered Chris's stomach, Chris stiffened and tried to break free from his father's hold as he let out a scream that carried through the doctor's count of five.

"Okay, Chris it is over," Dr. Sherman assured him. "You did just fine, Chris."

Diane rushed into the room when she heard Chris's scream. She pulled her weeping son into her arms. "My baby, you're okay. It's over." She fell into a chair and rocked Chris. He welcomed the safety of her arms.

"He isn't a baby, although he acts like one," Frank chided, shaking his head.

"The boy did just fine," the doctor said, placing his hand on Chris's sweat-drenched head.

"Mommy, it still hurts! It burns, Mommy, it burns!" Chris wept as Diane rocked him in her arms. Chris's body was wet with sweat. The nurse brought the boy's clothing to Diane. Diane moved toward the gurney to dress him, but as she did, Chris screamed out and tightened his hold on her. Frank turned and glared.

"Sweetie," the nurse said to Diane, "just have a seat there and I'll help you dress him."

As Doctor Sherman made his way out of the room, Chris heard him tell Frank that he should bring Chris back at the same time tomorrow. "Mommy, I don't want to come back," Chris begged as he pulled her face toward his with both of his hands.

"I know, baby, but you have to."

"No, Mommy, please, no more." Chris buried his head in Diane's neck and clung to her.

"Listen, honey, if that dog that bit you is sick you will get very sick, too. Mommy doesn't want you to get sick."

"But, Mommy, if I get sick then I'll come back. Please, Mommy, please, I promise I won't get sick."

"I know, baby, but we have to do what the doctor says."

"Stop calling him that," Frank said with disgust. "He isn't a baby."

"Stop it, Frank, not now," Diane answered, without looking at her husband.

"Listen to me," Frank said to Chris, grabbing the crown of Chris's head and forcing Chris to look at him. "You embarrassed me tonight," Frank continued, looking at Chris, who strained to turn his face away from his father's view. "Are you my son?"

"Yes, Daddy. I am." Chris tightened his hold on Diane's neck.

"Then you'd better act like it. Tonight you acted like a sissy. I'm ashamed of you."

Mary turned and looked at Diane as she rose to leave the office. Mary reached over to stroke Chris's hair as she said, "Mr. Bellesano, your son did just fine. Really, he did." Her voice had a tone of softness that was meant for Chris, but her face had a look of impatience as she stared into Frank's eyes.

"That's not for you to say, now is it?" Frank replied, as he tried to take Chris from Diane. Chris threw his arms around his mother's neck and held on.

Lies That Bind

"Frank, stop it," Diane insisted. "He isn't making you look bad, you are doing a good job of that yourself." Diane gave Frank her back in an effort to stop him from putting his hands on Chris. "What the hell do you want from him, anyway?"

"I want him to act like a man, not a sissy," Frank insisted.

Mary interrupted. "But he isn't a man, Mr. Bellesano, he is only a boy, a five-year-old boy," she said as she left the room.

Frank watched as Mary left the office, then he turned to Chris and said, "Doctor Sherman is going to be giving you shots for the next two weeks and I never want to hear you scream or see you squirm like you did tonight. Do you understand me?"

"Yes, Daddy," Chris answered as his father stared at him. When Frank turned away Chris whispered into his mother's ear. "Mommy?"

"What, honey?"

"Am I going to get shots for two weeks?" Chris continued in a whisper.

"Yes."

"Mommy if I stop being a sissy, do I still have to get them?" Chris asked, again holding his mother's face in his hands as he looked up into her eyes.

Gently stroking his face and desperately trying not to cry, Diane again tried to explain to Chris why he had to get the shots as she carried him from the hospital to their car. He was now almost limp with exhaustion. "Honey, try to get some sleep," Diane said, laying Chris down in her lap as they began their drive home.

"Mommy. I want Grandma and Grandpa," Chris pleaded, as his eyes neared sleep.

"Okay, I'll call them and tell them to come over and tuck you in," she whispered, stroking his face. As Chris closed his eyes, Diane quietly wiped tears from hers. *Saint Anthony,* she silently prayed, *please help me help my son through this. Make me strong enough...*

Frank interrupted her thoughts. "You've made that boy into a sissy," Frank said as they drove across town on Seventy-ninth Street.

Diane shook her head. She could not imagine why her husband always seemed to have so much contempt for their son. Yes, that's it. Contempt, she thought. It had never been clearer to her than now; contempt. "Don't be ridiculous, Frank. Did you see that needle?" Diane said. She was trying to separate herself from her anger as she had so many times in the past, but the contempt she saw in Frank's face for Chris was fueling her building hatred of him. She turned and stared out the car window as they drove through Central Park and then said flatly, "I'd like to see you take that shot."

"Fuck you, Diane!"

"You bastard. Boy, would I just love to see you on that table." The tone in her voice surprised Frank. He was accustomed to her anger, but this was different.

"Don't call your parents," Frank said in an oddly conciliatory tone. "He doesn't need them. I can't stand the way they fall all over *my* son."

"*Your* son, now he's *your* son?"

"What does that mean?"

"Before, you asked him if he was your son or if he was a sissy. How do you think he feels when you say that?"

"I don't care about how he feels. He has you for that. I only care about how he behaves."

"You only care about how you think he makes you look."

"Don't call them. He's asleep, anyway."

"I *am* calling my parents," Diane snapped back. "He seems to think he needs them, and that's enough for me," she said, stroking his face. "You were supposed to be watching him. And what the fuck were you doing? You were bullshitting with your friends, weren't you? I'm calling my parents, Frank, and I'm going to tell them not only to come over tonight, but also to come with us to the hospital from now on. You're the one who's out of control, not Chris." Diane was desperately trying to control her anger. Once again her son was hurt, and once again Frank had a hand in it.

Frank tightly gripped the stirring wheel. "Damn you and your family. He's my son, you know. They act like he's theirs."

Fuck you! Diane thought, but decided the best way to survive this was to end the conversation and do what she intended. Diane was a rare mix of charm and strength. She was slim, about five feet five, and had an athletic build. She had long, dark-brown Bernadette Peters-type curly hair, high cheekbones, full lips, and a strong angular nose. If one were to take each of her features separately it would be difficult to say they were attractive, but when put together they made her a very striking woman. She looked good in tennis shoes, blue jeans and a tee shirt, or in her four-inch heels and a tight black draped silk dress. She was a challenging combination of sophistication and street smarts that almost no one but women from New York could pull together.

Lies That Bind

As they drove through Central Park, Diane, staring out the car window, thought of her first and only love, Richard Patrona. She imagined what her life might have been like if she had been allowed to marry him. She glanced down at Chris, stroked his head, and again drifted away. She could not wish for that, she thought. Without Frank she would not have Chris, and Chris was all that made her life worth living.

Her thoughts drifted back to happier times, when she was fifteen. She thought about her best friend Ann, who was dating Bill Patrona and who introduced Bill's younger brother Richard to Diane. Soon they started dating, and soon they decided they were desperately in love. Diane remembered how her body ached to be with Richard. Now all she had of him were memories.

Anthony Dinato allowed his daughter to date Richard only because he knew Richard's family well. When Richard and Diane turned eighteen, Richard asked her if she would marry him, but her father insisted that they wait until Richard was better able to support a family. Soon after, and without discussing it with Diane, Richard joined the Navy. Realizing that being drafted was inevitable, he had seen the Navy as an avenue to an education and a career. Diane was both crushed and angered when Richard informed her that he had enlisted. She felt betrayed. After his training, he was given orders to go to sea. Before leaving, he asked if Diane would wait for him to return. Her pride dictated her response. She returned his ring and asked him never to contact her again. Ann, however, who remained Diane's best friend and later married Bill, always kept Diane informed of what was going on in Richard's life.

Frank Bellesano was Bill's best friend, and knew both Diane and Richard while they were dating. After Diane's breakup, and against her father's wishes, she began dating Frank. Diane was angry with her father and blamed him for the loss of Richard. She believed that if her father had allowed them to marry, he would not have joined the Navy. The more her father wanted Diane to stop dating Frank, the more defiant she became.

What Anthony knew of Frank was that he had a terrible relationship with his father. Anthony told Diane that a man who did not have respect for his parents could never be a good husband or a good father. Frank, however, claimed that his father was critical, unreasonable, and at times physically violent, and therefore, did not deserve respect.

After Anthony and Josephine Dinato tucked their grandson into his bed they sat and listened to Diane explain the procedure and the fact that there would be thirteen more shots. They agreed to accompany Chris to the hospital each night. When they left, Diane and Frank launched into one of their worst arguments. Diane blamed Frank for what had happened, and Frank blamed Diane for raising his son as a sissy. The argument finally ended when Frank struck Diane. Chris, hearing Diane's screams, rushed from his room into their bedroom. He explained frantically to his mother that his father had been sitting with him on the stoop, and that Frank tried to make the dog go away, but the dog had bitten him anyway. Then he promised his father that he would not be a sissy anymore. He pleaded with them not to argue as he continued to apologize to his father.

The next evening Anthony and Josephine accompanied their grandson to Lenox Hill Hospital. Anthony held Chris's hand in the car on the way to the hospital, throughout the procedure, and on the way home. Josephine sat with Diane in the waiting room and held her hand. When Dr. Sherman administered the anti-rabies injection Frank again held Chris to the table. Although Chris was terrified and could feel himself trembling, he resisted the urge to scream out in pain; this time he did not move or make a sound. That night Chris had what everyone thought to be a very strange reaction to the anti-rabies serum. After arriving home, Chris began to salivate so much that saliva streamed over his lips and down his chin, much as the blood had the night before. Diane held his head over the bathroom sink and watched as the clear liquid poured from her son's mouth. Dr. Sherman said he had never heard of a similar reaction to the serum, and recommended that Chris be watched carefully. During the next two weeks, Chris had the same reaction more often than not.

After his promise to his father not to make a scene, no one had to hold Chris to the doctor's table to receive his shot. Anthony sat beside his grandson, held his hand, and watched. Frank was proud of Chris, and proclaimed that his son was a little soldier. However, everyone else was concerned as they watched Chris's eyes glaze over before each injection. Josephine told Diane that she had only seen Anthony cry once before, when his mother died, but that he cried when he told her what he witnessed in the hospital room.

"Chris, you did good," Frank said, as they drove home after the last day of treatment.

Diane cringed. She wanted to scream: you dumb ignorant dago bastard!. You graduated high school, my father never got to go to school. You were born in this country, English is my father's second language, and your English is just as bad as his. But her anger was not about his use of

Lies That Bind

grammar. She hated Frank for the way he emotionally tortured *her* son.

"Chris, did you hear me?" Frank asked, glancing into the backseat of the car where Chris was seated between his grandparents.

"Yes, Daddy. Grandpa, can I sit on your lap?" Chris asked in a weakened voice.

"Sure, Sonny." No one knew when Anthony had started calling his first-born grandchild Sonny, but it was a nickname that no one else used for him. Chris crawled onto Anthony's lap and wrapped his arms around his grandfather as he leaned his head against his chest.

"*Questi qua sta sudando,*" Anthony said to Josephine, remarking that Chris was wet with sweat.

"It's hot, Pa," Frank said.

"*Io non sudo,*" Anthony impatiently answered Frank, telling him that he was not sweating. "Do you understand what I am saying?" Josephine put her hand on Anthony's leg and shook her head, signaling Anthony to be calm.

"*Il figlio sta tremando,*" Anthony mumbled to Josephine. Josephine reached over and stroked Chris's back and felt that Anthony was right. Chris was trembling.

Diane turned in her seat and put her hand on Chris's head. His hair was wet, and she, too, could feel him trembling. She glanced up at her father as tears filled her eyes.

"*Non piangere, figlia mia,*" Josephine said, pleading with Diane not to cry.

"Grandpa," Chris whispered into Anthony's chest.

"What is it?" Anthony answered, as Chris glanced up at him and then looked away. "What is it, Sonny?"

"I forgot," Chris said faintly, rubbing his stomach.

Anthony put his lips to Chris's ear. "Sonny, are you okay? Talk to grandpa." But Chris did not answer. Everyone sat silently as Frank made his way through cross-town traffic.

"Grandpa," Chris again whispered.

"*Che cosa?* What?" Anthony asked, as Chris pulled Anthony's head down toward his own.

Chris whispered, "I love you, Grandpa."

Anthony's voice trembled. "*Carissimo mio,* close your eyes and rest. Grandpa loves you too."

"All the macaroni in the world, Grandpa?"

"All the macaroni and more." Anthony fought his tears.

Diane wanted to scream as she sat there. She did not know how much longer she could stay married to Frank, but she was afraid she could not make it on her own. She felt trapped. Her feelings for Frank were clear—contempt. Her feelings toward her father were changing.

As Chris knelt waiting for Father O'Brien, he thought, This isn't like *Alien*, she escaped. This is like *Jaws*. He thought of the girl in the opening scene, the moment she struggles to the surface of the water after first being pulled under; naked and defenseless, a terrified and knowing look upon her face as she realizes what is about to happen.

* * * * *

I felt my stomach churning as I listened to Christopher speak about his father. I swallowed hard, trying to relax the clenched muscles in my jaw. I reached for my coffee and took a sip. I wrote down his first associations. His fear fantasies: he either survives by killing me off or he is devoured in the therapeutic process by the re-living of his disavowed pain. Would I be cast as the neutral Dr. Sherman, as his sadistic demanding father, as his nurturing but ineffective mother, or as his caring grandfather?

Chapter Two

"Powerful Images," I repeated, feeling the weight of his pain now sitting on my chest. "Perhaps, we can find another metaphor."

"What do you mean?" he asked, glancing up at me.

"Well, a metaphor in which you don't have to destroy the monster in order for you to survive, as in *Alien*, or be devoured by the shark, as in *Jaws*. Understandably, you've come to see your survival as a matter of kill or be killed."

Chris nodded. There was a long silence.

"Earlier you referred to being in a hospital. Is that what you were talking about?" I asked. Chris nodded, again staring at the floor. He was closing down. "Christopher, what are you thinking about?"

"Can you call me Chris?"

"Okay."

"I guess I was thinking about being a kid, being with my grandparents, living in the Bronx."

"How old were you when you moved from the City?" I asked.

"I guess when I was six. I went to Saint Dominic's School. We lived near the Bronx Zoo. My granddad used to take me. We could walk there." I nodded. I knew the area well.

He looked toward me. "Can I get some water?" he asked, rubbing his stomach.

"Is your stomach bothering you?" I asked. He glanced down and looked to be surprised by what he was doing. He shook his head, no.

"Go to the nurse's station and ask Nurse Greene for a cup. You can get water from the fountain." When he left the room I took a deep breath and found my focus falling on the Ansel Adams print of "Winter Storm Over Yosemite." I sat back in my chair and let my mind wander.

Like Chris, I had grown up in the Bronx. Much of New York City is made up of areas that are, or were, known by their ethnic minorities. The area where Chris's grandparents lived is an Italian/Jewish neighborhood. The buildings in that area are mostly row houses; two- and three-family homes. I grew up in a single-family home, five miles to the north, near

Albert Einstein Hospital where my father worked. My father was a medical doctor, a born-again Christian, and a social conservative, as they like to be called. My oldest sister, Claire, followed in my father's shadow and became a cardiologist. My other sister, Janet, attended New York University Law School and now worked on Wall Street. Being my father's only son, it was his plan that I also attend medical school. But, for the first time in my life, I decided to follow my own path, and enrolled in graduate school at Columbia University. My father was disappointed.

As a child, I had been all that my father wanted in a son. We were the model white suburban professional Christian family. And although my father weathered my going to graduate school, allowances for my independence ended when, after I received my doctorate, I announced to them that I was gay. My mother cried; my sisters tried to console her. At first my father was quiet. Finally, he spoke. "I want you to know something," he said to me. "When your sister," meaning Janet, "was born, your mother and I decided not to have any more children. Her pregnancies had been extremely difficult. When they told us that you were a boy we cried with joy and your mother decided to go to term. Now I wish we had had you aborted." He then rose to his feet, walked me to the front door and said, "I want you to leave my home and never return. You are now forever dead to me."

Chris returned to the room, sat down, and sipped his water. "Is there anything you want to know?" he asked.

"Do you want to continue where you left off? You were with Father O'Brien."

He looked at the floor. What life there was in his face once again disappeared. His eyes half closed. He glanced at me. I imagined that he was sizing me up. He shrugged his shoulders. I nodded. "Okay," I said, looking at my notepad. "You said something about hospitalizations. Were there other visits to the hospital besides what you've told me?"

"No, I mean that's not where we left off. We left off when I told you that we moved to the Bronx when I was six."

"Oh, okay. That's right," I said.

"Can we talk about that and then we'll talk about Father O'Brien, okay?"

"Okay."

Chris nodded, seeming relieved. "Actually, we moved to the Bronx because I had to go to the hospital again for the third time. The second time was for the shots. I don't remember why I went to the hospital the first time. I mean I remember little things, but it's probably from hearing stories from my family."

"I'll be talking to them later today. They can fill me in on what you don't remember."

He nodded. "They're coming here today?"

"I understand that they were in the lobby until midnight last night and that they were coming back this morning." He turned his face from me, but I could see his chin trembling. "It's okay to cry, Chris."

He shook his head and composed himself. "What I remember from the first time is that when I would try to go to sleep there was this thing on my head. When I told my mother that I remembered this she was surprised, because I was so young. I guess I was about eighteen months old. She said that she had come home from seeing an opera with my cookie grandma, my father's mother, and I was lying in a pool of blood. My father said I fell, but . . ." he stopped. "Another time was when I was almost six. I remember more about that time.

"That was the year after your rabies shots?"

"Yeah."

* * * * *

When Chris was born Frank and Diane lived in Manhattan, in what was then thought of as a poorer neighborhood of Manhattan, the upper west side. They had a small two-bedroom apartment on the third floor of a building that had no elevator. Diane loved the neighborhood. Her street was lined with maple trees. Three blocks west was Riverside Park, which bordered the Hudson River. Closer to her was Central Park, where she often met her two best friends, Camilla and Ann. Camilla, who was only four years older than Diane, was actually her aunt by marriage. She had three sons, who were six, four, and two years old when Chris was born. Ann, Diane's friend since elementary school, had just had her first son three months before Chris's birth. Diane was also just a short subway ride away from her mother-in-law, and her parents, who lived in the Bronx.

Frank and Diane lived on the upper west side until one day in May, when they had a fight. Chris was six years old, and once again, Frank hit Diane, but this time he also hit Chris and drew blood.

Since Chris had been born, Frank and Diane had many arguments, and on several occasions Frank had "used his hands." Diane decided not to tell her father about how bad her marriage had become. Her pride dictated her decision; her anger at her father festered. Since consequences were nonexistent, Frank's anger was getting worse with each fight. And with each argument Diane's contempt for Frank grew as her self-respect and esteem dwindled. She had made a bargain with Saint Anthony that as long as Frank did not hurt her son, she would do her best to make her marriage work. But this, she thought, was a lost cause beyond even a saint. On several occasions Diane had been afraid that Frank might strike Chris. After each incident she thanked Saint Anthony for once again protecting Chris. But as Chris grew older, Frank became more strident with him. It was not until Chris was six years old—it was on Mother's Day—when Diane's worst fear came to pass.

Diane woke Chris to ready him for a visit to her parents' home for the day. It had been a long tradition that Anthony's family had holiday dinners at his apartment. In Anthony's family, Mother's and Father's Day were special occasions: cards and gifts were always exchanged. It was also a tradition that on Mother's Day Anthony would prepare the dinner for his family. This was one day of the year that Josephine could sit back and enjoy a meal she had not cooked.

Tensions began over breakfast before Frank and Diane left for the Bronx. Breakfast was over, and neither Chris nor Frank had wished her a happy Mother's Day. "It's Mother's Day, or had you forgotten?" Diane said to Frank angrily as she was drying the breakfast dishes.

"You're not my mother," Frank yelled with a smirk and a shake of the head. Frank gritted his teeth, realizing that he was about to hear again how, in Diane's eyes, he had failed as a husband and as a father.

"What about your mother? I asked you to take Chris and have him buy cards for his grandmothers. Did you at least get them cards?" Diane yelled, as she followed Frank into the living room.

"It's not Grandmother's Day, and I stopped giving my mother cards years ago." In his mother's eyes, he knew he had failed her as a son long ago.

"'It's not Grandmother's Day,'" Diane mocked. "You're a horse's ass. Do you know that?" she sneered as she threw the dishtowel at the wall.

"Watch it, Diane! Watch your mouth," Frank warned. He was sure she just loved it when he screwed up. For a moment he considered apologizing, but he refused to look weak.

"You are the boy's father. You're supposed to teach him to respect me. On Father's Day last year I had him pick out a card and gift for you."

"Mommy, I can pick out one for you, too. Mommy, don't yell." Chris said, following Diane from the living room back into the kitchen. "Mommy, I can buy you a card!"

Lies That Bind

"Diane, I didn't ask you to do shit." *Now* I'm the boy's father, Frank thought. When I tell him to do something and he doesn't listen I'm not his father, I'm too demanding, I'm too hard on him, I'm too impatient—*now* I'm his father, Frank raged to himself. "If you want a card from him take him out and have him buy you one. And while you're at it, if it's so damn important to you, have him buy one for my mother, too," Frank called out as he started searching the apartment for a pack of cigarettes.

"Now you want your mother to have a card?"

"Diane, get the fuck off my back," he yelled from the bedroom. His frustration was growing as he slammed one drawer after another trying to find his cigarettes. He stopped; he sat on the bed and took a deep breath. He was dreading spending the day at his in-laws, especially now that he remembered his mother would be there also.

"You guinea bastard," Diane mumbled under her breath. "Where the hell do you think I could get cards on Sunday morning?" She knew how far to push it with Frank. Her anxiety level was her cue to back off. She turned her attention to Chris, who had also become anxious.

"Diane, where are my cigarettes?" She did not answer.

"Mommy, I can make a card for Grandma and for Cookie Grandma. I can, Mommy. Mommy, don't get angry," Chris pleaded, pulling at Diane's arm to get her attention. They both knew the situation could escalate. Chris's eyes kept darting toward his parents' bedroom, where Frank continued slamming drawers.

"Okay, sweetheart. You and Mommy will make both your grandmother's cards for Mother's Day."

"Okay, Mommy. I can make you a card, too. Really, I can."

"I know, honey. We don't have time right now. Tonight," Diane said as she kissed Chris on the head.

Frank stormed into the kitchen. He hated the way they spoke to each other. "Where are my cigarettes?"

Diane shook her head and thought to herself, you'd know if they were up your ass. "If you have any, they're in your nightstand." Frank grabbed his keys, put on his jacket, and left the apartment, slamming the door.

Diane and Chris sat at the kitchen table trying to design two Mother's Day cards. They decided on flowers. Diane drew tulips on two pieces of colored construction paper, and Chris colored them with his crayons. Then Diane lightly traced, "Happy Mother's Day, Grandma" across the top and bottom of each page so that Chris could follow her markings.

There had been a time when Diane had a great deal of patience for Frank's moods and temperament, but that was in the past. In his youth, Frank had been a striking man: tall, broad-shouldered, and slim at the waist. He had straight raven-black hair, big brown eyes, and a friendly smile.

When Frank was drafted into the Army Diane married him. After basic training, Frank was sent to Vietnam; he was an infantryman. When he returned from Vietnam, Diane believed he was no longer the man she married. She thought that Frank had survived physically, but that emotionally it had destroyed him. Frank no longer had a smile. His eyes were no longer rich with life. Rather, he was sullen, cold, withdrawn, and cruel, both physically and emotionally. When once he would laugh, now he raged. When once he was gentle and loving, now he was harsh and demanding. He often bragged to Diane about all the girls he and his friends "did." What love Diane had had for Frank was now dead. Their love-making became torturous for her, but luckily it never lasted long.

Soon after Frank's return from Vietnam, Diane's friend Ann had informed her that Richard was still in the Navy, but remained unmarried, and often asked about her. Diane decided she wanted a divorce. She realized her mistake in marrying Frank, and decided that she wanted to be with Richard. When she told her father of her plan to leave Frank, he forbade it. "No daughter of mine will be divorced," he insisted, "it would be a disgrace to the family." He was punishing her for disobeying him. Diane backed down and promised her father that she would give her marriage a chance. She secretly held to the belief that eventually her marriage would fail.

After Frank's discharge from the Army, Diane and Frank moved into their apartment in Manhattan. Frank found a job as a machinist in the garment district. Both Frank's mother and Diane wanted him to use the G. I. Bill to attend college, but Frank refused. Although both of his parents and his sister were college-educated, Frank considered college to be a waste of a man's time. As Diane bided her time she became pregnant with Chris. A depression gripped her as she realized that now her future was surely tied to Frank.

"Now print your name here," Diane said, pointing to the lower right-hand corner of the paper.

"Here, Mommy?"

"Yes, sweetheart."

Chris mumbled each letter as he printed his name, "C H R I S T O P H E R."

"Very good, honey. You know they'll love these."

Lies That Bind

"I know," Chris agreed.

Frank did not return to the apartment. Instead, he joined his friends on the corner and had a beer. When Diane and Chris emerged from their apartment building, Diane called out to him several times before he would acknowledge her. Finally, he left his friends and met Diane and Chris at their car. During the drive to Frank's mother's home no one spoke.

"Now remember to wish Cookie Grandma Happy Mother's Day when she gets in the car. You can give Cookie Grandma the card when we get to Grandma's house."

"Okay Mom, it will be a surprise," Chris said smiling.

All of Chris's grandparents had been born in Italy and immigrated to the United States. Diane's mother had been born in Southern Italy, in a small town outside of Naples. She was a small woman, just five feet tall. She had straight black hair that was beginning to gray, and had beautiful eyes. They were so dark in color it was hard to see where her pupils ended and her irises began. She spoke in a wonderfully unique Italian-American slang that was her own combination of English words with a Neapolitan accent. She never cursed in English—never used "dirty" words—but in Italian, Diane would say, her mother could embarrass a sailor. Of course, at those times no one would ever translate what she said.

She made up for being small by being strong in other ways. She always made her opinions and her feelings known, often to Anthony's dismay. If they disagreed, Anthony would try to persevere, but eventually whatever Josephine insisted upon was what came to pass. While the world knew it was the Italian men who ran "The Family," Italians knew it was the women who ran the family. And she did, with love, respect, and a very strong voice.

When Anthony argued with Josephine, sooner or later he would break into a litany of Italian curses that Chris never understood, but that he knew were his grandfather's and only his. Each time Anthony would start reciting his list of curses, which, oddly, seemed to always rhyme, Chris would listen attentively and try to learn them. He knew they had something to do with all the saints in heaven, but he was never able to get beyond the first few words. When Chris asked his grandmother what Anthony said, she would only shake her head and say, "If he doesn't watch out, God will hear him and he'll go to hell." Usually, after his litany, he would acquiesce. "Okay, Okay, Jo, enough, enough," Anthony would concede. Josephine did not like her given name. She wanted to be called Josie, but at times like this Anthony called her Jo.

Anthony had been born in Sorrento. He was a quiet man and, like many Italian men, could be emotionally distant and demanding. However, when it came to his grandson, Anthony's presence, his touch, his tone of voice, although strong, were always comforting and protective. Frank might have been physically stronger, but Anthony commanded respect. Chris came to understand that his father feared Anthony. This knowledge gave Chris courage, a feeling of power; a willingness to face his father even in his rage.

Diane loved telling Chris that when he was an infant, his grandfather would sing an Italian song to him, always the same song. Anthony held Chris so that his feet barely touched the surface of the kitchen table. She told him how his face would light up, and that he would kick his legs and wave his arms as his grandfather sang. When Anthony stopped singing Chris would be still. Then Chris would kick his legs, as if to say, "Sing again, Grandpa." Everyone would laugh, and Anthony would sing and Chris would smile and dance for his grandfather.

Often on Saturdays Chris and Diane would take the subway and visit Frank's mother. Frank seldom accompanied them. Chris's cookie grandmother had been born in Milan and had attended the University of Milan, where she met her husband, who was studying to be a master chef. After their marriage, they moved to New York City and started a family. She was an elegant woman, large in stature, but delicate in presence. She had a smile that lit up her face, a laugh that was soft and gentle, but would often bring tears to her eyes. She had long, beautiful, straight brown hair that she wore braided and layered like a crown upon her head. Her voice was high pitched, and seemed to fade when she ended a sentence. When she sneezed, she would barely make a sound. Although Chris never heard her speak in an angry tone, he knew from stories his father told that she could be a firm disciplinarian. In many ways, she was like the roses in her garden, bright and bold and stunning to the eye, yet so delicate to the touch, so light and fresh in their aroma. But, his father seemed able to see only the thorns.

Whenever Chris visited her, there were two things he could depend upon. There would be opera playing on her stereo and freshly baked cookies on the kitchen table. She loved Italian opera, the theater, and Shakespeare, interests that she and Diane had in common. After arriving and going through the rituals of greeting, Chris would stand patiently waiting for her to pour his milk. After that, she would sit down at the table and gently place him upon her lap. While Diane and Cookie

Lies That Bind

Grandma talked about the latest play or opera they had seen, she would put one arm around Chris's waist and, with her other hand, gently stroke his arm or leg while pressing her lips against his head. Her lap was a wonderfully warm and safe place to be. Here too, Chris knew he was loved. No one was ever sure when Chris had started calling her his "Cookie Grandma," a name that always brought a loving smile to her face. Frank's mother, who was now widowed, often spent holidays with Anthony and Josephine and their family.

This Mother's Day, after they arrived at the Dinatos', and after Chris wished both his grandmothers Happy Mother's Day and presented them with his hand-made cards, Anthony readied his grandson for their usual Sunday walk. Anthony gave Chris a new dollar bill every Sunday. Today, on this walk, Chris asked his grandfather if he could use his allowance to buy his mother a card and a gift for Mother's Day.

Every Sunday Anthony stopped at the drug store to say hello to his friend Paulie. Chris liked Paulie because he was always so happy to see him and his grandfather. Paulie and Anthony always spoke to each other in Italian. They were neighboring business owners, both had opened their stores the same year, but, more importantly, they were both men born in Italy. This time Chris and Anthony left the store with a candy bar for Chris and a bottle of perfume for Diane that Chris chose because he liked the oval shape of the bottle and the blue color of the perfume. When they left the drug store Chris insisted that he had to buy a Mother's Day card for his mother. He explained to his grandfather that he felt sad because he had not remembered to buy her a card.

"The card store is closed on Sundays," Anthony explained to Chris, as they tried the door.

"But Grandpa, I have to buy my mommy a card, please." Chris pleaded looking up at Anthony. Chris knew Anthony was a "champean" problem solver.

"Okay, I know where the card lady lives. We can walk to her apartment house and see if she is at home. If she is, maybe, she will sell us a card."

The card lady was at home. And she, like everyone else in the neighborhood, knew and liked Anthony. He made the most generous Italian hero sandwiches in the neighborhood, especially for other storeowners. It was a mistaken belief, held by people who were not Italian, that what was called a "sub" sandwich was the same thing as an Italian "hero." Italians know that there is no sandwich like an Italian hero, and people in the neighborhood said that there were no better heroes in New York than the ones made by Anthony. As with most Italian food, it was an art form.

Whenever someone entered Anthony's store for the first time, and asked for this or that kind of sub sandwich, Anthony would put his hand on the counter, bow and shake his head and say, "But how can you come in this store and call what I make a submarine? Take a breath, smell the wonderful aromas," he would say, as he waved his other hand through the air. "That is like saying that what Michelangelo did was carve rocks. He took marble and created works of art," he explained, as his hands waved through the air as if he was directing traffic. "I take the best bread, meats and cheeses, the freshest lettuce, sweetest tomatoes and roasted peppers, and create an Italian sandwich that is called a hero. Now if you want an Italian hero I'll make it for you. If you want a submarine, go and get lost." When the customer smiled and asked for an Italian hero, Anthony would smile back, and say with his Italian accent, "Now you talkin'. I'm gonna make you a hero that when you eat it you will think 'this is better than sex.'"

When Chris explained to the card lady how important it was for him to buy his mother a card, she said she would be happy to open the store. Inside the store, Chris looked through several cards and finally settled on one that was covered with flowers—purple violets. After she slipped it into a small brown paper bag and handed it to Chris, he reached up and gave her his dollar allowance. She gave him seventy-five cents change and winked at Anthony, who thanked her for her troubles. On the way home they agreed that Chris should wait until he returned to his apartment that evening and surprise his mother with the card and the gift. As they walked to Anthony's apartment Chris held his grandfather's hand.

"Grandpa, will you carry me?" Chris asked, as he skipped to keep up with Anthony's quick pace.

"Aren't you a little too old to be carried?" Anthony asked, looking down at Chris.

"Yeah, but Grandpa you're strong, you can carry me." Anthony loved seeing himself through the eyes of his grandson.

"Okay, but for just a little ways. Okay?" As Anthony held Chris, Chris wrapped his arms around his grandfather's neck and his legs around his waist.

"Grandpa," Chris whispered with his head lying on Anthony's shoulder.

"Yeah?"

Lies That Bind

"I love you, Grandpa," Chris said, drawing his arms tighter around Anthony's neck. Anthony felt ten years younger; his chest filled with pride.

"Grandpa loves you, too," Anthony said, kissing Chris on the cheek, "More than all the macaroni in the world." Chris laughed.

"Wow, Grandpa, that's a lot. Isn't it?"

"Yup."

"Do you love me even if I'm a sissy?" Chris whispered as he moved his head closer to Anthony's ear.

"I love you no matter what." Anthony's tone was one of concern. He had heard Frank complain about how Chris was sensitive, delicate and gentle in his manner, much the same way Anthony's brother Mike had been when he was a young boy. He also remembered how Mike had suffered for it.

"Me, too, Grandpa. I love you, too," Chris said, relaxing into Anthony's arms.

Anthony felt the heat of anger building in his face. "Are you okay?" he asked.

"Yes, Grandpa. I'm okay."

"Is there anything wrong?" Anthony's tone was now more one of anger. Frank, he thought.

"No, I just miss you, Grandpa."

"Well I just saw you last Sunday," Anthony said. He reached up, put his hand on Chris's head and messed up his hair. Chris laughed again.

"Yeah, I know, but I miss you every day, Grandpa," Chris said. Then he put both his hands on Anthony's head and messed up his hair. They both laughed and hugged.

"I miss you every day, too. You know you're my 'champean' grandchild. But don't tell your cousins. Okay?" Anthony said, giving Chris another kiss on his cheek.

"Okay," Chris said with a smile, and then kissed Anthony's cheek. "Grandpa, you can let me down. I can walk now." Anthony felt an odd mixture of sadness, pride, love, and protectiveness, which came together as tears in his eyes, an ache in his stomach, and a smile on his face, as he watched Chris running ahead of him. He could not remember ever feeling this depth of affection for any of his own children.

That night when Chris returned home he gave Diane the perfume and the card. Both were in a brown paper bag that Chris was able to hide from her until they arrived home. When Diane opened the bag she found the perfume that Paulie had wrapped for her, and a smaller bag that contained the purple violet unsigned Mother's Day card. Diane was pleased and thanked Chris, kissing him repeatedly on his face. He laughed.

Chris was in bed when Frank returned after finding a place to park their car and buy another pack of cigarettes. Before long, Diane and Frank were arguing. Chris sat up in his bed. He got up and moved to his door to listen.

"I wasn't being sarcastic, Frank. Why wouldn't I think that you took the boy out to buy the perfume?" she asked, with building frustration. "I just assumed you bought the gift and the card."

"I don't want to hear any more about it," Frank demanded.

"My father must have bought them when he and Chris went out," Diane said as she turned to leave the room.

"How sweet, now you have your father buying you Mother's Day gifts. You and your family are sick," Frank said with contempt.

"Shut your mouth about my family," Diane said hearing Chris's bedroom door opening.

"Mommy, I bought you the card. I used my allowance," Chris explained from the hallway.

"Get to bed!" Frank screamed so loudly that Chris jumped.

"Don't yell at him like that, you scared him," Diane said, as she moved toward the hallway. She glanced once toward Chris, then her focus returned to Frank.

"Don't tell me how to talk to my son, God damn it. I am so fucking tired of you and your family, and the way you pamper and spoil this kid. That's why he's such a brat." Turning in his chair to face Chris, Frank glared and pointed to Chris's bedroom saying, "Now, get in there." Chris turned and slowly made his way into his bedroom. His stomach churned with fear, his eyes filled with tears, and his face burned with anger. His skin tingled with anticipation of what he believed would happen next.

"If you're angry with me, don't take it out on the kid," Diane said calmly, trying to turn Frank's attention toward her. "I just made a mistake, Frank." She too feared that Frank was beyond reason.

"Diane, I'm telling you for the last time—don't tell me how to deal with Chris," he yelled.

"Okay, Frank, I won't." Diane prayed. She could feel every beat of her heart in her neck. She realized her mouth was dry. She thought about going to the kitchen for water when she heard Chris call to her.

"Mommy."

Lies That Bind

"Honey, go to bed. Mommy will be in to tuck you in, in just a minute," Diane answered, keeping her attention on Frank. She was now acting purely on instinct.

Diane watched Frank watching Chris. "Chris, this is the last time I'm telling you to go to bed," Frank yelled.

Diane knew that Frank was close to going into one of his violent rages. "Chris, mommy wants you to go to bed, *now*." Her voice was stern.

"Mommy, are you okay?" Chris called out, his anxiety breaking through his words.

"That's it, you little bastard, now you're going to get it," Frank shouted as he got up from his chair.

"Don't you lay a hand on him! Frank, don't," Diane screamed, jumping between Frank and the entrance to the hallway. Without hesitation, Frank shoved Diane so hard she crashed into the wall. Hearing the commotion Chris came running out of his room. Diane screamed when she saw Chris enter the hallway. Fighting to get to her feet, she tried to keep Frank from getting into the hallway. "Chris, get in your room," she shouted. "Mommy's okay."

As Frank brought his arm back to strike Diane, Chris ran to his father, yelling, "No, don't! Don't hit my mommy!" Instead, Frank, in his rage, hit Chris so hard that the boy was knocked from his feet and crashed into a coffee table. Then both he and the lamp hit the floor.

"Frank, stop it!" Diane screamed.

Diane ran to Chris and lifted him from the floor. She saw the right side of his face was covered with blood. "Oh my God. Frank, he's bleeding." Blood was pouring out of what seemed to be his eye. Chris remained motionless. He did not make a sound.

"Jesus Christ, Diane. Don't start getting hysterical," Frank shouted.

"Frank, it looks bad. It's bleeding a lot." Diane stood with Chris in her arms and braced herself against the wall for strength. Her legs were shaking.

"Just put a Band-Aid on it," Frank said, after glancing at the blood on the floor, and now all over Diane's blouse.

Diane moved into the bathroom, put the light on, grabbed a towel, and sat on the edge of the tub. "Oh my God, Frank," Diane whispered in horror. "This is bad. He's bleeding out of his eye. Frank, I can't see his eye." Chris remained quiet in her arms. "Frank, get the car, we have to take him to the hospital."

"Stop exaggerating, Diane." Frank said, entering the bathroom. "Just put something on it." Frank sounded almost contrite.

"Chris, baby. Talk to Mommy." Diane felt herself break into a cold sweat. "Frank, get the car." Chris clung to his mother.

"I am not going to say this again, Diane. No hospital."

"Okay," Diane said, as she carried Chris into the living room. "Go into the kitchen, wrap some ice in a dishtowel and bring it to me." When she heard Frank open the freezer door she quietly stepped out of the apartment, holding a washcloth over Chris's eye. She flew down the steps.

Spotting a parked cab on the corner, she ran. Opening the door, she shouted, "Roosevelt Hospital, emergency!" to the half-asleep cab driver.

"Yes, Miss," he answered, starting the engine. Cutting through a red light and turning south on Broadway he explained, "I know a fast way; I'll get you there right away."

Diane glanced down at Chris, who was staring up at her. He had not made a sound since Frank hit him. He asked, "Mommy, are you okay?" in a strangely flat tone. His voice expressed no feelings. He was limp in her arms. He did not cry. He just stared.

"Yes, honey. I'm fine."

Then he asked, "Mommy, am I okay?" without emotion.

"You will be, sweetheart, I promise you, you will be," Diane said, her voice trembling.

When they pulled up to the hospital the cab driver jumped out of the car and helped Diane into the emergency room. As she realized she did not have her purse, the cab driver told her that he had never turned on the meter. He wished them well, and left.

As soon as Chris was admitted into the emergency room, Diane called her parents and told them where she was and what had happened. Soon, Anthony arrived, and joined his daughter who was talking to Chris's doctor.

"Your son was lucky," the doctor said. "There was no damage to his eye. He bled from a gash over his right eyebrow. But because it's a jagged cut and above his eye, we can't stitch it. We're going to help stop the bleeding, and then butterfly bandage it."

Anthony carried Chris to his car. Diane began to weep. "Daddy, he hurt my baby. I thought he'd lost his eye." Anthony reached over and stroked her face as he drove them to the Bronx. "Daddy, I can't stay with him any longer. He goes into rages."

Diane spent the week with her parents. Finally, Anthony called Frank and told him that he wanted to speak with him. Anthony gave Frank a choice. Either divorce Diane, or move from Manhattan to the Bronx into the apartment above Anthony. Frank assured Anthony that it would never

Lies That Bind

happen again, and agreed to move to the Bronx. Anthony believed all that was necessary to stop the violence was for him and Josephine to be living in close proximity to his son-in-law.

Chris was happy about their move to the Bronx. He loved living above his grandparents. Now he could visit them every day. Every night before going to bed, Diane sent him downstairs to kiss his grandparents. Typically, Chris was gone for half an hour or until Diane went downstairs and reminded him that it was time for bed. Returning to their apartment, Diane ordered him to kiss his father. It was a moment that Chris had come to dread. Being physically close to Frank now always gave rise to an unpleasant collection of physical and emotional sensations. Anxiously, Chris would walk into the dark living room and try to anticipate Frank's mood. As he approached his father, usually dragging his feet so as to get his attention and not surprise him, Chris's nostrils filled with the stench of cigarette smoke. Frank sat dressed in what Diane called his "guinea tee shirt" and his gray work pants. He was typically sprawled out in his Lazy-Boy chair, the ashtray on his stomach and his eyes glued to the television. His forefinger was yellowish-brown from the stain of nicotine. He always seemed so far away. When Chris finally made himself noticed by shuffling his feet or stepping into view, Frank would slowly turn his head to look at Chris. Never smiling or saying a word, he would turn his cheek toward Chris to kiss.

Now that Chris was living above his grandparents, he and his grandfather had a new Sunday morning ritual. Diane would wake Chris early and ready him for his Sunday morning walk with his grandfather. They would head out, regardless of the weather, to buy bagels, or crumb buns and crullers, or Kaiser rolls, and then stop at Anthony's grocery store and get two or three fresh loaves of Italian bread. As they walked, Anthony would put out his forefinger for Chris to hold; it would fill his entire hand. Anthony was only about five feet eight inches tall, but Chris had to take two steps to every one of Anthony's. As they walked, Chris would often have trouble keeping up with his grandfather. Sometimes Anthony asked the boy if he was getting too tired to continue walking. "Are your legs getting rusty?"

"Yeah, Grandpa."

Anthony would smile and say, "Well then, if you're too tired to walk, maybe you should run." At six, that made sense, especially when explained to him by his grandfather. So he would run ahead of Anthony, then stop and rest while he waited for his grandfather, then he would run ahead of him again. When Chris grew tired of running, he would take his grandfather's finger again and walk with him.

After their early morning foray, Chris would help his grandmother make the tomato sauce for Sunday's mid-day family dinner, which included her five children, their spouses, and their children. Dinner always consisted of some kind of macaroni covered in a meat tomato sauce, which in his family was called gravy. The meat in the sauce could be cubes of beef or pork, Italian sausage, chicken, or meatballs. However, no matter what kind of meat was used, Josephine would always make four or five meatballs for Sunday lunch. After the meat was browned, the sauce was made and left to simmer for two to three hours.

Josephine had a rule. None of the fifteen family members, who would wander through her apartment at various times of the day before dinner, were allowed to sample the sauce or the meat. "If everyone dips into the sauce there will never be enough for dinner," she explained. There were to be no exceptions; well, almost none.

Every Sunday, Anthony would sneak Chris into the kitchen. He would take a large piece of fresh Italian bread and submerge it into the sauce and tell Chris to count to ten in Italian. Each time Chris called off another number, Anthony would put up another finger on his hands. Then he would remove the gravy-soaked bread, along with two or three meatballs from the saucepot. Anthony would cut up the meatballs and place them on the soaked bread and sprinkle it all with Parmesan cheese. He would hand Chris a fork and wink as they both dug in.

"Yum, Grandpa, it is *so* good. Grandma's the best cook." Chris delighted in their secret ritual.

"Shhhh, *mangiare, non parlare.*"

"Okay, Grandpa. I *mangiare* the meatballs, Grandpa."

"Shhhh, eat, eat."

After they were finished Anthony would clean all traces of their secret indulgence and say, "Give grandpa a kiss."

It did not matter to Anthony or Chris that Diane and Josephine knew of their furtive Sunday lunches. It always remained their secret.

* * * * *

What a wonderful memory, I thought. Grandparents can be a powerful source of a sense of well-being. "You enjoy talking about your grandparents," I said. At first, he smiled and nodded, then his smiled turned to a frown.

Chapter Three

"ARE YOUR GRANDPARENTS LIVING here now or are they visiting from 'the City'?" I asked.

"They're visiting," Chris said with a smile. "My graduation."

"They're very important to you," I added. Chris nodded in agreement. We sat for a while, and neither of us spoke. Then I asked, "Can we get back to Father O'Brien?"

"How long am I going to be here?"

"Most likely through the weekend. I want to get to what happened to you yesterday."

Chris continued to stare at his feet, "Have you ever read any of Stephen Hawking's books?" he asked.

"Yes, why?"

"Isn't he the one who talks about parallel universes?" he asked.

"What about parallel universes?"

"Well, you see, there is a universe just like ours moving in the opposite direction. It's dark, so we can't see it."

"Okay."

"There are people like us on that parallel universe, but doing the opposite of this."

"And what would that be?" I found myself at first feeling frustrated. I wanted to know what had happened in the confessional. I took a deep breath and allowed myself to accept his anxiety. My frustration then turned to curiosity about how his thoughts and emotions would be revealed. Again, I felt open to him, and although I was certain my face did not show it, I felt my eyes smiling.

"I don't know. I was just wondering that myself."

"Take a guess."

"We'd be sitting outside someplace." Chris hesitated. "Near water. Maybe swimming in water, in the ocean or a pool. But there would be sun." Again, he hesitated and then looked at me and smiled. "You're from New York City, aren't you?"

"How did you know?" I wondered why I was surprised that he picked up on that. Usually, I am nothing more than a listening object to many of the kids I treat. But I knew Chris was taking in everything I said, sizing me up. Maybe my surprise was his willingness to be so direct.

Chris smiled, looking pleased. "Before, you said, 'the City'. No one calls New York City 'the City' except people from there, and you also have an accent." It was good to see him smile; his face relaxed and his mood lightened. "Is it okay that I said that you have an accent? I mean I do too, but I like that I do."

I was not surprised at how quickly he worried that he had offended me; not unusual for a survivor of abuse. "I'm not offended in the least. I like my New Yawk accent, too," I said, smiling.

"Are you a New York chauvinist, too?"

"Yes, I've been accused of that."

"But you're not Italian," he smiled.

"No, I'm not, but my best friend in New York is Italian. I spend a lot of time with his family. And, yes, being Italian is something he's proud of also."

"I mean, I really don't think I'm better than anyone else, but if you have to be something…"

"…there's nothing better than being a New York Italian," I finished. We both smiled.

Chris chuckled and said, "That's cool," nodding his approval. "When I was a kid we used to go to Orchard Beach. Do you know where that is?"

"Yes."

He smiled and nodded again, "You must be from the Bronx then. Right?"

"Yes," I said, smiling as he glanced at me. His smile was contagious.

"Wow, that is too cool. I mean think of it, two guys from the Bronx, here."

I struggled with whether or not to answer his questions, but my sense was that he desperately wanted to find some common ground. I guessed that he was needing a way to connect with me, and to deny him the opportunity would be counter-productive. Avenues that led to building trust were sometimes hard to find. He was working toward telling me something; looking for a reason to trust me. Perhaps, this would do.

There was now an energy about him I had not seen before. "I love that my family is Italian. I guess I've said that." He glanced at me and smiled. I nodded. "Sometimes I think that that's weird. I mean I'm an American,

Lies That Bind

but I love that my family is from Italy." His voice sounded light and pleased. "I've never been there. My grandfather said that he would send me to Italy for a summer when I graduate college. What I want to do is take a semester and go abroad while I'm in college—and go to Italy, of course."

"Of course," I said smiling. It was clear to me that his attachment to his grandparents brought him a sense of identity that he was proud of and took pleasure in; a sense of belonging, security and well-being.

"My grandfather is the oldest of thirteen children and my grandmother is the oldest of nine. They were born in Italy, but some of their younger siblings were born here. Once I went to a wedding of one of my mother's cousins, and there were over a hundred people there from just my grandfather's family. They were all my aunts and uncles and cousins, and I knew them all. Isn't that cool?" His smile filled his face. "I mean, they did this thing during the dinner, where the photographer said, 'Everyone with Dinato blood please gather here for a family picture.' Over seventy people got up." He had become animated. "I mean, that meant that all the people who married into our family, they don't have Dinato blood, so they wouldn't be in the picture." He paused, his chest puffed out as he sat up straighter in his chair. "My grandfather calls them the in-laws, '*i stanieri*', the strangers," Chris said, delighted. "Man I loved being in that picture. My grandfather sat in a chair in the middle and I knelt in front of him. He had his hand on my shoulder." Chris looked at me and said, "Can't you just see it? It was too cool, I will never forget that, never."

"Yes, it is 'too cool'," I said. "Family is very important, and it sounds like you are very important to them." I sometimes wondered why some of these kids fought on, while others tried to take their lives. In Chris's case the answer was obvious. He no longer felt as alone as before. "You asked me about Orchard Beach?"

"Oh yeah. It isn't all that great a beach. I mean, no waves like at the beaches here. But when I was a kid I loved going there."

* * * * *

Often, during the summers of Chris's childhood, his family had picnics at Orchard Beach, on the northeastern coast of the Bronx. Since it faces a bay, and not the Long Island Sound or the Atlantic Ocean, the water was warm, the waves were small, and the weather was usually mild. Adjacent to the beach was a large park with trees, picnic tables and barbecue pits.

Thomas Domenici

Memorial Day was always their first family outing. Anthony would send several of his brothers ahead to secure an area large enough for at least fifty or sixty people. All his brothers and sisters, with two exceptions, were married and had children, some of whom, like Diane, were married themselves, with children of their own. It was expected that at least once during the summer everyone would show up for one of the family picnics. Since the death of his mother and father, Anthony was considered the head of the family, and therefore attended all family functions.

One topic that always came up at a family event was the breakdown of the family. Anthony's parents had raised their children in Little Italy in Manhattan. As each child married, which was the only condition under which they were allowed to leave their parents' home, they found an apartment somewhere in Little Italy. Josephine and her parents also lived there. After the end of World War II, several of Anthony's brothers and sisters and their families moved to the Bronx. Anthony moved, first his business, then his family. One by one, the rest of his brothers and sisters and their families followed. But they were scattered in various neighborhoods throughout the Bronx, and even though they all lived within ten miles of each other, and some lived on the same block, they worried that the family unit was threatened. Picnics, special occasions, and holidays took on a special significance, they were an expression of the value of the family. Not the family values of fundamentalist Christians whose families had come from northern Europe, but of ethnic peoples from southern Europe.

As soon as they arrived at Orchard Beach someone would start a fire and place a very large pot filled with water on the barbecue grill. While other families might use such a pot to boil corn on the cob, they did not. There was an unwritten rule in Chris's family that on an "occasion," and a family picnic was an occasion, there had to be pasta. So, along with barbecued Italian sausages, grilled onions, red and green bell peppers, loaves of freshly baked Italian bread, and salads of all kinds, there was macaroni for everyone.

Chris loved family picnics. He loved seeing all his uncles and aunts, who always fussed over him. He was always impressed with all the food that was being cooked. And he loved to play in the water. He guessed that was why his grandmother gave him the Italian nickname "Peschadelle," which, literally, means "little fish." Chris and his cousins would spend the day digging holes and building sandcastles and forts, and running in and out of the one-foot waves. On this Memorial Day Chris, who was now seven years old, decided that he was going to be brave and learn to swim.

Lies That Bind

Anthony carried him into water that was over the boy's head. His grandfather placed a hand under Chris's stomach and told him to kick and move his arms. Gently, Anthony removed his hand, and watched as Chris tried to keep his head above the water.

"Grandpa, Grandpa, I can swim!" Chris shouted, exclaiming at his newly discovered ability.

Anthony smiled, "You are learning. This is your first time. But soon you'll be a 'champean' swimmer. Just like your Grandpa," Anthony assured him. To be like his grandfather was always the highest of compliments.

"Grandpa, when you were seven, were you a 'champean' swimmer?" Being thought of as a champean by his grandfather, at anything, was a badge of honor that Chris treasured.

Diane always cringed when she heard Chris speaking in broken English, and Chris often pronounced words as Anthony would, just to get a reaction from her. The boy knew how to pronounce the word "three" correctly, but also loved to watch the look his mother gave him when instead he said, "tree," like his grandfather. His favorite was "helicocker." "Helicopter, helicopter, Chris," she would shout. "You don't have to do everything like your Grandpa."

"No, I wasn't 'champean' until I was ten." Anthony replied. "Did I tell you how I became a champean swimmer?" He asked, as the two of them sat at the water's edge. Anthony was a storyteller at heart. He took any opportunity to tell the stories of his childhood. When Josephine was present, she would smile and say in Italian that he loved to stretch the truth, and that his stories changed a little, becoming better with each telling. "Well, I was ten years old, and my brother Mike was eight. We were very poor, we had just come from Italy, it was the Depression. During the summer we would try to find different ways of earning money. After my father would leave for work, he sold garlic on the Avenues, your Uncle Mike and I would walk to the river where they were working on the piers. We would hang around and wait."

"For what?" Chris asked, fully engrossed in his grandfather's story.

"Sometimes the guys working dropped one of their tools and it would fall into the water. Then I would jump in and try to find it. If I did, they'd give me a nickel. In those days a nickel was a lot of money." Anthony lay down on the wet sand, and Chris stepped over him and straddled his chest and then sat down on his grandfather's stomach.

"Really, how much money was it?"

"Oh, like two quarters today." Anthony was in his glory. He loved an audience, and Chris was his favorite. No one else seemed to give him such undivided attention and hang onto his every word. He smiled as Chris's eyes gleamed with anticipation.

"Well, my brother Mike wouldn't jump in because he didn't swim good."

"Dad," Diane complained, "it is 'Uncle Mike was not a good swimmer.'"

"Ma, that's what Grandpa said. Uncle Mike couldn't swim good," Chris repeated. Diane sighed and shook her head; Josephine smiled.

Ignoring Diane, Anthony continued, "The water was strong and it was very hard to swim. You had to be very strong."

"You were very strong then too, Grandpa?" Chris asked, as he put both his hands on Anthony's chest and looked him in the eyes.

"Oh, yeah. One day I jumped in after a hammer fell in the water. There were other kids there, too. They wanted to get the hammer so they could get the nickel. I jumped in and down I went. It was very deep and dark, you could hardly see." Anthony's tone was full of drama. Chris's mouth fell open. Diane and Josephine smiled at each other. Diane decided to join them on the sand. Anthony continued, "But I got to the bottom and finally found the hammer."

"Wow!" Chris exclaimed, his eyes as big as saucers.

"When I came up and started to swim to the ladder with the hammer, I heard people yellin' that Mike fell in."

"Uncle Mike fell in?" Chris asked with surprise. He glanced up at Diane who smiled and nodded.

Anthony nodded. "When I saw him, he was being pulled down the river. I dropped the hammer and started swimming to him. 'Hold on, Mike. Hold on, I'm coming,' I yelled. When I got to him he was pretty scared and very tired."

"I bet he was happy to see you, Grandpa," Chris said as he looked up and scanned the crowd, looking for his Uncle Mike.

Again Anthony nodded. He couldn't help smiling as he continued, "So I grabbed him and I had to swim really hard for both of us to get back to the pier. Finally, I got us there and got us out."

"Wow, Grandpa. Do you think he might have drowned?"

"Yeah. That was the day I became a champean swimmer."

"Wow, Grandpa. You were really a champean that day. You saved him. Is that why Uncle Mike works for you in the store?"

"No, he works for me because he is my brother and I love him."

Lies That Bind

"Why did Uncle Mike fall in, Grandpa?"

"I found out that the guy that got the hammer, after I dropped it, pushed him into the water."

"They pushed him in so they could get the hammer?" Chris asked, with his mouth still open and his eyes wide.

"Yup."

"Wow, that was mean," Chris added. Again, he glanced through the crowd of family members, looking for his Uncle Mike.

"Yup, when I found him the next day I beat him up."

"Really, Grandpa?" Chris was filled with awe.

"Anthony," Josephine complained, "don't fill that kid's head with stories."

"Yeah, that was the day I became a champean boxer."

"Really? Wow. Can I become a champean boxer?" Chris asked as he made two fists.

"Sure, I taught your mother to be a boxer." Anthony glanced toward Diane. He tried to quell his smile, but he loved watching Chris's face light up with delight. As Diane listened, she was caught between the bitterness she had felt toward her father for as long as she could remember, and the comfort she experienced in Anthony's devotion to her son.

"My mom is a boxer?" Chris stared up at Diane, who sat there smiling. She had heard this story countless times. She nodded and smiled.

"Ask her! Your mom is a champean boxer. She can box better than her brothers." Diane leaned over and kissed Anthony on his forehead.

Chris did ask Diane, and learned that Anthony had taught Diane to box when she was eight years old. Anthony had wanted a son, and Diane was his third daughter. It was not until five years later, when Josephine had borne him his fourth child, that Anthony got the boy he so desperately wanted.

There was a story told that when Diane was born, Anthony was so disappointed that she was a girl he suggested to Josephine that they swap Diane for a boy. He said he knew a couple that had three sons and were trying to have a girl. Their fourth child, another boy, was born a month before Diane. Of course, Josephine refused. Unfortunately, Diane learned at a very young age of the rumors of her father's proposed swap from her sisters. When Diane was fourteen a cousin informed her that the story of the proposed swap was true and that she knew the boy Diane was to be traded for. He had also learned of the story. Diane had only half believed the teasing of her older sisters, but this information changed the rumor into fact and her anger into contempt—a contempt that survived any efforts he made to win her love and respect. Diane spent her childhood, and much of her young adulthood, on the one hand trying to win her father's attention by being athletic, tough, and independent, and on the other hand being defiant, which she knew would anger him. Either way, Diane grew up a tomboy. Recently, however, watching Anthony's consistent devotion to her son, Diane had found herself able to set aside her pain.

Later the same summer, Cookie Grandma invited Frank, Diane, and Chris to a private club in the Bronx. It had a swimming pool. They were going to meet her there along with Frank's sister, her husband, and their son. Chris's cousin Rudy was eight years old and, much to Frank's often expressed disappointment, could "do everything better than Chris." Before leaving the house that day, Frank reminded Chris that his cousin Rudy knew how to swim. But, so did Chris. Or so he thought.

"I heard that your cousin Rudy can swim good," Frank said. Diane grimaced, making every effort not to correct Frank's grammar. She often voiced her fears to her mother that Chris would grow up sounding like a guinea from the Bronx.

"I can swim, too. I swimmed with Grandpa," Chris exclaimed proudly. "He said I'll be a champean."

"Swam Chris, not swimmed," Diane interrupted.

"That wasn't swimming. I was there, that was not swimming. He held you up. You're no champean," Frank said in his usual tone of derision. "You're going to swim with me today."

Chris tried to maintain his enthusiasm, but he worried about being compared again to his older cousin. "Uncle Rudy said he'd teach me, he taught cousin Rudy," Chris said warily. "He's a good teacher."

"I am going to teach you," Frank insisted sternly. "And I don't want to hear any sissy whining from you," his tone carried unmistakable disgust.

The drive to the Castle Hills pool, although closer to them than the beach, seemed to Chris to take much longer. He was so excited about his new adventure, that he almost became carsick. He had never been in a pool. When they arrived, they met his cookie grandma, his uncle, and his aunt. Rudy was already swimming. Chris was ready to jump in, but first they had to change into their swimsuits.

The locker room was underground and was dark and damp. It smelled musty, and the concrete floor was cold against Chris's bare feet. As Frank and Chris walked through the locker room, Chris noticed men walking around in the nude. He had never seen a naked adult before, and was surprised by the sight of their pubic hair. When Frank finally found and

Lies That Bind

opened their locker, he instructed Chris to undress. After Chris undressed he turned to his father and handed him his clothes. As he did, he noticed Frank's pubic hair. Becoming aware of Chris's stare, Frank quickly covered himself. He then spun his son around so forcefully Chris fell to his knees. Pulling him to his feet, Frank told him to face the locker.

"Don't move," he said contemptuously, with his mouth pressed against Chris's ear. Chris had grown accustomed to Frank's disdain.

What did I do? Chris wondered; his heart was pounding. *He always gets so mad at me and I never know why. He just hates me.* Chris heard Frank put on his bathing suit, put away their clothing. When Frank slammed the locker door closed, Chris jumped.

"Put on your bathing suit and meet me outside," Frank said as he walked away, leaving Chris standing naked in a dark maze of gray metal lockers and strangers. *What did I do?* Standing alone, Chris's eyes welled up with tears. *I hate him, too.* Drying his eyes, Chris put on his swimsuit. Finally, after several failed attempts, and a great deal of anxiety, he was able to find his way out of the locker room to where his father, mother, and cookie grandmother were waiting for him. Chris glanced into his father's eyes and saw that Frank was glaring at him. But Chris's sadness had, somewhere in the darkness of the locker room, turned to anger. He defiantly continued his stare at Frank, refusing to give in to his father's silent threat.

"What's wrong?" Diane asked, glancing from Chris to Frank and back again.

"Nothing," Frank said, continuing his stare.

"Frank, don't get on him. Not today. He has been looking forward to today," she pleaded.

Chris tried to make his way over to his cookie grandmother, who was standing near his mother. But as he passed his father, Frank took him by the hand. Chris could feel his father's anger in the strength of his grip. Chris's excitement began to return as they approached his uncle and he heard Rudy calling out to him. "Mom," Chris yelled, "can I go in?"

"Not without an adult," she insisted. "You don't know how to swim that well and the water is over your head."

"I'll learn, Mom, I promise," Chris yelled to her. "Uncle Rudy, will you teach me how to swim now?" Chris asked his uncle with excitement.

"I'm going to teach you how to swim," Frank said, taking Chris by the hand. Instead of running to keep up with his father's quick pace, Chris began dragging his feet.

There was a slide at the pool. Chris watched as his cousin Rudy climbed the ladder, sat at the top, and slid into the water. Under he went, and then he swam to the surface. Frank, still holding Chris by the hand, brought him to the slide. As he bent down to speak, Chris realized his intention. "Daddy," Chris said, staring down at his feet, "I don't want to go down the slide. The water is over my head. And it goes too fast."

"You'll be okay. You wait until I get into the pool. Then, when you go down the slide, I'll catch you," he assured Chris.

"No, it goes too fast," Chris began to whine. "Can't I just jump in from the side?" he pleaded, as he began to play with his fingers.

Frank grabbed Chris's arm and said, "Don't you dare embarrass me. Do you want everyone here to think you're a sissy?" Frank knelt down to be at eye level with Chris. When Chris looked into his father's eyes he saw the glare of disdain. "You climb that ladder, slide down the slide, and stop when you get to the bottom. Then jump in and I'll catch you. I promise." Chris looked away, shaking his head. "Look at me, Christopher." Again he shook him. "Now, march."

It had to have been the tallest ladder Chris had ever climbed. After struggling his way to the top, one rung at a time, he sat down, and then noticed a steady stream of water flowing down the slide. He gripped the railing of the slide with all his strength. As fear gripped him, he could feel his insides trembling. He contemplated climbing back down the ladder, but as he turned, he noticed a kid standing behind him.

"Go," the boy yelled, "don't be a scaredy-cat!"

Frank was in the pool staring up at Chris. Neither said a word, they just stared at each other. Chris repeated Frank's words to himself—*just stop at the bottom and jump in. I'll catch you, I promise*—over and over. With all the courage he could muster, and with the hope of making his father proud, he let go of the railings and started down the slide. But, before he could take a breath, his legs flew up into the air as he slid down. Then he felt himself launched though the air for what seemed to be a hundred feet before he hit the water butt first. Of course, he could not stop at the bottom of the slide. And, of course, Frank did not catch him as he had promised. In the shock of hitting the water Chris opened his mouth to take in air, but instead, he found himself inhaling water. His eyes strained in hopes of finding the surface. His ears registered every sound that echoed through the water. He could no longer make sense of which way was up or down; space no longer had direction. Everything was moving slowly; time no longer had meaning. He felt helpless and

Lies That Bind

alone, and was sure he was about to drown. In a matter of seconds, he went from feeling fear to feeling suspended—neither in space nor time—but on waves of pure terror, as he realized he couldn't swim.

"You're okay," Diane said, pulling Chris to the surface. Trying to calm him, Diane took the boy to the side of the pool and sat him on the edge. Chris was choking and coughing, and desperately hanging on to Diane. "Don't cry, you'll only make him angry," she warned. But Chris was not crying, it was no longer something he did. He was trembling.

"Mommy, don't make me swim with him anymore. He's mean and I hate him."

"Chris, don't say that. Please. He just wants to have fun with you."

"Fun!" Chris shouted. "Is it fun to drown me?" Josephine, who had given Chris the nickname of Peschadelle, had recently given him the name "The Lip." She claimed that Chris had an answer for everything and always had to have the last word.

Frank was laughing as he made his way to Chris. Pulling him back into the water, he said, "Come on, that wasn't so bad. Actually, it was pretty funny." Frank again warned Chris not to embarrass him. "Relax! Let go of me! Don't be afraid. Sissies are afraid. You've had the worst of it," he said, "now you can learn to swim."

Chris was no longer afraid; he was numb. Instead of fighting Frank, he acquiesced and did what he was told. However, Chris's compliance was no longer an effort to please Frank, but rather a mask for the first sparks of hatred. His eyes were fixed and his mind was focused. He was determined to learn to swim. His newfound contempt for his father brought about a determination to be all that his father demanded and more. He promised himself that never again would he allow himself to be humiliated by his father or anyone else.

As Frank held onto the seat of Chris's swimsuit, he promised that he would not let go of him. Moments later, when Chris finally started to relax, Frank picked him up out of the water, threw him into the air and back into the water. It was the sink-or-swim learning method, and that day Chris learned to swim.

Before they left the pool Frank insisted that Chris go down the slide again. "No!" Chris said, crossing his arms across his chest. He no longer stared at his feet in deference to his father; rather, he stared at Frank in defiance.

"Why? Now you can swim good," Frank insisted.

Chris answered, "I know I'm a good swimmer, now. But I don't care. I'm not doing it." Chris continued the stare.

Frank caught Chris's not too subtle grammatical alteration of what he had said. He heard Diane's voice in his son. *You little shit*, he thought to himself. "Go down the slide," Frank demanded. "I'll stand at the bottom of the slide in case you drown." Frank's face burned with anger.

"No! You didn't catch me before. And I don't care if you call me a sissy. I won't do it," Chris said, in a strangely matter-of-fact way.

Frank considered slapping the boy, but then he noticed his mother staring at him with the same look of contempt he now saw in Chris's face.

"Leave the boy alone, Frank," she insisted. She took Chris by the hand and walked him away.

On the way home Frank lectured Chris. Instead of praising him for learning to swim, Frank was still angry. "Why didn't you go on the slide again?"

"Because I didn't want to."

"That's not good enough," he said, turning his head to face Chris in the back seat. Chris was no longer surprised or even frightened by how ugly his father's face became when he was angry.

"Yes, it is," Chris insisted, refusing to show fear.

"When I tell you to do something, you'll do it!" Frank suddenly screamed, slamming his fist against the steering wheel.

"I did, I tried it, I did what you said," Chris insisted. "But you didn't do what you said. You said you'd catch me. And it wasn't funny and you laughed."

Diane pleaded, "Frank, leave him alone. He did okay. It was his first time, and you were too rough with him. He's only seven."

"Did you see how your cousin was swimming?" Frank continued. "He can swim good." Frank heard himself and heard Diane sigh. He bristled at the idea that his son would correct him again.

"Yeah, well, he's eight and Uncle Rudy taught him how to swim last year. If Uncle Rudy had taught me how to swim last year," Frank turned and glared at Chris, "I would be a better swimmer than he is." Chris hated being compared to his cousin. He knew he would always come up short in his father's eyes. Sissies always do, he thought.

"I tried to teach you how to swim."

"No, you didn't, you tried to drown me," Chris snapped. The anger in his voice surprised everyone. Diane's breath became shallow, she swallowed hard. Again, Frank turned and glared. Diane reached back from the front seat and waved her hand at Chris as if to say, "don't say another word". By now, Chris knew he was in trouble and so did Diane.

Lies That Bind

"Frank, stop it! Leave him alone!" she insisted. "Chris, you hush up." Diane turned and shook her head at Chris.

"You're making him into a sissy," Frank shouted. "And I won't have a sissy for a son."

"I don't care if I am a sissy," Chris yelled. "And I don't care if you think I'm a sissy…"

"Chris, stop it," Diane shouted.

"…and I don't want you to teach me anything ever. I don't care if you don't want me for a son, because I don't want you for a father. I'll have Grandpa for my father," Chris screamed.

With the skill of a marksman, and without swerving the car, in one sleek swift move Frank turned his body, swung his right arm, and backhanded Chris in the face so hard that the boy's mouth bled, but Chris did not cry. Diane screamed as she heard the sound of the slap across her son's face.

"That didn't even hurt," Chris sneered, refusing to give his father the satisfaction of seeing his surprise and pain. As he tasted the warm blood in his mouth, Chris said, in that same strikingly flat and matter-of-fact tone, "And I am going to tell Grandpa you hit me."

When they arrived home, Diane ordered Chris into his grandparents' apartment as she and Frank went upstairs to their apartment. Chris knew that once he was out of the way, their fight would begin. When Chris walked into his grandparents' apartment, Anthony saw Chris's face and recited his litany of Italian curses. Josephine found a washcloth and began to wash the blood from Chris's mouth and chin. All their eyes glanced at the ceiling as their attention turned to the commotion upstairs. Frank and Diane were screaming at each other, and someone was throwing and slamming objects against the walls and floor. Chris turned to run toward the door, but Josephine grabbed him and held onto him. "Anthony," Josephine shouted as she glanced up toward the apartment upstairs.

Anthony stood up from his chair, clenched his fists, and shouted toward the ceiling, "This time no second chance!"

With Anthony now upstairs, the commotion grew even louder. Now there were three voices, but soon only two. When Diane entered her mother's apartment she was crying, but her tears were born of rage. Josephine asked if Frank had hit her. Diane explained that she didn't give him the chance this time. "Daddy always said, when you think you're going to lose the fight, at least get in the first blow. He never saw it coming." Diane showed her mother her reddened knuckles. "That son-of-a bitch hit my son and drew blood for the last time. No one hits my son. No one!"

Although voices could no longer be heard from upstairs, there was now a great deal of movement. Later that evening, after dinner, Chris watched television while lying on his grandparents' couch with his head on Josephine's lap. She held an ice cube wrapped in a cloth napkin against his lower lip. Anthony did not come down for dinner. That night Chris slept in his grandparents' apartment. When Chris made his way upstairs the next morning in search of his mother, Frank was gone. Anthony had finally decided that Diane was right; Frank could not control his anger.

No one ever talked to Chris about what had happened that night. Adults in Chris's family never talked about things like that, especially in the presence of children. That was another rule in Chris's family. Chris came to regret what he had said to his father, and blamed himself for his parents divorce. Diane's only regret was the loss of the friendship she had shared with Cookie Grandma.

Nearly a year passed before Chris saw his father again. By then visitation had been arranged; Saturdays from ten in the morning until four in the afternoon. Chris was told that he had to wait outside for his father's arrival, since Frank refused to come to the door. Chris sat on the stoop and waited. The first Saturday Frank was two hours late. Diane sat by the window and fumed. Finally, Frank, driving a new black Ford, turned the corner and pulled up to where Chris was waiting. As the boy stood up, he glanced up to the window where Diane stood watch. She blew him a kiss. Chris took a deep breath and started toward the car. As he approached the vehicle he looked toward Frank. When Chris was seated and strapped in, he again glanced toward Frank, who continued to stare straight ahead as he began to drive. Part of Chris wanted to jump up, throw his arms around his father and say he missed him and was sorry for what he had said. Another part of him refused to show "weakness." He decided to do as his father did. Neither of them said a word.

The drive seemed endless. Chris fidgeted with the seat belt as he tried to decide what to say. He had only seen his cookie grandmother twice in the last year, and he missed her terribly. Finally, Chris blurted out, "Dad, can we go see Cookie Grandma?"

Frank replied, without hesitation, "She's dead. She died two months ago."

Chris was shocked. He felt as though someone had reached for his stomach and was forcing it up through his throat. His face suddenly felt on fire. With a trembling voice he asked, "Why didn't you tell me?"

Lies That Bind

Frank said, "I didn't think you'd care."

Chris knew not to cry. If he did, Frank would get angry and say, "Girls and sissies cry."

Instead of crying, Chris stared out the car window and swallowed hard. He was trying to put any thought of his cookie grandmother out of his mind. He hummed a song to himself, over and over again. He sat silently and watched as his father drove them to Frank's sister's house to spend the day. After lunch, Chris sat and watched Frank while he washed his car. Uncle Rudy and his son played catch on their front lawn. Chris prayed for the afternoon to end. No one mentioned his cookie grandmother. He thought of her loving touch, her arms wrapped around him tightly as he sat on her lap, the smell and taste of her cookies, and how she smiled each time she first saw him. Pain filled his chest and seemed to tear at his heart when he realized that he had not said goodbye to her. Each time his chest filled with pain he did everything he could to think of something else; something that made him angry. Watching Frank washing his new car, Chris wished his father had died instead of his cookie grandma.

Finally, it was time to leave his aunt's house. Again, the drive seemed to take forever. Neither Chris nor his father said a word. As Frank turned the corner of the street where Chris lived, Chris saw his mother and grandfather sitting outside their apartment building. Frank stopped the car in front of Chris's building. He turned and looked at Chris and said nothing. Chris turned and looked at Frank. And for the first time, Frank saw in Chris a reflection of himself. He recognized in Chris's eyes the hatred Frank had so often felt for his own father.

Chris slowly unbuckled his seatbelt and opened the car door; never taking his eyes off Frank. As he stepped outside the car and was out of his father's reach, and feeling the strength that came from the presence of his grandfather, Chris said to Frank, "I loved my cookie grandma. You are the one who didn't love her. She told Mommy that you can't love anybody." Then he shouted with the same disdain for Frank that Frank seemed to have for his son, "And I do care," as he slammed the car door. Frank stared at Chris as Chris stared back in defiance and, without a word, Frank drove away. Quickly, Anthony stood as he watched Frank drive off. Diane ran to Chris, who was still standing in the middle of the street. Chris told Diane that his cookie grandmother was dead, and that his father had said he did not think Chris would care. Chris kept repeating over and over, "He said that I don't care." Diane cried, and said, "Of course you do; we all do."

Anthony's only comment was, *"stu faccima,"* the Italian for "bastard."

Chapter Four

"I THINK THAT'S MY grandfather's favorite curse word," Chris said. "My mother uses it a lot too." He smiled. "*Stu faccima,*" he repeated slowly, using his hands as I imagined his grandfather would.

Stu faccima. I'll have to remember that one, I thought. It has a nice ring to it. Why was I thinking of Adam right now, I wondered.

When I first moved in with Adam, I told him I thought California was "God's country"—what can I say, I was in heaven. Once, we drove to San Francisco along the Pacific Coast Highway. There were hundreds of spectacular sites along its hundreds of miles of magnificent coastline with its many rock-ribbed bays and beaches. It took us two days to drive four hundred miles. Adam had a book with a map that showed the beaches where people usually swam naked. We stopped at many of them. The first winter that I was there Adam took me skiing at Squaw Valley. When we flew to Reno, I saw the Sierra Nevada mountain range for the first time. They curved like the backbone of a giant reptile along the state's eastern side, and held snow-covered peaks, lakes, and national parks. I had never skied before. Adam , an expert skier, suggested lessons. That was the first time I experienced the sting of his disdain. He seemed to be embarrassed by my lack of athleticism.

Running down the center of the state is the Great Central Valley, with its lush farmlands. South of the valley spreads Southern California, with the edge of the world's largest ocean to the west, and, east of the Sierras, the Mojave Desert, including Death Valley. California is also the home of the largest living trees, the giant Sequoias, and the oldest living things on earth, the Bristle Cone Pines, which are over four thousand years old. But, like my relationship with Adam, California is also paradise gone wrong. The Sequoia are near extinction, and the smog that drifts eastward from California's largest city, Los Angeles, threatens the Bristle Cone Pines. Los Angeles, known as the City of Angels, is also known for its depravity.

Los Angeles has two contradictory faces. Interestingly, this contradiction is, and always has been its lifeblood. There is an energy-producing

Lies That Bind

tension between the utopian dream of sunshine, winter-blooming flowers and a life of unlimited possibilities, and its shadow of endless miles of spaghetti-like car-jammed freeways, mindless middle-class culture, racial strife, poverty, despair, and violence—an energy that works on the collective psyche much as the San Andreas Fault works on the terrain.

I read in a Southern California tourist guide books that Los Angeles has more area codes than any region of the country. It is the home of more university graduates per capita than any U.S. city. It has more colleges and universities than all of Massachusetts, but also has large segments that are cultural and intellectual wastelands. While Los Angeles has problems financing its public schools, libraries and health-care system, it has more fitness centers, psychiatrists, psychologists, and plastic surgeons than any city in the nation. The residents, rather than invest in public places and services, fight to save their money for private pleasures. Los Angeles is the City of Angels, but the angels are child-like, narcissistic cherubs. And as in all narcissism, nothing is as it seems. Everything is borrowed, and illusion substitutes for reality. And if that weren't enough, while giving the appearance of immovability, the city is moving north at the same rate as a fingernail grows. In ten million years it will be San Francisco's neighbor.

As so many others have, I escaped to Los Angeles to live my dream: a new job, a new love, a new circle of friends, and an emotionally and physically healthier life. In New York it had often been a struggle to survive the intensity of "The City" and its people. In Los Angeles, one had to survive the split between surface perfection and underlying emptiness and despair. Los Angeles is the house on the hill above the Bates Motel, except the outside has been renovated for the cover of *Exteriors* magazine, an illegal alien manicures the front lawn, and the fence has fresh white paint. Inside Mrs. Bates' son Norman still talks to himself, and she remains dead but not buried.

As I had, Diane and Richard also came to Los Angeles to live their dream: a new beginning, the hope of recapturing their youthful love, and freedom from oppressive family ties. Chris's coming to Los Angeles was his nightmare.

"I didn't see him often after that," Chris said. "He got married again and his wife and I didn't like each other." He shrugged his shoulders, "He'd pick me up and drop me off at my aunt and uncle's house, and then pick me up in time to drive me home."

"He wouldn't spend time with you?" I asked.

"No. Eventually, he just didn't come anymore. I guess it was okay with me. I used to spend the time playing with my cousins. That was cool."

"And then you moved to California."

"Yeah. I hated that. I really didn't want to move. At first, I really hated Richard. But he's pretty cool. He makes my mom really happy, and that makes me happy too. But when I moved I didn't care. I just wanted to stay with my grandparents."

* * * * *

The flight from New York to Los Angeles was difficult for Chris. He did convince his mother, with the help of his grandfather, to put it off until the last possible week. But now he had to leave. He would be starting eighth grade at Saint Patrick's Middle School in a week, and Diane wanted Chris in Los Angeles. Richard, well aware of Chris's resentment of him, would have been content to have him stay in New York.

Richard had married early in his naval career, but his wife had died in a car accident when they were stationed in Italy. Ann, Richard's sister-in-law and Diane's best friend, had convinced him to call Diane during his last assignment, which happened to be in New Jersey. They started quietly meeting for dinner in Manhattan. They had not seen each other since Richard had joined the navy. Neither of them believed in second chances, but this was proving to be theirs.

Diane talked to Anthony and Josephine about her feelings for Richard, but Chris was kept in the dark until Diane and Richard decided to marry. Chris met him for the first time when Diane invited Richard to have dinner with her family the weekend of Chris's twelfth birthday. It was then he was told that Diane and Richard were going to marry. He was happy for his mother. Secretly, he was excited about the possibility of having a "dad." However, all his excitement turned to resentment, which he did not hesitate to express, when they announced their planned move to Los Angeles.

Richard had put his time in the Navy to good use. He had earned a college degree, and then had attended law school. He became a JAG lawyer and, now after twenty years of military service, had retired as a major with a pension and various excellent job opportunities, one of which was a partnership in a firm in Los Angeles. With his pension, the salary from his new job, and the investments he had made from an inheritance, Richard and Diane were now able to afford much of what they wanted.

"Grandpa, please, I don't want to go to L.A.," Chris pleaded.

Lies That Bind

"Sonny, trust me. It will be good. You belong with your mother." He reached out to his grandson saying, "Give your grandpa a kiss." Chris hugged him, and kissed him on the cheek.

"I love you, Grandpa," Chris said. He was afraid that he might not ever see them again. In actuality, it was his father whom Chris would never see again.

Diane smiled when she saw her son exit the airplane. "Give your mother a kiss," she said, as she opened her arms and pulled him toward her. Chris's face reddened with anger. He gave in to her hug, but then pulled away. Richard extended his hand, but Chris ignored him.

During her efforts to enroll Chris in Sacred Heart Middle School, Diane met Jack Payden, who taught eighth grade there and was a Boy Scout leader in Sherman Oaks. She had heard that space might become available in Payden's class, so one afternoon she went to the school, hoping to meet with him. As she stood outside his classroom, she overheard a very heated conversation between Payden and a man she thought she heard him call "Taylor." Suddenly a handsome man, dressed in slacks and a short-sleeved shirt and tie stormed out. He almost tripped over Diane.

"Mrs. Patrona, come in," Mr. Payden said.

"I'm here because I heard there might be an opening in your class next September," Diane said as she sat down in a chair that he was pointing to.

"I'm sorry to disappoint you. I did think there might be, but Mr. Jarrett has decided to keep his son David at Sacred Heart, and in my class."

"Was that Mr. Jarrett?"

Mr. Payden smiled, "Yes, it was."

"Oh, I thought I heard you call him Mr. Taylor."

"No, his name is Paul Jarrett," he said, looking away.

"He seemed very angry," Diane said.

"That he is, but I really shouldn't be…"

Diane interrupted him, "I'm sorry. I didn't mean to eavesdrop, but I couldn't help but overhear. And I guess I'm a little disappointed."

"That's okay. Mrs. Patrona, I'd like to hear about your son and what concerns you."

"Please call me Diane.

"Diane, would you like to get a cup of coffee?" Mr. Payden asked, as he rose.

"Yes, I'd love a cup of coffee," Diane said. "Are you related to Mr. Jarrett?"

"Why do you ask?" Mr. Payden said, as he opened the door for her.

"I thought I heard him say 'our parents.'"

"Oh that. Well, our parents knew each other."

"I see," Diane said. "Well, I *was* hoping that a space might open for Chris in your class." Diane explained her situation to Jack over coffee. He promised her that if a space became available Chris would be the first boy considered. He informed her that many of the boys in his Boy Scout troop were Sacred Heart students and would be attending Sacred Heart High School with Chris. He explained that many of them, like Chris, would also be playing summer league baseball, and then be on the high school baseball team. He encouraged her to have her son join his troop as soon as he arrived in Los Angeles and that he would introduce him to "a really great group of boys." Jack delighted in the prospect of helping another boy with his struggle through adolescence.

"Chris is very social. He enjoys being involved, but he can also withdraw into himself," Diane told Jack. Her concern was apparent to Jack. "He'll be resistant to the idea of meeting boys his age at first, but I know he'll do it. Perhaps you can spend time with him. You know, help us get him settled and involved."

Diane left her meeting with Jack feeling both disappointed and relieved. Chris would mostly likely not attend Sacred Heart Middle School, but she had asked if Jack would agree to meet Chris when he arrived in Los Angeles, and Jack had promised to be a mentor.

As Chris grudgingly unpacked he heard the doorbell ring. A few minutes later Diane called to him. "Chris, come here. There are people here I want you to meet."

Chris entered the living room. Jack and his wife were seated there. They were talking with Richard. Diane moved toward Chris and walked him toward them. Jack stood. "Hi Chris. It's nice to finally meet you. Your mom has told me a lot about you."

"Hi, and why am I meeting you?" Chris asked dryly. During the summer, along with entering puberty, Chris had started to have "attitude." They shook hands.

"This is Mr. Payden's wife," Diane said. "She's a dentist." Chris nodded. "Mr. Payden is a teacher at the Sacred Heart Middle School where we wanted you to attend, and he is a scoutmaster for the local Boy Scout troop. He was a Marine. Then he went to college and became a teacher," Diane explained. Her nervousness was apparent; she was rambling. Chris glared at his mother. He could not believe that on his first day moving into his new home he had to deal with some ex-Marine and his wife. He promised himself that he was going to make her life as miserable as she had made his.

Diane continued, "We have a surprise for you: he's taking some of the troop out this weekend for a camping trip. He's offered to take you along. You'll get to meet some of the kids in the neighborhood and kids that will be in your class when you get to high school."

"You're kidding me," Chris said to his mother with disgust. "I just got here and you're sending me off into the mountains with people I don't know?" Chris said, with a huff, and a rolling of the eyes. He was enjoying his new attitude.

Jack interrupted, "Chris, you'll enjoy it, the guys are great and I've told them about you and they're looking forward to meeting you."

Now it was a caustic smirk coupled with a tilt of the head and a loud exhalation. "Excuse me! I was talking to my mother, not you." He knew he was being brutal.

September in Los Angeles is often very hot. There are days when the temperature reaches a hundred degrees. And, if it is a hundred downtown, it is at least 110 in the San Fernando Valley, which was where they were. It never cooled off that Tuesday night. At nine on Wednesday morning it was already eighty degrees. This was the beginning of what would be a sweltering week.

Chris had started smoking that summer; Camels in the flip-top box. It was all part of his new attitude. He had not had a cigarette since he left New York. After breakfast he decided to go for a walk and have a cigarette. "Mom, I'm going for a walk to check out the neighborhood before it gets too hot."

"Where are you going?" Diane asked.

"I don't know, just around. Don't worry, I'll be back in about an hour."

"Honey, be careful," Diane said. "Do you want me to come with you?"

"I don't need company. This is Los Angeles, remember, not Harlem."

"Wait up," Diane insisted, "I'd like to get some exercise. Let me put on my sneakers."

"Whatever," Chris sighed as he rolled his eyes and shrugged his shoulders. "I'll wait outside, don't rush." The knot in his stomach seemed to be getting tighter. As he waited for her, he smoked a cigarette. After walking for a while, with Diane leading the way, they passed Jack Payden's house. And he, coincidentally, was outside working on his lawn.

"Hey, Diane. Hey, Chris," Jack called out. "What are you two up to?"

"Chris wanted to take a walk and see the neighborhood. Maybe you could show him around?"

"Sure, I'd love to. I have the day free. I was trying to get this lawn taken care of before it gets too hot. But, any excuse not to work."

"Great. I have so much to do today."

Chris was furious with his mother. *Who did she think she was kidding,* he thought. While Chris had been sneaking a smoke back at their house, Diane had been inside making a phone call. Now he knew whom she had called. Diane kissed Chris and said goodbye. As Chris and Jack started their walk, Jack made small talk for about two or three blocks, and then asked Chris for a cigarette. He had not had a cigarette since he was discharged from the Marines, but he thought this would be a good way to make a connection with Chris.

"What are you talking about?" Chris snapped back.

"I know you smoke, I can smell it on you."

"Oh really, so you're a fuckin' spy, too?" Cursing was also new.

"No." He looked at Chris. "So, are you going to share? If not, let's walk to a store so I can get a pack." Chris turned and faced Jack, and then pulled up his tee shirt, reached down into the front of his shorts and into his jockey shorts and pulled out two cigarettes and a lighter.

"No one ever looks there for anything you're hiding." Chris said as he smiled at Jack caustically, thinking that Jack would not smoke the cigarette after it had been down the front of Chris's underwear.

"So, what else you hiding down there?" Jack asked, as he lit the cigarette.

"We're going to have to stop at the store anyway, *Jack,*" Chris said, saving the emphasis for Jack's name. "I only have one more, and it's mine." They bought a pack of cigarettes and some orange juice, and walked to a park, looking for some shade. They found a picnic table, sat down and opened their juice. After more small talk Jack turned and looking directly at Chris, asked, "Your mom told me that something happened between you and your dad. Do you want to talk about it?"

"Real subtle, Jack. And why would I want to talk to you about anything?" Chris snapped at Jack. "She put you up to this."

"She's worried about you," Jack explained. Jack opened the pack of cigarettes and offered one to Chris.

"Why would I tell you shit?" Chris said. Chris was deciding to head home. He was practicing the argument he was going to have with his mother. He took the cigarette from Jack, reached into his underwear, pulled out his lighter, and lit his own cigarette leaving Jack's unlit.

"I think she was talking about your father not coming to the airport when you left. And there was an incident before you left?" Jack took the lighter from Chris and lit his own cigarette.

"Mind your own business, *Jack*, I can't fuckin' believe she told you this stuff. God, she pisses me off," Chris growled, as he clenched both his fists. In a family where little was talked about, talking to strangers—and Jack was certainly a stranger—was a violation.

"Can I ask you something?" Jack said, looking at Chris. "And look at me when you answer, okay?" There was that middle school, boy-scout-leader tone to his voice that says, pay attention to me *now*. "Are you angry with me, too? Did I do something to you?"

Chris did not want to look at him, but he did. "No, you didn't do anything, and no, I'm not angry with you," Chris said defensively. "But why are you so fuckin' interested in me, anyway? I don't get it," he said, going back on the offensive.

"Why am I interested? I understand you were in the Boy Scouts. Is that right?"

"Yeah." Chris played with his cigarette.

"Well, your mom wants you to continue with the scouts, perhaps become an Eagle Scout. I can help you do that. I don't know what your other troop leader did, but I take a personal interest in my boys. You could have a difficult time of it; these boys have known each other since their first grade. Or you can have a very easy time of it. They are great guys. I'm here to try to make this transition easy on you. That's part of what the Boy Scouts are about. All I want to do is get to know you, help you out. There's nothing in it for me. Except to be a person who entices you into new and exciting experiences," Jack said, looking directly into Chris's eyes.

"Oh really, and what would those be?" Chris asked, scowling.

"We'll see," Jack said smiling. "The camping trip this weekend, for example. Where you can possibly make new friends." Chris took a deep breath. "Next year you'll be going to Sacred Heart High. They'll push you hard into sports. Some of these guys will be on the baseball team there. Next year you'll all be too old for Little League, but there is a summer league. So why not get to know them now? Make your life a little easier, Chris."

There was a long silence. They both sat there smoking, and glanced at each other from time to time. Jack broke the silence. "I heard what happened was pretty bad, and that you haven't talked to anyone about it."

Again, Chris tensed up. "Look, if I wanted everyone to know about it I would have told them. And I don't talk about things that happen with people outside my family. As a matter of fact, I don't talk to anyone inside my family, either," Chris said, placing his cigarette between his thumb and middle finger and flicking it as far as he could. He'd gotten pretty good at it, it was a New York thing.

"Okay, look, let's go back," Jack said, "Let's grab our bathing suits and towels. It's getting really hot. We have cigarettes. Let's go find a nice beach. It's too hot to hang around here," he said pulling at Chris's arm. "Can you swim?"

"Yes. I am a champean swimmer."

"Can you body surf?"

"I don't know, I've never tried."

"Oh yeah, well, I'm a great body surfer," Jack said. "And it will be only your first new experience with me." Jack smiled.

"Really," Chris said. "I guess that makes you champean."

"What's with this 'champean' stuff?"

"Never mind, just forget it. That's none of your business either," Chris said, displaying what Jack thought of as "the dreaded adolescent smirk" that, as an eight- grade teacher, he had seen countless times.

"Do you give everyone this much shit?" Jack asked.

"Yes, but especially assholes." For some reason Chris laughed. so did Jack.

"Well lighten up a bit and let's try to have some fun at the beach."

On the way to the beach Chris decided to drop some of his attitude. He guessed that Jack was about thirty, and thought he seemed to be a decent guy. He asked Jack why he had joined the Marines. Jack explained that he was young, without direction, and without a way to support himself at the time. As it turned out, the military had paid for his college tuition. He was actually thirty-two, but Chris did not think he looked it. He was tall, blond, and blue-eyed. He was rather lean and muscular.

When Jack found a fairly deserted beach near Malibu he parked the car. Chris noticed that there was nowhere to change into his bathing suit. Jack suggested that they climb into the back seat and change there. As they were naked and struggling to get on their suits, Jack remarked, sounding surprised, "You have pubic hair."

Lies That Bind

"Yeah, so?" Chris said, feeling his face flush.

"Oh sorry, I didn't mean to embarrass you."

"I'm not embarrassed. Why are you surprised?"

"Well, you're only twelve. I didn't have pubic hair until I was fourteen. I didn't start masturbating until I was fifteen," he said so nonchalantly it shocked Chris.

Chris said, feeling anxious, "Well, I'm going to be thirteen in about six weeks." Chris tied the drawstrings on his bathing suit. "I started about six months ago," trying to sound as nonchalant as Jack.

"Having pubic hair?" Jack asked.

"No," Chris laughingly said, "jerking off," as if it were a badge of honor. He had never admitted to an adult that he masturbated, although it was common talk with guys his own age. Admitting it to Jack made him feel a bit queasy.

They made their way across the hot sand and down to the water; the waves were breaking at five feet. They unfolded and laid out their towels. Jack had brought a tube of sunblock, and insisted that Chris allow him to spread the lotion on his already tanned back. "I really don't need this stuff," Chris explained, as Jack continued to rub the lotion onto Chris's back. "I'm Italian, we don't burn."

"Just stand still, I'm almost done with your back," Jack said. Chris remained tense as Jack slipped his hand below the waistband of Chris's swimsuit and along the upper cleavage of his buttock. Jack had not seen such a muscular buttock on such a young boy. Again, he ran his fingers below the waistband of Chris's swimsuit, this time more slowly. He hesitated as his fingers fell into the divide. Timing, he thought. He felt Chris's back muscles tighten. "You have a very muscular back. That must be from playing ball."

Jack knew that Chris was hurting emotionally. It was also clear to Jack that Chris needed attention from a man. Most boys this age do, he had come to learn, and most boys never get it; even those with live-in fathers. He knew that with his move to Los Angeles, Chris was now isolated and looking for friendship and guidance. "Now turn around and let me do your chest," Jack said, as he moved his hand along the small of Chris's back.

"I can do that, really," Chris said, holding out his hand, asking for the lotion.

"I'll do it." Jack said as he began rubbing the lotion onto Chris's smooth chest.

"You've got a nice build for a twelve-year-old. Your mother said you like to play baseball."

"Yeah." Chris was feeling extremely uncomfortable, but acquiesced to Jack's demands. Underneath all his bravado, he desperately wanted to fit in, and Jack had promised him an opportunity. After all, Chris reasoned, he is a teacher and a Boy Scout leader.

"Several of the guys I want to introduce you to also play. You'll like them," Jack said, as he rubbed the lotion on Chris's stomach, again reaching his fingers below the waist band of Chris's swimsuit, feeling the beginnings of Chris's pubic hair. Jack then noticed what he thought was a growing bulge in the boy's swimsuit. "Here," Jack said, handing the tube of lotion to Chris, "now you do me. I'm blond and I do burn." As Chris passed his hands over his back Jack felt a chill of excitement run up his thighs.

Chris could not remember ever doing anything like this before. He wanted to say no, but decided again to acquiesce to Jack's wishes. Jack then turned, and it became apparent to Chris that Jack wanted him to continue spreading the lotion onto his chest. Chris again felt a wave of queasiness, and a blush came to his face as he realized he had the beginnings of an erection. Jack continued, "Peter Cartola is a good ball player and so is Derek Powell. They're great guys and they're coming on the camping trip this weekend."

Jack had long ago dedicated himself to helping these boys through the turmoil of adolescence. "Timing, it's all timing," Jack said with a smile, "you have to do your thinking beforehand. Then you just have to wait for the right moment. Then go for it. If you wait for that right moment, everything will always fall into place. Once you've committed to the action, don't second-guess yourself. Don't let your anxiety stop you, but rather just go with the adrenaline rush, the danger makes it all the more of a high," Jack said as he put his arm around Chris's shoulder and pulled Chris close to him.

"What are you talking about?" Chris asked.

"Catching a wave, body surfing," Jack said, pointing toward the surf.

Although Chris did know how to swim, he had never learned to body-surf. Jack loved to bodysurf, and enjoyed teaching Chris how to catch the waves. By the end of the day Chris was sailing through the breakers. He did not know who was more excited by his learning how to take the waves, Jack or himself. But Chris did love the attention and the cheers every time he successfully caught a wave.

Jack would take a wave and then shout to Chris to wait for the next one. Then Jack stood on the beach and watched as Chris caught the next one. It lifted Chris along its edge, he could see Jack yelling and waving his

Lies That Bind

arms with excitement. Jack would then grab him and pull him back out into the water saying, "You're doing great. Doesn't it feel great? The power of the waves, wow, what a high! Don't you love it?" More than a high from the power of the waves, Chris was feeling a high from the power of Jack's excitement about how he was doing, or what they were doing together.

By late afternoon Chris felt both exhilarated and exhausted. They decided to walk along the beach to where they could get something to eat. About two miles down the beach they found a hamburger stand and each had a burger, fries and a coke. Chris telephoned Diane to tell her that they were having a great time, having a late lunch, and that he would not make it home for dinner. She was happy to hear him sound so excited as he explained how Jack had taught him how to bodysurf. When they returned to the car, Jack decided they should go for a swim and wait for the traffic to die down before heading home.

"We should have bought another pack of cigarettes," Chris said, as he counted four left.

"I bought another pack, it's in the car."

"You won't tell my mom that I smoke, will you? If you do, I'll really be in shit up to here," he said, touching the top of his head.

"If you ask me not to, I won't. You can trust me."

"Trust you? There are only two people I trust, my grandmother and my grandfather. You better not tell my mom or anyone else."

"Okay," he paused. "Let's go swimming naked," Jack suggested.

"I don't think that's allowed," Chris said nervously.

"There aren't many people on the beach, and if we're quick no one will notice. Have you ever gone swimming naked?"

"Only in my bathtub," Chris said, half jokingly.

"Ahh! Well then, this will be another new experience. Sometimes when I take the scout troop out swimming in the stream where we camp, we all go swimming naked. They love it," Jack explained. "We'll do that this weekend."

"Do people in California do this a lot?" Chris asked as he took off his bathing suit.

"Oh, yeah," Jack answered.

"Fruits, nuts, and yogurt, and swimming naked," Chris said with a shrug.

"What?"

"Oh, people in New York say California is full of fruits, nuts, and yogurt," Chris called out as they ran into the water.

"Have you ever slept in the nude?" Jack asked, when they were past the breakers and treading water.

"Nah."

"We do that here, too. When you camp and sleep in a sleeping bag, it's best to sleep naked. You stay warmer that way, and besides, it's a great feeling."

Chris had to admit it felt wonderfully free to be out in the ocean, bodysurfing naked. A couple of times people walked by and noticed them, but they never gave them a second look. Treading water, he watched as Jack's naked buttocks rose to the surface of the water when he caught a wave. He watched Jack turn and run back toward the breakers. He could not help but stare at Jack's bouncing genitals. Chris decided that nudity was going to be part of his new attitude.

While driving home Jack explained that he and his wife were expecting a child. He said no one else knew but that he just had to share the great news with someone. He asked Chris to promise not tell anyone. "Can I trust you, Chris?"

"Sure, I can keep a secret." Now they both had secrets to keep.

"Can I tell you a weird story about something that happened to me several years ago? Well, actually, I'll have to tell you about my growing up. Do you want to hear about it?" Jack asked.

Chris shrugged. "Sure, I guess. If you want to tell me, I'll listen."

"I can trust you, right? I mean you won't tell anyone?" *And so it begins*, Jack thought, feeling the beginning of his arousal.

"No, I won't tell."

"Hmm, should I give you the long or short version?" Jack asked rhetorically. "I guess I'll give you the short version; just the important details. I guess I should start with the fact that when I was born I was given the name Andrew Jackson Payden."

"You're kidding, right?" Chris asked laughingly.

"No, that's my name. And I have a brother who is five years older than me and his name was Zachary Taylor Payden," Jack added.

"No way. What do you mean 'was his name'?"

"I'm not kidding. He changed his name, but I'll tell you about that at the end of my story. Okay? Anyway, my father's name was Henry and my mom's name was Melissa. They're both dead." Chris turned slightly toward Jack, who stared into the traffic in front of him. "They met at the University of California in Berkeley while my father was working on his doctorate in history. That's up north near San Francisco. He was an American History professor, which is why he picked those names for my

Lies That Bind

brother and me. He had just come out of the Army after serving in the Second World War. My mom was a lot younger than him when they met. I think she was in her second year of college. He was her teacher or something. Anyway, I guess she became pregnant and they had to get married, because six months after they were married my brother Taylor was born. She dropped out of school; she was going to be a nurse." Jack could see that Chris was listening intently.

"When he finished his doctorate at Berkeley he found a job teaching at a city college in Santa Barbara, which is about one hundred miles north of here, on the coast. Do you know anything about Santa Barbara?" Jack asked, happy that Chris was interested in his story.

"No. I don't think I've ever heard of it."

"My dad was doing what he loved to do: teaching, writing, and surfing. I guess my mom wasn't all that happy. She wanted to be working and just when she thought she might be able to get out—Taylor was starting school—I was born. And I guess I was a difficult baby. My mom became severely depressed and my dad stayed away more. He started to have affairs with his students and my mom started to drink."

"How did you find out all this stuff?" Chris interrupted.

"My mother's sister told me most of it. Well, when I entered elementary school my dad told my mom to go back to school, but she was drinking so much she didn't do very well. I guess she felt like a failure and felt trapped and really hated my dad because he was cheating and stuff. So she drank more and more, and then I guess things started to get really bad. My dad became violent. The drinking and the violence became pretty regular. I can remember a lot of yelling and hitting and stuff like that. When Taylor and I would come home from school she'd be drunk and ranting about something, or she'd be passed out."

"I thought his name was Zachary," Chris said, now turned in his seat so that he could see Jack as he told his story. Jack looked into Chris's eyes, and then he glanced at his tanned naked chest.

"Oh, well, my nickname is Jack, from Andrew Jackson, and my brother's was Taylor, from Zachary Taylor." Chris nodded. "Taylor had it worse than I did, I guess. He really tried to keep my mom sober. Tried to make her happy. He always wanted everything to be perfect. I think he believed that if he could make everything right she'd be happy and she wouldn't drink. I just tried to stay out of her way." As Jack continued, he saw again in his mind's eye the picture of Chris naked and diving into the waves.

"She'd get crazy though, and sometimes start hitting us for no good reason. One time she hit Taylor with an extension cord she pulled from a lamp. I got so scared that I peed my pants. When she saw that I was all wet she went nuts and started to come after me, but Taylor got in her way and I ran. He got a worse beating for that. I remember that he always tried to protect me from her. He was the best big brother a kid could have. If it hadn't been for him, I think she would have killed me."

"What would he do?" Jack noticed that Chris looked distressed. Jack felt pleased with himself. This is sure-fire stuff, he thought.

"Well, he'd get up really early in the morning before we'd go to school and he'd make sure our room was really clean, he'd make the beds, and he'd make us lunch. He would get me ready for school and make sure we didn't wake her up. When we left the house he always made sure everything was perfect. When we came home he'd always go in first and see if she was drunk. If she was, he'd keep me out of the house until it was safe to come in. He'd often make dinner for us and then clean up. He always helped me with my homework so that I'd get good grades so she'd be happy. He did a lot of stuff."

"If everything was perfect why did she get angry?"

"You've never been around a drunk, have you?" Jack asked, as he glanced over at Chris.

Chris remembered his father drinking but he never thought of him as a drunk. "Not really, I guess not."

"Sometimes we'd come home and our bedroom would be torn completely apart. All our clothes would be on the floor and the beds turned upside down. Something would be wrong and she'd scream that I had made a mess. Taylor would make sure that I didn't come home until he had straightened everything up, and usually by then she'd be so drunk she didn't care if I came home. But it was always something that I did that made her tear things apart."

"Wow, I bet that scared the shit out of you," Chris said. Jack smiled to himself.

"Anyway, one day my dad had a heart attack while he was out swimming in the ocean. He went out for a swim one morning and they found his body later that day. Things got really bad for us after that. My mom went through all the money we had. Then my aunt, her sister, came down from Seattle. They put my mom in a hospital to sober up. When she got out, they sold our house and we moved to Seattle. My mom worked as a saleswoman and my brother and I went to school. My brother graduated

Lies That Bind

from high school and came down to Los Angeles to go to UCLA. About a month after he left, my mom found out that she had liver cancer. Less than a year later she died."

"Damn, you lost both your parents when you were a kid. Damn," Chris said, shaking his head. "Oh wow, what happened to you and your brother?"

"Well, I went and lived with my aunt and uncle and cousins. My brother changed his name and never came up to Seattle again. Not even for my mother's funeral."

"No shit? You've never seen him again?"

"Well, after I graduated high school I went into the Marines. After I was discharged I moved to Los Angeles and attended college at Cal State Northridge. That's where I earned my teacher's credential. While I was there I was able to find my brother. Like I said, he had changed his name, but I was able to find his graduation picture in his yearbook and his new name was in there."

"Did you ever see him again?"

"Yeah. I went to his house. But he wouldn't invite me in. We stood on his front steps and talked for about thirty minutes, and he told me that he never wanted to talk to me again. He said he had put everything behind him and didn't want to be reminded of any of it."

"Oh man, that sucks so bad." The compassion in Chris's voice excited Jack. "Do you ever see him?"

"Yes, once in a while, but we don't speak. We just ignore each other."

"Wow, if you were Italian that would never happen. Man, that really sucks. I'm really sorry for you."

"Well, thank you, but my life is good. I have a great wife, a great job, and a baby on the way. I love teaching, and I love being a scout leader. I try to be a big brother to my scouts like my brother was to me. Well, like he was when we were kids, not like he is now."

"That is so weird that he was such a great brother and then he just never wanted to see you again."

"He must have felt like my mother, you know, that it was all my fault. That I was the reason her life was so bad. Maybe it's true. If I hadn't been born she might have gone to school and become a nurse, and maybe she would have been happy."

"That's bullshit. Well, at least you're happy now, and fuck your brother." There was a long silence in the car. Chris glanced at Jack as Jack glanced at him. But neither of them spoke.

Thomas Domenici

Jack thought about what he hadn't told Chris: how Taylor was very protective of Jack, and struggled for perfection because their mother demanded it. But the goal was unattainable and Taylor's frustration with his mother's demands grew. As angry as he was at her, his fear of her dictated that he never express his building rage. However, when his father beat his mother Taylor began moving toward his bedroom door so he could watch. On one occasion, their parents had an argument about an affair Henry was having. Taylor watched as their argument turned from accusations about his sexual infidelity and her sexual frigidity to violence by both of them. This time Jack joined Taylor as he watched their father tear at Melissa's clothing. Before long he had her naked and pinned face down on the floor. They watched as their mother's drunken stupor took over and their father undressed himself and then sodomized her.

Henry had died several months after he raped Melissa. After Henry's death, Melissa had made her best effort not to drink. But, eventually the stress, anxiety, loneliness, and depression took over and Melissa was again using alcohol. Her drunkenness led to renewed verbal abuse.

When Taylor and Jack returned home from school and Melissa was in a rage, Taylor would try to protect Jack by attempting to reason with his mother, but when that failed he would hide his younger brother. Jack looked to Taylor for guidance, protection, affection and reassurance. Taylor was the only hold he had on sanity, and he idealized him.

Once, after Taylor had made Campbell's soup and peanut butter sandwiches for dinner, Melissa returned home from work drunk. As the boys sat in their room hoping that Melissa would quickly fall into a stupor, they heard her go into a tirade instead. Jack had left a mess in the kitchen. Knowing what was to follow, Taylor hid Jack under his bed. As she screamed for Jack, she started destroying the kitchen. Taylor made every effort to calm her, but her rage only escalated. Melissa finally fell into a stupor, but not until she had beaten Taylor with a lamp cord for refusing to turn Jack over to her. When Taylor returned to his room and knelt down to pull Jack from under his bed, he found himself kneeling in urine. In his terror, Jack had lost control. After cleaning the floor, Taylor and Jack undressed and washed their clothing so that no evidence would be found.

The boys went into the bathroom where they both climbed into the shower. It was unusual for them to shower together; Taylor was thirteen and Jack was eight. Jack noticed the welts all over his brother's arms and legs, and then noticed that Taylor had an erection. They started to explore each other's bodies, and Taylor convinced Jack that he should allow himself to be sodomized. When Jack protested because of the pain, Taylor threatened never to protect him from his mother's outbursts again. "Which pain do you think is worse, this or getting beaten by Mom?" Jack would do anything to escape his mother's tantrums and remain in Taylor's good favor. Soon, Jack was doing whatever Taylor demanded and whenever Taylor demanded it. Jack came to yield without protestation to what became Taylor's nightly demands.

As Jack had told Chris, Taylor had left Seattle to attend college in Los Angeles. When he did return to Seattle for Christmas before their mother's death he again demanded servicing from Jack. What was different this time, however, was Taylor's desire to inflict pain on Jack, and the obvious excitement that gave Taylor during their sexual encounters. This was the first time that Jack feared his brother. And yet, he still did not protest. What he suffered was nothing compared to what he thought Taylor had saved him from. In Jack's delusion, he labeled his willingness to submit unconditionally to his brother's demands as an act of love.

Finally Jack broke the silence in the car. "I hope you'll let me be a big brother to you. I really do want to introduce you to a bunch of really nice guys and to all kinds of new and exciting experiences." The movement in Jack's bathing suit alerted him to the initial stages of his own excitement. "I know you only trust a very few people, but I'm hoping you'll decide to trust me. I trust you."

Chris nodded. "I trust a lot more people than I say. Just not many people outside my family."

"I understand," Jack said.

"You seem pretty cool, though." Again there was a long silence. Jack was now fully erect. "Were your aunt and uncle kind to you?" Chris asked with clear concern.

"Yes." He wanted to reach over and touch Chris's naked chest, but he reminded himself that it was not the right time. "Very. My aunt was wonderful, and my uncle was pretty cool, too." Chris nodded.

During Jack's enlistment in the Marines he had had sexual encounters with a fellow Marine. He was surprised to find that it held very little excitement for him. Again, in college, he had the opportunity to experiment with a fellow classmate, but decided against it. He found that his sexual interests were strongly directed toward women. However, during his late twenties, after beginning his work as a teacher and Boy Scout leader, he found that boys—specifically boys who admired him, who reached out to him for his guidance and mentoring—sexually excited him. After his third successful assault on a pubescent boy, Jack came to understand that not only were his sexual interests connected to women, but also to teenage boys; or, more specifically, boys he mentored. At first, he wondered if it was fate or some unconscious drive that had steered him toward his profession, teaching adolescents. Later, he decided that it did not matter to him. What mattered was that he was saving these boys from the confusion and loneliness they were experiencing.

Eventually, he no longer waited for the occasional lonely boy to seek him out. Now he chose his targets. Of course, concerned parents like Diane often helped. His interest in their children was clearly transparent, something that might work against him, were it not for the trusted position he held. "This morning you said something happened between you and your father. If you want to talk about it, I won't tell anyone," Jack assured Chris, gently prodding him.

"I hate him. My father is a real asshole."

"What happened?" Jack asked, giving Chris a well-practiced look of concern. Jack noticed Chris looking out the passenger window. He took the opportunity to press the palm of his hand hard into his own crotch, enjoying the stimulation. He began to anticipate the coming weekend. He imagined his imminent pleasures.

"You can't tell anyone. I swear, if you do, I'll hate you, too."

"Okay, my word as an ex-Marine." They both laughed. The keeping of secrets, Jack thought triumphantly, they are the power behind the necessary and usually unspoken threat.

"I don't understand why you want to talk about this stuff. I was so happy when we left the beach and now I'm starting to feel angry again. What good does it do to talk about it, anyway?"

"You really should trust someone. You're too young to hold onto stuff. I hear you can get pretty depressed."

"I don't hold in my feelings. I get angry. Ask anyone who gets in my way. Ask my mother if I let my anger out."

"That's not what I mean," Jack said with an innocuous smile.

Again, there was silence in the car. Chris was angry, but what he did not say was that he was hurt and confused. He wanted to understand why he did things that seemed to be so natural to him, and yet always caused so much trouble. He sighed loudly. He decided to trust Jack, hoping that Jack might be different. He thought about all that Jack had experienced as a child, and the fact that he was a teacher and a scout leader.

Lies That Bind

"While I was staying with my grandparents this summer, I called my dad and told him I was moving to California. I hadn't seen him in over a year, and I figured he wouldn't miss me, but my grandfather kept on me about his being my dad, and that I had to respect him. Italians are big on the respect thing. My grandfather made me promise that I would call him. So I did, and I told him that I was leaving for L.A. and wouldn't be back to New York any time soon, and that I wanted to see him before I left."

"Why hadn't you seen him for so long?"

"Well, he had remarried, and his wife and I didn't get along. He would pick me up, drive me to his sister's house, leave me there, then pick up his wife and spend the day doing whatever. Then, he'd drop her off, pick me up, and take me home. I finally told him that if he wasn't going to spend the day with me not to pick me up anymore. So he didn't."

"Go on," Jack said, shaking his head.

"I called him in July. He said he'd come. I waited all day, but he didn't call and he never showed up. My granddad made me call him again. Same thing happened. Finally, the last weekend I was going to be in New York he came to see me. I was outside with my cousins and some of our friends. We were horsing around when he drove up. When I walked up to him, he looked right at me, and said, 'Can you tell me where I can find Chris?'"

"He didn't recognize you?"

"No," Chris said. His voice was still changing, but this cracking in his voice was sadness. " By now it had been almost a year since I had seen him. I had grown a lot. But still," he shrugged. Jack felt the weight in Chris's voice wash over him.

"How was that for you?"

"It made me mad," Chris said, this time the sadness almost breaking through. He took a deep breath before he continued. Jack reached over and rubbed Chris's leg.

"I really hate him."

"Yeah, but he's your dad."

"Screw you, Jack. You sound just like my grandfather," Chris said, shaking his head. "Anyway, I said, 'Dad that's me.' He looked surprised. He said 'You got tall.' I got into the car and we pulled away. I told him that Mom had remarried, and that I was going to live in California. I think I wanted him to ask me if I really wanted to go. I think I wanted him to care. Maybe he'd say, 'Come and live with me.' I mean, I wouldn't have, but…Anyway, we drove about a mile and stopped at a White Castle hamburger place. He gave me money and told me to get myself something for lunch. I got a hamburger and a shake. I guess I was confused. Why was he still in the car? Why here? There was a restaurant just across the street. I got back into the car and told him that I probably wouldn't be back to New York for a while. He didn't say anything. He started the car. He pulled out and started heading back to my grandparent's house. He parked in front and said, 'Well, be sure to write.' That was it."

"Just like that? 'Be sure to write'?" Jack asked in disbelief.

"I said, 'You drove here to see me for five minutes?' He said, 'Well, Jean'—that's his wife'—'is at the restaurant and I don't want to keep her waiting.' I lost it at that point. 'Jean is at the restaurant?'" Chris, reliving the event, was now quite animated, raising his voice and waving his hands. "'You drove here to see me for five minutes, to buy me a fuckin' hamburger and shake and then you're off to have lunch with her?' I was yelling. My father's eyes got bigger, but he didn't move or say a word. Then I pushed open the car door, but when I did I spilled my shake all over my lap and the seat of the car. I saw him coming at me and I threw myself out of the car onto the ground. As I stood up I yelled, 'You may never see me again, and you spend only five minutes with me? That's how much you care about me? Fuck you! I am going to move to California, I am going to change my name, and you'll never hear from me again!' Then he got out of the car. He looked boiling mad. I had seen this look before. I knew what was next."

"What?"

"I was about to get hit. I still had the hamburger in my hand. I lost the shake someplace; I guess when I rolled out of the car. He started around the car. I threw the hamburger at him and told him that if he tried to hit me I was going to hit back. By now, my cousins were standing behind me. He got back into his car and one of my cousins closed the other door. He started the car and drove away. I don't think I've ever been so angry. When I went inside, I had the milk shake all over me. My grandfather asked me why I was back so soon and what had happened. All I could say was, 'Fuck you. And leave me alone, God damn it. Just leave me alone. This is all your fuckin' fault.'"

"You cursed at your grandfather?"

"Yeah," Chris conceded, his voice now quiet and his body again frozen in place. "He got really angry, but my cousins told him what they had seen and he left me alone. Later, he came into my room and kept asking me to tell him what happened, but I wouldn't."

"Are you going to change your name?" Jack asked, glancing from the road to Chris and then back again.

Lies That Bind

"Hell, no. It's just as much mine as it is his."
"Do you think you'll ever see him again?"
"No."
"Would you want to?"
"It doesn't matter what I want. He'll never want to see me again," Chris said. Again, his voice betrayed his sadness. "I shouldn't have gotten so angry. I got scared. I thought he was going to hit me. I'm always doing and saying stupid stuff to hurt people and make them hate me. I always provoke people. I think I may be just bad," Chris said with a sigh. "I think I was going to hit my own father," and with that, Chris started trembling.

"Are you okay?" Jack asked. But it was immediately obvious that Chris was not okay. Jack took the next exit off the freeway and pulled the car off the road and stopped. He moved toward Chris and held him as Chris continued to shake uncontrollably. Jack was surprised to realize that Chris's body was covered with sweat. "Are you okay, Chris? Chris, are you okay?"

Chris doubled over as saliva began to pour from his mouth over his chin and down onto his chest. Jack, remembering his childhood bouts with anxiety, recognized the signs of a panic attack, but he had never seen anything like this before. He held Chris in his arms as Chris's breathing began to calm. Jack continued to stroke Chris's head.

"I'm going to puke," Chris whispered, opening the car door. Jack watched as Chris's body tensed as he vomited all he had eaten. Jack moved so that he could hold Chris head. When Chris was finished vomiting he sat up, closed the car door and said, "I think it must have been something I ate."

Jack sat back and said, "Probably." They both sat silently.

"Chris, I'm sure, if you want to see your father, you can write to him and he'll see you."

"You don't know my father," Chris said, as he took deep breaths, trying to calm himself. "He's a real bastard." Chris made full eye contact with Jack and in his most vulnerable and pleading voice said, "I don't want you to tell anyone what I told you about my father. Please!"

"I won't. It's our secret." Jack assured Chris, sounding concerned. But, as he held Chris and comforted him, Jack's body responded with arousal, reminding him again of his real desires.

"We don't talk about things like this in my family. And don't fuckin' tell them about what just happened, either."

"Or what, you'll beat me up?" Jack asked, as he continued to hold Chris.

"I'll tell that you're having a baby," Chris said jokingly. Chris began to feel the discomfort of their physical closeness and began to pull away. Jack gave him the space he needed. Timing, Jack thought.

"Are you okay, Chris?"

"I'm fine. I guess I got it all out. You know, the hamburger."

"I really think you should come on this camping trip with me and the troop this weekend. These are a bunch of great kids that you'll like, I'm sure of that," Jack said as he started the car.

"It'll just be too weird," Chris said, wiping his face with his tee shirt.

"How so?" Jack asked, again touching Chris's leg. Chris made no effort to stop him. He hardly seemed to notice Jack's touch.

"I don't know, being with all those guys that know each other. And then there's me. I don't know anyone."

"You know me. Look there are only six other guys going. You and I will make eight. That's a good size group. We're going for three nights. We take two-man tents, so you can sleep with me in my tent." Jack explained, as a flush moved from his face to his chest to his groin. "I especially want you to meet Peter and Derek. They're really good baseball players and I'm sure they'll be on the high school baseball team. Your mom says that you're a great first baseman, and that your batting average is three-ninety. Is that right?"

"Yeah, I'm champean," Chris said, with a smile on his face.

"So, you'll come with us?" Jack's heart was pounding so hard that he could feel his heart beat in his neck. "I promise I'll take good care of you. There's the beautiful stream we camp along. This time of the year the water is warm, so we can all go swimming—I told you we swim naked. And you'll get to sleep nude for the first time in a sleeping bag, and in my tent. Really, we'll have a great time."

Chris's expression was pensive and somewhat distant. Then he turned and looked at Jack and said, "Sure, that sounds okay," flashing what Jack thought was a perfect smile.

That evening as Chris lay naked in his bed, he began to run through everything he had done for the first time this summer. *Wow, swimming naked and sleeping naked for the first time and on the same day. This summer is almost over but I've had a lot of firsts. Smoking, driving, French kissing, bodysurfing. Pretty good for one summer, and I'm not even a teenager yet.*

Chris recalled his cousins teaching him how to smoke. He and his cousins, in the middle of the night, had rolled his uncle's BMW out of the garage and driveway, and then hot-wired it so that Chris could learn

Lies That Bind

to drive. His first time driving a car, and it was stick shift, too. He French kissed Julie. He smiled at the memory of his first French kiss, just a few weeks ago. Chris was sure it counted, even though she was his cousin's girlfriend and almost four years older than him. When she found out that he had never French kissed, she pulled him aside and started kissing him. His legs had shaken and he had become lightheaded.

Lying there, Chris thought about what a great time he had had at the beach, and that maybe he did feel better after talking to Jack. He decided that Jack was pretty cool, and that he was glad he was going on the camping trip after all. That would also be a first: camping in the mountains. He wondered what other new experiences he might have before he became a teenager.

Lying on his stomach, he thought about swimming naked, his upcoming camping trip, and making new friends. His penis, becoming erect, moved against his stomach and the sheet he was lying on. He pushed his hips into the mattress and enjoyed the sensation. He lifted his hips, moved his hand under his stomach and began to slowly stroke his penis. Now, there was hardly a night that Chris did not masturbate before falling asleep. Tonight his body seemed to be exceptionally receptive to his touch. As he neared orgasm his breathing quickened. His hips and legs moved in rhythmic motion until he rolled over onto his back so he could capture the explosion of his cum on his chest. His fantasy, as he reached orgasm, was always the same, he imagined the feel of an unknown boy's mouth upon his own. He delighted in his forbidden desires; they remained safely his own.

Chris used his dirty underwear to wipe himself clean. Feeling only partially sated, he remained erect. He grabbed his pillow, wrapped his arms around it and continued thinking about the coming weekend.

After masturbating again, he quickly fell asleep with the comforting thought that, compared to what happened to Jack as a child, he didn't have it that bad.

* * * * *

"Did you enjoy your camping trip?" I asked. I wanted to get to the particulars of what had happened before our session ended. However, I had learned long ago that forcing an adolescent into revealing himself emotionally did nothing more than get us into a power struggle. He shook his head, no.

Chapter Five

I LOOKED AT MY watch, worried that we were almost out of time. "Do you want to talk about it?" At this point, it was not only important for Chris to talk about what had happened to him, but for me to understand how *he* understood what had occurred.

He remained silent. He had noticed me glancing at my watch. He sighed.

"I know it is difficult to talk about, Chris."

"I guess I'll tell you about the confession," he muttered. His words were again labored, his voice was flat, his eyes looked to be fighting sleep, and his mouth fell into a frown. We both took a deep breath at the same time. I could hear waves of anxiety moving through his body as they rode upon his exhalations.

* * * * *

Father O'Brien was an elderly man of dark moods and excesses. He was short and overweight. What little hair he had was white and looked to be glued to the crown of his head. He walked bent over, and he had an angry redness to his face. It was rumored that he was an alcoholic, and was marked as a smoker by his hacking cough and constant throat-clearing. On one occasion, he had had to leave the altar during a mass, due to one of his coughing spells. On another occasion, during a sermon, people in the front of the church had heard him curse at an airplane that had just taken off from the Burbank airport. He actually shook his fist at it as it drowned him out.

All the students except Chris had returned to their classes. The church was quiet except for Father O'Brien's occasional coughing, the muted sounds of someone confessing, and the rustling made by people on their knees as they mumbled their prayers. In some ways, this particular Friday was no different from any other. Neighborhood women were waiting in line to have their confessions heard by Father O'Brien. Those who had already confessed were now saying their penance.

Lies That Bind

Chris's mind raced as he knelt at the altar railing, saying his penance before the statue of the Blessed Virgin Mary. Glancing at his rosary beads, he noticed his hands shaking. He could feel his shirt sticking to his sweat-soaked torso. Every sound pierced his skin; Father O'Brien's phlegmatic cough hacked through the church. Chris's heart was pounding; his stomach churned so wildly he thought he might vomit. Saliva filled his mouth. When there was more than he could swallow, it streamed uncontrollably over his lips and down his chin like tears might flow from his eyes if he allowed himself to cry. He watched in amazement as his entire body continued to tremble.

Perhaps this was his first glimpse at the reality of what had happened or, now, what he believed he had made happen. How was he to understand it?

Hail Mary full of grace, the Lord is with thee.
Blessed are thou amongst women,
And blessed is the fruit of thy womb, Jesus.

Why didn't I stop him sooner? Was I enjoying what was happening? As Chris repeated Father O'Brien's questions to himself, he wiped saliva from his chin.

Father O'Brien's voice was harsh, his questions accusatory. "Did you want this to happen?" Father O'Brien asked. *Did I?* Chris could not remember.

"Bless me Father, for I have sinned. It has been six months since my last confession. I missed mass on Sunday five times. I've sinned in thought, word, and deeds. I've lied."

"What deeds?" Father O'Brien mumbled. Chris answered. As he heard the words coming from his mouth he felt dizzy with fear.

"How old are you?" Father O'Brien asked sharply.

"Twelve, but I'll be thirteen in two weeks," Chris replied, hoping that would make a difference.

As Chris continued, Father O'Brien's tone grew harsher and Chris became more frightened. He wanted details. Chris could feel himself trembling, as he remained kneeling in the confessional.

"Why did you allow this to happen?" Father O'Brien asked.

"I don't know, I just did," Chris answered. Chris kept telling himself not to cry, not to show fear. "I don't know why I let it happen."

Then Father O'Brien asked a question that terrified Chris. "Do you ever think about men with pleasure?"

Chris wanted to lie and say no, never. But could he lie to a priest in confession? Wouldn't that be a sin, and wouldn't Father O'Brien and God know he was lying?

Chris heard himself say yes, but now in a calm and steady voice. It was as if his thinking and speaking self were now separate from the rest of his body, which was trembling. He had learned how to look and sound strong and confident when he was frightened. His father had taught him well.

Father O'Brien began to lecture him in a low but stern voice. Chris imagined that everyone in the church could hear him. "You must stop this, put it out of your mind." He paused, "if you don't, your soul will be damned. You must not think of it, you must pray to God."

Holy Mary mother of God pray for us sinners,
Now and at the hour of our death.
Amen

As Chris continued saying his penance, Father O'Brien's questions flooded Chris's mind. *Why didn't you stop it sooner?* Chris again noticed that his body had not stopped trembling. Chris felt like Father O'Brien's questions had opened a hole and left him alone to fall into it. Whatever rationalizations he had created for what happened were ripped away, and accusations and a threat of eternal damnation were put in their place.

Hail Mary full of grace, the Lord is with thee.
Blessed art thou amongst women,
And blessed is the fruit of thy womb, Jesus.

Chris tried to stop his mind from racing and take comfort from the familiar prayers, as he had so many times in the past.

Holy Mary mother of god pray for us sinners,
Now and at the hour of out death.
Amen

As he did, he watched as his body continued to tremble and saliva continued to flow from his mouth. He tried to calm his body, but he could not. Father O'Brien coughed again. Chris had lost track of time. He could not remember how many times he had been around this chain of rosary beads.

Holy Mary, mother of God, pray for us sinners,
Now and at the hour of our death.
Amen

He focused on the statue of Jesus on the cross and remembered what He said: "Forgive them, Father, for they know not what they do." *"Maybe I did not know what I was doing. Maybe, I just did not know. Did I tell him that? Did I?"* He tried to remember.

"What deeds?" Father O'Brien asked.

Lies That Bind

"I masturbated. And," Chris said, and then hesitated, his heart was pounding. "And I touched a man then he touched me."

"What do you mean?"

"I masturbated him, and then he masturbated me."

"How old are you?"

"Twelve, but I'll be thirteen in a couple of weeks."

"And how old was this man?" Chris could hear anger in the tone of the priest's voice.

"Thirty-two."

"Where did this happen?"

"While we were on a camping trip," Chris said, as sweat began to soak through his shirt.

"Were there other people there?"

"Yes. There were six other boys, but they were in other tents. I was alone with him in his tent." Sweat ran down from his forehead, along the side of his nose, and then turned the upper ridge of his lip. Chris tasted the salt of his own sweat as he licked his lips.

"Did you make this happen?"

"What do you mean?"

"You said that you touched a man and then he touched you. Did you enjoy it? Did this happen once, or did it happen again?"

Chris froze. "It happened again," Chris conceded.

"Then you must have wanted it to happen."

"I don't know."

"Did anything else happen?" Father O'Brien's tone was stern.

"He put his mouth on me."

"And did you do the same to him?"

"Yes." Sweat was running down Chris's back. His legs were shaking as he knelt in the confessional. He was sure he was about to vomit.

"Did he make you do this?"

"What do you mean?"

"Did he force you, or threaten you?" the priest snarled.

"No. Well, not until later."

"What happened?"

Chris could swear that he heard crashes of thunder flood through the church, but it was only in his head. "The second night he woke me up again." Chris's stomach was knotting and his entire body trembled. "He put my penis in his mouth."

"Did you ejaculate?"

"Yes." Chris admitted. "Then he rolled me over and got on top of me. He wanted to put his penis inside my butt, but I said no. I knew it would hurt, because of what he did the first night. He said it wouldn't. I said no, I didn't want to. He was hurting me. I kept telling him not to, and kept moving so he couldn't, but each time, he held me down harder. Then, I said that if he didn't stop I was going to tell. Then he stopped. I promised not to tell anyone if he wouldn't try to put it in me. He said okay." What Chris didn't tell the priest was that Jack agreed, but under one condition to which Chris reluctantly acquiesced. Jack took Chris by the hair and forced himself into Chris's mouth where he quickly ejaculated. Chris stayed awake the rest of the night. The next night Chris shared a tent with Peter. Derek Powell moved into Jack's tent.

"So you were able to stop it," Father O'Brien said accusatorily. "Why didn't you stop it sooner?"

"I don't know."

"Yes, you do. You wanted this to happen and you enjoyed it. Do you know what a homosexual is?" Father O'Brien asked, lowering his voice so that he could barely be heard.

"Yes, it is a man who has sex with a man. But…" the priest tried to interrupt him, but Chris continued. "…he's not a homosexual. He was a Marine, and he's a Boy Scout troop leader and a teacher. He is married," Chris said, naming the icons of masculinity and heterosexuality.

"I am not talking about him. I am talking about you," Father O'Brien hissed. "You made this happen didn't you?"

"I guess."

"Do you want to be a homosexual?"

"Me?" White spots began to appear before Chris's eyes. "No."

"Homosexuality is a sin against God. Homosexuals go to hell for eternity." More thunder, Chris thought. "Do you know that? "

"Yes." Chris realized that it finally happened. He was no longer feeling his body. He seemed to escape, or break free from the torturous emotions he was experiencing as he heard Father O'Brien ask him, "Do you think of guys with pleasure?" Chris's voice was now harsh, "Yes, but I'm not a homosexual," he insisted.

"If you do think of boys while you masturbate, you will become a homosexual. You must never think like that again. If you allow the devil to fill your mind with these imaginings, your soul will be lost. You must not masturbate either, or you will remember what you did with this man."

"I won't, I'm not a homosexual," Chris asserted without equivocation.

Lies That Bind

"You must pray to the Blessed Virgin Mary to guide you to her Son. For your penance, say the rosary. Now say the Act of Contrition."

"Yes, Father. Oh my God, I am heartily sorry for…"

Kneeling at the altar, Chris assured himself that all he had to do was put everything out of his mind; everything that had happened, everything that, as the priest said, he had made happen. He continued watching his hands tremble, but saliva no longer flowed from his mouth. Finally, he left the church, but he did not remember to return to class as Sister Bernadette had instructed. Instead, he slowly walked home. Memories, like fast-forwarded movies, raced through his mind as unfelt feelings, like undifferentiated energy waves, coursed through his body. Memories of his grandparents calmed him; memories of his father disquieted him; he fought to block any memories of Jack.

On his walk from the church to his home, Chris resolved to never masturbate again. If he did not masturbate, he knew he would never again think about Jack or any other guy in that way again.

That was Chris's last confession that year. He received communion that Sunday in Saint Patrick's church for the last time. By week's end he failed in his resolve not to masturbate. He agreed to continue with the scouts—knowing he would have contact with Jack, which made not thinking about what had happened impossible—but only if Diane agreed that he would not have to continue being an altar boy, making it possible for him to avoid going to confession. Although there were many times in the coming year he wished he could go to confession and clear his mind of all that was burdening him, he could not bring himself to kneel before a priest and be vulnerable, especially Father O'Brien. Chris had not been ready for what had happened with Jack. He was not yet able to make sense of it. He also had not been ready for what Father O'Brien had said to him.

As his high-school years passed, Chris's friends and family thought of him as complex, mysterious, intense, independent, heterosexual, and gorgeous. His friends often teased him about the fact that he could have most any girl in school as a girlfriend, and that the girls thought of him as being "too cool." It would take another life-defining moment at the end of his senior year to bring the weight of all his secrets to critical mass; secrets that almost destroyed him.

* * * * *

Chris seemed emotionally exhausted. I was in an emotionally familiar place; torn between wanting to comfort a victim and to destroy the perpetrators.

And as usual, the list of perpetrators was long. "I am going to meet with your mother later," my voice strained, betraying my emotions.

"You can tell her whatever you want. I don't want any more secrets," he pleaded.

"Okay," I said. We sat there silently. "I am going to tell her that you were sexually victimized by Jack, but I am not going to get into any of the details." My choice of words surprised me.

Chris turned his head and stared at me for a moment and then said, "Okay."

I nodded. "Okay, we're going to have to stop soon, but I will see you again tomorrow. But before we stop there are a couple of things that I want to clear up in my own mind."

Chris asked, "Do we have to stop now?"

"Yes, I'm afraid so, but I'll see you tomorrow." He nodded. "You said," I looked at my notes, "you told this priest that first you touched Jack and then he touched you. Then you said…"

Chris interrupted, "Oh that," he sighed, and his mouth turned downward sharply. "I said that I didn't start it. What happened was that I was asleep, and when I woke up," he hesitated, "somehow I had moved and was lying up against Jack. He was lying on his back. My hand," he said as he moved and stared at his right hand as though it had betrayed him, "was around his dick. I just froze. I couldn't believe what I was doing. I didn't move, I was so afraid he'd wake up and get really angry. I mean, what could I say?" Chris was sounding angry; angry with himself, I guessed. "I decided then to slowly move my hand away, but as I did, he woke up. I didn't know what to say. I could feel myself starting to shake inside. I pulled my hand away. Then he said, 'You started this, so let's finish it.' He took my hand and put it back on him, then he put his hand on me." Chris became silent. Again, his eyes closed and slowly opened.

"I understand," I said. "One other thing. You said that you knew it would hurt," again I referred to my notes, "because of what happened the first night." I could feel my face reddening. I tried to relax my face and keep my anger at bay.

Chris shrugged and shook his head. "It was really weird. After we were done I was lying on my stomach facing him, he was lying on his side facing me. I was feeling really confused. I felt weird about what we did, but I started it and I guess I thought about him like that but it felt wrong with him. I remember that I wanted to go home. He was running his hand up and down my back. I wanted him to stop really bad but , , , " he paused.

"Then he put his middle finger in his mouth. It looked like he was sucking on it. He looked right at me while he was doing it." Again he hesitated and again sighed deeply. He kept shaking his head.

I realized I was breathing quickly. I could feel the tension in my neck moving up into my jaw; my stomach churned. I was sure I knew what was next. Genet wrote about this in one of his novels. It was what a man in prison would do to someone he claimed as his bitch.

Chris turned his head away from me. He filled his chest with air and said, "Then he put his hand on my butt and shoved his finger in. I almost screamed, it hurt so much. Before I could pull his hand away he put another finger in and pushed really hard. I guess I rolled away from him. Then he just smiled, rolled over and went to sleep. Later, I guess it was almost morning, I woke up and he had his mouth on me. That's when we had oral sex the first time, but I wouldn't let him get his hand near my butt." I nodded.

Chris turned his head toward me. We made eye contact. "Do I just leave now or what?"

"Yes. Please give the cup back to Nurse Greene. Then you can go back to the dayroom. I'll see you around noon tomorrow." He hesitated. "Chris, I know this is very difficult to talk about."

"Tomorrow is Saturday."

"I know. I'm on call, and I'll be in tomorrow."

Chris nodded and left the room. His sadness was palpable. As soon as the door closed I felt anger grip my jaw. I decided I had to sit alone for a time before I met with his mother and grandparents. Clearly, Jack was not new to this, I was sure of that. He knew how to approach Chris, how to disarm him and win his trust—he had set him up. Then he marked him—his trophy. The anger I was feeling surprised me. I thought of my father. I was to have been his trophy, not literally marked by his finger up my ass, but marked just the same. I was to have been something he could be proud of or nothing at all.

Soon I would be meeting with Chris's family. I knew I would have to maintain my detached, clinical persona so that they could have the space to respond as they saw fit.

I met with Diane and Chris's grandparents in my office. We sat and talked about what Christopher could not remember. When we were nearly finished I carefully explained to them that Chris had been sexually abused. Perhaps it would have been better to have Chris tell his mother, but right now what was important was for her to know, and for me to make my report to the proper authorities.

I was no longer surprised at how differently parents respond to the news that their child has been sexually molested. Some parents become very protective of their child, blame themselves, and then the perpetrator. Other parents minimize the assault, and others blame the child.

Carl, another patient of mine who was currently on the ward, was caught "servicing" his two older brothers. His oldest brother had begun molesting him when Carl was nine years old. A year later his other brother joined them. Carl informed me that at first he tried to stop what was happening, but was threatened with rejection and physical harm. Carl came from a very conservative Christian family. His brothers were both athletic and masculine while Carl was fairly effeminate. His parents believed their older sons' claim that even though they were heterosexual, their homosexual younger brother had seduced them. Carl tried to hang himself when they informed him that, for the sake of their older sons' souls, he was going to be moved out of the family.

Diane's response was as I expected it would be—she was shocked, and she became pale. Josephine moved to her and put her arms around her daughter. Anthony could no longer sit still. He stood up, paced around my small office clenching his fists and muttering something that seemed to rhyme in Italian. When I explained to her who had molested Chris, Diane wept—"I brought that son of a bitch into my home. I sent my son off with him. I did this." Josephine continued to hold her as Anthony paced the room. I told them that their feelings were understandable, but that right now we all had to focus on Chris and his healing process. The police would take care of Jack Payden.

Within moments Diane's sadness and guilt turned to rage—"I'll kill that fuckin bastard! He hurt my son." Anthony sat down, his eyes filled with tears.

Diane watched me looking at Anthony. Anthony asked, "Is my boy going to be okay, Doctor?" his voice quivered, and his nostrils flared under his piercing eyes.

Diane cried. "Pa, I'm sorry, Pa. Oh God, Daddy, I am so sorry. I've brought so much pain into my son's life." Diane moved to sit near her father.

Anthony put his arm around his daughter and stroked her face, and then kissed her cheek. "*Figlia mia*," he said to her in a whisper, "*non pian-*

Lies That Bind

gere, none of this is your fault. We have to stay strong for the boy." He looked at me and asked, "This man, he will go to jail?"

I informed them that I would be reporting the molestation and that there would be an investigation. I told them that in cases like this it is likely that there would be other boys who had been molested, and that, right now, their concern had to be with Chris and not with Jack. I assured them that the police would do their job.

I told them that Chris was clearly depressed, but that I did not have him on medication. I informed them that I would be seeing Chris tomorrow, that I wanted to have a family meeting Monday afternoon, and that it was my hope that Chris would be returning home no later than Tuesday.

During our meeting Diane told me that Chris's father had passed away a few months ago. I was surprised, since Christopher had not mentioned it to me. She explained that Christopher had learned of his father's death in a letter he received from his stepmother. She said that he had not shared the entire contents of the letter with her, but that she would try to find it and bring it with her tomorrow. She said she was not surprised that Chris did not mention it.

Later, I met with Karen and summarized all that I had learned.

"Well, let her do what she wants, but I wouldn't read the letter until you talk to Chris about it."

"Okay. I was concerned as to what I should do," I said.

"He just found out a couple of months ago in a letter," Karen repeated, shaking her head. "God, how do you grieve a parent like this man, and yet, he was his father."

"I know. His mother said he just put it all aside. Seems like, from what his family told me, he is "champean" at avoiding his feelings. Not unusual for an abused boy."

"'Champean?'"

"It's a private joke," I said, smiling, but feeling my throat tightening with sadness. Having met Anthony, I understood the love contained in this expression that they shared, and it touched me deeply. I thought about the importance words like that could hold; the depth of their meaning, that to an outsider would go unnoticed. Everything he talked about in regard to his grandparents painted a picture of a boy held in love and pride: simple family traditions and rituals, meals, nicknames they gave to him, the Dinato family picture. I understood why he was calmed by these memories.

"Did you tell him you were going to report the molestation?" Karen asked.

"No. I was over on the time and I had yet to speak to his mother. I did tell her," I added.

"When did you report it?"

"After I talked to his mother. His grandparents were with us. They seemed as I thought: very nice people. Very concerned. His grandfather was moved to tears a couple of times. He calls him, 'my boy' when he asks about him." I found myself swallowing hard as my throat again tightened with sadness. I was deeply touched and envious of the concern and affection they had for Christopher.

"Do you think we can discharge him by Monday? If not, I'll make arrangements." Karen sounded concerned.

"Yes. If not Monday, then definitely Tuesday. I want to keep him here until he talks to the police. Besides, he has a lot more talking to do, but I'll be in tomorrow and perhaps Sunday."

"I don't want you to come in on Sunday. Chances are the police won't get out here until Monday afternoon or Tuesday. Let's think Tuesday."

As my conversation with Karen continued, I felt myself sliding into depression. I guessed Karen had noticed. "Carol Underhill, she's who I called to report, asked me if I had her phone number on my speed dialer. We laughed." I shook my head. "It really isn't funny." Karen nodded. "I can't believe the number of kids I've reported being molested since I started working here. Yesterday, I heard on CNN that they arrested some guy in Northern California who molested over a hundred and fifty boys and girls. God, Karen, what is going on?"

"It's a good time for you to be taking a break. Working with abused kids is tough work. You should also take a break from your research."

"Oh, I don't know."

"Bobby, you are studying child molesters and working with molested children. Work that has to be done, but…"

"Exactly, Karen. Work that has to be done."

"Take a break. Pull your life together. Then get back into it."

"I am, this summer. I'm hoping I can just figure out what it is that stops these boys from telling an adult when they've been victimized. But, then, look at Chris. He did tell someone, a priest," I said, shaking my head. "God, I'd love to have wrung that prick's neck. This Jack guy. I'd bet my last dollar he's a serial molester. I mean he really has it down. Find the lonely isolated kid, a confused boy, gain his trust, involve him in secrets, and pounce." Then I explained to her how Jack had marked Chris. We agreed that it was part of a ritual. Serial molesters typically ritualize their behavior. It seems to be part of the obsession. I could see the anger in Karen's face. Unflappable Dr. Torrel, I thought.

Her lips tensed. "You called the District Attorney's office and gave them a heads-up?"

"Yes," I said. "I did. I wanted to be sure someone is here on Monday to interview Chris. At least he has a mother who supports him, and grandparents. His father was a real prick."

"Your own issues getting in the way here?" Karen asked.

"Yes, my issues. But they're not getting in my way."

"When you get back to New York, you should really try to resolve things with your parents. Age mellows people out."

"Karen, I do appreciate your advice, but , , , " I was surprised by the sudden anger in my voice.

"Okay, sorry," she said cutting me off. "Back to Mr. Bellesano. No medication for tonight. I'll put you on call for him. They can reach you at home?"

"Yes."

"One suggestion," she continued. "This boy has no reason to trust you. He seems to, but in terms of past relationships, other than his grandfather, what male figure does this boy have to base any real trust in? He's telling you that he trusted his father and he betrayed him. He then opens up to Jack and is molested and nearly raped…"

"He was orally raped," I interrupted.

"Yes, you're right, of course. Well, he has to be struggling with whether he can trust you or not."

"Yes, I was thinking the same thing. He seemed to want to connect with me. It opened him up some, and his associations were to his grandfather, but then back to his father." I was finding it hard to sit up straight in my chair. My neck was tiring from the weight of my head. The tone of my voice had gone flat and I noticed my eyes feeling grainy. Karen was right. Maybe it wasn't the priest's neck I wanted to wring. More than likely, it was my father's.

"I suggest you start tomorrow's session by talking about your concerns regarding his trust of you. At some point you'll have to tell him that you reported the molestation. Don't have that be a betrayal of his trust in you."

"I know, I know. I'm hoping I didn't screw up. He's got it in his head that he made the molestation happen. Damn, I wanted to address that, his idea that he's responsible for what happened. That priest and his idea that this kid made this all happen! I mean, what the fuck was that priest thinking?"

"The priest. Another betrayal," she reminded me. "Clearly, the priest needs to see sexually abused boys as perpetrators rather than victims."

"You're right. And, Chris doesn't see any of them as abusing him."

"Anyway, no doubt it will come up again," she smiled at me. "What are you going to put down for a diagnosis?"

"Post-traumatic stress disorder. There are also dissociative processes going on."

"Okay. Call me tomorrow if you need to. I'll see you the first thing on Monday. Whoever comes out to interview him, tell them that I want to see them first. That should be it."

"Karen, about before. I wasn't trying to be rude. It's just fresh on my mind. You know I talk to my sisters often, especially Janet, who calls me at least twice a week. They tell me that my parents are well, and that my father doesn't ask about me, nor does he allow my name to be spoken. Recently, however, Claire informed me that my mother asked about me. She said that my mother met with Janet and asked if, when I returned to New York, I would meet with her for lunch."

"That's great, Bobby."

"Not really. The catch is that my dad mustn't be told of our meeting. I told Claire to tell Janet that I refused to participate in my mother's self-imposed subjugation to my father's tyrannical demands. Claire said that I should tell Janet myself. Also, my sister Janet is getting married in September. She's marrying a friend of mine. We were classmates at NYU when I did my psychoanalytic training. I introduced them to each other and they asked me to be their best man. I said yes, but now I'm going to have to back out."

"Oh?"

"I was told that my father said if I was in the wedding he and my mother wouldn't come, and that they would tell our side of the family not to come to the wedding."

"Your sister un-asked you?"

"Janet? No, not at all. But, I just can't let that happen."

"I see. And you think that will be the end of it?"

"Actually, no. Claire told me that they said they didn't care if I came to the church, but that if I came to the reception they would not come."

"And?"

"I'm going to tell Janet that they can go to the reception, that I won't go."

"Bobby, I care about you. I think what they're doing to you stinks."

"I know, but…"

"Bobby, I've been there. Don't waste any more years of your life suffering their insanity."

"I know."

"Both your parents threw you away. Worse, your father wished you'd never been born," Karen reminded me.

She paused and looked thoughtful. Then she said, "But about your mother wanting to meet you for lunch—Bobby, that would be a start. So she's weak. If she weren't, she wouldn't still be married to your father. But she's acknowledging her need to have a relationship with you, her youngest child and her only son. You know, small steps, like the ones you took when you were coming out."

"Forget it!"

"You need to forgive her as much as she needs to be forgiven by you, and she's giving you an opportunity. You need to…" There was a knock at her door. She glanced at her watch. I smiled and stood. "I'll see you Monday." I nodded and opened her office door. "Dr. Kendrell. Please come in," she barked.

I drove home with the top of my Porsche opened. Kevin, a psychiatrist who was doing a fellowship on the children's ward at UCLA, met me at my apartment. Our plan was to change into our swim suits, shop for dinner, and then head to the beach for a swim, after which we would meet his wife Barbara, a resident at USC Medical Center, at my apartment for dinner. They were both from New York.

The water was wonderful: cold but refreshing. We swam against the current for about fifteen minutes and then swam back again, leaving the easy part for last. When we were back to where we started we decided to tread water for a while.

"Robert. Barbara and I were talking," Kevin said between breaths. "We decided that we are going to really miss you, and that we miss 'The City.' So, next year when I'm finished with my fellowship, and she's finished with her residence, we're moving back to New York. Is your apartment big enough for us to stay in with you while we find a place to live?" Kevin asked, smiling.

"Do you think you'll really come back?"

"Yes. I decided that I'm going to start looking for a hospital job in New York City. Barbara will be looking for a job there, also." He swam toward me and said, "Did you think you could get rid of us just by moving east?" He laughed and splashed water at me.

"That's wonderful. Of course, you can stay with me," I said. I couldn't stop smiling.

Kevin smiled and said, "Imagine, we had to come three thousand miles to find you."

"I am glad you did," I said.

"You know, I'd be jealous if you weren't gay."

"What do you mean?"

"Barbara absolutely loves you."

I laughed and splashed water back at him. "I love her, too."

"Oh, and what about me?"

"Oh yeah," I said laughing, "it's good to be your friend, too."

Kevin smiled and shouted, "If you don't have a boyfriend by the time we get there, Barbara said she's going to find you one. She has a friend she wants you to meet."

I smiled and nodded, but thought, *Fuggedaboudit*.

Part Two: Saturday

Chapter Six

THE PROSPECT OF KEVIN and Barbara moving to New York lifted my spirits. We talked at length, excitedly, about their living there. Barbara also mentioned a gay friend of hers who lived there too. She insisted that we would enjoy getting to know each other. I tried to look interested, but I hate blind dates. So I lied, and told her I would call him. Happily, she believed me, and her efforts at matchmaking ended.

Driving into the parking lot of the hospital I realized that I was looking forward to meeting with both Chris and Carl.

"Good morning, Ron," I said, entering the nurses' station.

"Good morning, Dr. Mitchell," he said. "Carl had a tough time of it in Dr. Torrel's group yesterday afternoon. But I think he had a good night's sleep." Ron relaxed in his chair. His professional persona eased. His smile was warm. "Christopher spoke up a bit in group, and he was very supportive of Carl at one point. After group they sat and talked."

"Really?"

"I wandered over there a couple of times. Sounded like the talk was mostly about what happened with Carl, but they were talking about you, too," he said with raised eyebrows. Later, he ate dinner, watched TV, and then went to bed. But I don't think he slept much. Night shift said he was up several times during the night."

"Where is he?"

"Day room. His mother stopped me on my way out at about six last night. She wanted to know how he was doing," he said, as he read through one of the charts. "She seems like a nice lady."

"Seems so to me, too," I agreed, as I finished reading Karen's notes on Carl. "Is treatment room four free?"

Ron laughed and then winked. "Like someone else is seeing patients today." Again with the RuPaul routine. "So. Wednesday for lunch?" he asked. "I'm off the next three days. And I don't come in on my days off for anyone."

"Wednesday it is." I quickly read through Karen's note on Chris. Ron had one of the attendants bring Chris into the treatment room.

"Good morning, Christopher," I said, closing the door behind me.

"Good morning, Dr. Mitchell." He didn't stand, but he wiped his hands on his pant legs and offered me one, which I shook.

"How did you do last night?"

"Okay, I guess. Wishing I was home in my own bed."

"You will be soon, probably Tuesday at the latest," I said, opening my notebook. Chris nodded, pushing his hair out of his eyes. "I want to see you on Monday, and then I thought we would have a family meeting in the afternoon." Chris's gaze went toward the floor. "I know this is tough, Christopher."

"Please call me Chris," he reminded me.

"Right, Chris. And I know it's hard to open yourself up to a complete stranger. Especially with all that's happened. Seems like a lot of the men you've turned to have failed you, at best." Chris began to interrupt, but I went on, "except, of course, your grandfather."

Chris nodded, "Father John, too. He's someone I trust."

"Who is Father John?" I asked, feeling hopeful that there might be another safe avenue for him into his pain.

"He's a teacher at Sacred Heart High. He's probably the best teacher I've ever had."

* * * * *

The Church of the Sacred Heart of Jesus occupies the corner of a two city-block square complex. Adjacent to the church are the elementary and middle schools and the rectory. Across the street from the church is the high school and the adjoining faculty office building.

The church was built in the Spanish Mission style and is one of the San Fernando Valley's most imposing buildings. It is a massive but graceful structure with two Moorish-Corinthian spires and a red Spanish tile roof. Atop the taller of the two spires, which housed the church bells, is a blue-green tiled half-dome sphere; upon it, stood an impressive statue of Jesus with hands outstretched to the city below. On each side of the front of the church is a brilliant flower garden which borders the twelve steps leading to three large wooden sets of doors.

The exterior of the church is a reverent introduction to an impressive interior. The vaulted arched wooden beams support a domed ceiling. Along the sides of the church are glittering bays of votive candles beneath soaring stained glass windows. The lengthy center aisle leads to an imposing altar with a gold-covered tabernacle under a large wooden cross. To

Lies That Bind

the left of the altar is the pulpit, which is covered with carvings depicting the torture of Jesus and his resurrection. And, of course, the church has many painted statues of different saints. At the back of the church is the choir loft, where the church's pipe organ sits. The church of the Sacred Heart of Jesus is one of the few churches in the valley that has a choir and regularly celebrates High Mass.

The high school is a three-story building. Its old mission-type architecture is only the façade on an otherwise modern building with central air conditioning, closed circuit television, a gym with an indoor pool, and a large auditorium.

Next door, in the faculty center, Father John D'Agostino had his office, and Diane and Chris had a follow-up appointment with him one Monday morning.

Chris was at the end of his eighth grade, and had applied for acceptance to Sacred Heart High School. A week earlier, the school psychologist had given Chris a battery of tests. Diane was anxiously awaiting the results. When Father D'Agostino entered the lobby of the faculty center, Diane quickly rose to her feet. Chris remained seated until Diane pulled at his arm. After the priest greeted both Chris and Diane, he asked to speak first with Diane alone.

"Please have a seat here," Father D'Agostino said, closing the door behind her. He pointed to one of the armchairs in the corner of his office. He sat opposite her in another armchair.

"Thank you, Father," Diane said, pulling at her skirt so that her knees would be covered. Diane always took pride in her appearance, and today had taken great pains to dress appropriately. She wore a white and blue silk blouse and a navy blue knee-length skirt. She went for an understated conservative look that was quietly stylish. Her mouth was dry with nervous anticipation.

Father D'Agostino's office was very different from what she had imagined. She had expected statues of saints, a crucifix, and pictures of the Pope. Instead, one entire wall was covered with bookshelves; she noticed authors like Kierkegaard, Sartre, Victor Frankel, and Freud. There were travel posters, one with the words, "Ski Heavenly." She smiled and nodded at the poster. "That's cute. Ski Heavenly—the ski resort Heavenly, and you being a priest."

"I'm a skier, also," he said, returning her smile. "It's my passion, or perhaps was my passion. Do you ski?" he asked.

Diane laughed. "No, Father. I hate the cold. But we've been to Tahoe when the weather was warm. It's beautiful there."

"Does Chris ski?"

"No. Friends invited him this last year, but he refused to go, which is very unusual for him."

"Really, how so?"

"Well, it was with several of his friends: Peter, a boy named Derek, and others. He seemed interested. No, I would say he was excited about going. Then, with no explanation, he out and out refused to go."

"Was this the middle school ski trip?"

"Yes. We called Jack Payden and had him talk to Chris. He was going with the boys, he was one of the chaperones. But once Chris makes up his mind, that's that. I'd like to see him give skiing a try. I think he would enjoy it."

"We encourage all our students to be involved in sports. Once a year we take as many students skiing as we can manage." The priest stood, opened a desk drawer and fumbled around with some papers. He then returned to his seat and handed Diane a sheet of paper titled "Mammoth Ski Trip," and smiled at her. "I'm sure he'll have another opportunity this winter. Most of the kids who make the grades take advantage of the trip."

"Thank you, I'll be sure he goes along this time," Diane smiled. "It sounds like you decided that he will be coming to Sacred Heart next year."

"Yes, let's get to that," he said, reaching to a small table that was next to his chair. "Mrs. Patrona, I am glad that we decided to test Christopher—his scores are remarkable," he said, shaking his head. He picked up a folder, removed a set of papers from it, and placed them on his lap. "He's a very bright boy."

"The nuns at St. Dominic's school said he tested in the exceptional range," Diane said proudly, her nervousness beginning to subside.

"He does test as exceptional. As you know, we did more than just an IQ test on him. I'm glad that we did." The priest turned several pages of what looked to Diane to be a single-spaced typewritten report. Father D'Agostino stroked and then pulled at his eyebrow as he read. He glanced up at Diane and said, "He appears to be very anxious and depressed. Do you know what might be going on with him?"

Diane described Chris's relationship, rather his non-relationship, with his father and their move from New York to Los Angeles. She explained his closeness with his grandparents, cousins and friends, and how he typically dealt with change. They discussed the year he had spent at St. Patrick's, and his plans for the upcoming summer.

Lies That Bind

"Well, that helps, but it might be more than that. The psychologist also suggests he is having difficulty with trust. What you've told me might give us some direction." Diane was not surprised by what the priest was saying, but surprised they had gathered so much information. Father D'Agostino continued, "As you know, it's Sister Bernadette's recommendation that Christopher repeat the eight grade," he said, looking up from Chris's file.

"I would hate to see him have to do that," Diane said woefully.

Father D'Agostino reached up and rubbed his eyebrow as he read the papers in front of him. "So would I. So would I. Well, I want to talk to Christopher. It's my opinion that he's struggling with something, and it's also my opinion that if he is held back we may lose him. I have no doubt that…" he paused and again touched his eyebrow. "I believe if he applies himself he will do just fine with the academics here. I know he was active in the Boy Scouts, and that he has played Little League baseball. Has he made any friends?"

"As I said, Peter Cartola, Derek Powell, a boy named Gary, another named David, but I can't remember their last names. He hasn't really made a good friend, though. And that worries me. It's unlike him," Diane said, realizing that her meeting with the priest was drawing to a close. "He was always very close to his cousins. He doesn't have anyone like that since we moved to Los Angeles, and I know he misses it. He spends too much time alone, as far as I'm concerned. He's been very moody and withdrawn since he moved here." Diane's voice revealed the depth of her concern.

"What does he do when he's alone?"

"He reads. He's an avid reader."

"What does he read?"

"Everything. His favorite book seems to be Tolkien's trilogy. He's read it at least three times that I know of. He recently bought a Stephen Hawking book. Before that I think it was *The Count of Monte Cristo*."

"What else does he do?"

"He swims. He recently asked us to buy him a set of weights. Richard, my husband, set the weights up in the garage. At first they could hardly be in the same room with each other for more than five minutes, but lately they've been helping each other with the weights. They recently started jogging together, but Richard says that Chris hardly says a word to him. I tell him that at least Chris is spending time with him." Tears filled her eyes. "Perhaps I shouldn't have agreed to move to California. Perhaps it was too much for him."

Father D'Agostino handed her a tissue and stared at her as she wiped tears from her eyes. He glanced toward the window in his office and then asked, "You mentioned a boy, David?" Diane nodded. "Might that be David Jarrett?"

"Yes, that's his name, David Jarrett."

"Okay. Well, David is also a very bright boy who seemed to be very distracted this last year. Maybe it's just adolescence," he said. "If I remember correctly, I had a hard time with it also." His smile widened as he began to stand. He reached his hand out to Diane and helped her up out of the chair. He then walked toward the door, then hesitated and said, "Let me talk to Christopher. I have an idea. I'm going to give him some work to do during the summer. Perhaps we can accomplish several things at one time. Mrs. Patrona, I'll do what I can, both in prayer and with gentle pushes to help Christopher out of his shell."

Diane nodded and started to walk through the opened door. Then she turned and said, "Father, thank you very much. He is a good boy, he's just having a hard time of it."

"Let me see what I can do. If we all work together, and we do want your involvement, we'll get through these four years with as few bruises as possible." Father D'Agostino put his hand on Diane's shoulder and walked with her into the lobby, where Chris was sitting and staring into space.

"I don't think he bruises easily."

He smiled, "Actually, I was thinking about you, me, and the other parents." Diane smiled; she was feeling relieved.

"Christopher, hi. It's good to see you again," Father D'Agostino said, as he offered his hand to Chris.

Chris rose and shook the priest's hand and said, "Hello, Father."

"Let's go to my office."

Diane watched as Chris and the priest walked toward his office. She finally realized who he reminded her of,: Antonio Banderas without the accent. She was not sure if she had ever known a priest who seemed to be in such good physical shape. He was in summer wear: a black short-sleeved shirt, with his white collar and black slacks (she thought his waist was smaller than hers and his buttocks were probably firmer). Black was his color, she decided. It complemented his straight black hair and olive skin. Italian men, she smiled, shaking her head. She smiled as she wondered how big a sin it was to covet a priest.

Chris looked back toward his mother, wishing that she was coming with him. As they walked into Father D'Agostino's office, Chris audibly sighed. Father D'Agostino closed the door, pointed to the same chair that Diane had been sitting in and said, "Christopher, we've decided to accept you into the ninth grade here at Sacred Heart in September." Chris looked at the books on the shelves. "Your test scores show that your work at St. Patrick's was well below your abilities. They also show that you are suffering depression and anxiety." The priest waited for a response, but none came forth. "Your mother seems to think that this is due to the move you made from New York," Father D'Agostino said, and now decided to wait until Chris responded.

Chris glanced from the posters to the priest. "I guess," he finally volunteered.

"Your grade in math at Saint Patrick's is below average. At Saint Dominic's math was consistently one of your best subjects. Your math scores on the test we gave you suggest that you have very strong math abilities. Your verbal scores were even higher. Actually, they were exceptional."

Chris smiled. "I guess the game I play with my mom helps."

"What game is that?" Father D'Agostino asked.

"Oh, well, you see, my mom always worried that my verbal abilities would be limited, since I spend a great deal of my time with my grandparents and neither of them graduated elementary school." He felt defensive, as they did, about the fact that they had never attended school; it was not a lie to say they had not graduated elementary school, he reasoned. "So she made up this game. She gives me lists of words and we use them. For each word I use correctly during that week, I get twenty-five cents. When she uses one, and I know what it means and can spell it, I get twenty-five cents. But, if she uses one and I can't spell it, or don't know its correct meaning, I lose a dollar." Chris's attention turned from the priest to the books on the shelves. "I don't get my money until the end of the year. Actually, I get to pick out a special Christmas present. I'd do it even if she didn't buy me the present, it's kind of fun." He glanced at the priest.

Father D'Agostino listened as Chris's nervousness alternated between inattentive silences and chatter. "Well, I must say, I'm very impressed with your mother's inventiveness. It would seem that she wants you to be an erudite young man," Father D'Agostino said.

Chris's gaze returned to the priest after several moments of silence. "Are we playing the game?" Chris asked. Father D'Agostino nodded and smiled. Chris thought a moment and then said, "E-r-u-d-i-t-e-, someone who possesses a depth of knowledge."

Father D'Agostino nodded. "I like your game. We'll have to come up with our own modifications. Let's give it some thought. Okay?"

"Okay," Chris said, looking once more around the office.

"Christopher, here at Sacred Heart we assign boys male counselors and girls female counselors. Also, each boy and girl is assigned a priest as a confessor. At any time you can request a change in either. I am going to be both your counselor and confessor, and eventually, I will also be one of your teachers. Okay, so far?" the priest asked.

Chris shrugged his shoulders in response.

"Is that a yes, or I don't care?" Father D'Agostino asked in a direct but gentle way.

"No, it's okay," Chris said with some anxiety.

"Okay, let's talk academics. I'm going to assume you will apply yourself come September, so I've made up your class schedule. You'll be grouped with the other advanced students. Christopher, the average student at Sacred Heart tends to perform at the advanced level. I've given you several advanced-placement classes. If you find them too difficult we will tutor you. If you are still finding them too difficult even with tutoring, we will move you into regular classes. Okay?" the priest asked. He waited for some kind of verbal response.

"Yeah, sure. Okay," Chris answered, sounding as unconcerned as he possibly could. He was very excited about leaving Saint Patrick's. But he decided that it would not be "cool" to share his excitement with Father D'Agostino.

"You will be taking advanced placement classes in algebra, history, and English. You also have Spanish and physical education. You can think about either starting your science requirement this year or waiting a year. You'll have to take a year each of advanced-placement biology, chemistry, and physics. Here is a list of other classes you can think about taking," the priest said, as he handed Chris a sheet of paper.

"Your mother tells me that you and David Jarrett are friends. Is that right?"

"Yeah. I know him mostly through Peter Cartola. They're friends, but we've played ball together, too. He's a nice guy. Funny."

"Yes, he is a good young man. And he is very bright. I will be his academic counselor. I have already given him his algebra text and I am going to give you yours and ask that you work together this summer to complete the first five chapters.

Lies That Bind

Bullshit, Chris thought. "I'm going to New York this summer."

"Yes, I know. You leave at the end of this month and you will be returning mid-July. Is that right?"

Chris nodded.

"Is that a yes?"

"Yes."

"Okay. Then I want to see you both the week you return. David had trouble this year also. He seemed to be very distracted, as I believe you were. We'll set up a schedule for you to bring in your work each week. If you have any trouble I'll help you with what you don't understand. Also, I'm going to ask that while you are in New York you read *Romeo and Juliet*. It's required reading in your advanced-placement English class."

"I've already read it," Chris said nonchalantly.

"You've read Shakespeare's *Romeo and Juliet*?" Father D'Agostino asked. Chris nodded. "I'm impressed."

"Yeah. My grandmother and my mother like to be read to. Like when my mom irons and stuff like that. When I was a kid and I would have to wait for my dad to come and pick me up on Saturdays—most of the time he never showed up—I would read to them. I got kind of bored reading stuff like *The Swiss Family Robinson* and *Treasure Island*. So, my mom had me read *The Three Musketeers*—that was my favorite book until she got me *The Lord of the Rings*. That's my favorite now. The last book I read to my grandmother was *Romeo and Juliet*. That was probably my most prodigious undertaking," Chris said with a smile. He waited and then chuckled.

"Oh is that my word? Good word. P-r-o-d-i-g-i-o-u-s. Ah, let's see. It means large, or enthusiastic undertaking. Right? This is a good game."

Chris nodded and smiled.

"Well then, I am sure your grandmother would love to hear Shakespeare's *Julius Caesar*. Okay? That is also required reading."

Damn. Chris nodded. Father D'Agostino sat and stared at Chris and waited. "Yes, that's okay."

"Christopher, I think you will find Sacred Heart very challenging, but clearly you are up to the challenge. I also think that you will enjoy being here. We have a great athletic program. Baseball's your sport. Your mother said that you have a great swing and play a great first base. Right?"

"I guess so."

"I am sure you will be varsity before long."

"I hope so," Chris said quickly.

"Also, your mother said that you've never skied."

"No, I haven't."

"Well, I'm not a very good ball player, but I love skiing. Every year we take our top students from each grade on a ski trip, usually to Mammoth. Talk to Peter about it. He's gone several years, so has David Jarrett. As a matter of fact, David is an excellent skier."

Chris laughed and pointed to the poster. "Ski Heavenly. That's funny. I just got it. Yeah, I'd love to learn to ski. It seems awesome. Peter goes every year," Chris said, nodding enthusiastically. "That would be too cool."

"Great."

Chris suddenly felt his stomach churn. "Do you go, too?" Chris asked nervously.

"Definitely. I'm one of the chaperones. We usually take teachers and parents along as chaperones." Chris shrugged and looked away. "Perhaps your parents would come and chaperone you and six or seven other students. The more chaperones we have the more students we can take."

Chris smiled, "Oh, okay. That would be cool."

"Now I want to talk to you as your confessor." Father D'Agostino reached over to his desk and picked up his stole. "As you know, when I have this on anything we talk about will never be repeated by me. You know how it works," the priest said, as he placed the stole around his neck.

Chris's eyes widened as he took a deep breath. He felt the blood drain from his face.

"Your mother tells me it's been a while. Is that right?"

"Yeah." Chris's eyes became fixated on the priest.

"Christopher, one of my major concerns is your spiritual life, your relationship with Jesus. I'd like to talk to you about how I think of confession. It is in many ways different from what you might be used to." Chris took another deep breath. His heart began to race. He wondered if he could just get up and leave. "I guess I should tell you that around here, I am thought of as somewhat of an iconoclast." Chris looked puzzled.

"Go ahead, give it your best."

"I-c-o-n-o-c-l-a-s-t," Chris said, feeling the dryness in his mouth.

"Good," the priest said.

"Well, an icon is a religious object, but I don't know what 'iconoclast' means," Chris said, wiping sweat from his upper lip as he continued to stare at the priest.

"It is someone who doesn't stand by or accept traditional religious methods." Chris's distress was apparent to the priest.

Lies That Bind

"Ah," Chris said knowingly, "you are a rebel priest." Chris smiled, liking the idea of a radical Jesuit priest. He decided he was going to lie about his sexual imaginings, as Father O'Brien called them.

"Well, perhaps a bit overstated, but okay. I want to do things in a way that I believe will best serve the needs of my congregation. And in this case that is you and your classmates. Okay?"

"Sure," Chris said with a pensive edge to his smile.

"You're nervous."

Chris gave a shrug, "Yeah."

"Sure, I would be if I were you also," the priest said empathically. "Christopher, you have no reason to trust me and I don't expect you to. I understand that I will have to earn your trust. All I hope for is that you'll give me that opportunity. I understand that it takes a great deal of trust to open oneself to another person. I think taking your time to get to know me before you trust me is healthy."

Chris was surprised by both Father D'Agostino's statement and his sincerity. As he felt his anxiety lessen, his eyes filled with tears. He did not know why. His body relaxed into the chair as he wiped his hands across his pant legs.

"Therefore, when in confession we'll do two things," the priest continued. "You can talk to me about whatever might be concerning you, and then you and I will spend a minute in silence. During that silence you can confess your other sins directly to Jesus. I will spend that time praying as to how to be the best guide possible for you."

"Guide?" Chris asked.

"Spiritual mentor, guide along your life journey with Jesus. To help you deepen your relationship with Jesus," Father D'Agostino said, looking intently at Chris. "Shall we give it a try?"

Chris shrugged in resignation, and then said, "I guess," as he started to get up from the chair.

"Stay seated. You don't have to kneel, and you don't have to recite anything. Let's just make the sign of the cross." Chris and Father D'Agostino crossed themselves. "Is there anything you feel comfortable talking about?"

"I guess," Chris said. "I've been getting really angry at my mom, saying nasty things, cursing at her."

"Do you hate your mom?"

Chris was surprised by the directness of the question. "Oh no, no, not at all. I mean I get really angry at her, but I don't hate her."

"I didn't think so. Do you think she loves you?"

Chris shrugged and then said, "Yes."

"Are you sure? You seem tentative."

"No, I'm sure. I think she loves me more than she loves anyone in the world."

Father D'Agostino nodded. "That would be my guess also." Chris noticed that Father D'Agostino had the habit of stroking his forehead and pulling at his eyebrow when he was thinking. "When you are nasty, cursing at her, do you think she stops loving you?"

"No," Chris said, shaking his head.

"Do you think all your anger is at her or might you be angry about other things?"

Chris stared at the floor, but he could see that the priest was staring at him. "Probably about other things, but at her, too."

"You must feel safe with her. You must feel as though you can let go and she'll still love you."

"Yeah, I do," Chris said, his eyes fixed on Father D'Agostino's feet.

"Afterwards, are you sorry?"

"Yeah, it bothers me a lot, a lot," Chris said. "Sometimes I can't sleep at night because I can't stop thinking about it."

Father D'Agostino noticed the boy becoming more animated when he spoke. His nervousness seemed to diminish, and his words sounded heartfelt.

"I wish I wouldn't do it, but sometimes I just can't help it. I keep saying things and doing things that hurt people, and I don't know why," Chris said, shaking his head.

"Do you love her?"

"Yes, very much."

"Are you thankful she's patient with your outbursts?"

"Yeah, well, afterwards, but not when I'm having them."

"That's honest." Father D'Agostino chuckled. "Are there consequences to your outbursts?"

"Yeah, I usually get grounded; no TV, stuff like that." Father D'Agostino nodded. "I guess I deserve it."

"You probably do." He and Chris smiled at each other for the first time. "Now I'd like us both to sit in silence. Think of all your sins and ask Jesus to love you for your sins." Father D'Agostino stroked his forehead. "Jesus died on the cross for our sins. One way to join in the Sacred Heart of Jesus is to ask for his forgiveness." The priest and Chris bowed their heads and sat silently for a moment. "Oh I forgot to tell you about penance. I'd like for us to think of penance in many different ways. One way is reparation. How about this for penance? I want you to consider, the key word here is "consider," apologizing to your mother for your angry outbursts. I'm not asking you to stop getting angry. I think anger is good. Right now I'm not asking you to apologize either, but, rather, I just want you to spend some time thinking about it. Do you tell your mom that you love her?"

"Not usually," Chris said.

"I'd like you to think about doing that also, and think about thanking her for being a good mother. I want you to search your heart and see what feelings are there, and also think about what it might be like for you, and what it might mean to your mother."

Chris shrugged again, looking up he said, "Okay."

"Do you know why I'm asking you to do this?" Father D'Agostino asked.

"I guess it's only fair," Chris said, with a shrug of his shoulders.

"Well yes, but more than that. As I said, I believe Jesus is found in forgiveness, gratitude, and love, and that you walk with Jesus when you share those feelings with another," the priest said, trying to make eye contact with Chris, who was still staring at the floor. "How are we doing, Christopher?"

"Good," Chris said with a nod.

"Good. Let's cross ourselves." Father D'Agostino blessed Chris, saying, "In the name of the Father, the Son, and the Holy Ghost, Amen." Chris finally looked up at the priest. "Okay, Christopher," he said as he rose from his chair. "Here is your algebra book. I'll expect to hear from you and David the week you return from New York, and don't forget *Julius Caesar*."

"Yes, Father," Chris said, as he stood up and took the book from the priest.

"Is there anything I can do for you?" Father D'Agostino asked.

Chris hesitated. "Yes, actually, there is."

"What is that?"

"Well, unless you're angry with me, please don't call me Christopher. Can you call me Chris? I like that better."

"Sure, and you can call me Father John, I prefer that," the priest said as he walked with Chris toward the door.

"Cool, Father John," Chris said with a smile.

"Chris, I am looking forward to a great four years with you and your classmates. I will do my best to see that you have the best possible experience at Sacred Heart," Father John said as he offered his hand again to Chris. They shook hands and smiled at each other. "If there is ever anything I can do that will make your experience here better, please let me know." As Father John opened the door for Chris he placed his hand on Chris's shoulder. He then noticed Chris immediately tense his body. He gently withdrew his hand as he accompanied the boy into the lobby. "Mrs. Patrona, Christopher…" Chris looked at the priest. Father John smiled and continued, "Chris and I are finished. He'll explain the book I gave to him."

"Thank you again, Father D'Agostino," Diane said.

"Thank you, Father John," Chris said with a smile.

As they left the building Diane asked Chris, "What did you think of him?"

"He's pretty cool, but I'm not ready to trust him," Chris said without hesitation.

"What?" Diane asked with surprise. "Did he say or do something?"

"No. He was really cool," Chris said, pushing his hair out of his eyes. "but I'm taking my time before I trust him."

"Oh!" Diane paused and then turned to look at Chris. "Chris, he's a priest and a teacher. Aren't you supposed to trust him?"

"No." Chris said tersely. "I just think I want to take some time. See what he's like and all."

"Okay," Diane said, with some confusion. She put her arm around his waist and pulled him to her, and whispered, "You know, Christopher, sometimes you are a hard nut to crack."

Chris nodded and said, "Whatever," and smiled.

Diane asked about the algebra book as she pulled her skirt so she could step up into their Suburban. Chris explained Father John's instruction while he fastened his seat belt. As Diane started driving home, Chris asked, "Mom, can I ask David to come over to swim this afternoon? I mean not to do any algebra." They glanced at each other. "He's a cool kid. You know, he played shortstop on my team. You know, since we're going to have to study together this summer."

"Yes, sure you can. Do you want to stop there on the way home?" Diane was surprised. She could not remember any other time that Chris had asked to invite a friend to their home. Usually, it was David or Peter who tried to involve Chris in activities.

Lies That Bind

"Yeah, that would be cool. Can we ask his mom if he can stay for dinner?"

Diane felt a weight being lifted from her shoulders. "Sure, that would be nice." Diane imagined that the knowledge that he was leaving St. Patrick's had lifted his spirits.

"What are we eating?"

"Well, I was just going to throw something together, but if we're having company I could make something special. What do you want?"

"Spaghetti and meatballs," Chris said enthusiastically.

"For company?"

"Yeah, he isn't Italian," Chris said. They both laughed. "And besides you make great spaghetti and meatballs."

"Well, thank you. And you're right, I do make great spaghetti and meatballs. But let's ask him if he likes that." There was silence as they waited for a stop light to change.

"Mom," Chris said, looking out the passenger window of the car.

"Yeah?" Diane said, glancing over at Chris.

"I'm sorry I curse at you sometimes. I don't mean it." His voice sounded tender.

"I know you don't," Diane said, glancing toward him, "and thank you for your apology. It means a lot to me," Diane said, feeling her throat tightening with emotion.

"Thanks, Mom."

"For what?" she asked, breathing deeply.

"Everything," Chris said. He wanted to say that he loved her, but he couldn't. He, too, felt tightness in his throat. Diane turned and stared at Chris, who continued to stare out the car window. She reached over and touched his head. She could not imagine loving him more.

David was at home, and Helen, David's mother, said it would be fine for David to stay for dinner, but that he would have to be home by nine o'clock. David, with great excitement, climbed into the back seat of the Suburban. Actually it was Richard's tow-the-ski-boat car, but Diane enjoyed driving it. She hated L.A. drivers. The Suburban gave her a feeling of safety and a view of the traffic ahead of her.

"David, do you like spaghetti and meatballs?" Diane asked, as she turned and backed out of the Jarretts' driveway.

"In the jar or the can?" David answered.

"What?" Chris asked, turning to look at David. Diane just stared at Chris. They both grimaced.

"I don't like the stuff in the cans. You know, where the macaroni is cooked already," he said, with all seriousness. "But I like the sauce that comes in the jars."

Diane glanced forward and then looked at Chris who was looking at her. They both broke out into laughter. "We don't eat that," Chris said. "My mom makes her own gravy."

"You put gravy on spaghetti?" David asked with surprise.

Diane smiled, "No, David. We call tomato sauce, gravy. I am going to make my own tomato sauce with meatballs."

"You mean like in a restaurant?"

"Yeah, like that," Diane said, again looking at Chris with a smile.

"Oh wow, sure! I love that. Wow, Mrs. Patrona that would be great. Do you make garlic bread, too?"

"Okay, I can do that," Diane said, still smiling and glancing at Chris.

"Good move, David," Chris said, looking back at David.

"What?" David asked innocently.

"We are now having garlic bread. I love garlic bread, too," Chris said.

"Me, too," Diane said laughing. "Did you bring your swimsuit, David?"

"Oh no, I forgot it."

"Chris will give you one of his."

"I only have one," Chris said. "I'll swim in my boxers." Chris turned to look at David. "You can use my suit," Chris added. "I saw Father John today. He said that you and I have to do five chapters of algebra this summer."

"You and me together, or separate?" David asked.

"Together. We have to work together, and turn in our work each week to him."

"Oh. Cool. We could go swimming, too, sometimes, you know, when we get our work done and stuff." David sounded excited. "He told me that I was going to have to do five chapters, but I thought I was going to have to do them alone. Cool, us doing it together will make it fun."

"Yeah," Chris added, "and you can eat over sometimes, too. Right, Mom?"

"If it's okay with David's parents, I don't see why not. But we should wait and see if David likes my cooking."

"Oh, I'm sure I will, Mrs. Patrona."

Diane dropped the boys off at the house and told them to swim safely. She backed her car out of the driveway and went to the grocery store.

Lies That Bind

As she sat behind the wheel of her car she began to feel both excited and confused. She wondered what it was that had just happened. When Chris told her about the algebra work he would have to do this summer, she was sure he would withdraw into his room and become despondent. Instead, he seemed relieved. And now, there was this new-found excitement about David and their working together. Diane was thankful for whatever it was that Father D'Agostino had said to Chris.

As soon as Chris and David entered the house they raided the cookie jar. Diane baked cookies for Richard and Chris; she had all of Cookie Grandma's recipes. Then the boys went to Chris's room and undressed. Chris, who had been wearing a pair of white jockey shorts, searched his dresser for a swimsuit for David and a pair of boxers for himself.

"You can't find your suit?" David asked.

"It's here someplace. I only use it when we go to the beach."

"What do you usually use when you swim in your pool?"

"Here? Sometimes boxers, but mostly I swim naked," Chris said, continuing to dig through the dresser drawers.

"Really?" David sounded surprised. "Don't your parents mind?" David walked across the room and looked out Chris's window onto the pool.

"Nah," Chris said, finding the suit. As he walked toward David with it he noticed that David's buttock was bruised.

"Wow dude, what happened to your butt?" Chris asked with surprise.

"What?" David asked, twisting around to see what it looked like.

"Your butt is all bruised. Damn, like all over. Look," Chris said as he moved David into the bathroom so he could see himself in the mirror. As they both stood there naked and staring at David's butt, David lied, and said he had been skateboarding and had fallen several times and bruised himself. "Jeez, that must have really hurt," Chris said as he returned to his room and grabbed a clean pair of boxers to swim in.

The boys enjoyed their day together. When Chris left for New York he promised David he'd call him as soon as he got back into town.

Diane called Father D'Agostino while Chris was still away. She made an appointment for him and David. When Chris got back, the boys went to the appointment, and agreed to meet with the priest once a week and complete the first five chapters in their algebra text before the end of August. Their assignment was all the chapter exercises and all the problems at the end of each chapter. Both Chris and David were to turn in their work each week.

Diane and Helen agreed that the boys would get together three days a week, and that David would have dinner and sleep over Friday nights, with the promise to his father that they would continue their work on Saturday. Each week Father D'Agostino called the Jarretts and the Patronas to report on how the boys were doing. That was part of the agreement. Each week they were given a glowing report. Father D'Agostino was pleased with their progress, and that they had not needed his help. He asked if anyone was tutoring them, and was surprised to hear that they worked together alone. Everyone was pleased with their work; Diane was especially pleased with their friendship.

With two weeks left in their summer vacation, Chris and David had their last meeting with Father D'Agostino. After they turned in their work, Chris asked Father John if he would return their work to them. Father John declined. He explained that his intention was not to exempt them from working hard in class for the first ten weeks, but to prove to them that they were capable of doing much more than they had been doing. When Chris told Diane what Father John had said, David remarked that he wished they had kept a copy of their work. Diane smiled.

"I hear that he's a hard ass in class," Chris said.

"Yeah, I guess that's why he teaches the seniors," David agreed.

"But I think I like him," Chris added, looking out the window of the Suburban.

"I think he's a saint," Diane said.

"Mom, you have to do miracles to be a saint," Chris said.

"I think surviving four years with you boys will qualify," she answered. They all laughed and continued talking about the priest and the classes they would be taking in the fall. "I'm going to drop you guys off at the house. Are you going to go swimming?" Diane asked.

"Yeah," Chris said.

"It's got to be over a hundred degrees," David said.

"Okay, but be careful. You're staying for dinner, David, I talked to your mom."

"Cool. What are we eating, Mrs. Patrona?"

"It is a surprise dinner for the both of you."

"Something Italian?" David asked hopefully.

"Of course," Chris said with a smile.

"Okay, I have errands to run and then shopping to do, so I might be a while," Diane explained.

Lies That Bind

It was now customary for Chris and David to swim nude when no one else was at home. This had started earlier in the summer when at first they both took to swimming in their boxer shorts. When they dived into the pool the water typically pulled their boxers to their knees. One afternoon, Chris dove in the pool behind David and grabbed at his underpants. Having pulled them off, Chris raced out of the pool. He glanced around the yard.

"What are you going to do?" David asked, smiling. It had become routine for them to push and tease and play practical jokes on each other. Chris pointed to the garage roof. "No, don't. Bellesano, don't!" David shouted, laughing. Again, Chris pointed and then pitched them so they came to rest inches away from the apex of the roof. Chris danced around the edge of the pool laughing and pointing to the rooftop. "You are such a butt hole," David said, as he began to make his way out of the pool. Chris, seeing David move toward him, ran. David was in hot pursuit. David, still laughing, tackled Chris, stripped him of his boxers and tossed them onto the roof.

Laughing, Chris shrugged and jumped into the pool. "My mom will be home in a few minutes."

"Yeah, well she'll see you butt naked, too."

"She's seen me swimming naked before."

"When?"

"I swim here in the pool naked all the time."

"No way! Don't they get mad at you?"

"No." Chris explained that Diane and Richard swam naked. The arrangement was that when Richard and Diane used the pool and the Jacuzzi they would alert Chris so he knew not to enter the backyard. They put outside shutters on Chris's windows which overlooked the pool. When they went swimming they made sure the shutters were closed.

"But, doesn't it bother her or you?"

"I mean, I don't parade around or anything," he told David.

Eventually, Chris helped David get the ladder from the garage. David climbed the ladder, retrieved his and Chris's boxers and tossed them down to him. As he climbed down the ladder he laughed and said, "I guess I could have just gotten my jeans and put them on and climbed up there."

"That's no fun," Chris said, jumping into the pool. David jumped in behind him. "It feels kind of cool swimming naked, don't you think?"

"Yeah, it does," David agreed.

The first thing Chris and David did after being dropped off at the house by Diane, after their last meeting with Father D'Agostino, was to raid the refrigerator: peanut butter and jelly sandwiches, milk and cookies. With cookies in hand they headed to Chris's room, where they stripped down, grabbed towels, and headed to the pool. In the pool they raced each other and played ghost on the diving board. David won. They wrestled and tried to drown each other. Chris won. Then they found a volleyball to hit back and forth.

"Your turn to get it," Chris said, after David hit the ball across the patio landing between the rosebushes and the house.

David climbed out of the pool and walked across the patio. He reached over the bushes but could not reach the ball. "Ouch," he called out, pricking his arm as he tried to reach into the tangle of branches.

"Hey Mom, whatcha got there?" Chris yelled out to Diane as she entered the backyard.

"I made lemonade," Diane said, carrying a tray with a pitcher and two ice-filled glasses.. Diane noticed David as David jumped up and turned toward her.

"Oh my God!" David said. His mouth remained open. He quickly covered his genitals with both his hands, turned and ran back to the pool and jumped in. "Oh my God, Mrs. Patrona. I am so sorry. Oh wow, I am really, really sorry," David said in full blush.

"Don't be, David," Diane said laughing. Chris was howling with laughter and smacking his hands against the water.

"Oh my God, I didn't know you were home. Really, Mrs. Patrona, really," David went on, now with his hands covering his face.

"Don't worry about it, David. You made my day," Diane said as she set down the tray onto their poolside table. "I always thought you had a cute butt," Diane said as she wiped the tears from her eyes. "David, the expression on your face was priceless. Oh, that was funny," Diane continued, as she walked back into the house.

David moaned. "Oh my God. I can't believe that happened."

"Don't sweat it. It's no big thing," Chris said, smacking the water again. "It's no big thing, get it," Chris said laughing and wiggling his little finger at David.

"Asshole," David said, shaking his head and rolling his eyes.

"Come on, you know it was pretty funny," Chris said, making his way toward David.

"I hope I didn't offend your mom. Do you think I did?"

"No way. Did she look offended? Come on, don't worry about it," Chris insisted, as he jumped on David and started to drown him again.

Lies That Bind

"And besides, she said your butt is cute." Chris also thought that David had a cute butt, something he tried not to think about while with David. His worst fear was that his body would respond as it did at night when he thought about David's naked body as he pleasured himself using his hands.

That night Diane prepared one of Chris's favorite meals: veal parmigiano, rice, and a large green salad with her homemade Gorgonzola dressing. For dessert they had Chris's favorite Italian pastry: cannoli. As they all sat down to dinner Richard poured himself and Diane a glass of wine.

"Oh my God, Mrs. Patrona, that looks and smells awesome. What is it?" David asked, leaning over the table while smelling the various aromas. "I am feeling voracious."

"Good word, David." Diane cheered. Diane had invited David to play the game with the same reward she promised Chris.

"Rapacious," Chris said, and laughed.

"Avaricious," Diane added.

"Ah, good one, Mom," Chris said, nodding his head. "Good word, 'avaricious.'"

"Yeah, Mrs. Patrona, awesome word."

"Well, this is one of Chris's favorite meals. Veal parmagiano. I hope you'll like it," Diane said as she put the salad on the table.

"Are you kidding, I like anything you cook," David said enthusiastically.

"Give it a rest, David," Chris said as he picked up the bowl of rice and started to put some on his plate. "You're invited back, don't worry."

"Why? It's true, I do. Mrs. Patrona, you are the best cook," David said, taking the bowl of rice from Chris. Next they passed around the veal and then the salad. As David finished his first mouthful of veal he again remarked, "Oh my God, Mrs. Patrona, this is so good. You should open a restaurant. You could call it 'Bellafooda.'"

"What is 'Bellafooda?'" Diane asked. Chris got it and just shook his head.

"Good food in Italian. Bellafooda," David said, gesturing with his hand. Diane and Richard laughed.

Diane said, "David, I love you, cute butt and all."

"Oh yeah, that reminds me, Richard," Chris said as he cut into his veal with his fork. "David flashed mom today."

David looked at Chris, horrified, and then turned to Richard and said, "No, it was a mistake. Chris, tell him it was a mistake." David paled.

"Oh I don't know," Chris teased. David's face began to turn crimson as he kept looking from Chris to Richard.

"What happened?" Richard asked.

"It was an accident," Diane said, smiling.

Chris, kidding said, "He was naked in front of Mom."

"Why was he naked? Why were you naked, David?" Richard asked calmly, picking up his glass of wine.

Diane was laughing, "It was funny."

David's body tensed. "Mr. Patrona, it was a mistake, really. I'm sorry," he said, as tears filled his eyes and his lower lip began to tremble.

"David, what's wrong?" Diane asked as she put her hand on his arm. No one was laughing now. David began to cry. Diane had seen him tearful before, and had felt concern, but this was different.

"Mr. Patrona, please don't be angry. It was a mistake," David said, with his hands covering his face.

Richard said, "David, don't worry about it. I'm not angry. Mrs. Patrona can handle herself just fine."

Chris looked surprised. "David, why are you so upset? We're only teasing you."

David shook his head, "Maybe Mr. Patrona won't want me to come over anymore."

Richard was really taken aback. "Don't be ridiculous, David." Richard paused, the silence was only broken by David's sniffling. Everyone's focus remained on him. "David, you are always welcome here. We all enjoy you very much."

David wiped the tears from his face, but kept looking down at his lap. "Mrs. Patrona, please don't tell my mom about what happened."

"Okay, but I think she'd get a good laugh out of it," Diane said.

"She'll tell my dad, and I'd really get into trouble, and maybe he wouldn't let me come over anymore." He looked up at Diane. "Please don't say I was swimming naked," he pleaded. "Please don't tell them. I'd get into so much trouble." Diane assured him she would not tell his parents anything. She looked at Chris, who could not stop staring at David. Diane glanced at Richard, who was also staring at David, who continued to stare down at his lap.

Diane reached over and touched David on the arm. "David, it's okay, really it is. Okay? No one will ever talk about it again." Diane's voice sounded angry.

"Okay," David said, looking up at her.

"David, you're safe here," Diane assured him. Both Chris and Richard looked at Diane. "Chris, your teasing goes too far sometimes," she said sternly.

Lies That Bind

"David, I'm sorry." Chris felt a sinking sensation pass through his body. "I didn't mean it. I knew Richard wouldn't get freaked," Chris said as David looked at him.

"I thought he would," David said, again looking away.

Diane asked, "What did you think he would do?"

"Make me leave, tell me not to come back," David said as he shrugged his shoulders.

Diane stared at David. She had suspicions, but until now could not bring herself to ask. "David, does your father or mother hit you?" David shrugged, as tears filled his eyes again. Diane stared at Richard and shook her head knowingly. "We don't hit in this house. No one hits anyone. Ever." Diane reached over and pulled David to her and hugged him and then kissed him on the forehead. She then gave Chris a stern look.

"I'm sorry, buddy. You forgive me?" Chris asked, as he messed up David's hair.

"Yeah," David said. "I'm sorry, too,"

After a few minutes of silence they all became fully engrossed again in conversation. Diane explained to Richard that they had finished their algebra, and that Father D'Agostino was very impressed. Then David started to laugh.

"What's so funny?" Chris asked. David continued to laugh as they all stared at him, smiling. "Tell us!" Chris insisted.

"I bet the expression on my face was pretty funny," he said, wiping the tears from his eyes. David was laughing almost uncontrollably. Diane understood that David's emotions were typically close to the surface; all except for anger, she was realizing.

Again, Chris messed up David's hair as they all laughed together.

"Mrs. Patrona, you are such a good cook."

"Thank you, David."

"Oh my God, here he goes again," Chris said.

"So, Mrs. Patrona, do you really think I have a cute butt?" Everyone laughed. David blushed.

But, Chris's mood had changed. Outwardly, he remained jovial and talkative; inwardly, except for the tightness in his stomach, he now felt numb. It was as if some one had thrown a switch and turned off everything inside of him. He wasn't even sure he was hungry. He watched as everyone seemed to enjoy themselves. Even David seemed relaxed.

When David finished his dinner, Diane asked if he wanted more. David smiled and nodded. When they finally finished dessert, David reminded Chris that he had to be home by nine o'clock.

"I thought you were going to spend the night," Chris suggested.

"Oh, that would be great, but I didn't ask my mom if I could, and she said that I had to be home by nine o'clock."

"Do you want me to call her?" Diane asked.

"No, I better go. My dad might get angry."

Diane nodded, "Okay, well you have time yet. Richard will drive you home." She did not know David's father Paul well, but had decided she did not want to know him any better. After Richard and Chris returned, they joined Diane in the den and watched television until eleven o'clock.

In Chris's room there were two twin beds that rolled halfway under a corner piece. During the day the beds had pillows thrown on them so they looked and functioned like a couch. At night each one could be pulled out and made into a bed. Chris's nightly workout routine consisted of crunches, push-ups, and pull-ups that he did from a bar placed over his bathroom door. Tonight he undressed, skipped his routine, and just crawled into bed and agonized over his teasing of David at dinner.

His loneliness consumed him. His hope for friendship disappeared into the darkness of the night. Why had he said that to David? He cursed himself for his desires. He had been invited to sleepovers and on camping trips with friends, but he had refused. After what he did to Jack, he could not trust himself in his sleep. He lay there on his side with his knees drawn to his chest.

Chris finally fell asleep, wishing the wind he heard rustling through the trees outside would carry him away.

At about 2:30 in the morning Chris woke from a dream, his sheets soaked in sweat. He uncovered himself, sat up and put his feet on the floor. As he put his head in his hands he realized that his hair was wet with sweat. He began to recall the dream he had been having. It was a recurring dream that had several variations on the same theme. Sometimes the beginning was different, other times the ending changed, but it always brought with it the same feelings: confusion which led to sadness, which in turn led to dread, fear, terror, and then resignation.

This time Chris remembered the dream started with him and several other boys his age hiking with an adult. Their trek was on a dirt path that hugged the side of a steep canyon. Above them was open sky, below them

Lies That Bind

was a river they could hear, but could not see. Across the gorge is another steep canyon wall. They were each carrying backpacks, wearing tee shirts, shorts, and hiking boots.

Then the dream changed, the path narrowed, the sky was gray and a cold wind was blowing. The leader decided to stop for the night. They unpacked their gear as everyone tried to maintain their footing on the narrow path. A severe storm was moving into the canyon. The leader ordered everyone to suspend ropes from the cliffs above and secure them to their sleeping bags. Everyone stripped naked and got ready to climb into their sleeping bags. As they were stowing the clothing and shoes the wind blew one sleeping bag into the ravine. It was lost. Then a pair of shoes was lost, then a full pack of supplies and clothing.

The leader blamed Chris, and told him he would have to do without his clothing, shoes, and sleeping bag. Chris was confused. Everyone climbed into their bags and zipped up and disappeared. All that Chris had left were the ropes that he had suspended from the cliff above. He tried to decide if he should stay where he was, or if he should walk back the way he had come, but either way he was sure he would freeze to death. He considered leaving his rope attached to the canyon wall and swinging himself over to the other side, where he might avoid the brunt of the storm. But chances were he would either freeze to death there or his rope would come loose, causing him to fall into the abyss below. Besides, being naked in the freezing wind would kill him slowly no matter what he did. Looking into the ravine, he considered jumping to his death so that it would be quick and easy.

He decided to swing across the canyon to the other side. As he did he heard the roar of the river below. Fear filled his body. Hanging on the other side of the ravine, still feeling the freezing wind, he decided to climb out of the canyon. He untied his rope. Slowly he climbed the canyon wall. He stopped; he heard the roar of mountain lions above him. As he reached the top of the canyon, the rocks that he was holding onto began to break away. In an instant, he realized his fate. Just as he thought he had made it to the top of the canyon, he began sliding down the canyon wall and fell into the darkness…Then he awakened.

Sitting there, his thoughts turned back to what had happened earlier that evening. The berating voices that had started arguing in his head before he fell asleep began again.

You should have never asked him to swim nude. Why did you treat him like that? Why do you always hurt people that like you? I just wasn't thinking,

Thomas Domenici

I thought it would be okay. No, you weren't thinking, you never think about how you make other people feel. God, I always make people hate me. I don't know why I do it. He is such a cool guy, why did I do that to him? You made him cry. He was shaking. I bet his dad hits him. I think my mom thinks that, too. He must really hate you now. That's why he didn't stay the night. Maybe he won't want to be your friend anymore.

Chris sat with his head in his hands and his elbows resting on his legs. "God help me." Chris pleaded aloud. *Please tell me why I do these things. Please help me stop. I'll never have friends. No one will be your friend. David will tell everyone that you made him swim naked in your pool so that you could look at him. You are attracted to him. You wish he felt the same way, but he doesn't. He probably knows, and will tell other people too. I wish I didn't feel like this. I don't want to be attracted to him. You think about having sex with him, about kissing him, and he must be figuring it out. He doesn't want you, that's why you hurt him.*

Chris laid his chest in his lap and wrapped his arms around his legs; he was beginning to tremble.

I even laughed at him. God, I laughed at him. He must hate me. He's going to tell everyone at school that I made fun of him, and that I made him swim naked. Why didn't I think before I did it? You like to see him naked and you love to wrestle naked with him. Everyone will know what you did, and they'll hate you and they won't want to be your friend. You were just starting to make a friend and now you've blown it. Everyone at your new school is going to hate you. You were trying to get him to have sex with you, just like you got Jack to have sex with you. He'll never want to come over here again. Damn you, you are so fucked up. You fuck with everyone.

Please God, make me stop feeling attracted to him. Please God, I don't want to feel these feelings. Please, I'm sorry for everything, please make me stop thinking about having sex. Help me to not feel this way toward David anymore. Please help me not think about him that way. I want to have a girlfriend like everyone else. Please help me.

As Chris got up from his bed, he realized he was feeling dizzy. Holding onto the wall, and then the furniture, he made his way into the bathroom. Once there, he knelt down and put his head over the toilet as saliva began to pour out of his mouth. His stomach pulled tight and his back arched. But each spasm brought nothing but sound, saliva and air. Chris laid his head on the toilet seat and allowed the saliva to drain from his mouth as he continued to pray. Eventually, his stomach calmed. He thought he might not be finished, so he lay down on the cool tile floor,

Lies That Bind

brought his knees up to his chest, and wrapped his arms around his legs. The cold tile cooled his sweaty, naked body. He closed his eyes and felt the tension drain out. His limbs became heavy. A familiar and welcome numbness fell over him. When he opened is eyes, light was shining through the bathroom window.

Slowly he got to his feet and made his way back to bed. He checked the time; it was 8:14. He heard someone walking through the house. Not ready to start the day, he crawled back into bed and pulled the covers over his face. His ringing phone woke him from a deep sleep.

"Hey dude, are you still sleeping?" David asked.

"Not any more," Chris said dryly.

"It's ten o'clock, come on, get your butt out of bed. Let's do something today. I don't want to hang at home," David said. "Please, can we do something?"

"Sure. Whatever you want," Chris said sitting up in his bed; his heart raced. *Thank you God for a second chance.* "Why don't you ride your bike over, maybe my mom will drop us off to see a movie or something."

"Okay, I'm there," David said before he hung up.

Chris stood and stretched. As he recalled what had happened the night before, there was a knock at his locked bedroom door.

"Open up, it's me," David shouted. Chris unlocked the door and opened it slowly as he peeked out the door. "I called you from the kitchen," David said, laughing. "I've been here for a half hour waiting for you to wake up, but your mom said I should wake you," David said, pushing his way into the room. "You look like shit, dude."

"Thanks, I just got out of bed," Chris said, standing naked as he watched David undress. "What are you doing?"

"I thought we'd go swimming," David said as he removed the rest of his clothing. "It's, like, really hot outside."

Chris shrugged, "Okay. Did you bring your suit?"

"Yeah, but your mom and Richard just left so we don't need them," David explained, smiling, as he stood naked before Chris.

"Where did they go?"

"They said they were going to meet some friends of Richard's and then they were going to lunch and a movie. Your mom said you should make me lunch, and that they would be home about dinnertime. She said they'd bring pizza." David said. He went into Chris's bathroom, grabbed two towels, and threw one at Chris. "She also said that there's leftover veal, and that you're to make us sandwiches for lunch," David said, pushing Chris toward the door.

"Come on, let's go."

"Dude. I am sorry about last night, and all that," Chris said, putting his hand on David's shoulder as they walked outside.

"Me, too. I can't believe I was such a jerk about it," David said. "I can't believe I cried. I feel so stupid. I was afraid last night after I got home that maybe you wouldn't want to be my friend anymore." David's voice cracked with emotion. "I was afraid you'd think I was weird or something."

"Fuggedaboudit. We're always going to be friends," Chris said.

"I'm really glad we got to be better friends this summer," David said as he pushed Chris into the pool and jumped in after him. "I can't believe we're starting high school next week. We should study together a lot, don't you think?" David asked, sounding tentative.

"Yeah. Sure," Chris said, "if you really want to. I'd like that a lot."

"Too cool, dude," David shouted. "We could make sure we have all our classes together and study together. You know, like we did this summer. We could make each other get really good grades."

* * * * *

"The voice, the arguing back and forth, is that a voice you hear outside yourself, or in your head?" I asked.

"In my head."

"That wasn't the first time?" I asked.

"No. I guess it started getting bad mostly after the stuff with Jack, then the confession with Father O'Brien. I mean, it's just me yelling at myself."

"We all have voices in our head, but this sounds torturous," I said.

Chris shrugged.

"Does it happen often?"

"Mostly it happens when I'm trying to go to sleep." He looked around the room again. I found myself wondering what he expected to find. "Sometimes I just can't get to sleep. I just lie there hating myself," Chris said, turning to look at me. He did not make eye contact often, but when he did he seemed to be reaching out to me for something: understanding, assurance, support, an explanation. His stare was so powerful I could almost feel it physically.

We sat in silence. Silences can sometimes be restful, calming or soothing, but these were painful.

Chapter Seven

"Any special reason for hating yourself, or just generally?"

"My dad, arguing with my mom, things friends say, girlfriends, being gay—that mostly, I guess. But all that stuff." Chris turned his head and stared at the floor. Then he wiped his hands across his pant legs several times. He took a deep breath; he sighed and then rocked forward in his chair, resting his elbows on his knees and his forehead in his hands.

"Is that the first time you've said that out loud?"

He blew out a burst of air from his lungs and nodded. Then he sat back in his chair and stared up at the ceiling.

"You think of yourself as gay?" I asked.

"Now, yeah," his breath quivered with anxiety.

My chest ached, I wished I could make this easier for him, but this was the way out of the mess he was feeling.

He continued, "I guess, before, well, I don't know, it was mostly confusing. I mean, I dated girls all the time in high school, but I always had crushes on guys. I started having sex, you know, intercourse, with girls when I was a junior, but I really had a crush on David then." He stared at the floor.

"How long have you been having crushes on guys?"

"I guess the first real crush I had that I remember was my best friend in the seventh grade in the Bronx. We used to look at each other and touch each other and stuff," he said in a whisper.

"You masturbated together?"

"Yes."

"This is Larry that you mentioned?" He nodded. "Did you do anything else with him?" I could see that he was becoming more agitated with each of my questions. I felt as though I was pushing him, and perhaps too hard.

"No. I don't think he was gay or anything."

"You kept your crushes a secret?"

"Fuck, yes!" he shouted. He rolled his eyes and shook his head. I truly expected the next words out of his mouth to be, 'What are you, some kind of fuckin' idiot?' He hesitated, took a deep breath and continued, "I mean being on a team, in Catholic school. In high school guys hate sissies and gays.

"The guys on my team hated gays, but I guess there were people in my school who didn't. I just never hung around with them." He sat silently, staring at the floor for several minutes. Then, as if he had suddenly awakened, he glanced toward me. His depression was visible. "It's weird," he said, nodding his head and turning to talk to the floor.

"What is?"

"Well, nothing has changed. I mean my fantasies have always been the same, you know, attracted to guys. But, before, I still believed that I was straight. I mean, I knew I was straight, but I just had these thoughts. Then I had sex with Jack." His voice sounded heavy and he sighed. He looked at me. He shrugged his shoulders and winced. "Then, I guess, I thought I might be gay, but that no one would ever know. It would be a secret all my life, and I would just never do anything. Never, no matter what. I thought about becoming a priest." A smile crossed his face. "A cool priest, like Father John; not that he's gay. I mean, I don't know if he is or isn't. But then I had sex with a girl. I was so happy it all worked and stuff. I figured now all the thoughts about sex with guys would stop. So, then I imagined I could get married. But the thoughts didn't stop. So, I figured I could just keep it all a secret and no one would ever know. I guess I was really happy then." His body and voice became more animated as he spoke. "It's weird, though. The more everyone, including me, thought that I was straight, the more the dreams and the voices seemed to scream at night. I mean it should have been the other way around." His focus disappeared into the floor.

"Where are you?" I finally asked.

"I was thinking about one time last year, during my junior year."

"Tell me."

* * * * *

After running eight laps around the high school track, David, Peter, and Chris, followed by their teammates, headed for the shower room. The three of them had become inseparable. Both Chris and Peter had played varsity baseball the year before, as sophomores, but this was David's first year on the varsity team. Gary, Derek, and Kyle were also juniors and new to the team. They had hopes for making it to the city finals this year, but the team was currently two games out of the running, and it was near the end of the season.

Lies That Bind

"Good practice, Peter," Coach Fraser called out. "Jarrett, you've got to work on your hitting. Chris, you should take some time with your friend there and teach him how to hit a ball. If I'd had another hitter like you this year we'd be going to state."

"Will do, Coach," Chris called back to the coach as the three of them entered the locker room.

"He calls you Peter, and he calls you Chris, and he calls me Jarrett. He says nice things to you guys, and he tells me to work on my hitting," David complained.

"Stop whining. You should work on your hitting," Peter said.

"Yeah, you're only a little better than Derek, and that isn't saying much," Chris added.

After making their way to their lockers, they undressed. Gary and Derek and the others had just entered the locker room as Peter, David, and Chris started for the showers. Gary was ranting about something and then turned and punched his locker. The sound echoed through the room. Chris turned and stared at Gary. *Asshole.*

As they entered one of the shower rooms, a couple of guys from the gymnastics team were leaving. "Hey Chris, Peter, David. What's going on out there?" one of them asked.

"Hey Mike, Howard. One of the guys on our team slamming lockers," Chris said with a grimace.

"You guys on the baseball team are a bunch of troublemakers," the other one said shaking his head. Peter pushed him and they both laughed.

"Hey, Chris." Mike called Chris aside. "I'm really fucking up in chemistry. We've got that test on Tuesday. I was wondering if we could get together this weekend. I really need help."

"Sure. Actually, David is better in chemistry than I am, but he'll be coming over, so why don't you join us? He can tutor both of us."

"Cool. Thanks, Chris. I'll call you tonight." Mike turned and joined his friends in the locker room.

There were two large shower rooms, separated by a smaller room where, during regular physical education classes, one of the coaches sat and handed out towels. After three o'clock, when only guys who were playing team sports were allowed in the locker and shower rooms, towels were piled up on a bench for the taking. In each of the shower rooms were six showerheads on each of three walls, and four large metal columns in the center of the shower room, each holding four showerheads.

After Chris turned on his shower he asked Peter if he knew what was going on with Gary. "He's all pissed off." Peter answered. "Says he was at the mall last night with his girlfriend and some guy winked and smiled at him. Says his girlfriend saw it, too," Peter said, as he turned on a shower that hung from one of the columns.

"So why is he punching lockers today?" David asked.

"He said that if his girlfriend sees guys winking at him she might think that he's gay. Now he wants to go to West Hollywood and look for the guy," Peter said, shaking his head.

Chris laughed, "He's a nut case. Why is he so threatened by that? So some guy winked at him," Chris said, standing under the shower.

David turned the shower on that was closest to Chris and said, "Like all the gay people in L.A. live in West Hollywood. What a jerk."

Gary stepped into the shower room, followed by Derek, Roger, and Kyle. The rest of the guys on the team were using the second shower room.

"Hey, dude," Roger said, addressing Chris, "I heard that you're thinking about running for student body president."

"Yeah, I am thinking about it, but I haven't decided. I've never run for anything before."

"Do it," Derek chimed in, "That'd be so cool. One of us as president."

"Derek," Gary yelled out as he turned on a shower that was against one of the walls, "When it comes to you there is no 'us.' You're in a group no one else wants to be in." Everyone laughed, as Roger high-fived it with Gary. Chris turned to Gary and gave him a thumbs up.

"Fuck you, all of you," Derek said as he turned on a shower next to Gary. Gary then shoved him as they all continued to laugh.

"Are you really thinking about running?" David asked Chris.

"I want to find out who else is running before I make up my mind."

"A guy named Andrew is running, and so is Cheryl," Roger said. Roger was a senior and on student council.

Gary shouted, "Andrew the fairy? Oh man, Chris, you've got to run."

Chris reiterated, "I haven't decided."

"Oh man, that guy is a fucking faggot. You can't let him be our president," Gary insisted. Chris felt his jaw tightening and his stomach sinking. He didn't know if he wanted to leave the shower room or kick Gary's ass.

"How do you know that?" David asked.

Lies That Bind

Derek chimed in, "He's such a prissy little queen. God, he turns my stomach." Chris turned and glared at Derek and then looked at Peter, who just shook his head.

"That's bullshit," David said, shaking his head.

"Why, he isn't prissy?" Gary asked.

"Well, maybe he's a little feminine, but that doesn't mean he's gay," David said, wishing he'd not said anything.

Derek persisted, "And how do you know he isn't gay, David? Did he say no when you tried to blow him?" Although no one except David seemed to notice, Derek was always quick to call David's heterosexuality into question.

"Eat shit, Derek," David mumbled, giving him the finger.

"Knock it off," Chris demanded, staring at Derek. "I'm going to have to decide this weekend. I think Monday is the last day to sign up. Right?" Chris asked, looking to Roger. Roger nodded in agreement.

"Come on, Chris. You have to run." Gary insisted. "You can't let some fairy be our president. We need a stud as our president."

Chris asked Gary, "Why don't *you* run?"

"No one would vote for him," Derek said jokingly. Gary then turned and made a fist and swung short of Derek. Derek jumped back so quickly he crashed into the wall. Again, everyone laughed. David just shook his head and stared at Derek.

"Fuck you, Jarrett," Derek yelled.

"Chris, if you don't run, then we'll have some 'brainiac' or some faggot." Gary said.

Chris thought, *Yeah, If I'm president you get both in one.*

"David, why are you always showering near Chris?" Derek asked contemptuously.

"What?" David asked.

"I said, queers are deaf," Derek responded, laughing loudly and pointing at David.

No one else laughed. Peter shook his head and said to Chris, "Some people never make it out of grade school."

"Derek," Chris asked Derek, "How is it that you notice where David showers?"

"What?" Derek asked. A roar of laughter echoed through the shower room. Derek looked confused. "What, what did I say?" Then he understood and said, "Fuck you guys."

"David," Chris said, "Move over. Derek, come here and shower next to me."

"Forget it," Derek shouted, as everyone laughed. "Fuck you guys."

"Come here, Derek," Peter chimed in, "I need to have my back washed."

"He always showers near Chris," Derek insisted.

Peter, who seldom showed anger, shouted, "Like, who the fuck cares, asshole." Then he said to Chris, "You should run. You'd be a good president."

"I'll be your campaign manager," David volunteered.

"The man behind the man," Derek muttered. Peter turned and glared at Derek.

"I guess. I'll think about it," Chris said thoughtfully.

After Peter, David, and Chris finished showering and horsing around in the locker room, they dressed and started their short walk home. As always, they walked home together. Peter's house was the first on their customary route home, then David's, and then Chris's. As they approached Peter's house he broached the subject of Chris's running for student body president again. "Why wouldn't you run?"

"I'd feel stupid if I lost."

Peter shook his head, "You won't lose. I bet if they hear that you're running, no one else will run."

"I agree," David said. "You'd get to work a lot with Father John, and you'd get class credit, too."

"Yeah, I know." Chris had been aware of feeling anxious ever since they had left the shower room, but he was not yet sure why. "I mean even if I did lose, I guess it wouldn't be so bad."

David insisted, "You won't lose, dude. And like I said, I'll be your campaign manager."

"The man behind the man," Chris said, poking at David and smiling.

"God, I hate him. And when he's around Gary he's such an ass," David insisted.

Chris asked, staring at the ground. "What's with all that fag stuff today? So some guy winked at him. Why does he go off like that?"

"He's always going off on some group," David said. "If it isn't gays, then it's Mexicans or Blacks or Jews or Italians." David smiled, "I mean, I can understand going off on the 'eyetalians.'" Peter Cartola and Chris jumped on David and wrestled him to the ground. "My uniform, my uniform! Guys, watch out. If you tear my uniform my dad will kill me," David warned. As they let him get to his feet, they each promised that they would get even with him when they next saw him.

"See you guys Monday," Peter said.

Lies That Bind

"Hi, Mrs. Cartola," David shouted, seeing her waving from the door. Chris waved to her too. David ran up to the house. He and Peter's mother hugged and began to whisper to each other.

Chris and Peter smiled at each other, watching David hug Peter's mother again and then kiss her on the cheek. "He's such a kiss-ass," Peter said laughing.

"I know. He's got my mom wrapped around his finger, too," Chris agreed.

"Julie's mom wants to adopt him." Julie, who had been David's neighbor, was now Peter's girlfriend. She was considered one of the more attractive girls in their class; cute, very smart, and athletic. "Is there anyone's mom who doesn't fall all over him?" Peter asked.

"Yeah, *his* mom," Chris said. Peter looked at Chris, winced and nodded in agreement.

As Chris and David walked the three blocks to David's house, David noticed that Chris seemed to be sinking into a mood. "What's up with you?" he asked, giving Chris a friendly shove.

"Just thinking," Chris mumbled.

"About what? Running?" David asked.

"Ahh, yeah, I guess."

"Are we getting together tomorrow?" David asked. Chris looked blankly at David. "We have appointments tomorrow with Father John," David said. "Remember?"

"Is that tomorrow?" Chris asked, looking lost.

"What is going on with you, dude? Yeah, remember. Mine is at three-thirty, and I think yours is at three."

Chris took off and dug into his backpack and pulled out a sheet of paper. "Yeah it is at three. I forgot all about it."

"You should talk to him about running. He'll tell you to run."

"He never tells me what to do. He just asks questions," Chris said, stuffing the sheet of paper back into his backpack. "Yeah, okay. Let's get together tomorrow. Call me tonight."

"Okay," David said. Chris watched as David walked up the driveway to his house. David's mood was now also changing.

Chris turned and shouted to David, "Hey, Mike asked me to help him with chemistry for the test on Tuesday. Why don't you come over before lunch? The three of us can study, and then you and I can go over to school together."

"Great," David shouted, smiling. "I'll be over at ten. Or should I come over earlier?"

Chris smiled, "Ten is good. Tomorrow, dude," Chris said, waving to David as he walked away.

Chris sighed. He had the physical sensation of falling. It was not the feeling of falling down, but rather, of falling away from himself, or falling into himself. He was never really sure. It was followed by a numbness, a loneliness that engulfed him; what everyone called his mood. It started in the pit of his stomach, first with a feeling of queasiness, then a sinking sensation which was followed by an eerie calm, or perhaps a deadness that felt like a calm. Then a numbing cloud enveloped him, resulting in an absence of all emotion. He was never sure why, but only that it happened. His face felt heavy, his sight drifted toward the ground, sound seemed to pass through his ears unnoticed. He became most conscious that it was happening when he felt himself trying to smile. Every muscle called for a special effort that he had to think about. His breath was mostly shallow. Deep breaths were accompanied by a quivering sensation that moved through his chest and into his stomach.

As he walked up the driveway to his house he realized he had no recall of the six-block walk from David's house. His thoughts were about Andrew. They had several classes together and were, at best, cordial. Andrew had his own circle of friends, mostly girls. He was attractive in an effeminate way: tall, lean, and soft. Andrew's prissiness always scared Chris.

Chris worried that it might be far more important to Andrew to win than it was to him. However, he was sure that Cheryl would win if he didn't run. Gary was right, no one wanted a sissy for a student body president. Chris tried to assure himself that the only reason he wanted to be president was for his resume. It had to help with his application to Columbia. "Hi, honey," Diane said, greeting him as he entered the house through their side door, which opened into the kitchen.

"Hi," he replied in an monotone. He walked to the kitchen counter and opened the cookie jar.

"Dinner is in about an hour, don't spoil your appetite," Diane said, walking toward him to give him a kiss.

"It's my appetite, if I want to spoil it I will." Chris said caustically, as he flashed her an angry glare.

"Don't be snippy with me, young man," Diane demanded.

"Whatever," Chris said, slamming the lid down and walking away empty-handed.

"What is with you?" Diane asked with concern. These downcast moods were nothing new, but Chris seemed more distraught of late.

Lies That Bind

"Just leave me alone." Chris picked up his backpack from the counter, and turned toward his bedroom.

"Come back here," Diane demanded. She had been worried for some time now. She had decided to sit back and listen for clues as to what might be bothering Chris. But, it was finally time to take him on.

"What?" His tone was edgy.

"You can't just walk in here and give me attitude like that."

"Whatever." he said impatiently, and waved her off.

"Chris, don't start with 'whatever,' I hate that. And don't you wave me off like I'm some annoyance to you." Chris turned and faced her, now doing his best to stare her down. "What is with you?" Diane stared back.

"Duh. You are with me. Do you see anyone else around here yanking my chain? You know, if you'd just back off, everything would be fine," he growled.

"Back off. Back off," Diane repeated with irritation. "Just who do you think you are? And whom do you think you are talking to? This is my house, and as long as you live in it you are going to show me a modicum of respect. If not, your life will not be worth living, I promise you that," Diane shouted.

"Whatever."

"Christopher, you sit down right now," Diane demanded, as she pointed to one of the kitchen chairs.

Chris threw his backpack to the floor, slapped his hands against the sides of his legs and sighed loudly. "Jesus Christ, why can't you just leave me alone? I've had a long, hard day at school, and the first thing you do when I get home is get in my face."

"Christopher, you are treading on very thin ice. I suggest you think about what comes out of your mouth before you next speak." Chris sat down in a huff, crossing his arms over his chest and staring at his mother. "And don't you stare at me like that. If looks could kill I'd be dead right now." Finally he looked away, as some of the steam seemed to escape from his anger. "Chris, I don't know what gets into you. I really don't."

"I don't either," he said, shaking his head.

"What gets you so irritable?"

Chris glared at her. He wanted to start another assault on her, but he thought it wise to remain silent. Besides, he had no idea why he was angry with her. All he knew was that she was the object of his anger. He took a deep breath, and then sighed. "I'm thinking about running for student body president."

"Okay, and you are angry at me because…?"

"No, just changing the subject."

"Do you think it will interfere with your school work?"

"God, Mom," Chris said in a huff. "I have the highest grades of anyone in my class. Do I look like someone who lets stuff interfere with my school work?"

"Sorry. You're right. I was out of line. Sometimes I can't help but hover."

Chris hesitated. He hated it when she was reasonable, especially when he was being so unreasonable. "Hovering is okay," he said. She sat and waited. "I think it would look good for getting into college."

"I'm sure it will, but Chris, you don't have to worry about college. You won't have any trouble getting into UCLA."

"Whatever."

"Chris, can we have a conversation without you using the word, 'whatever?' I swear I'm going to destroy that tee shirt the next time I find it in the wash." Chris had bought a tee shirt that said "WHATEVER" in big green letters. He had put it on one night under another shirt. During a conversation at dinner, when it seemed most appropriate, Chris opened his shirt to reveal his new tee shirt. Richard had smiled. Diane had made every effort not to laugh, but finally she had had to admit that she enjoyed the moment. However, "whatever" remained her second most hated word.

"I still want an answer to my question. What do you think gets you so irritable?"

"I don't know," Chris said, shaking his head and drawing circles with his finger on the kitchen table. "I have an appointment with Father John tomorrow at three. It's for my class schedule for next semester. He had to schedule appointments after school this semester, but because I have baseball practice he scheduled me for a Saturday. David's appointment is at three-thirty, so we'll go together."

"Okay."

"He and Mike are coming over tomorrow at ten. We're going to study chemistry. We have an exam on Tuesday. Then David and I will go over to school." He glanced up at his mother, looking contrite.

"Okay," Diane said, not dissuaded from where she was heading. "I'm waiting."

"For what?" Chris asked impatiently. Again, he tried to stare her down.

Lies That Bind

"I want an answer to my question. Your irritability."

He raised his hands into the air in frustration, "Damn it, Mom, I don't know."

"Then I want to ask you something. And I want the truth." She took a deep breath. "Christopher, don't lie to me. If I find out you've lied to me your life will become what is now unimaginable to you."

"Geez, Mom. A little dramatic, you think?" His heart began to race. He worried anxiously as to what she thought she knew. "What's with you?" His ears began to burn red.

"Drugs." Diane said, staring at him, trying to gauge his first reaction.

"Really? What are you on?" Chris playfully asked, as he began to relax. She refused to break her stare. "Okay. God, Mom! Get a sense of humor. I am not doing drugs," he said, staring her straight in the eyes. "No lie, no drugs. None. Well, I mean I am doing caffeine." He paused. "some Coke, once in a while," he said with a smile, "and Pepsi, too." Diane refused to be amused. "Mom, I am not doing any drugs. Really, I promise."

"Have you done drugs?"

"Damn it, Mom. Do you want my history?" She continued her stare. "Okay, look I've done nicotine, but you knew that, right?" he asked grimacing.

"When?"

"The summer before I moved here, but I stopped when I started school and I haven't had a cigarette since then. No lie," he said, waving his hands at her. "I've done alcohol, but mostly with you and Richard or Grandma and Grandpa. You know, wine at dinner and a beer with Richard, and stuff like that."

"No other drinking?"

"Well, yeah. I got drunk at a Halloween party. You know about that. But that was it."

"Nothing else?" Diane insisted.

"No. Look, I've been offered dope, speed, blow, and I've turned them down. Mom, I am *not* lying to you."

"Christopher, I believe you. But that still doesn't answer my question."

"Why do I get irritable?" He shook his head. "Mom, I don't know. Maybe it's low blood sugar. Maybe it's stress. Maybe I'm horny," he said, laughing. *Oh my God, why did I say that?* "Mom, that's a joke, we need a joke right now, right, Mom? You know, in *Moonstruck,* when the grandfather said, 'somebody tella joke.'" He used his practiced Italian accent and hand gestures. "You know, when they were all tense sitting around the table. Like we are, right now." He waited and hoped that he could make her smile.

"That brings me to another subject."

"No way. No way. We are not having the sex talk. No way," Chris said, waving his hands and shaking his head. Again, his heart began to race. Could he lie and have her not know? He doubted it.

"I am not an idiot. I know you don't need any sex talk."

"Thank God. You had me freaked," he said, shaking his head. "What's the next subject?"

"Are you having intercourse with Cathy?"

"Oh, Mom," Chris shouted, shaking his head 'no' and rolling his eyes. "We are not having this conversation. Fuggedaboudit. End of discussion. Period. *Finito*."

"Chris. I was talking to a friend and she told me that Cathy had an abortion last year. You two have been dating for…" Diane counted the months on her fingers, "five months now. I am not some prude who can't figure out what's going on here."

"Then why ask me?" he asked, exasperated.

"I want an answer."

"No way," he said as he got to his feet, picked up his backpack, and started for his room. Then he turned back to the kitchen. "That reminds me. What drugs have you done?"

"Nicotine, caffeine, alcohol," she said. "Marijuana, dope as you call it. That's it."

"Mom, you smoked dope?" Chris asked in astonishment. "Really, when? What was it like?"

"It was after you were born. I was at a party with your father. He was smoking it with some of our friends. They offered it to me, so I tried it. To tell you the truth, I didn't particularly enjoy it. I got high, but I also got a headache. Didn't appeal to me." Diane had been practicing her answer to this question for some time. She knew if she questioned Chris about his drug use, he would ask her about hers. She had long ago decided that if she treated her son with the respect due to him, he would in turn show her the respect she expected. Mutuality in honesty was part of the mutuality in respect she insisted upon.

"Wow, I'm impressed," Chris said enthusiastically.

"Why would you be impressed with my smoking dope?"

Lies That Bind

"No. Actually, I figured that you had. I'm impressed that you told me. Thanks for being so open, that was cool. And no, I don't want to know if you're having sex," he added while shaking his head.

"Don't worry about it. That's none of your business," Diane insisted.

"Exactly, Mom," Chris agreed, flashing her the dreaded smirk. "Oh, and that reminds me. David, Jeanine, Cathy, and I are going out Saturday night. I need the car," he said as he started toward his bedroom.

"I'll let you know," she shouted back to him.

Hr turned and walked back into the kitchen. "What do you mean, 'you'll let me know?'" he asked, as he reached into the cookie jar. "Just two, okay?"

She noticed that his mood had completely changed again. And again, she did not know why. "It's my car. I'll let you know if you can use it."

"Now who's being contentious?" Chris asked with a smile.

"Whatever," Diane said, returning the smirk. Chris stood there and stared at her, trying to decide if she was being serious. "Good one, Mom. Good one."

"Whatever."

Chris had a restive night. He tried reading. This was his fourth journey through Tolkien's *The Lord of the Rings*. He turned his light off at eleven. He lay there and wondered what his mother would do if she knew he was attracted to guys. He stared at the ceiling, remembering his night with Jack. His stomach churned, he wished for the millionth time that it had never happened. When Diane had confronted him earlier in the day he thought for a moment that she found out. But how could she, he reassured himself, no one except Jack knew what had happened. And he was sure Jack would never tell anyone. *No one would ever think that I am bisexual. Besides, being bi isn't so bad, as long as you aren't a" fem." It's not like being gay.*

He was sure that if the guys on the team knew about what had happened with Jack they would never shower with him. He was glad he no longer had a crush on Peter. But his crush on David never seemed to fade. As he imagined having sex with David he could feel the beginnings of his arousal. Lying there, he forced himself to imagine himself with Cathy. But his efforts failed. He gave in to what allowed him pleasure. Moving his hand to greet his erection, he imagined David beside him. He imagined David aroused, touching him, lying on top of him, kissing him. He imagined what he would say to David, and what David would say to him. He could hear David breathing deeply, wanting him. Imagining passionately kissing David, his body became tense and then began rhythmically contracting. Each contraction brought with it a release of liquid that splashed onto his neck and chest. He lay there for several minutes as he sadly acknowledged to himself that he would never realize the passion of his desires.

Later, the voices started. First came the guilt he felt about his sexual desires. Then the guilt over the betrayal of those he loved, especially David. He worried about the distress he caused his mother.

He was sure that if his mother found out she would be disgusted, angry, and rejecting, and she might even never speak to him again. His grandfather would not be angry, but Chris could hear the disappointment in his voice as he told him that he was no longer his champean grandchild. His grandmother would just shake her head, turn her back and ignore him. Cathy would tell everyone she knew. David would feel horrified, embarrassed and violated—all that naked wrestling. David would never forgive him. But, he assured himself, no one would ever find out. He promised himself he would be his own best-kept secret. No one would ever really know him. It was the only way he could survive.

He wrestled his pillow until two in the morning, and then took his guitar into his bathroom, closed himself in his shower, sat on the bench, and played until he felt calm settle over him. It had become the only thing that could distract him from his torment. When he last looked at his digital clock it was 3:44 a.m.

At ten o'clock there was a pounding at his locked bedroom door. It was David and Mike. They studied until noon, when Diane made them lunch. At two-thirty, Chris left with David and Mike in Diane's Suburban. Chris drove Mike home, and then drove himself and David to the high school for their meeting with Father John. They had already decided what classes they would take together: AP Physics, AP Algebra IV, AP Senior Composition, and Father John's philosophy and religion class. Chris decided to run for student body president, much to David's pleasure, so he would have credits for civics. David would take another year of computer graphics at the local junior college with Julie, Peter's girlfriend. And he and David would have another year of physical education, which was required because they were going to play varsity baseball again next year.

The first half of Chris's meeting with Father John went as he expected. They talked about his schedule of classes for the fall semester. Father John suggested that Chris also take another college course, perhaps

Lies That Bind

English literature, as he thought this might be his college major. They talked about his choice of colleges and the application process, and about his running for student body president. Father John thought the experience would help Chris strengthen his public speaking and leadership abilities, skills he thought Chris would find indispensable in the future.

"Well, I do agree that being student body president will help you with your applications, especially with schools like Stanford and Columbia. But, to be candid with you, Chris, your resume is looking good as it is," Father John said. By now he had come to know Chris well. He knew when he was upbeat and light-hearted, and when he was pensive and remote.

"Yeah, I agree, but I think it would be fun, too," Chris said.

"Well, since we have time here, perhaps this would be a good time for me to hear your confession," the priest said, putting on his confessional sole.

"Oh yeah, well, I guess."

"Chris, I know you well enough to know that something is troubling you," the priest said as he blessed Chris.

Chris, in return, made the sign of the cross. "I've talked to you about going off at my mom. Well, it's getting bad again, really bad, I guess. I mean I don't know why I do this, but all of a sudden there's this anger that gets so strong, and I just explode."

"This happened again, recently?"

"Yeah, yesterday." Chris explained to Father John the argument and conversation he had had with Diane the day before.

"You were angry before you got home?"

"No. I don't think so. More like just tired, I guess."

"Did something happen at school or on your way home?"

"No. Well, maybe. I mean there was all this talk about me running for president."

"Where did this happen?"

"After baseball practice. In the showers. The guys wanted me to run," Chris said unconvincingly. "Actually, they want me to run because they don't want Andrew to win. But Father, I was thinking about running before that." Chris recounted much of what was said in the shower room, but made every effort not to use names.

"Why don't they want Andrew to win?"

Chris stared at Father John, who remained silent. "Wow, this is hard to say." Chris hesitated. "They don't want him to win, because they think he is effeminate and gay."

"I see," Father John said nodding. "But this was not what motivated you to run?"

"No. When I was thinking about it, I didn't even know he was going to run. But I think part of me feels like they feel. I think maybe that really bothers me."

"That you want to beat him just because you think he is a sissy and gay."

Chris had confided in Father John how his father berated him as a child for being a sissy.

"Yeah," Chris said, staring down at his feet and shaking his head.

"And your anger at your mom?" Father John asked.

"I don't get it, really."

"Do you think that hearing someone being berated the way you were as a child by your father brings up your anger?"

"Yeah, maybe that's it."

"Chris, there is something else troubling you. Some burden that you are carrying. It is clear to me that the filial love you have for your mother and both your grandparents is unwavering. As I've said in the past, I don't believe that is what all this anger is about. I do not believe your anger rests with her moving you from New York. Whatever it is, it haunts you, and you may not yet be ready to share the reason with me. But I've seen the effects it has on you. I've seen you when you are gregarious, animated, and full of humor, and unequivocally erudite. Then I've seen you when you are laconic, staid, and oddly diffident…"

Chris interrupted, "I don't know that one, 'diffident.'"

"Timid and shy. Which is so out of character for you on the one hand, and yet so you on the other. Am I off base here?"

"No."

"And my guess is this. When you are feeling morose, sullen, devoid of feelings, it is a quick shift to your anger. And your mother becomes the target. The question that seems to elude us is why." He paused. "My guess is this. You are testing her love for you. Although, your love for your family is unwavering, you do not yet believe, for some reason, that theirs is unwavering for you. And I believe part of you would rather destroy it than have it taken away from you." Father John nodded as he spoke, his head always supported by his right hand as he rubbed his brow. "I believe your anger at your mother arises when you believe she would abandon you like your father did. The question is why you would believe that."

"That's what I like about you, Father. You never mince words," Chris said, making eye contact. He often thought he could talk to Father John

Lies That Bind

about his attraction to other guys, but he feared the conversation would lead back to Jack.

"Do you want me to?"

"No. I do appreciate what you say." Chris hesitated. "There is something else. I've been having sexual intercourse with my girlfriend. I know it's a sin and all, but I haven't had the nerve to say anything to you about it."

"Until now," Father John commented.

"Yeah. I guess it's been bothering me that I haven't said anything to you about it. I am using protection, condoms."

"And do you have any notion as to why you feel compelled to tell me this now?"

"Just because it came up with my mother."

"I see," Father John said, sounding unconvinced. "Do you love this girl, Chris?"

Chris looked into Father John's eyes. He knew what the right answer was, but he did not want to lie. "No, I guess not. I mean, I like her, and I enjoy being with her. But, no, I'm not in love with her."

"Chris, I want you to search your heart. I want you to think about what this is all about for you. Also, you know the church's position on premarital intercourse. I want you to come to some understanding as to your own moral position on the issue. I want you to make responsible choices." Father John paused. He rubbed his brow and sighed. "Do you tell this girl that you love her?"

"No, Father. I'm not being deceitful. I've been very clear and so has she. But you're right. There is something that's bothering me about it. But I can't say exactly what it is."

"Think on that." Father John bowed his head. Chris thought he was done, but then the priest continued. "Chris, I am going to do something I usually don't do. I am hoping you trust me enough to know that I have your best interests at heart."

Chris felt the blood draining from his head. He had never lied to Father John, a man he respected and trusted as much as he did his grandfather. "Of course, I know that. What is it?"

"Your mother asked you about drugs."

"Really, Father, I'm not using."

"I have no doubt about that."

"Then what?"

"I've often wondered," he hesitated. "Well, I know we've talked about your father and the physical abuse. I guess I've sometimes wondered if you have ever been sexually abused."

Surprised, "By my father?" Chris asked.

"No, no. I was asking in general. Were you ever sexually abused?"

"No, Father. No, I haven't been," Chris answered honestly. He never thought of his sexual experience with Jack as abuse.

"Okay, then. I guess I was off base. I guess your mood swings, your outbursts, your depressions still remain a mystery to us," the priest said as he began to bless Chris.

Chris bowed his head and again made the sign of the cross.

They rose to their feet and walked to the door. At the door, Chris hesitated. Before he left the priest's office, Father John would always put his hand on Chris's shoulder and give it a squeeze. Then they would look at each other and smile. Chris always left feeling comforted and reassured after Father John's absolution. He sincerely believed that Father John was his conduit to Jesus.

As they started to leave the office, Chris stopped before the door. "Father."

"Yes, Chris."

"Can I hug you?' Father John nodded and they embraced.

Chris did not move as Father John started for the door. "Chris, is there anything wrong? Are you in any kind of trouble?"

"No. Not at all. Just thinking about stuff, personal stuff."

"Allow me one more question, please."

"Sure."

"Are there times when you are depressed that you think about committing suicide?"

"Oh no. Really, no, not at all."

"Okay. I didn't think so, but…" Chris smiled. "Why you are smiling?" the priest asked.

"I know you care about me, Father."

Father John nodded. "Chris, when you're ready to talk, I'm here. Okay?"

"Father, you don't have to worry about me." Chris felt queasy. He could hear himself telling the priest about what was troubling him, but he backed away from disclosure.

"Chris?"

Lies That Bind

Chris shook his head. "Father there is stuff bothering me, but please I'm not ready to talk to you about it. Please," Chris said, "I just don't want to talk about it now. But, I will, when I can. I promise."

"Chris, as I said, I am here for you whenever you need me. I trust you to know that, and I do respect your desire to keep what is bothering you to yourself until you feel comfortable talking to me about it." Chris reached out and, for the second time in all the years he had known the priest, he hugged him.

"Father John, you're champean with me." The priest smiled and nodded. Chris opened the door and exited the office.

Hey," Chris called out to David. "I warmed him up for you."

"I guess," David said, "he kept you over by ten minutes. You must have had a lot of sins to confess."

Chapter Eight

I SQUIRMED IN MY chair as Chris talked about struggling with the possibility of being gay. How well I remembered the process. The homosexual fantasies and desires under the mask of heterosexuality—the self-hate. The power of denial, the energy wasted. Then came the slow self-recognition, the redefining of myself, but only to myself—the guilt I felt because of the betrayals of those close to me. Then I suffered the anxiety, at times the overwhelming anxiety, as I revealed myself to others and tried to find myself a place in the world without rejection.

But I knew I had to be careful not to disrupt his train of thought, so I kept my mouth shut.

"I won the election," he said with a faint smile.

"Did anyone run against you?"

"Cheryl did."

"And Andrew?"

"He ran for class secretary and won," Chris said, with a shrug and a smile. I was embarrassed to notice that we both smiled for the same uncomfortable reason.

"David and I went to New York last summer. I told him it was payback for being a great campaign manager. He was really excited; he'd never been there. I was excited as well. We had a great time," Chris said, looking painfully wistful.

I couldn't help myself, so I said, "Tell me about your trip." I quickly regretted my decision.

He smiled, "Okay."

I hoped my feelings were in accordance with his thoughts, because otherwise I had just distracted him from where he needed to be going. Trust the process, I told myself.

"I guess it was an exciting trip for both of us. It was exciting for me, because I got to share my grandparents with David, and I got to spend the whole week with him; and for David, because he got to be away from his dad."

"What do you mean?"

Lies That Bind

"Well, I knew his dad beat him, but he never really talked about it a lot. I think he was really ashamed of it. You know, they say that abused kids always blame themselves." I nodded. "Like it was his fault. He mentioned some of it on the plane back from New York. But he told me a lot more during the year."

* * * * *

Chris listened as they announced the flight over the airport loud speaker. "Ladies and gentlemen, final call, Los Angeles flight. We are about to close the doors." He was saying goodbye to his cousin. As he glanced over at his grandfather he noticed Anthony beckoning to David to give him a hug.

This year Chris's trip to New York was shorter than usual; only a week. That was all David's parents would allow him to be away from home. They had been lucky; the weather had been ideal. "Mr. Dinato, thank you very much for a wonderful week," David said as he hugged Anthony and then kissed him on the cheek. David had learned that when saying hello or good-bye to Anthony or Josephine, a kiss was in order. David was not accustomed to hugs and kisses from family members. In David's family, touch was usually associated with pain.

This was David's first trip to New York, and it was far more exciting than he had anticipated. David's parents allowed him to accompany Chris to New York to see all the architectural wonders the city had to offer. His parents' goal for him was that he become an architect. Due to exceptional hand-eye coordination his drawing abilities were remarkable. Many of his teachers were amazed at the skill he showed in translating what he saw in three-dimensional space into two dimensions. His drawing skills, coupled with his gift for math and science, led his parents to decide that he should be an architect. Only Chris knew of David's desire to be an artist.

"You are my grandson's best friend," Anthony said, as he turned his cheek for David to kiss, "and you are always welcome in my home. He is a good boy and so are you."

"Grandpa, we have to go," Chris said, tugging at Anthony's shoulder. Chris put his arms around his grandfather and kissed him on the cheek. "I love you, Grandpa. You take care of yourself and Grandma, too. I'll see you in June for my graduation, right?" When saying goodbye to his grandparents, Chris always worried that he would never see one of them again.

"Yes, we'll be there," Anthony assured him.

"Remember, Grandpa, you promised me that I'll be able to go to college in New York."

"If you get into Columbia or NYU I will pay for your college. I've been saving money since you were born. My grandson a college boy, you make me so proud," Anthony said as he pinched Chris's cheek.

"Grandpa, I love you."

David was touched by the affection he witnessed. He knew that Italians were demonstrative, but he was surprised at how tender and loving Anthony and Josephine were with Chris. Each day when he and Chris returned to the Dinatos' home, the first thing that Chris did was kiss them both. Anthony held out his hand to David to shake, and Josephine turned her cheek for David to kiss.

Chris sat near his grandfather at the dinner table. David sat near Josephine, who made sure that he had more food on this plate than he could eat. There was always pleasant and animated conversation at dinner, which seldom occurred in David's home. David was struck by how often Anthony touched Chris during the course of one of their conversations. He had always envied Chris's ability to literally reach out and touch people, and now it all made sense to him.

"*Carissimo mio, guaglione*," Anthony said as he kissed his grandson. "Now get on the airplane. Do you have the meatball sandwiches your grandmother made for you and your friend? It is a long flight, and the food they give is crap."

"Yes, Grandpa, David has them," Chris said as he handed his boarding pass to the ticket taker.

The flight was only five hours, but Anthony was right, it was long. The flights from New York to Los Angeles were always long for Chris.

"The steward put your guitar, or as your grandfather says, 'geetar,' in the closet up front," David said, settling into his seat. Chris glared at David. "Oh man, I wasn't making fun of the way he talks, really. God, I love your granddad. Really, I think he's wonderful," David insisted. Chris nodded, then David sadly said, "I am so jealous. I wish I had grandparents that loved me the way they love you. Really, Chris, I'm serious," David said, pulling at Chris's arm.

"Okay, fuggedaboudit. I guess I'm just a little tired or something," Chris said, as he turned to stare out the window. He felt sleep pulling at him.

"You're getting your New Yawk accent back." Again Chris turned and stared at David, and audibly sighed. "Oh man, lighten up. Your accent is cute," David said, smiling.

"Cute, my accent is cute." Chris looked amused, but tried to hold to his stern demeanor. "Boy, this is going to be a long flight."

Lies That Bind

"Yeah, but we have 'meataball' sandwiches." David said, making exaggerated hand motions, and with that, both of them began to laugh.

"Chris, I'm serious, I think you're so lucky to have your grandparents. I really mean it. They love you so much. No one in the world loves me like they love you. I'd trade you everyone in my family for either of them." The truth of his statement was made obvious by the tone of his voice and the sad turn of his mouth.

"Your mom loves you," Chris said, understanding what David was trying to tell him.

"She spends too much time being afraid of my father to show love to anyone," David said, with his head pushing back into his seat. "You know, she's the dutiful obedient Christian wife. It's sick, Chris, really sick."

"Well, maybe she doesn't show it, but you know she loves you," Chris said softly.

He wanted to say something more, but he never knew what to say at moments like this. Chris understood that he was regretting the flight to Los Angeles because of what he was leaving, but that David's regrets were about his returning home.

"What did your grandfather call you?" David asked.

"When?"

"You know, when we were leaving and he kissed you, he said something in Italian."

"Oh yeah. Forget it, you'll make fun."

"No, I won't, really."

Chris stared at David, sighed, and then said, "*Carissimo mio, guaglione,*" with the same Italian accent that his grandfather used. "He's always called me *carissimo mio*. I used to think that was my name in Italian. I guess it means something like, you are of my heart, or you are in my heart. It means I'm special. *Guaglione* means like, well, tough guy, a teenager who is a tough guy, but not bad. It's the opposite of a sissy."

"Wow, *carissimo,*" David said, trying to wrap his mouth around the unfamiliar sounds. "That's nice. You're lucky, dude. Really."

Chris nodded, "My grandfather says that you know God by the mark he makes on the earth. Like mountains, rivers, the rain forest, and the diversity of people and animals. He says that you know a person by the mark they make on someone's heart. So I guess *carissimo mio* says something like that, that I have made a mark on his heart. I don't know, I think you have to be Italian to understand."

"I get it, I do. That's nice." David said, thinking about his father.

Paul Jarrett, David's father, was a born-again Catholic, since his conversion during college. He was now a deacon at Sacred Heart Church, and often helped with serving the mass. He believed in a strict or conservative reading of both the Bible and canon law. He considered Pope John Paul II's positions on birth control, a woman's role in the church, abortion, and homosexuality moderate in comparison to his own. David wondered what the Italian word was for the marks Paul left on him.

"This has been the most perfect week. My first time in New York coupled with meeting your grandparents." David thought, but could not admit to Chris, that spending a week with him was by far the best part of their trip. He said, smiling, "Your grandmother kept calling you something different, but I didn't get it."

"Forget it!" Chris said shaking his head.

"No, come on. It sounded like she was calling you a fish. I mean fish in Spanish is *pescado*, and it sounded like that, but in Italian." David reached over and tentatively shook Chris's right leg. He was trying to be more demonstrative.

Chris could see that David was nervous, but he assumed it was because he was pressing him, which was something that David ordinarily never did. "Fine, she calls me fish," Chris said sarcastically, rolling his eyes and shaking his head.

"But why? I don't get it." David loved to tease Chris. It was their favorite way of sparring with each other.

"*Peschadelle*, she calls me *peschadelle*. Little fish. I used to think that was my name in Italian, too."

"Little fish," David repeated. "Damn, you had a lot of Italian names when you were a kid." He smiled at Chris and nudged him. "You mean like *peschadelle* would have been, like, your Native American name, like Little-Bear, but only in Italian?" David laughed. "Were you born on a Friday?" David was in a good mood and he could not stop needling Chris. "Get it? Friday. Fish."

Chris rolled his eyes and sighed, "It's what you call a little boy. You know, little fish," Chris said as he wiggled his little finger, "meaning little penis. It's a term of endearment."

Of course David broke out into laughter. He put both his hands up over his face and rocked back and forth. "She calls you little penis, I can't believe this." He had never heard of anything like that before. "Oh my God. Little penis."

Lies That Bind

"I swear, Jarrett, if you tell anyone, I'll kick your butt." David continued laughing. Chris smiled. "It isn't that funny. Besides, it isn't little anymore," Chris whispered and nudged David in the side with his elbow.

"So, I've heard." David's face was bright red. "Your grandparents are too cool, dude."

"What does that mean? What have you heard?" Chris asked poking David in the side.

"Cathy says you're hung, lover boy. The word is out," David said as he winked and smiled at Chris. He was in full blush.

"Cathy has a big mouth." Chris said as he hung his head and shook it back and forth. David nodded and they both laughed. Now Chris was also blushing, which was unusual. "You really are a butt, you know that, don't you?" Chris said, as he turned toward the window.

He stared out the window as the plane took off from John F. Kennedy International and headed to LAX where his mother would be waiting for them. He thought about his chances of being accepted into Columbia University. He had worked hard for three years. His grades were excellent and his SAT score was over 1500 and there was a good chance that he would be class valedictorian. This year, as a senior, he would probably be the captain of his high school baseball team. He still played first base and had the highest batting average on the team. Last May he had been elected student body president. He and David had been doing volunteer work at a local hospital, and twice a month worked with Richard in the kitchen at Meals on Wheels. Last year they had taken classes at the local junior college. And they were Eagle Scouts; he hoped that would count for something. Even he thought his resume for his college applications would look impressive.

Chris knew Richard would be okay with him leaving, but Diane would fight to keep him close to home. She was always talking to him about his going to UCLA and living in the dorms.

"What ya thinking about? You're being so quiet," David said, leaning over toward him.

"Oh, going to Columbia. You know how much I want to go to school in New York. I think it would be so exciting. Plus, I'd be near my grandparents." Chris paused and then asked, "Were you serious when you said that you'd like to be roommates if we get into Columbia or NYU?" Chris asked.

"Sure, of course. I think that would be great. You and I would be great roomies. Don't you think?" David asked.

"Yeah, absolutely," Chris said.

"I can't think of anyone I'd rather live with than you," David agreed. "I've always hoped that we'd go to college together and that we'd be roommates, but I'd never really thought seriously about going to school on the east coast. But after seeing all the stuff in New York, I really want to go," David said.

Chris was fighting that sinking sensation; he could feel his stomach tighten. He found himself caught in between two desires. He wanted to hold onto David's friendship, be his college roommate, but he also wanted to get away from everyone he knew in California. He hoped to make a new start in the City.

One afternoon Chris had heard guests on Oprah talking about how they carried around "excess baggage". He had listened as they explained how their pasts got in the way of their present and their future. He had also heard one of the priests at school talk about building armor against the temptations one would face in the world. Chris's hope was to shed his armor, his past, rather than carrying it into the future. He was coming to see his armor as weighing him down rather than protecting him from the future. His hope was to leave it, and everyone involved with it, behind. He thought it would be an easy way not to have to deal with all his lies.

"Do you think your parents will go for it?" Chris asked, sure that David would say no.

"Not really, but I have my college trust fund that my grandparents set up for me in their will, and as long as I go to an accredited college I get my tuition and living and college expenses paid for. My grandmother wanted us to be able to live at college. I'm pretty sure I can get scholarships or some financial aid, which should really help."

"Oh yeah, that's right. Who set up your fund?"

"My mom's parents had money, and after my grandfather died my grandmother set up a trust fund for me and my brothers. I was about nine when she died. She had all her money put into a trust, and it's supposed to be used only for our college education. She really didn't like my dad, and she didn't want him to get any of her money. Whatever doesn't get used goes to charity. She was pretty smart that way."

"Was there anything in particular about him or just because he's such a dick?"

"She never liked him. I heard my aunt tell my mom that my grandmother thought he was a self-righteous religious bigot. One time she called him a boorish brute."

Lies That Bind

"You and I have that in common, I guess."

"Yeah, but you don't have to live with yours. And even though Richard can be a dick, he's nothing compared to my dad."

"True, he is mostly okay, I guess. I hated him at first, but after we got used to each other we decided to be friends." Chris said, as he watched David sit back in his seat. Staring at David, Chris noticed his steely blue eyes, and that they seldom seemed to smile. His straw-colored straight hair was now long and combed over the top of his head, like Chris's, and always falling down into his eyes. His lips were full, his teeth were white and straight, and his nose turned up at the end. Chris remembered that when they had first met, David had a mouth full of silver braces, and had been lanky and very awkward.

But now he was tall and lean and quick on his feet. He was the shortstop on their high school baseball team and had become an exceptional athlete. He was not muscular like some of the other guys on the team, but his body was tight and well defined. He had the type of muscles that did not bulk up, but allowed him to be agile. The girls often said that David looked like a young Kevin Bacon, and he was never without a girlfriend.

"What was your favorite day or thing that we did?" Chris asked.

"Wow, I think meeting your grandparents and all the good food. Homemade ravioli. You just don't know how lucky you are. I've never had food like that before. I mean, homemade macaroni. Who makes homemade macaroni?" David asked rhetorically.

"No, I mean something that we did."

"You know, I still can't believe that you play guitar. I've known you for four years now, and you're, like, my best friend ever, and you play and sing and you're so good, and I never knew you even had a guitar. Your voice is great, too. Why didn't I know that? Where do you keep it?"

Chris noticed something changing within himself. He was always very private, and there were parts of himself he would not share with anyone. Lately, he was more willing to share himself with David. He had not invited a friend to New York, although the opportunity had presented itself in the past. He never shared his guitar playing with any of his friends, nor told anyone of his plans to attend college in the City. His recent openness with David was surprising even to him.

"Under my bed."

"You are so good. Why didn't you tell me?"

"I play for myself and no one else. I like that it's just mine. I feel like it's the only thing that I enjoy that's just mine."

"But you brought the guitar to New York and played for me and your grandparents."

"When I was a kid, after my parents divorced, my mom decided that I should take violin lessons. No way was I doing that. We argued about it and then I said I wanted to play guitar. She said that a guitar wasn't an instrument. So she rented a violin and it just sat there."

"Didn't she know how stubborn you are? David asked. Chris reached over and grabbed David's left leg just above the knee and squeezed. The strength of his grip was like that of a vise. David jumped and wrestled the hand free. "Well, you're the most stubborn person I know," David insisted. "Ouch! That hurt."

Chris continued. "For Christmas my granddad bought me a guitar and he paid for lessons. I would come home from school and practice while my mom was at work, and he'd listen to me play. He'd tell me I should learn to play in Italian."

"Hey, that's funny. Play in Italian." David said, smiling, fully engrossed in the story. He had always thought that Chris was the best storyteller.

"He meant Italian songs. So then after about a year of taking lessons I was getting to be pretty good and everyone would ask me to play and I was always too nervous, and would just say 'no, I only play for my grandma and grandpa'." And, so I've only played for them."

"But you played while I was there. I heard you. You were great. Will you let me hear you play again?

"Sure, if my grandparents are there. Next year."

"No, dude. I mean like next week."

"No," Chris said.

"Really, why?"

"Are you dense? I just told you. I only play for myself. It's for me."

"And your grandparents," David added with resignation. "You are so stubborn."

"So, you didn't answer my question," Chris reminded him. "What was your favorite thing that we did?"

"Going to the City with your grandparents, and going for Chinese food and then going to the Museum of Modern Art. Your granddad was such a kick. He was telling me about how Michelangelo was the greatest sculptor of all time. That only an Italian could put that much feeling into stone. I guess it's pretty cool, being Italian."

Chris smiled, "and being from New York."

Lies That Bind

"Yeah, that's cool, too."

"Where are your parents from?" Chris asked.

"My mom's family is from central California. I think before that they came from Germany."

"Your dad?"

"I don't know much about his family. My dad doesn't much talk about his family. They died when he was a kid. First, his dad died. Then his mom died; I guess she had cancer. I think his dad was a college teacher," David explained.

"Oh yeah, you told me about this before. He had an older brother, right?"

"No, I don't think he did," David said without confidence. "He really never says anything. I guess I've just heard stuff from my mom."

"My father's parents were born in Italy and they went to college, but my mom's parents didn't graduate high school. They were very poor." David listened intently. "It's weird, my mom has always been interested in cultural stuff, but my dad...," he paused, "My mom said that my dad's idea of a cultural event was standing around on a street corner wearing a tee shirt with no sleeves, drinking beer, and bullshitting with his friends."

David laughed. "Your mom is so funny. I really love your mom." David sounded sad. "You are so lucky."

"Anyway, so even though they didn't graduate high school..."

David interrupted, "When we were in the modern art museum your grandfather said that he wanted to show me his favorite painter and his favorite painting."

"At the Museum of Modern Art?"

"Yeah. I just figured it would be something Italian, but it wasn't."

"Oh, I know what he was talking about," Chris said knowingly.

"It was Vincent Van Gogh's *Starry Night*. I've seen it in books, but Chris, it is awesome." David explained what Anthony had told him: "*Starry Night* was painted in 1889 while Van Gogh was in an asylum at Saint-Remy in France. Van Gogh looked out from his window and saw a bright star before the sun came up; Venus. He stayed up all night for three nights and painted *Starry Night*. Can you imagine he painted that in three nights?" David always had a hard time looking into Chris's eyes. He feared that someday Chris would see the depth of his desires. "Damn, Chris, I'd love to be able to paint with such emotion. I mean, he was so imaginative. He believed that the stars were a map to heaven, and that when you die you follow them like you follow road signs."

Chris couldn't take his eyes off of David as David stared back at him. Chris said, "He was certainly a great artist, I guess a genius." Chris had had crushes on other guys in the past, but they seemed to quickly pass. His crush on David was different. For one thing, it had never faded. As a matter of fact, the more he knew David the stronger his feelings had become. Although he knew he'd never act on his desires, his crush on David always felt comfortable. Perhaps the comfort came from the look of admiration and friendship that he always found in David's eyes and tone of voice. His attraction, however, was to something much deeper. As he sat there, he imagined again what it would be like to kiss David. He felt safe in allowing himself his amorous thoughts as he sat there with a blanket covering his lap and his head cradled in the airline pillow. He imagined what David's naked body would feel like under his.

"Are there more things I don't know about you?" David asked.

Chris laughed, somewhat surprised by the timing of David's question.

"Of course, there are a lot of things you don't know about me. I am sure there are many things I don't know about you," Chris said.

"Not really, you know me pretty much. Tell me something I don't know," David insisted.

"Bullshit, you know that there are things that I don't know about you."

"Not really."

Chris sat up and moved close to David. "Oh, really. So there aren't things you've done or things that have happened to you that you wouldn't want to tell me. You don't have deep dark thoughts or desires that I don't know about?" Chris asked, looking directly into David's eyes. "How can you say stuff like that to me?" David's blond complexion instantly betrayed him. A red blush covered his white skin and a panicked look fell across his face. He was surprised at how quickly Chris got in his face. "Okay, tell me that one. The one that made you get so red," Chris said instantly.

David looked almost frightened and had to look away. Neither of them said a word for a while.

"Okay," Chris said, feeling guilty about how abrupt and harsh he had been with David. "I'm sorry. I'll tell you one thing that no one knows about me. But you can't ever tell anyone. Never! Anyone! You have to promise, like your word as my friend that you will *never* tell *anyone*."

"I promise. It will be our secret," David said, still feeling unsettled.

"You can't think I am weird, or if you do, you have to tell me," Chris said as he looked at David.

Lies That Bind

"Okay," David said.

"Well, sometimes I just can't go to sleep. I mean I just lie there in bed and I just can't stop my head. It's so weird; sometimes it gets so bad I feel like I'm going to throw up. So I get up. You know I sleep naked, right?" he asked rhetorically.

"Yes, I've noticed," David said, as he watched Chris staring at the back of the seat in front of him.

"Well, I get up and get my guitar and go into my bathroom and close the door. I sit on the bench in my shower and play my guitar and sing. I sit there naked, playing my guitar and singing. I don't know why, but it relaxes me. For some reason it stops all the noise in my head."

"What do you mean, like voices in your head?" David interrupted. Chris shrugged. "You mean you yell at yourself, like 'I can't believe you did that, you stupid idiot!' Stuff like that?"

"Exactly!" Chris said, surprised that David understood.

David nodded, "I read this book and in it this woman called the voices her demons. Night Demons."

"Wow," Chris said. "Well, after playing and singing for a while I feel calm enough to go to bed and go to sleep." He turned again and looked at David, waiting for some kind of reaction. "So what are you thinking?"

"When we're roommates and can't sleep at night can I sit with you in the shower and sing, too?" he asked with a smile.

"Sure." They both smiled and nodded and laughed.

Chris was surprised that David understood "Night Demons." But maybe everyone had that voice that wouldn't be silent at night, he reasoned. The music and words must be unique to each person. Chris's voices sang to the music of criticism, harsh accusatory melodies with undertones of guilt and shame that always led to overwhelming anxiety. The words were condemnations of desire, reminders of hypocrisy and the solution of false living. Everything he did, or knew to do, led to the same end: feelings of absolute isolation, the extremes of loneliness. Everyone who knew him knew him as someone other than who he knew himself to be. He was valued for a performance, an act. The only time he was honest was in his fantasy life, alone, with secret desires.

Chris considered whether he envied David with his demons. He knew what it was to have a sadistic father. He thought that David's demons were those that spoke the words of hatred and dread and fear, but that it must be better to have your hatred directed toward someone else, and not toward your own desires. It must be easier to dread your life with someone else, than to dread your own life. At least David could escape his father.

"You are weird, I mean really weird," David said with a smile. "But you are too cool, dude."

"You owe me, you have to tell me one of your secrets."

"I don't have secrets like that. I mean I have secrets, but yours are cool secrets. Your secret name is little penis." David laughed. "You sit naked in your shower at two o'clock in the morning and play your guitar and sing. I don't have secrets like that," David said, unconvincingly.

"David, you always think other people's families and their lives are better than yours. Come on, a secret is a secret. They don't have to be a special kind," Chris said.

"Shit!" David had been considering what secret he might tell Chris. He sighed and shrugged, "Let me pick one from my long list of secrets." He paused, took a deep breath that shook his chest and then turned to look at Chris. "Okay," David said as he realized his back was wet with sweat. "I wet my bed until I was thirteen years old. My father had this punishment," David's voice cracked with sadness as he stared down at his hands. He did not know if he could go on. Even what he called "war stories" were difficult for him to share. He was terrified that Chris would humiliate him.

"I can imagine. Your father is such an asshole. A lot of guys wet their bed, David. I did sometimes." There was a long silence that was painful for Chris. He reached over and gently touched David's leg, much like Anthony would often touch his. David looked comforted by Chris's touch. "You don't have to tell me if you don't want to."

David looked at Chris again, sighed, and then looked away. "You know what you do when a dog pees on the floor?" Tension covered David's face. His toothy smile was now flat and the pout that was so familiar to his eyes returned. "Well, he'd push my face into my sheets, he'd take my wet pajamas off me and rub them in my face and then he'd take me into the bathroom and push my face into the water in the toilet bowl and he'd hold my head there while he flushed the bowl. I'd be standing there naked and, of course, he'd do all this in front of my brothers."

"David, couldn't you fight back or something?"

"I did once, I refused to let him put my face in the toilet. Then he beat me with a belt until I did it. So, it was just easier to just let him do what he wanted and get it over with."

"That fucking asshole." Chris felt himself becoming angry.

Lies That Bind

"You won't tell anyone, will you?" David said, as he placed his hand on Chris arm. David's eyes were filled with tears.

"Never." Chris's voice was filled with concern, but his jaw was locking in anger.

"I shouldn't have told you," David said, sensing Chris's awkwardness. "I wish I had a cool secret to tell you."

"You just think mine is cool. It doesn't feel cool when I'm sitting there in the dark in the middle of the night feeling crazy. It feels very lonely."

"Well bro', next year we'll both sit in the bathroom and sing," David said.

"And you can pee your bed anytime you want," Chris said with a smile, as he reached over and messed up David's hair. They both laughed. The more they shared with each other the stronger Chris's feelings for David deepened. He felt a great deal of empathy and compassion for him. He also felt a greater depth of guilt for the betrayal.

"So, what was your favorite thing that we did?" David asked with a smile, pushing his hair back into place.

"My favorite thing we did," Chris wondered out loud. "Well my favorite day was the day we went to Central Park and saw the area called Strawberry Fields. You know, dedicated to John Lennon. 'Imagine' is one of my favorite songs to play and sing to quiet the night demons."

"Wow, cool song," David agreed. "Yeah, that was really a cool place, and the park is so big. I didn't know it was so big."

"It's like eight or nine hundred acres," Chris guessed.

"Really? It is so cool that they saved it. You know what it was like from a long time ago. All the trees and stuff."

"No! It wasn't like that then. I think it was probably just flat dirt or something. Two architects designed it back after the Civil War. They planted all those trees and bushes. They even brought in all those rocks and stuff."

"I didn't know architects designed parks."

"St. John the Divine Episcopal Church, that was cool, too." Chris said.

"It figures that the largest church…"

Chris cut David off mid-sentence, "Gothic church."

"The largest Gothic church in the world would be in New York City. And it is too cool that they have an altar dedicated to all the people who have died of AIDS."

"You're becoming a New Yorker, and in just one visit," Chris said, feeling affirmed in his love for New York and excited by the prospect of living there with David. David was smiling again.

Chris smiled, but a nervous roiling in his stomach returned as he fixated on David's full lips and smile. "I loved the ride on the Staten Island ferry when it was dark. I've taken the ride before, but never at night," Chris said, continuing to stare at David. "I mean, I could feel myself kind of getting lighter or something, my pulse seemed to quicken and my ears and eyes strained. You know, when you could see the skyline of Manhattan as the ferry pulled out. Ellis Island, the Statue of Liberty, the Verrazano Bridge, all those lights."

David nodded and smiled. "Yeah, the World Trade Center, and we were there just the day before. Over a quarter of a mile up. It was like a city in there. You're right, I am becoming a New Yorker, I can feel it. It's in my blood, I am being transformed," David crooned dramatically. "This is the most exciting thing to ever happen to me. Shouldn't I have thrown a coin in something so I'd be sure to come back?"

"You're coming back. School next September."

"Would we live in the dorms or in an apartment?" David asked.

"Well, we'd both have to go to the same school for the dorms and I think an apartment would be so cool. I mean it would be a studio apartment probably, but it would have to be bigger than a dorm room." At one moment, Chris was excited by the idea of them having an apartment together; in the next, he hated himself. What was he doing to himself, he wondered.

"Yeah, and think of all the shit we'd have to put up with in the dorms."

Chris agreed. "We should come back to New York right after we graduate and spend the summer looking for a place. We could stay with my grandparents until we found a place. And I bet I could get us jobs working in one of my granddad's stores." He could not stop himself. His desire to hold on to David was stronger than his desire to "come out."

"Oh wow, that would be so cool. I really need a job so that I don't have to ask my parents for anything. You know, maybe being an architect wouldn't be so bad. I mean it's like being an artist. Isn't it? I mean, if you design a skyscraper that goes up in Manhattan then you are being like an artist. I mean, New York City is like a painting of building and lights," David said, filled with excitement. Chris listened, filled with desire. "I'd change the whole look of it with my new buildings. And all those people would look and see a view that was made new by what I designed. Right?"

"David, if you want to be an artist you should be an artist. If you want to be an architect, then you should be an architect."

"I would love to be an artist, but I...I can't even imagine it," David said softly.

"You should imagine it," Chris said and then he recited in a whisper, "Imagine there's no heaven,
It's easy if you try,
No hell below us,
Above us only sky,
Imagine all the people living for today."

Chris stopped. David's eyes were fixed on him. His look would have betrayed his love and desire if Chris had allowed himself to see it.

"Do you know all the words?" David asked. Chris nodded. David pleaded, "Do you sing that song when you play your guitar?" Chris nodded. "Will you sing it for me?" Chris shook his head no, and turned toward the window. "Fine, then I'm going to sing," David said, as he began to sing: "It's meataball time right now, and I'm so hungry", and he laughed, and reached into his backpack and pulled out two meatball sandwiches on Italian bread.

"Thank you for asking me to come to New York with you. It was really cool of you. Don't think that I'm gay or anything like that, but you are absolutely my best friend, dude, and I love you," David said carefully.

Chris fought against his smile turning into a frown. He felt his face flush. "Dude, I know you're not gay. Don't sweat it."

"I can't believe your grandparents paid for my ticket," David said, unwrapping a sandwich and handing it to Chris.

Chris smiled, "It was my birthday present."

"What do you mean?" David asked in surprise.

"Well, you know, every year they send me a ticket to come to New York to visit them. Well, this year I asked them if when I came if I could bring a friend. They said yes, and then I asked them if for my birthday they would buy your ticket."

"No shit? I'm your birthday present? I've never been a birthday present before. When do you unwrap me?" David said, trying to joke. He pulled back into his seat and tried to compose himself. The thought of being valued by another always forced this reaction within him: a sinking sensation in his chest, tightness in his throat, accompanied by the downward pull of his smile into a frown and then tears to his eyes.

Chris stared at him, and could see how touched he was. Sometimes he envied David's ability to show his emotions. "I was hoping you'd get New York fever and might think about going to college there. You know, so we could be roomies. But don't let it go to your head," Chris added, as he messed up David's hair again. They smiled at each other and then both turned their attention to their sandwiches. Chris wished he could say he loved David, but he was afraid of the love he felt. Again he admired David's ability to share his feelings.

As an airline attendant passed their aisle, he said, "I was wondering where that wonderful aroma was coming from. I knew it was something Italian. It smells like my grandmother's meatballs." He smiled. "The smell has filled the entire cabin. If you have any left over, please let me know."

Diane was not alone at the airport. Cathy had convinced her that Chris would be surprised and happy to see her. Diane liked Cathy, but she was concerned that Chris and Cathy's relationship had become too serious. Whenever she questioned Chris about whether he and Cathy were sexually involved, he continued to avoid giving her a direct answer. He assured Diane that this was just a senior year romance without, as he would say, "any legs".

Chris was neither happy nor surprised to see Cathy at the airport.

Chapter Nine

"You're being pulled in all these different directions," I suggested, "and it seems as though you're the one pulling all the strings." Chris nodded. "You're dating Cathy and you're sexually involved with her." Again, Chris nodded. "You have a crush on David. Actually, you're not talking about a crush. You both love David and have a strong sexual attraction to him," I said cautiously.

"True," Chris acknowledged.

"You want to move to New York, free yourself of everyone in Los Angeles, start over in New York, but then you invite David to be your roommate."

"It seemed pretty crazy to me, too."

"Not crazy, but complicating. Also, I was wondering. Maybe your asking David to come to New York was more a sign of your ambivalence about 'coming out.' Perhaps, asking David to live with you in New York was a way for you to stay in the closet. You know, he'd be your gatekeeper."

"What do you mean?"

"Well, part of you wanted to explore your possible homosexuality. Another part of you wanted to maintain what you had—David's friendship, dating girls." Chris shrugged. "Chris, sometimes we think the trouble we know, the pain we are used to, is better than the pain of making a change. Part of you wanted a wide-open future and the freedom to explore with the safety of your grandparents far enough away so you would have that freedom, but close enough so you would have their support. Perhaps another part of you, the part that is so frightened of that future, wanted David, your best friend, there to keep a lid on all of that."

"That all sounds so selfish. I guess I was using him, but I do care about him."

"Of course you do. Chris, we all use each other in some way. I don't believe you were being malevolent."

"I think I was being most unfair to Cathy, by being confused, or really, just being a coward. I am really just a coward."

"Do you really think of yourself in that way?"

"Yes," Chris answered, his eyes filled with tears. "There were times I really looked down on Cathy because all she wanted to do was have people like her. But, at least she was honest about it. I lied to get people to like me. I can't believe I was so condescending to her. All the time it was really me. I was the phony."

"Well, perhaps it wasn't a lie. Perhaps, you were doing the best you could."

Chris sighed. He shook his head and glanced up at me. "I was a dick at the end. I was never honest with her. I was never honest with anyone."

"How did your relationship with Cathy end?"

* * * * *

"Why can't we go out alone sometime?" Cathy asked angrily. "Next week is Thanksgiving and that weekend is like our one-year anniversary and I don't want to double date with David and Jeannine," Cathy complained as Chris started the car.

"We're going to a party, Cathy. It's Derek's birthday. And we are going with David and Jeannine. We'll be alone after the party," Chris said, tired of having the same conversation each time they went out. "Every time we double with them you start on me. You know my mom gets all over me if you and I go out alone. And, besides, David isn't allowed to go out with Jeannine unless he doubles. And his parents check up on him." Chris wondered why he continued dating Cathy. Recently, he thought that his mother was probably right about their relationship becoming too serious. But it was his senior year, he reasoned, and what would a senior year be without a girlfriend?

"Can't they, like, do stuff with someone else? Like, I feel like you're more, like, with him, you know, than, well, like you're with me."

He found himself counting the number of times she used the word "like" in one sentence. "Jeannine doesn't seem to have a problem with double dating," Chris said.

"That's, like, because she'd rather be with you than David." Cathy knew where she was going with this conversation. She had been wanting to separate Chris from David for months, and now she thought she had what she needed.

"Cathy, I hate your possessiveness. That is so much bullshit." Chris realized that his hands were clenched and his jaw was tightening. "I don't want to argue, really. David is my best friend. I like dating you and I like having him around. And that's the way it is, *like*, okay?" Chris said, trying to calm himself. He had asked her countless times not to use the work 'like' more than once in a sentence. Now all he had to do to make his point was to use the word as she did.

"Fuck you. And it isn't okay. And I'm not possessive. Jeannine has as much as told me that she'd rather be with you than David. Did you know that she and David aren't having sex?" The tone in her voice when she was angry and petty was always the same; she sounded like a shrew.

"And just how would I know that?" Chris glared into the traffic ahead of him. "Contrary to what you might think I don't talk about what we do sexually. And David doesn't either. Although, he did tell me that you do." Again, he noticed his hands clenched around the steering wheel of his mother's Suburban. Chris wished everyone could be happy and everything would just work out right.

"Well, they're not. And it isn't because she doesn't want to either. Like she's even taking the pill and, like, they still aren't having sex. David can't do it, and this is not the first girl I heard that from."

"God, you are vicious. Why are you so angry at David?" He found himself pushing and pulling at the steering wheel.

"I'm not angry at him. I think he's gay, and I think he wants you." He was amazed at how triumphant her voice sounded, as she placed her hand on his leg.

He could feel the blood draining from his face. "Jesus Christ, Cathy." His voice was angry as he pushed her hand off his leg. "First it's Jeannine who wants me, and now it's David. How can you say that about David? He's my best friend, and if he were gay don't you think I would know it?" Chris said, slamming his clenched fist thunderously against the steering wheel. "Maybe it's all that religious stuff, all that guilt and fear that his father fills him with." Anxiety ran through his body like the pulses of a neon sign. "Or maybe he just hasn't found someone as easy as you." As he turned his head to look at her he felt her hand across his face. A slap that, oddly, seemed to quiet him. He heard her sniffling.

"Okay, I deserved that. That was cruel. Cathy, I don't want to hurt you, really. But, you're out of control with this David thing." He looked at her and could see that she was crying. "Cathy, I'm sorry. David is a good guy, and he isn't gay. Believe me, I'd know." He hated himself when he struck a person where they were most vulnerable. Cathy was a beautiful girl with a fantastic body. And she knew it. She had been using it since she was fourteen. Maintaining her popularity among the boys was her number one priority. Being the head cheerleader, and prom queen this year, were more important to her than graduating. Her last relationship had ended when she became pregnant and had an abortion. Two months later Chris and she were dating, and she had started taking the pill.

"Derek says that David is gay. He says a lot of guys on the team think so, too."

"Derek told you that David is gay. Cathy, Derek is always saying shit like that. And besides, how would Derek know that David is gay?"

"You can't tell anyone this," Cathy whispered, even though there was no one else in the car. "Derek said that David told him that he had a crush on him. He also said that the guys on the team notice that David checks guys out in the shower, and that he is always checking you out." She reached over again and touched Chris's leg. Her tone was one of concern, but Chris knew that it wasn't beyond her to be feigning.

"He doesn't check me out," Chris insisted. "If what Derek told you is true, why would he tell you and not me?" Chris's stomach was churning so much he was afraid he might vomit.

"The same reason that no one tells you anything. You don't like people to say bad things about your friends. You defend, like, every one of them. You hate conflict. Everyone knows that they're not supposed to talk shit about anyone to you or, like, you'll jump on them just like you jumped on me. Everyone wants you to like them." Cathy rubbed Chris's leg. He felt himself recoiling. "You're Mr. Wonderful, everyone looks up to you and wants you to be their friend, and everyone is, like, so afraid to get on your bad side." They both sat in silence. Then Cathy said, "Derek would give anything for you to pay as much attention to him as you do to David. Fuck, I would do, like, anything to get you to pay as much attention to me as you pay to David. Even when we have sex you seem to be someplace else." Cathy was sounding pleased with herself.

"You seem to enjoy it enough." Chris said, grabbing his crotch.

"I do, believe me, I do. You're the best I've had. But, you know, sometimes I think I enjoy it more than you."

"Shit, Cathy, do you know how lascivious you sound?" Chris asked, as he shook his head in disgust. His stomach felt as if it were on an ocean liner crossing the Atlantic in a midwinter storm.

"I hate it when you call me stupid," Cathy growled.

"I didn't call you stupid," Chris said, shaking his head and rolling his eyes.

"Whatever. But it's true. You seem to enjoy it less than any other guy I've been with."

Lies That Bind

"And if that's true, is that saying something about me or you?" Chris said as he felt himself getting lightheaded.

"I don't know."

"So now what are you saying, that I'm gay, too? It could be that you're just a lousy lay, Miss all-I want-to-be-is-prom-queen. All you pretty much do is lie there and moan."

They continued the drive to David's house. They both realized that they had said too much. "Cathy, I'm sorry. You're right about one thing. I don't like it when people bad-mouth my friends. And that includes you. I mean, I don't like it when people say shit about you, and I guess I don't like it when you say shit about my friends."

"When David bad-mouths people do you jump on him?" Cathy could never let things go, and Chris began to realize he was more than finished. Not with just the conversation, but with Cathy as well. He knew that once she knew of his plans to go to college in New York she would break up with him and hunt out another boyfriend.

"David doesn't bad-mouth our friends to me," Chris said with a sigh.

"To you, he doesn't."

"Well, I can't do anything about what he doesn't say to me," Chris said as he parked the car. What he wanted to do was to take Cathy home and spend the evening with David, but then there was Jeanine. "We're here. I am sorry, really. You're a wonderful lay," he said, laughing and pulling her toward him. She smiled and teasingly pulled away, but then kissed him on the mouth and gently bit on his lower lip.

"We'll see how good a lay I am later," she said grabbing his crotch. Chris walked around the car and opened the car door for her. "I hate this house," she said as they knocked on the Jarretts' door. Mr. Jarrett insisted they always come into his home and give a detailed account of their plans for the evening. He would explain David's curfew, and then explain to David the consequences of a late return: the belt. Chris stared at the floor, wondering how David tolerated humiliation so well. Jeannine was always at David's house when Chris and Cathy arrived. Paul Jarrett made it his policy to have Jeannine present when David was released for the evening so she, too, would be aware of his demands.

Chris's hands never failed to sweat when he shook Paul's hand. Since David had revealed to him some of the physical abuse he endured, Chris often became flushed with anger when Paul spoke to him. Chris decided that David's father must have been a very insecure, angry man who, like Chris's father, felt inferior, and who, unlike his father, had found Jesus and become secure of his place in heaven. Unfortunately, he was still an angry man who now felt superior; or as David put it, Paul was a self-righteous prick. Chris often wondered how someone so full of "The Lord" could be so full of contempt and could engender so much misery in his family, especially David.

Chris and Cathy decided that they wanted to see a movie. David would have done whatever Chris asked, but Jeannine wanted time to make out with David. Chris and David had long ago found ways to get around Paul's strictures. They would take time during the week to see a movie that they would then tell David's father they were going to see on a Friday night with dates. They always called in advance, making sure the movie wasn't going to change, and then checked the time the movie showed. David told Chris he did not think Paul really cared about what he did; rather, it was just another way for Paul to exercise his control and authority. David said it was more like a game. Paul would use the excuse of broken rules to do what gave him most pleasure, inflicting pain. The trick for David was to do what he wanted and not get caught, something David believed he was getting much better at. That night they saw a movie.

After Chris dropped David and Jeannine at their homes, he and Cathy parked at their usual place on a dirt road, in the hills, just off of Mulholland Drive. The back of Diane's Suburban was the perfect place for two teenagers wanting a place to make out. Chris had long ago figured out that before he backed the car out of his garage he had time to sneak a sleeping bag into the back.

Both of them worked quickly to put down the back seat and unfold the sleeping bag. Cathy removed her shoes and made herself as comfortable as possible under the sleeping bag that was now open and spread out. Chris also removed his shoes and his shirt, and then covered both of them with the sleeping bag. Cathy was always amazed at how the sight of his naked chest excited her. His shoulders were broad and muscular; his chest was tight and molded. Chris had grown from a skinny boy whose mother had described him as frail, into a long and lanky adolescent, and now into a young man with a strong and well defined torso. There was not a hair on his chest or his flat stomach. Unbeknownst to anyone but David, and now Cathy, Chris had had his navel pierced in New York that summer. He had been told that it would take upwards of three months to heal.

"How is your navel ring doing?" Cathy asked as she passed her fingers over it.

Lies That Bind

"Good. It's looking like it's all healed. I wash it with alcohol like they said. I think it's hot," he said, as he held her hand there. "You like it, don't you?"

David loved the idea, and wanted to have his navel pierced also, but, while Chris knew he could probably successfully hide it from Richard and Diane, David never knew when he would be made to stand naked before his family and take the position for a whipping. Chris also knew that, although Diane would scream at the sight of his piercing, she would do nothing more. David had applied to both Columbia and New York University. He was sold on the idea of living with Chris. Having a navel piercing was number one on his to-do list for his freshman college year.

"Yes," she said, as she began to unfasten his pants and move her fingers along his lower abdomen where there was the first sign of hair. She ran her hands along his waist, around his hips, which were smaller than hers, to his buttocks.

Chris moved so that he was now partially lying on top of her. He slowly moved his hand under her blouse and around to the small of her back. He was always slow with his hands. Just what she loved: soft touch, slow and gentle fingers. She had come to appreciate the paradox he seemed to be. He had a powerful presence, physically and personally, yet he was gentle and soft in his lovemaking. His way with her was to always have her desire precede his advances. It made her feel safe, safe enough to allow herself to experience the extent of her excitement. She never doubted that she could ask him to stop at any point and he would respect her wishes.

As Cathy continued to undress Chris, he buried his face in her neck and smelled the fragrance of her hair. Smells always turned him on, as did the sound of her slow and rhythmic breath in his ear deepening as he began to move his hand under her blouse. He believed that lovemaking was an acquired skill, one that he practiced. He noticed her every moan, and stored it away for future reference. He knew just how long to tease his hand along the lower edge of her bra. He loved to fumble with it until just before the moment her frustration caused her to push his hand aside and unhook it herself. Then, miraculously, he knew what to do.

She pulled his face to hers and began to kiss him, hungrily searching for his tongue, which he held back just long enough. When he finally gave her the full force of his opened mouth and tongue, he sucked at her lip and then took her tongue into his mouth. Her reaction was always the same. The tension in her lower back seemed to ease and her breathing began to quicken. Slowly her hands moved down his back and began to push at his pants and underpants until they were down below his buttocks. He laughed as they both wrestled his pants off and then used their feet to kick the clothes off. He reveled in her eagerness for him.

As she again settled under his naked body, he started to kiss her by running his tongue slowly over her lips, then pulling her lower lip into his mouth and gently sucking and releasing it. As he ran his tongue against her teeth and over her lips, he moved his hand over her breast, so that his fingers lightly caressed her nipple. She moved under him so that now he was completely on top of her. This was the art of lovemaking, he thought. He settled on top of her so that his hips fell between her now spread legs. His slow and gentle rocking movements against her pelvis, and the teasing touch of her breasts, were his beginning move to slowly bring her to orgasm.

As Chris more aggressively caressed Cathy's breasts with his hand, Cathy began to remove her blouse. She pulled his face to hers again and kissed him, she unbuttoned her jeans, and they both kicked them and her panties over her feet. He smiled as she pushed his head down to her navel. He thought of himself as a considerate lover. He always tried to bring her to orgasm using his mouth before he began intercourse.

"You don't need that, I'm on the pill," Cathy said as Chris searched for his jeans to find a condom. "Please don't use it."

"Shhhh," Chris said as he opened the package.

"Chris, you don't have to use it, really, I promise," she pleaded and tried to pull him back on top of her.

"It's either my way or no way, Cathy," he insisted as he maneuvered the condom into place.

Gently he began to run his tongue over her breasts and slowly moved his fingers along her inner thighs.

Could Derek be right? he thought as he began to move his head down toward her navel. *Could David be gay?* His heart raced as he considered the possibility. *But why wouldn't I know?*

He had never trusted Derek, anyway. After their first meeting on a camping trip at the end of Chris's first summer in Los Angeles, Chris couldn't bring himself to trust Derek. David was always a good friend, while Derek was always a wise ass. And it was evident to Chris, and almost everyone else, that Derek was jealous of David's friendship with Chris. Chris was sure that Derek just wanted to bad-mouth David. *Derek is just hoping to turn me against David, that has to be it.*

But again his heart raced, as he thought of the possibility. He had noticed David checking him out, and David had remarked about what good shape Chris's body was in, but some of his other friends made

Lies That Bind

similar remarks. Then there were all the times David wanted to swim naked in Chris's pool; but Chris knew it was he who had first suggested it. Chris reassured himself that this was all Derek's imagining. *Could David have a crush on Derek? Impossible, that proves it's all bullshit.*

Chris remembered that this was not the first time Derek had set out to destroy some one's reputation. Derek could never just dislike a person. He wanted everyone to hate whomever he hated. Derek always gathered up all his ammunition before he moved in for the kill. He could be, and had been, merciless. Last year, he had destroyed the reputation of a girl who broke up with him. She was so overwhelmed by the gossip he spread that she transferred before her senior year.

Cathy's moaning from the pleasure of her orgasm distracted Chris from his musing. She pulled at him as he began to run his tongue up to her breasts and her neck. As he again settled on top of her, she again pleaded, "Chris, please, please don't use the condom."

"Shhhh," he said. He was surprised at how excited he was. He had completely lost awareness of his erection. He told himself that it was impossible for David to be gay, or to have a crush on Derek. Even if he did, he would not be stupid enough to tell Derek. But the possibility of David's being gay excited Chris more and more. He began to kiss Cathy again as he slowly and gently began to move his hips. He was always slow to enter her. She often remarked at how rough other guys had been with her and how they left her frustrated. He never wanted to be thought of in that way.

As he entered her and began to slowly move on top of her, he wondered whether, if he asked David if he was gay, David would tell him. He then realized the absurdity in that. Chris would never admit to what he thought of as his bisexuality. Chris wondered what he would do if David were to ever confess a crush on him. He thought of the possibility of David's naked body beneath him, which brought him to the point where his orgasm was inevitable. As he felt the rhythmic contractions in his groin begin, he withdrew himself from Cathy. His orgasm was far more intense than usual as he continued thrusting his hips against Cathy's stomach. He moaned loudly, as was his way.

Collapsing on top of her, his breathing fast and shallow, his body still making involuntary movements, his muscles still contracting and relaxing, Cathy murmured in frustration, "Damn it, Chris. Why do you do that?"

He did not answer. His body slowly relaxed. He moved himself off of Cathy and onto his side.

"If you're wearing a condom, why do you do that?" she said, more hurt than angry.

"Condoms break," he said, reaching down to remove it.

"But I'm taking the pill," Cathy insisted as she searched for her blouse.

"Cathy, I just don't want to take any chances, okay? And, besides, it's my orgasm. I can't believe you're doing this right now." They both remained silent as they continued to dress. Their routine was always the same. Chris put the seats back into their upright position, while Cathy rolled up the sleeping bag.

"You make me feel so dirty. I got an HIV test. It was negative. Like how many years are you going to punish me for what happened before I was seeing you?"

"Years?" He knew he was opening a door that he would not be able to close.

"Yeah, why do you say it like that?" Her voice held pained anxiety.

He took a long sigh and asked, "Do we really have to do this now?"

"I want to know what you're thinking. I mean if it ends, it ends. But it's like you know it's going to end."

"I'm going away to college, and well…" he hesitated.

"I know, you're going to UCLA. It's only twenty minutes away. So you live in the dorms, so what?"

Again he sighed as he backed the car down the dirt road. "I'm not going to UCLA."

"Your mother said you applied there."

"I did, but I applied to ten different colleges, Cathy."

"You'll have no problem getting into UCLA. You're the smartest person in our class and your SAT scores , , , "

He interrupted her, "You're right, but I'd only go to UCLA if I didn't get into any of the other nine. It's my last choice, not my first."

"But your mother said…" she sounded close to tears.

"Never mind what my mother said. I'm going to college, not my mother. Look, we have months ahead of us. We'll have a great senior year," he said, trying to assure her.

"Damn you!" Cathy shouted through her tears.

"Cathy, come on," pulling her near him while he was driving the curves of Mulholland Drive. "Cathy, don't cry, please Cathy," he pleaded as he looked over at her.

"Damn you!" she said again, and she slapped his face for the last time.

Lies That Bind

"That I didn't deserve. And that is the last time you'll do that," he said angrily. No one except Cathy had hit Chris since his father had. Diane forbade it. Cathy knew how Chris felt about physical violence, and had promised several times in the past that it would never happen again. This time there were neither promises nor apologies. Neither of them said a word during the rest of their drive to her house.

As he pulled up to her house, and before he could take the car out of gear, Cathy opened her door. "Don't call me anymore, Chris. It's over between us. I love you, but you can't use me like this—*you can't use me to have fun during your senior year!*" she screeched as she slammed the door of the Suburban and ran up the walkway to her house. He waited and watched as she closed the house door.

Driving home, he wondered if he should be feeling something. He decided he was feeling relieved. After he parked the car in the garage he put away the sleeping bag. As he walked toward his house he again thought of the possibility of David being gay and what that might mean. Considering the possibilities, he began to become aroused. He looked into the house through the window in the kitchen door and saw a light on in the living room. He glanced down at his crotch; he wished he'd worn jockey shorts and jeans, rather than loose fitting boxers and his khakis. His erection pushed against his pants, creating a noticeable bulge. He covered his erection by pulling his shirt out of his pants.

When he entered the house, Diane was waiting for him; she usually did. "Hey Mom, you know you don't have to wait up. I'd call you if something happened."

Diane got up from the couch where she had been reading and asked, "Are you hungry?"

"A little."

Diane poured a glass of milk for him and put the cookie jar on the table. "I made them today. Your favorite, oatmeal chocolate chip," she said as she sat down at the table across from him.

"Thank you, Mom. You made them for me, didn't you?" he asked with a smile. "Cookie Grandma's recipe." She smiled and nodded. As he broke a cookie in two, which was his habit, he said, "I just broke up with Cathy."

"Really? Are you okay? Is she okay?"

"Yeah, I guess I'm fine. I think she's taking it badly." He shrugged his shoulders.

"What happened?" Diane asked.

"I don't know. She's just too possessive, or maybe I just don't want to be with her as much as she wants to be with me."

"It's probably for the best. She's sweet, but…"

Chris interrupted her, "But she isn't for me, right?"

Diane reached across the table and put her hand on his arm, "You're young, and you'll fall in love with lots of girls."

"I haven't yet," Chris said, to her surprise.

"You will, I promise you," Diane assured him. "Are you sure you're okay? If you want to talk I can stay up," she offered as she stood up.

"I'm okay, Mom."

"Okay, then clean up your mess before you go to bed."

"Thanks for making me my favorite cookies, Mom," he said with a smile as she bent over and kissed him on the forehead. "I love you, Mom."

"Good night, honey. I love you, too."

Chris cleaned up as Diane had asked, and then went to his room with a handful of cookies. He could not stop thinking about David. The more he thought about it the more agitated he became. By one in the morning he had paced around his room for almost an hour. He thought about grabbing his guitar and heading to the shower, but then he decided that he had to talk to David, and it couldn't wait until tomorrow. Paul Jarrett did not allow phone calls after nine in the evening and David did not have his own phone, but David and he, in the past, had shown up unexpectedly at each other's bedroom windows and talked about first dates, break-ups, and other things that could not wait. Chris decided that his break-up with Cathy certainly warranted a late night visit. Besides, it was Friday night. David could catch up on his sleep tomorrow.

Chris climbed out the bedroom window. He put a note on his pillow in the unlikely event that Diane broke into his room searching for him. If she found the note she would be angry that he had left the house after curfew, but she would get over that. He knew he would be home long before either she or Richard was awake, but it had occurred to him in the past that Diane would go nuts if she ever found his bed empty and did not know where he had gone. It was much easier to face her in her anger than in her fear.

It was well after one o'clock when Chris jumped over the wall that surrounded his backyard. It was six blocks to David's house and Chris ran the entire way.

Chapter Ten

THE JARRETTS' HOUSE WAS on a corner lot, making a surreptitious entry into their back yard easy. The wall surrounding it was about six feet tall, but that was not the problem. David's parent's bedroom was closest to the street, and the area where Chris had to climb the wall was close to their bedroom window. If he went to the end of their property, which was the farthest from their window, he would land in juniper trees and shrubs. He decided the junipers were his best bet.

Chris hesitated as he gripped the wall. He began to reconsider. *Why are you here?* The night was dark, it was a new moon. The air was still. A nearby streetlight cast a shadow along the cinderblock wall. *What are you going to say?* In one steady muscled motion, he pulled himself up onto the wall. Slowly, he eased himself down into the bushes, where he stood quietly for several seconds. The house remained quiet. His ears strained for sounds; he could hear his breathing, the crunch of leaves under his feet, but nothing from the house. With each step he recalculated his escape route over the wall and his way home.

He studied the house. Everything remained quiet. His eyes strained at the ground in front of him as he tried to see what might be hidden beneath each bush. Cautiously, he made his way across the yard, keeping one eye on David's bedroom window and the other on the rest of the house. He smiled to himself when he was able to discern that David's bedroom window was open.

"Chris," David whispered. He was squatting against the garage wall, keeping out of view of his parents' bedroom window. Chris's legs weakened, he fell to his knees immediately, his heart almost jumped out of this chest. He was about to turn and run, when his brain finally processed the words he heard. "Over here."

"Shit! You scared the fuck out of me," Chris whispered, realizing it was David.

"I scared you! How do you think I felt when you came flying over the wall? What the fuck are you doing here?" David asked.

"What are you doing outside? Are you naked? Chris asked as he crawled on both knees and moved toward David. "What's that smell?"

"Damn it, Chris. Why are you here?"

"I had to talk to you. Cathy and I broke up. What are you doing out here? You were smoking weed." Chris said, sniffing the air. "Why are you naked?"

"Let's go inside. Be careful, we have to go in through my window. Be very quiet," David ordered. As David stood he self-consciously covered himself with his hands. "Can't this wait until tomorrow?" David asked as he climbed through his window. He signaled Chris to follow him. Once inside, they both stood very still and listened to hear if anyone in the house might be moving about. "Remember, if you hear someone coming, get in the closet," David said.

It was a large house, much like Chris's, but David had two younger brothers who shared a room across the hall from him. Unlike Chris, David was not allowed to have a lock on his door. He did, however, pile his dirty clothes in front of it whenever he wanted privacy. Chris moved across the room and sat on the bed. David fumbled around in the dark looking for a pair of sweatpants he had earlier tossed onto his pile of dirty clothes. As he sat down on his bed next to Chris he pulled the sweatpants on. "So what happened between you and Cathy?"

"I'll tell you, but first you tell me what you were doing outside," Chris said as he made himself more comfortable on the bed.

"Can't we just skip it?" David asked, knowing that Chris would persist.

"Tell me," Chris said poking at David.

"Shit, Chris." David said as he lay down on his bed, almost putting his head in Chris's lap. "Can't you let this go?" David asked, knowing Chris's tenacity would win out.

"What is going on?" Chris reached over and shook David by his shoulder.

David had smoked a whole bowl and was feeling pretty loose. "I really fucked up. Really fucked up," David said as he moved his knees up to his chest and rolled over on his side.

"How long have you been smoking weed?"

"Shit, I don't know. Years."

Chris was surprised. "Wow, I can't believe I didn't know."

David looked up at Chris and said, "I almost told you on the plane coming home from New York. Remember you told me about your guitar playing? Well, I do the same thing, only with weed. I was too afraid to tell you." David turned away from Chris. "Do you hate me now? You're so straight, and I, well, I…"

"David, just because I don't smoke weed doesn't mean I'd hate you if you did. My cousins in New York smoke weed. I'm just surprised I didn't know. But why outside, and why were you naked?"

"The smell. I can't take the chance that it would smell up my room. So I go outside. Then one morning I got up and I could smell it on my tee shirt and boxers."

"God, if your dad ever found out…"

"I'd be dead." David said, unable to look at Chris. He just lay on his bed and stared into the darkness of his room. He wished he was not stoned.

"What did you mean you fucked up? Did you get caught? Where do you get it from?"

"The fucked up doesn't have anything to do with this. Well, maybe it does kind of have something to do with it. No, I didn't get caught."

"What is the fucked up thing?" David could feel himself in a cold sweat. He had decided he would have to talk to Chris about many things, his weed smoking being the least of it.

"Why don't you tell me about you and Cathy?"

"David, that can wait. What happened?"

"Fuck, Chris, you are so stubborn." There was a long silence. Then David sighed loudly and rolled over so that he was facing the wall. "I really fucked up. I'm really afraid to tell you," David said, sounding as if he was about to cry.

"David, I am your friend. I promise you that will not change. You can tell me anything." Chris moved closer to David, took him by the shoulder and rolled him over so that he could see David's face. "Tell me."

"Derek got into the school computer. He was able to get the tests for both math and physics. He got all the physics exams for the year. Father Anthony always gives the same test, so that was easy. Father John must make new tests each semester, but Derek has the code and he got the next mid-term for math too."

"Fuck, that weasel. What a fuck." David started to roll over so as to face the wall again, but Chris put pressure on his shoulder and rolled him onto his back. "What does that have to do with you?"

"Well, he sold it to four or five other guys, guys on the baseball team. But, of course, they were having trouble working out some of the problems. They said that they would give me a copy if I would work with them and give them the answers. At first, I said no. Then Derek said he wouldn't sell me any more weed if I didn't work with him."

"He's the one who sells to you?" Chris was surprised.

"Yeah, me and half the team, and other guys, too. You remember Richard Allen? He was a senior a couple of years ago. He used to sell, but now he just sells to Derek and Derek sells to everyone else." David glanced up at Chris. He wanted to turn away.

"Why didn't I know about this? Forget it, never mind." Chris said.

"Then I started to really worry about Father John's test and I caved. I called Derek and I agreed to help them out." David could not take Chris literally looking down at him. So he rolled onto his side and folded both his arms across his chest, afraid of Chris's condemnation.

"I thought Derek got a B on the physics midterm."

"He did. The idiot. He copied the exams at the beginning of the year and decided that he didn't have to study. He hadn't even read any of the chapters. So, even though he saw the problems worked out and saw my answers to the physics exam, when he got in there he still couldn't work some of the problems. He is such an idiot. Gary also had the exams and he got a C on the algebra midterm."

"He got a C and he had the test? What a jerk. Serves him right."

"Well, I'm not much better than they are. Maybe I'm worse. I got an A, but I cheated to get it." David closed his eyes.

"You would have gotten the A anyway."

"Maybe, but I cheated. This time they're going to take a filled-in exam into the room with them and switch it at the end. They figure they'll give themselves about a 92 or 93 on the exam and that they'll each make a different mistake so that Father John and Father Anthony won't get wise. But they still need me to work out the problems, because they're so far behind now that they have no idea what's going on."

"What are you going to do?"

"First I said no, then I said just once more. So I saw the test and helped them out with the problems and then I said never again. Now Derek is really pissed. He's making all kinds of threats. He can't do anything about the cheating without getting himself into trouble and he can't tell anyone about the weed either. But he can stop selling to me. And there's other stuff, too. But please don't ask me about anything else right now, please." David knew he had said too much. Chris never let anything slide. Was it the weed, he wondered, or was it time? He had to tell Chris eventually, he reasoned. His eyes filled with tears.

Lies That Bind

"So, what are you going to do?" Chris asked.

"I don't know. I think I'm going to have to help them. He said that I have to help him through the year, through physics next semester and through pre-calculus. I don't care about helping them, I just hate that I'm cheating, too. And what if we get caught? I really fucked up."

"So you have to help them, right?"

"Yeah."

"All we have left are the finals, right?"

"Yeah."

"Okay, you help them with the exam. It will be like you're tutoring them. Then you can get sick for the final exam, and they'll have to give you a make-up exam. It won't be the one you saw."

"I guess that would work. But I'm still helping them to cheat."

"Yeah, but your grade will be your grade."

"Yeah, I guess."

"Tell them that you'll help them through the semester. Tell them that if they take pre-calculus and physics next semester you won't help them if they want to take tests into class let them. If you take a different test you're cool."

Chris hesitated. He could feel the wetness of his sweat being absorbed by his tee shirt. "So, what other stuff can Derek do to you?"

"I can't tell you. Please, I can't." Again David sounded like he was crying. "Maybe you'd better go, Chris." David's anxiety was growing. Several times in the past, while on weed, his anxiety had grown into panic attacks. He began to feel as if he was going to jump out of his skin.

Chris took a deep breath.

David could no longer tolerate the silence. "I guess I am going to have to continue helping them," David said. "He said he was taking physics next semester because it was required, and that he was also taking pre-calculus. You know, if my father ever finds out about any of this I'm dead. I can't even imagine what he'd do if he knew I cheated. I wouldn't have, but I was so afraid I was going to do badly on that algebra test that I caved in." He started to ramble. "God, I am so fuckin' stupid, Chris. I mean I don't need the stupid fucking A in the class. My grades are fine to get into college, but I didn't want a bad grade. I just couldn't go through it again."

"Go through what?" Chris asked.

David sat up on the bed, took a deep breath, his insides were shaking. He explained to Chris how his father punished him for each bad grade he brought home. Paul Jarrett was a severe disciplinarian who used a leather belt on naked buttocks to instill in his children the desire to achieve perfection in everything. The Sacred Heart Schools assigned number grades instead of letter grades. Paul delivered one lash, as Paul called them, for each point by which David or his two younger brothers missed an A on a report card. A grade of 85 in Spanish had brought him five lashes at one midterm report card. However, he had also received Bs in English and history, and was given a total of thirteen lashes. His grades were all A's on his final report card that semester. Breaking curfew brought lashes, as did other behaviors that Paul thought unacceptable. "Get naked," Paul would order, "bend over, and grab the back of the chair." All corporal punishment was delivered in the living room with the entire family present. Paul believed that fear instilled through a combination of pain and humiliation was the cornerstone of effective discipline. He often remarked on how seldom he had to whip his two younger sons.

Paul quoted biblical passages to justify his actions. He believed that children were born in sin and therefore had evil within them. He would have David recite from the Book of Proverbs, before and after a beating, "He who spares the rod hates his son, but he who loves him is diligent to discipline him."

"Oh man, how do you deal with him?" Chris said, louder than he realized. "Fuck, I really hate your father."

"Shhhh, Chris. Don't even wake up my brothers." David said as he leaned against the wall next to Chris.

Chris sighed, "David, it'll work out. Agree to help him until the end of the semester, then he can find someone else."

"Don't get involved. Derek is an asshole. Whatever you do, you can't let him know you know any of this. He'll really fuck me over then." David looked at Chris as if he wanted to curl up in Chris's arms and go to sleep.

"Derek won't fuck with me. Believe me. But he *is* fucking with you." Chris decided that he was going to tell David what Derek had said. Besides his own carnal interests, there was the fact that Derek was gossiping, and eventually, David would hear about it. And there was no one better to hear it from than Chris, he decided. He figured that David would probably just deny it, but that maybe it was what David was so worried about. "Cathy told me that Derek was talking about you to her."

David immediately pulled his knees up to his chest and wrapped his arms around them. His face disappeared in his legs. David thought that Chris knowing was bad enough, but he could not survive everyone else knowing.

Lies That Bind

Silence. Chris hated these silences. It suddenly became clear to him that this was what David feared. "What did she say he said?" David asked. He was crying.

"Shit, David. I'm sorry. I thought…Shit. Maybe…"

"Just tell me, please," David insisted.

"He said that he thinks you're gay. That you told him that you had a crush on him." Again, there was silence. Chris didn't know what to do. He placed his hand on David's back. "David."

David jumped up from the bed and started pacing around the bedroom with his hands on his hips. Then he began taking deep breaths. He looked up at the ceiling, then squatted and stared at the floor. Again he stood and began pacing with his arms tightly wrapped around his chest. Suddenly he stopped and lay down on the floor, continuing to take deep breaths. His mind was racing.

Chris crawled over toward him. "David, David. Are you okay?" Chris asked, as he moved closer to him. "David. Are you okay?" He knelt over David, whose head and chest were now gleaming with sweat. "David. Talk to me!"

"Oh, God," David sobbed loudly.

"Shhh, David, don't wake your brothers." Chris reached over and put his hand over David's mouth. "Shhh, don't shout." David's hair was wet. "David, are you okay?" He realized David was trembling. "David, look at me." David's eyes seemed to be rolling in his head. Suddenly he was up again, and again pacing.

"Maybe you should leave, Chris," David said as he continued to cry. "Oh fuck."

"No way, David. Please talk to me."

David continued to pace, taking deep breaths. He found the corner of his room and stood there pushing his head against the wall. Then he collapsed and curled up on the floor. Chris moved toward him and put his hand on David's sweaty back. David got to his knees and doubled over, wrapping his arms around his torso. Gradually, he rose to his feet and put both his hands over his mouth and looked wide-eyed around the room. Quickly he lunged toward the open window. Chris watched David's entire torso go into convulsions, tightening and then relaxing over and over again. Remarkably, David was vomiting without making a sound. Chris opened the door that went from the bedroom into the hallway, it was quiet. He made his way into the bathroom that David shared with his brothers. Quietly he filled a glass with water and brought it to David, who was now lying on his bed. He was still wet with sweat, but no longer trembling.

"Are you okay?" Chris asked as he sat down on the bed and handed the glass of water to David.

"It's happened before. The nurse at school says it's just nerves. Stress. Panic attacks or something," David said as he pulled his legs tight to his chest and began to cry. "Chris, please go. Leave me alone, please. I'll be okay."

"No. I'm staying." Chris pulled closer to David. "What were you thinking? Why would you tell Derek that? Did you think you could trust him?"

"It was three years ago. We were…" David hesitated and then shook his head. "I don't want you not to be my friend anymore."

"Damn it, David, I said that wasn't going to happen. I came over here tonight, didn't I?"

"We were having sex. But it was mostly that I was, well, I mean, he didn't do much but lie there and I…" David could not bring himself to say it. He had never said it.

"You gave him head." Chris said, finishing David's sentence.

"Yeah, and then I told him that I had a crush on him and he freaked out. That was the last time. Now he says that I was his bitch in between girlfriends."

"Listen to me," Chris said, pulling himself closer to David's ear. "Listen to me, he won't say another word about this. I promise you. As a matter of fact, he'll even tell Cathy that he lied to her about you having a crush. David, I promise you that this is over. It won't go any further," Chris paused. "David, look at me."

"Please go," David pleaded, tightening up into a ball.

"David." Chris's mouth was almost to David's ear.

David pushed Chris away. "You don't have to be my friend if you don't want to be. We don't have to be roommates next year. I was going to tell you before. I just didn't know how to, really. I wouldn't have let us be roommates. I promise. I just had to figure out a way to tell you. I was too scared. Please believe me," David said with whispered tears.

"Stop it, David. Shut up and just listen to me," Chris said. His mouth suddenly went dry; his tongue seemed to stick to the roof of his mouth. He had also never said the words to anyone. He could not imagine what they would sound like to David or to himself. For years there had been a war between what he desired and what he thought he should desire; thoughts and desires that had lived only in his heart and mind.

Lies That Bind

"I'll be okay, Chris. Really. It's okay if we're not roommates. I understand that you don't want to live with someone who is gay. I just don't want you to hate me. Do you think we can still be friends?" David was calmer; he was no longer crying.

Chris took a deep breath, "I guess I was kind of jealous when I heard that you had a crush on Derek." The muscles in his arms reflexively began to twitch. He wondered if he was going to have to start pacing around the room.

"Had, or thought I had. Fuck, Chris, I don't have a crush on him. Be serious. And why would you be jealous? You know you're my best friend. I hate Derek." Strength returned to David's voice.

"I guess because…well, I, you know…I've thought about stuff with you."

David rolled over and half sat up on his bed. He looked down at Chris. "What are you saying?"

"That I have…" Chris struggled for the words to use. "That I think about what it would be, you know…"

"You mean, what it would be like for me to give you head like I gave to Derek?" David asked, sounding offended.

"Fuck no. I've thought about all this for a long time," Chris said as he sat up and moved to get up off the bed. "Asshole, you had a crush on Derek and I've had one on you," Chris barked. He found his voice. They were both shocked to hear what he had said.

David pushed Chris back down onto the bed. "Are you serious?" David whispered. "What are you saying…?" David paused. "Damn, I just never imagined that you felt the same way as I do."

"Yeah, well, imagine it," Chris whispered.

"I mean, I've had a crush on you for as long as I can remember, but I never ever thought you might have one on me." David lay down beside Chris again. They both lay there without saying a word, and both of them too afraid to move. Again, there was that awkward silence that Chris hated so much. Finally, he reached over and pulled at David so that David half lay on top of him with his head on Chris's chest. David put his arm around Chris's waist as Chris moved his fingers through David's hair. Neither of them said a word. David could hear Chris's heart pounding. He wondered if it was from fear or excitement. Chris continued to stroke David's hair.

David finally broke the silence. "Tell me about what happened between you and Cathy." Chris gave him the long-drawn-out version, trying to put off another long silence, hoping that something would just happen.

When he finished the story, he again found himself lost as to what he should do next. David lifted his head and stared down at him.

"Let me brush my teeth. My mouth tastes like puke," he said, as he started to get up from the bed.

Chris pulled him back onto the bed and half rolled on top of him. They were both breathing heavily. David lay still as Chris looked down at his naked chest. David watched as Chris ran his fingers along the edge of David's sweat pants. Chris could see David's erection pushing up inside his sweats. Chris moved to kiss David. "You're right, you should brush your teeth," Chris said, and laughed. David got up from the bed, slowly opened his door and disappeared into the darkness of the hallway.

Chris sat up and pulled his tee shirt over his head. He kicked off his shoes and pulled off his socks. When he had dressed for his run to David's he had thrown on a pair of jeans and white briefs. Now he wished he was wearing his loose-fitting boxers. He decided to remove his pants before David returned. By now he had a full erection pushing hard against his ribbed white-cotton Calvin Klein briefs.

He heard David rinsing his mouth. His mind raced, anticipating what he imagined was about to occur—David's naked flesh against his, the wetness of David's mouth, the sound of his passion—David's and his orgasm. Chris put his hand on top of his erection and felt dampness. His penis was pulsating. He thought he might climax with another touch of his own hand.

David returned to the room, closed the door, and stuffed clothes around the door. As he approached the bed he saw that Chris was in his underwear. He hesitated, then whispered, "Where are your clothes?"

"I put them in the closet just in case I have to…"

"Oh, okay."

David sat down beside Chris. Then he did something he had wanted to do for years. He slowly ran his hand over Chris's stomach and his chest. "I can't believe this is happening. I never imagined it would," David said.

Chris lay there. He watched David, who watched himself touching Chris. Chris reached up, putting his hand on the back of David's head and pulled David toward him. David eagerly gave in to Chris, lying on top of him.

When their lips met there was, from both of them, an audible sigh. Chris held David's head so that their mouths became locked tightly

Lies That Bind

together. David put his tongue deep into Chris's mouth as Chris opened to him. David had one arm under Chris's head and with the other hand he held his face. David lifted his head and looked down at Chris. He ran his fingers over Chris's mouth. Chris opened his mouth and sucked in two of David's fingers.

"Oh, Chris," David said as he began to lick at Chris's neck. Chris turned his face in to David's neck and gently bit down. As he ran his tongue over skin he could taste the salt of David's sweat. Chris sucked harder. His body responded instantly; he was writhing in pleasure. David began to grind his hips into Chris's pelvis. Chris took David by the shoulders and rolled him over so that now he was on top. As he did, David lifted his hips and slipped off his sweatpants, leaving himself naked. Chris glanced down and for the first time saw David's naked arousal. He slowly ran his fingers along the outside of David's hip and across his leg, then to the inside of his thighs. He looked up into David's eyes. They smiled. Chris then slowly brushed his tongue over David's lips as he teased his fingers through David's pubic hair and caressed his erection. David moaned. "Oh, Chris." There was a tremor in his voice.

Chris was in ecstasy. He moved his fingertips along David's scrotum. His testicles drew upward in response to Chris's touch. Chris moved his hand and wrapped his fingers around David's penis. He smiled, feeling the strength of his erection, the softness of its head. Chris watched as he stroked David's cock. He could hardly take in all that he was feeling. His body was running on automatic. His skin felt on fire. He felt tingling in his hands and arms, then running through his chest and groin down through his legs to his feet; it was like a fever. David's moans sent another wave of electricity through Chris's body. He was amazed that he was near orgasm.

Chris's gaze moved to David's closed eyes. He leaned in to David and kissed him again. Then he kissed David's neck, ran his tongue down to his navel. David's penis pressed against his chin.

"Wait, stop," David said. Chris stopped and looked up at him. "Let me undress you first," he said, looking into Chris's eyes. "You still have your underwear on. I want to unwrap your package." They both smiled at each other, and David began to blush. Chris moved off of David and lay on his back.

"Go ahead," Chris said in a whisper.

David got up from his bed and started to fumble around at his desk.

"What are you doing?"

"Looking for matches." David struck a match and lit two candles that he brought to the nightstand near his bed. "I want to be able to see you."

"Don't move," Chris whispered.

David froze. His ears strained for the sound of someone on the move. His body immediately responded; his muscles tensed. "What?" he said, pointing to the closet. "Turn to the side, I want to see you from a better angle," he said, directing David with his hands as he began to laugh.

David, realizing that Chris was gazing at him, struck a pose as he began to laugh. First, he did a full frontal muscle flexed, he flexed his arms and shoulders and turned to one side, then the other. He turned around and flexed his buttocks. Although there was no one he would rather be doing this for, he felt embarrassed. However, he reveled in the feeling, his embarrassment added to his excitement.

"Sexy, dude," Chris whispered. "You are so hot."

"Shut up," David said smiling. He returned to the bed. Kneeling, he straddled Chris at his hips and then sat down on his thighs. Chris ran his hands up and down David's legs and then moved to the inside of his thighs, while David stroked Chris's chest and stomach. "Damn, you feel even better than you look," David said. Chris smiled, and then he sat up and kissed David, taking David's erection in his hand. David moaned as Chris ran his other hand up David's thigh, between his legs and around to his buttock. The sound of their moans added to each other's pleasure.

"Lie down," David insisted. "Let me." David pushed Chris to the bed. Chris lay down, but kept running his hands up and down David's thighs. David took hold of Chris's hands and stopped him. "Relax, Chris, just stay still," he said, as he caressed Chris's torso.

"But I want you, too."

"I know. Stop trying to be in control," David said, smiling. "First let me unwrap you." Chris propped his head up on the pillow so that he could watch David "unwrap" him. He had never seen David so animated, excited, and eager. He had often noticed how attractive David was, but suddenly he thought that David was strikingly handsome. The sight of his straight blond hair falling over his face, the strong angle of his high cheekbones, the white, toothy smile that filled his face, his broad shoulders and smooth defined chest and abdominal muscles in the flickering of candlelight left Chris in reverie.

Time seemed to be standing still. Everything around him except David disappeared. And every sound was magnified by his yearnings. He quickly sat up and ran his tongue over David's chest, coming to a stop on his nipple. Then he collapsed on the pillow, but again his body tensed with pleasure. "Do it then."

David, too, was overwhelmed with what was happening. Just moments ago his body ached with fear that he was going to lose Chris's friendship, and now his body ached with desire. David stroked Chris's stomach. He could see the outline of Chris's erection straining against his white cotton briefs. He pressed the palm of his hand against the bulge; Chris's cock pushed back. Not yet giving in to his desire to see Chris naked, David ran his fingers under the waistband and along the shaft and head of Chris erection. "Oh fuck, Chris. That ain't no *peschadelle*," David whispered, as he slowly pulled the waistband down, exposing Chris's erection. Chris's chest shook as he tried not to laugh. David moved off Chris as he pulled Chris' briefs down and over his feet. He stood by the side of the bed, just staring down at Chris.

Chris sat up, grabbed David, and wrestled him down onto the bed. Their bodies became intertwined, and for only a brief moment David resisted Chris. Then he gave in to Chris's strength as Chris rolled him over and put all his weight on top of him. Their hands roamed all over each other's bodies, exploring, grabbing, holding. Their mouths searched, kissed, licked, and sucked at each other. With their legs intertwined their hips ground into each other.

David rolled on top of Chris, their mouths locked together. David continued grinding his hips into Chris's stomach; their penises rubbing against the other's sweaty groin. Chris's body began to tense, his breathing quickened. "David, I'm close."

"I know." David quickened the rhythmic grinding of his hips.

"David," Chris moaned.

"Shh," David whispered, putting his mouth over Chris's, just as Chris had imagined. His passion exploded as David's mouth fell upon his. Feeling the warmth and wetness of Chris's orgasm, David quickened his movements. He buried his face in Chris's neck and moaned as he began to come. Chris wrapped his arms around David's shoulders, his legs around his hips, and held him close. Slowly their breathing calmed, their bodies relaxed, their lips gently caressed each other. When David tried to move, Chris tightened his hold. "Don't."

"Let me get something to clean you off."

"No, it feels good," Chris whispered. David relaxed on top of Chris. They remained quiet for several minutes. They continued to gently kiss.

"What time is it?" Chris asked.

"A little after four. My dad gets up at six. He helps serve mass at seven. You'd better go by five-thirty."

"Cool. That gives us time."

"For what?" David asked.

Chris rolled David over so that now he was lying on top of David. He moved his hand between them, grabbing David's penis. He looked at David and smiled.

David laughed. "Not so loud this time."

"I can't help it."

David smiled and said, "You are so hot."

"Shut up," Chris said as they began to kiss.

On Monday, at school, Chris waited for a good time to confront Derek. He watched him through physics, their first period class. Chris kept him in his sight all morning. Each hour Chris's anger grew, each hour he plotted. Several times they made eye contact. Derek smiled, Chris glared. Derek wrinkled his brow as if to say, what? Chris glared. After each class Chris looked for an opportunity to get Derek alone, but someone was always hanging on. Finally, at lunch, he made his move.

"Hey, Derek," Chris called out from the table where he was eating his lunch. "Wait up. I want to talk to you." Chris told the guys he was sitting with that he would talk to them later.

"What's up?" Derek asked, slowly walking toward Chris. Chris glared as they exchanged handshakes. Derek winced questioningly and said, "The word is out that you and Cathy broke up last Friday night. What happened?"

"That's what I want to talk to you about, dude," Chris said, focusing his stare on Derek's eyes and tightening his hand around Derek's.

"What? About you and Cathy?" Derek said. He looked puzzled. "What's going on?"

"You really are a bastard." Chris still had not let go of Derek's hand and continued to apply pressure.

As Derek pulled his hand out from Chris's grip he said, "What are you talking about?"

"You love spreading gossip, don't you?"

"Oh man, it's not me. Cathy has been telling everyone. Really."

"Cathy told me that you told her that David made a pass at you." Chris waited for Derek to say something, but he didn't. "Look, dude, I don't care if it's true or not, but not only is she going to be the last person you tell, you are going to walk over to Cathy right now and tell her

Lies That Bind

that you were just bullshitting and that you thought she knew you better than to take it seriously."

"Yeah, well, I wasn't bullshitting. He did." Derek moved from one foot to another and then scratched his head.

"You are not getting this, Derek," Chris said, moving close to him. "Maybe you need to be taking notes. So let me say it again." Chris spoke slowly. "I don't care if he did or he didn't." He put his hands on his hips and looked down at the ground, then he looked up again. Derek was about to speak when Chris put his hand up to Derek's mouth and shook his head. "If you continue with this, David will have a really hard time of it for the rest of the year, and I don't want that to happen. If it does happen, and this is not a threat, Derek, it is a promise, I will make sure you have a much worse time of it," Chris said with about six inches between his mouth and Derek's ear. "Derek, I promise you. And let me say this slowly. I will make your life, in a word, fucking miserable."

"That's two words." He smirked. "And just how would you do that?" in a tone he quickly wished he had not used.

Chris dropped his head and took a deep breath. He looked up and into Derek's eyes and said, "Don't fuck with me, asshole. I know your game." He poked his index finger into Derek's chest and continued. "You see, I have all kinds of shit on you and you have none on me. Isn't that the way you play the game, asshole?" Chris said, speaking softly through his teeth.

"What shit do you have on me?" Derek asked, defiantly trying to cover his nervousness.

"Well, that's part of the game, isn't it? You just don't know what I have on you. Do you? But I promise you this, Derek," and again he began to poke him in the chest, this time harder. He poked him hard enough to knock Derek off balance. "You don't scare me like you scare the others."

Derek grabbed and held onto Chris's hand so he would stop poking, but he was too afraid to say a word.

Chris held onto Derek's hand and began to squeeze. "You know I have the coach's ear. You are not that good a player. One word from me, and you won't play. What is it called? Team cohesiveness. There are two juniors who would jump at the chance to play varsity next semester. And that is just the start of it, Derek," Chris said, squeezing Derek's hand tighter. "I am not kidding. You fuck with David or any other guy on the team and I promise you, I will find every way possible to fuck you over."

"Okay, okay." Derek pulled his hand away. He glanced around, sure that everyone was watching them. "But, I have a question for you. Is this about David or about the team? If he were spreading shit about me would you be pounding his chest right now?" Derek asked in a most pitiful way. It looked to Chris as though he might cry.

"In a heartbeat. You know you're one of my best buds, dude," Chris said with a smile. He reached out and pulled Derek to him and gave him a hug and a slap on the back. "I just don't want to see the team fucked with. David is an important player on the team and we have a good chance to go to state. I'm the captain of the team, you know, like the Don of the family, Don Bellesano. I just want harmony amongst the players."

"Don Bellesano," Derek repeated with a tortured grin. "That's good. Should I kiss your ring?" Derek said. "I guess I was mistaken about David. Are we still friends?"

"Derek, absolutely nothing has changed between us, I promise you that," Chris said with a caustic smile. "Cathy's over there," Chris said, pointing to where she was sitting. "Be sure she understands that you were only joking, and that you were very surprised to hear from me that she took you seriously."

"Okay," Derek said as he started to walk toward Cathy. Chris could see that Derek was both scared and angry.

"Hey, Derek," Chris called out. "I won't have a date for your party. Am I still invited?"

"Well neither do I, so you can be my date," Derek called out.

"Derek, was that a pass?" Chris said laughingly. *Who was it that said that there is truth in every joke?* Chris wondered.

* * * * *

"So, you and David found each other?" I said surprised. I thought I had figured out what brought Chris to this place. He had told David he was attracted to him, David had become upset, and their friendship had ended. Then everyone had found out that Chris is gay. That had been my guess.

"Yeah," Chris said with a smile.

"You had no idea he was attracted to you?"

"Looking back, maybe I did. But, maybe I didn't want to know, or something like that."

"The time wasn't right for you. Psychologically, emotionally, at least until…When was it that this all happened?"

"Seven months ago. Last November," Chris said. I noticed a look of distress come over him.

Lies That Bind

"What just happened? You were looking energetic, present, available, and then you seemed to slip away," I said. "Do you know what I mean?" He nodded. Then there was a long silence, only broken by the sound of Chris's breath. He looked at me. His agitation was apparent. "What's happening?"

"I have to stand up," he said. He got to his feet and began pacing until he moved to the corner of the room.

"Are you feeling anxious?" I asked. He nodded, pulling his arms tightly around his chest. "Can you talk about what's happening?" He sat on the floor with his back pressed against the wall, his knees pulled up to his chest. "Are you more comfortable sitting there?" I asked, noting to myself the physical distance he had put between us.

"I mean I just realized that I told you about David and me having sex. I was just thinking that you, well, people like you, think people like me are sick."

"I see." I said nodding. I had just become one of his rejecting demons. "First, let me say it seems to me that you put a great deal of stock in what others think of you. And with all that you have told me about your father, I would say that you do that for good reason."

He shrugged and sat silently. I wrestled with whether or not to continue, but he seemed to be deep in thought. "How else would I know how to be? I mean, that's the problem now, I don't know how to be."

"Tell me more."

"Before, I knew how to be. I just did what other people wanted. My father said, 'Don't cry', so I didn't cry. My grandfather wanted me to play ball, so I did that. My mother wanted me to be smart, so I am." His voice grew louder. "Everyone says you're supposed to be straight, so I was. I always knew how to be." He paused. "I don't think I know how to be anymore. I feel like I've been thrown from an airplane. I've got a parachute on, but there's no one there to tell me how to open it. I'm just feeling out of control." He looked up at me and asked, "Can you tell me what you are thinking about?"

I paused, "Actually, I was thinking about the incident at the pool, going down the slide." His eyes filled with tears, he drew his knees in closer to his chest.

He nodded, "Exactly."

I was sure he was wondering if I would be there to catch him. I decided to leave his expectation of rejection until later. "I know this will seem somewhat ridiculous, but you just moved from your chair to the floor."

He looked up at me. "How did you know to do that? I didn't tell you to do that, nor did I tell you that it was proper or not proper. You felt a need to move across the room, that is what made you most comfortable at the time." He shrugged. "How did you know to do that?"

He stared at me intently. "I just knew I had to move."

"Okay, so something told you how to be. It came from inside of you. Not from me, right?" I asked rhetorically. He nodded. "Chris, you have allowed others' expectations and opinions of you to dictate who you are and how you feel about yourself. You can go on doing that, but you know well the pain in that. The alternative to that is to learn who you are, but then you can't let yourself make other people's opinions of you become your opinion of yourself." More silent.

"Chris, I don't believe you no longer have a self. I believe it's buried deep, but it is there. I also believe that self is probably much of who you are, but a lot is also a false self—an adaptive self, but not freely chosen. Rather, chosen so as to survive." I noticed that our time was short and before I went into greater depth I wanted to hear more from him.

"I don't understand."

"There's a quote from Kierkegaard that I think is really useful. Have you read him?"

"Yeah, sure."

"I'm sorry, of course you have. I used to know it verbatim, but that was a while ago." I noticed that his stare was less intense. For the first time I thought I saw in him an openness that moved me; a desire for the possibility of hope. "It goes something like this: 'The most common despair is to be in despair of not choosing to be oneself; but the deepest form of despair is to choose to be other than oneself. On the other hand, to will to be that self which one truly is, is indeed the opposite of despair, and this choice is the deepest responsibility of Man.' I think that's pretty close."

"That sounds like Kierkegaard," he said, nodding.

"Chris, what you've known is despair, deep despair." He nodded. "You can choose anew. It's a long journey—lifelong. Kierkegaard believed that Jesus chose to be himself. To live his life, his destiny, and not the life others would have chosen for him. He also believed that we each have to struggle in those choices." He nodded.

"We are going to have to stop soon," I added. "But before we finish I do want to get to a couple of things." He nodded. "Did your love for David feel sick to you?"

"No. It made me happy. But it scared me, too."

Lies That Bind

"Well, there is the conflict, isn't it? You know what feels right to you and you know that the people around you will disapprove. Can we look at what you said before, so I can better address your concerns?"

"What? I mean sure. Okay," Chris said, shrugging.

"You said people like you, meaning me, think people like you are sick. Who are people like me?" I asked.

"Doctors, psychiatrists."

"I am a doctor, but I am not a doctor of medicine. I have a Ph.D., and I am a psychologist," I said. "You also said, people like me, meaning you."

"Gays," he shrugged.

"I see, and sick means what?"

"I don't know, I guess sexually fucked up, perverts."

"Okay. Generally, most psychologists and psychiatrists do not think that gay men and lesbians are mentally ill. But, you are right that there are still some who hold to that belief. I definitely do not believe that being homosexual means you are mentally ill. There are mentally ill heterosexuals and mentally ill homosexuals, and there are very healthy heterosexuals and very healthy homosexuals.

"Now, specifically with regard to you, what I believe is that you are in a great deal of pain." Chris sat silently staring up at me. "Can I ask you something?"

"Sure."

"Have I said or done anything to give you the impression that I think your being gay means that you are sick?"

"No." Chris paused. "Well, before, I forget when, you seemed uncomfortable. I guess I figured it was because I was talking about gay stuff."

"I am glad you said something about that. You are right, I was feeling distressed. But it was not about you being gay. It was when you talked about the rejection you anticipated and the pain and anxiety around all that."

"Okay. Cool," he said nodding.

"I would like to ask you, if you can, to please tell me if I do anything or say anything that makes you feel rejected or judged."

"Really?" Chris asked, making eye contact. I nodded. "Okay," he said with a shrug.

"I do respect your being cautious with me. I will make every effort to be as honest as I can be with you."

"Thank you," Chris said. He seemed calmed.

"Well, like I said, we are going to have to stop soon. I am going to see your mother, and probably your grandparents. "I want to be sure you understand that I am here as your therapist, not as a family therapist or mediator. When I meet with your mom, I'll do my best to keep what you talk to me about to myself."

"You can tell them anything. They know most of it." Chris got up from the floor.

"Okay. When I talked to your mother yesterday, she mentioned that you found out in a letter that your father had passed away." Chris nodded as he sat down in the chair. "You hadn't mentioned that. Your mother said she was going to try to find the letter and bring it in." Chris shrugged. I continued. "I believe she wants me to read it. What do you want?"

"Bring it in here. We can read it then."

"Good, excellent. Also, you said something about Jack Payden not being homosexual because he was a marine, married, et cetera. You told that to Father O'Brien. Well, I don't know if he is heterosexual or homosexual, but what I do know is that he is a pedophile. Well, actually, that isn't accurate."

"What do you mean?"

"Well, a pedophile is someone who is exclusively attracted to prepubescent children. My guess is that he is attracted to post-pubescent boys. And that probably his attraction is also to adult women. It can be very complicated. I have a word for you."

"What's that?"

"E-f-i-b-o-p-h-i-l-e," I spelled out for him. "It is pronounced "eh-FEE-bo-phile." It is a person who is attracted to adolescents. Jack is an adolescent molester.

"Yeah, I guess I realized that a couple of months ago. He molested David, too."

"Really? My guess is that there are other boys that he victimized besides you and David."

"Yeah. I guess." Then, in a way that sounded like a thought exploding from his body, he blurted out, "I was not victimized."

"What do you mean?" I asked.

"You said I should tell you when you say something. You said that before, too. Well, I wasn't victimized. You're wrong about that." There was a strength to his voice that was not angry, but filled with conviction.

"Well, I think that is a common reaction among boys who have been sexually abused. It's hard for boys to accept being victims."

"No, that's not it. I thought about that, but I was not a victim," Chris insisted. This was a strength that had previously only been suggested. I was impressed with his polite insistence.

Lies That Bind

"Chris, I know you see yourself, if not as the initiator of what happened with Jack, then a willing participant. What you are not acknowledging is the inappropriateness of what took place. Jack was an adult and Jack, regardless of what that priest said…" He seemed to want to interrupt me.

"Oh, you mean Father O'Brien."

"Right, Father O'Brien. Even if you did grope Jack, he should have removed your hand from his penis, rolled over and gone back to sleep." I hesitated. "First let me say this. It is very common for boys at the age of twelve, thirteen, and fourteen to want to have a sexual experience with another person. Clearly, you understand this. Although, an adolescent may be physically ready, he is not psychologically ready to handle having a sexual experience with an adult. That is why it is called a molestation. Not because force or manipulation is used, although that is often the case. Rather, it is because the adolescent does not have the psychological capacity to make sense of all that is going on."

Chris's gaze was intense and filled with pain. I was once again struck by the awareness that inside this very young adult lived the soul of a very wounded young boy. I began to have one of those experiences where you hear yourself talking but your thoughts are elsewhere. I could feel in him a deep longing to be listened to and understood, to be accepted and loved for who he was. I had a sensation in my stomach that felt as if it was both empty and full at the same time. As I spoke, my thoughts returned to him lying on the hospital table waiting for his rabies shot, looking into this father's eyes and pleading to be held.

I continued, "In your case, what Jack used instead of force was friendship, trust, your desire to belong, your need to open up to someone. Having used that and your curiosity and sexual desires, he was able to successfully make you a 'willing participant.' But you are correct; it would have been different altogether, if Jack had 'raped' you. In that situation you would have also lost trust in yourself, but in a different way."

"How so?"

"Well, not being able to defend yourself against the attack. Adolescent boys see themselves as, well, 'men in training,' and a man is supposed to be able to defend himself against aggression. We do not raise boys to freely admit to being victimized. In our society, it is more acceptable for a girl to admit to being victimized than it is for a boy. Let me be clear, no one should be victimized. In our society it is very difficult for anyone to be taken seriously when they claim to have been victimized. Usually, society re-victimizes them. Men, therefore, seldom see their molestation, or a young boy's sexual experience with an adult, as an assault. They usually describe it as an early sexual experience. But, it is not just an early sexual experience. It is also a molestation. If you and David had been sexual with each other when you first met, then you would have been two emotionally and psychologically immature boys expressing their desires. When there is an adult involved there is an issue of power, and that power, when used in sex, is damaging.

"More specifically to what happened with you, this is partially the power that I am talking about. You were seduced into revealing what you felt was a very private part of yourself by a man who had an agenda. He tricked you into trusting him, at a time when you were feeling extremely vulnerable; Chris, he knew what he was doing. He then used that as an opportunity to molest you. You were tricked into talking about a man who was emotionally out of control to a man who was sexually out of control.

He shook his head, "I guess, but the whole victim thing, I don't know, it just doesn't feel like what happened."

I was painfully aware that we were again going over our time. I decided not to continue with this now. "We are going to have to talk about all this tomorrow."

"Tomorrow, sure," Chris said, with a smile.

When I met with Mrs. Patrona I told her that I thought Chris was doing well. I informed her that I hoped that he might be released on Monday. She said that she had heard that the police had visited Jack Payden and that he denied the allegations. She also told me that she had found the letter regarding Frank's death and had it with her. I asked if she planned on coming to the hospital tomorrow and she said "Of course". I asked her to bring the letter in tomorrow, and told her that I would see her before I saw Chris.

Mr. Dinato asked if he could speak to me alone. He expressed his anger regarding Chris's molestation. He also asked me to tell Chris that he loved him. I explained to Mr. Dinato that soon he and his family and I would meet together and that he could tell Chris.

As I left the waiting room, I found myself thinking about my parents and wishing I could experience the love that so clearly surrounded Chris.

It was not until I was in my car and on my way home that I remembered that tomorrow was Sunday. I thought about calling the hospital and telling them to tell Chris that I would not be in, but then I remembered the look of relief on his face and decided that if I couldn't make it in, I would call tomorrow.

Part Three: Sunday

Chapter Eleven

IT WAS NOT A typical June day in Santa Monica. Usually, the mornings are cool and overcast, with the sun not breaking though the cloud cover until afternoon. It has something to do with the inversion layer; it's a California thing, I guess. This morning, however, the sun was bright, and there was a wonderful ocean breeze moving through my bedroom window.

I spent most of the morning working my way through my closets, separating what I would pack and what I would give to charity. Eventually, I became bored and decided most of what I owned would go to Goodwill, making my life and packing much easier. I poured my fourth cup of coffee, went up to my roof—I was living in a condo-townhouse with a private roof deck—stripped to my boxers, and made myself comfortable in the sun. I decided that I would go to the hospital after lunch.

I had been thinking about both Carl and Chris all morning. My preoccupation was always the same. Why do these boys wait to break their silence? It had always been clear to me that there was no single answer. And, whatever the factors, they were further complicated by the vicissitudes of adolescence.

I had learned that one of the factors adding to the pressure to keep silent was the nature of the sexual act itself. Often, the molester was a man. Often he was heterosexual. However, for the boy to admit to the molestation, he must admit to a homosexual encounter. Regardless of whether the boy was homosexual or heterosexual, the prospect of being thought of as a homosexual, putting his sexual identity into question at such an early age, created more anxiety than most boys could tolerate.

Society closely links—incorrectly, I believe—sexual orientation to gender identity. Homosexual men are "feminized," lesbians are "masculinized." For a boy to acknowledge being molested, he believes that he is admitting to being either a willing participant or a victim. He believes that admitting to being a willing participant makes him a homosexual, thus feminizing himself. If he claims to have been victimized, he then de-masculinizes himself. Either way he jeopardizes his gender identity.

In the short term, silence seems to be the most bearable solution. A solution which is a compromise to save a wounded ego caught in a double bind in the midst of the psychic storm better known as "the teenage years." A solution based on a very complicated form of denial now resting on an often previously weakened psychic structure. Typically, the conflict becomes overwhelming, and these boys void themselves of all emotions, falling into depression, drug abuse, aggressive and/or self-destructive behavior.

There is always a secret involved in the molestation of these adolescent boys: either a secret the abuser threatens to reveal if the molestation is revealed, as was the case with Chris, or the secret of the molestation itself, which contains its own threat. Very often the family knows the abuser. He or she may be a family member, a respected friend, professional, or neighbor. The relationship between the abuser and the parents is seen by the boy to be more substantial than that of the boy to his parents. Or the adult is in a position of power and believed by the boy to be more credible. The boy becomes convinced the parents will not believe him, or might even blame him. Sadly, sometimes that is exactly what happens.

I had long hoped that if I could, in some small way, shed light on what makes these boys keep their secrets, I could interrupt the process and help them in breaking their silence. Thus, they could start the work of repairing their wounds much earlier, and stop the wounds' insidious effects. But when the silence is maintained, it's their adolescent drug abuse, aggressive behavior, severe depression, and suicide attempts or nervous breakdown that brings them to our attention. Many others go unnoticed into adulthood, where similar symptoms affect their behavior. The rest abuse themselves or their families.

The ringing of my phone brought me back to reality. First ring. *Damn, can I make it before my machine answers?* Second ring. *It's probably Janet. Damn, I better get it.* Third ring. *I'm going to break my neck running down these stairs.* Fourth ring. *Gotcha.*

"Hello."

"Hello, Robert? This is Josh Rosen."

"Hi?" *Damn, and what are you selling?*

"Am I disturbing you?"

"Probably. Who are you and why are you calling me on Sunday?"

"Ah. I'm Barbara's friend. She said she was going to tell you that I was going to call." He paused; I guessed I was supposed to say something. He continued. "She didn't call you?"

Lies That Bind

"No. But..." *Damn, damn.* "Sorry, I wasn't expecting your call. Where are you?"

"New York. I'm sorry. I talked to her for about an hour last night, and she said she had talked to you about me, and that it would be fine for me to call you. She gave me your number, but she promised she'd call and..."

"Oh, Josh. Oh, okay. Josh, I'm sorry." *Sorry I didn't let my machine get it.* "Yes, she did tell me about you, Friday night when we had dinner." *I thought I was supposed to call him when I got to New York.* "Okay, let's start over again." I laughed. "Hi, Josh, Barbara told me all about you. It's good to hear from you." *I hate this, I really do. I know this is how it's done, but I do hate it.*

"Hi, Robert. Is it Robert, Bob, or Bobby?"

"Well, I do prefer Robert," *you call me Bob and I'll hang up,* "but some people get away with Bobby."

"Okay, I'll call you Robert. I don't want to push it."

Good idea. "So, where about in the City do you live, or are you a train or tunnel person?" *That's what city people call commuters.*

"Upper West Side. West 80th Street, between Columbus and Amsterdam."

"Nice, near the park." *An uptown queen.*

"Yeah, it's great to go for a run."

"You do that often?" *Damn, hang up the phone—another physical fitness freak. Damn Robert, lighten up. Give the guy a break. He had the courage to call—that's more than you would do.*

"Nah, I just wanted to sound like I'm really athletic. I do swim, though."

Nice, a sense of humor. I laughed. "Swimming is good. Where do you swim?"

"The gym I belong to has a pool. It's on 8th Avenue and 50th."

"So, you talked to Barbara."

"Yeah, she said you were driving back to New York soon. She said you were driving your Porsche across the country."

"Yeah, I'm leaving here in about two weeks. I'm going to take the long way back and see the country." I walked across my kitchen and poured myself another cup of coffee. I lifted myself up and sat down on my kitchen counter. I had a nice view of the beach from there.

"Are you planning on living in the City?"

"Yes. Actually, I bought a place in Chelsea." I paused, but he said nothing. "Yeah, I know, a Chelsea queen. It comes available August 1st."

"What are you going to do with your car?" he asked.

"Well, I have a sister, she and her future husband have a place in the Hamptons. They said I could keep it there as long as she could use it when I'm not."

"Sounds like she's getting a pretty good deal. Barbara tells me you're a psychoanalyst."

"And you still called?" He laughed. "I'm impressed." Actually, I was impressed. My attitude helps keep my nervousness from taking over. If it did, I'd either ramble on and on, or I would not say anything.

"She also told me that you teach, that you have a job at John Jay College."

"She's told you a lot. What else did she tell you?"

"Oh, that you're thoughtful, funny, honest and straight forward, kind, intelligent..."

I began to feel butterflies in my stomach. "Are you sure you called the right number?" Self-deprecation was an old hobby of mine.

"And she said you are—and these were her words—knock-your-socks-off good looking."

"Damn, now I know you've got the wrong number." I felt myself blush.

"On the bad side, she said you and I are a lot alike in that we're independent, like our space, and take life too seriously."

I guess she didn't tell you that I hate blind dates. "Well, she has me there. Josh, since you know so much about me... Well, can I ask you a few questions?"

"Fire away."

"What do you do for a living?"

"I also teach. I'm a photographer, and I teach at Parson's School of Design."

"You're a photographer," I said, impressed. For some reason I lost my nervousness. My internal sarcasm also stopped.

"Yeah, I've had a couple of shows, small stuff, but nice."

"What do you shoot?" I found myself engaged by the warmth of his voice.

"Well, for money I do cover work."

"What is that?"

"*Rolling Stone*, other magazine covers, and I've done shots for album covers. But, my artwork is mostly black and white artsy stuff. It gives me a good reason to travel and then to spend time in a darkroom."

Lies That Bind

"Sounds wonderfully creative." I was feeling interested. His voice sounded warm, sincere, and solid.

"I love teaching, and I love my work, so I'm one of the lucky ones."

"Nice. How old are you?" I was now doodling. I hear there are books written about what doodles mean. Mine are always the same, curved lines with shading, suggesting the waves of the ocean, or ripples in a pond. Then I remembered that it means that I am sexually frustrated. I put down my pencil.

"Thirty-four. And you?"

"Thirty-one," I said. "Barbara described you as soft spoken, genuine, creative, and funny, but she didn't tell me you were a photographer. I must admit I'm impressed that you called. To tell you the truth, I'm not sure I would have had the courage to call you." I then felt surprised by my admission.

"She told me that. She said that if I waited for you to call me when you arrived in New York I wouldn't hear from you."

"She does know me," I said, feeling embarrassed.

"I'm not sure I would have called you once you were here, either."

"Really, why not?" I liked his honesty.

He was silent for a moment. "The distance between us makes it safer, I guess. I mean if this call went poorly, we could just lose each other's number or something. If you were here the pressure would have been more immediate."

Nice, he also thinks things through, with some self-awareness. "True, but I'm still impressed." I hesitated. "So how is it going?"

He laughed, "Good. So one point for me, right? For calling?" I laughed. "So, are you curious about what I look like?"

I laughed, I guess we were both nervous, "Yeah, but I thought I'd call Barbara when we hung up and get all the info from her."

"I'm five- foot nine, about one-fifty. I'm Jewish, but you probably got that from the name. I have black straight hair. It's short, a great smile, and a goatee. People say I'm easy on the eyes."

"You don't have to do this. You sound like a decent guy. I'd like to meet you. Like I said, I appreciate your willingness to make the effort."

"Great, how should we leave it?" he asked.

"Well, I'll be there and moving in, like I said, around August first. Why don't we plan to have dinner that week? Give me your number and I'll call you."

"Okay," he said, sounding a bit dejected.

"Better yet. Do you really want to do this?" I asked.

"Yes."

"Okay, let's set a date to meet for dinner."

Okay, but here comes the bad news. I have a really severe gluten allergy, and…"

I interrupted, "You can't eat wheat, barely, oats, or rye."

"You've heard of it."

"Sure. No problem. Let's meet in front of my favorite Thai restaurant, Kin Kaho on Spring Street in Soho. I love to introduce people to this place, and I'm sure there is a lot you can eat there."

"I've eaten there many times. I love the food."

I laughed, "That's two points for you."

"When and what time?"

"The first Friday evening in August at eight," I said. "You're not going to be able to cancel, I won't have a phone yet."

"I'll be there. But why don't we meet at six, have an early dinner, and then go uptown and see a show? I'll buy us tickets for something. My treat. That will make it an official date."

I smiled, "Oh nice. I'd love that. It'll be my first Broadway show since my return to New York." I do love being courted. "It will also be my first date in a long while." I could not believe I had said that. *Jackass, he's going to think you're a real loser.*

"How about *Cats*?" There was a silence that was painful. "That was a joke, Robert."

I laughed, "That was good. You had me going for a second. I like you," I said without thinking. *Damn it Robert, edit, edit.*

"Thank you. That was kind of you to say. Okay, dinner at six and then a show. I'll get tickets for something light and fun."

"Great, Josh. I'm really excited. Really, I am. And thank you for calling."

"Thank you, Robert. Have a safe trip across country. Take lots of black-and-white photographs."

"Okay, I will," I said.

"See you in August."

"Bye." I hung up the phone and stared at my doodles. *Damn, I must have doodled the name Josh ten times in the last twenty minutes. Will I always feel like an adolescent on a first date?*

I decided it was time to leave my apartment. Janet was sure to call, and I was feeling too good to talk to her. The drive to the hospital was

Lies That Bind

wonderful. All the traffic was heading in the other direction toward the beach. I opened the roof on my Targa and made my way into the valley, where it was a warm eighty degrees. I decided to stop and have lunch before going to the hospital. Nearby is a wonderful outdoor restaurant that serves the best Cobb salad in town. Feeling content, I decided to walk the six blocks to the hospital. When I entered the hospital I saw Diane, Anthony and Josephine sitting in the lobby. When they saw me they rose and walked toward me.

"Hi, Dr. Mitchell," Diane said.

"Hi, Mrs. Patrona, Mr. and Mrs. Dinato, I do understand your wanting to be here, but…"

Diane interrupted me by putting her hand on my arm. "Actually, we came here because we wanted you to talk to David."

"David Jarrett?"

"Yes, and I wanted to bring that letter we talked about," Diane said.

"Oh yes, the letter. I'm not sure that it's a good idea that David and I speak yet, Mrs. Patrona."

"No, it isn't about Chris, but well… Anyway, the police are investigating Jack, and he is denying he ever touched Chris. He said that Chris was crazy and making it all up."

"Well, that's not unusual," I assured her.

"I understand that they'll be out to talk to Chris tomorrow," she said.

"I think so, yes."

"David was also molested by Jack, and not just once or twice. David knows of other boys who were…"

"There are others," I said nodding.

"David wants to talk to them tomorrow too, and we thought the police should talk to him before they talk to Chris. Maybe, you know, since Chris is in the hospital, if David talks to them first…"

"I see." David entered the lobby carrying a cup of coffee. I recognized him immediately from Chris's description of him. "What about the other guys?" I asked.

"Peter Cartola, Derek Powell, and I'd bet others, too," Diane said, turning toward David.

I asked her, "Can they speak to the police also?"

David joined us. "David," Diane said taking his arm, "This is Chris's doctor. Dr. Mitchell, this is David Jarrett." I shook David's outstretched hand, and noticed his eyes filling with tears; his nose flared and his mouth fell into a frown.

David spoke. "I know Peter wants to talk to the police. He told me he does. But I don't know about Derek," he added.

I asked, "Will you be here tomorrow, David?" His lips quivered, his sadness was undeniable.

"Yeah, I'm coming with Mrs. Patrona," he said, his eyes never leaving mine.

"Okay, I'll arrange it so that you can talk to the police before they talk to Chris. I'm going up to see Chris now. Mrs. Patrona, can I have the letter?"

"Sure." She reached into her purse. "I read it, and I can't believe what it says."

I took the letter from her. "Chris and I decided that he is going to read it to me. So I'll hear all about it then."

David asked, "How is he?" His voice cracked.

"Well, I'm hoping he'll be going home tomorrow afternoon after he speaks to the police." I turned to Diane and said, "You'll have your son home soon."

David tried to speak again, but tears began to roll down his cheeks. "I feel like this is all my fault," he said to Diane. He turned and walked away with Josephine. I watched as he sat down and covered his eyes with his hands. Josephine sat beside him, looking genuinely concerned.

"He's very emotional, and he's been blaming himself for what happened." Her chest rose as she took a deep breath. "I'm afraid I tore into him this morning."

"Really?"

"I don't like being lied to, and they both played me for a fool and betrayed my trust." I could hear the anger in her voice and see it in the rush of tension that washed through her.

I nodded, "That's not unusual..." She interrupted me.

"I know, but I had to let him know that I don't like being lied to. If he's ever going to be welcome into my home again, he's going to understand that is one thing I will not tolerate."

I decided to remain silent and just nodded.

"My son is going to hear from me about this, also." She paused and looked at me and said, "That is, after I tell him how much I love him."

I nodded again and glanced toward David, as did Diane. Clearly, he could hear what she had just said. "I'll talk to him," Diane said. "He'll be okay in the short term, but I worry about him." She hesitated. "You talked to me about Chris being in therapy in the future, to work through

Lies That Bind

all that is bothering him." I nodded. "Would it be inappropriate for you, at some point, to talk to David about starting in therapy too?"

"No, not at all. I could do that," I said. I had no doubt that David did need to be in treatment.

As I walked toward the ward I turned to look at David. He wiped tears from his face. Both Josephine and Diane sat at his side, trying to comfort him. I smiled to myself, noticing that his hairstyle was the same as Chris's. And, like Chris's hair, it fell over his face when he leaned forward. Chris was right—David was very attractive.

Chapter Twelve

ENTERING THE NURSES' STATION I expected to see Ron, but today was his day off. It was my day off too, but I felt too good to be packing up boxes, and decided that coming in today might facilitate Chris's leaving tomorrow. "Good afternoon, Nurse Ortiz."

"Hi, Dr. Mitchell. I can't believe you're here on a Sunday—are you seeing a patient today?"

"First, Chris Bellesano, then I'll see Carl. How are they doing?"

"Chris couldn't sleep last night. They told him they could call you and get authorization for a sleeping aid, but he said no. He had breakfast and then asked if he could nap until lunch. He seems fairly depressed. He's in the day room now, reading."

"Could you bring him to treatment room four? I'll see him there." I watched through the windows in the nurses' station as Nurse Ortiz approached Chris. He did look depressed. I noticed his face come alive when she explained to him that I would be seeing him. He quickly closed his book and followed her to the treatment room.

"Hi, Chris," I said, as I entered the room.

"Hi, Dr. Mitchell. You're here on Sunday."

"I'm on call this weekend Chris, and when I am, I often come in and read through the charts. Since I am here I thought it would be a good idea if we talked. It might help us get you home before too long." He smiled. "They tell me that you didn't get much sleep last night. Night demons?"

"No, not really. Just remembering stuff. Mostly about David. Happy times, not so happy times."

"Anything you want to share with me?"

* * * * *

The skiing conditions at Mammoth Mountain had been poor until the day after Christmas. A cold winter storm that originated in Canada made its way down through Washington and Oregon, then northern California and the Lake Tahoe area. The storm moved south and dumped over a foot of snow on Mammoth Mountain. Three days later another storm came across the Sierras and it snowed for two more days.

Lies That Bind

When the Sacred Heart High School group arrived at Mammoth the evening of January first, it was clear; the air was still, and only twelve degrees. The next day promised to bring near-perfect skiing conditions. The group was staying at a condominium at the top of Lakeview Drive near Canyon Lodge. It was as close to a ski-in/ski-out condo as one could find at Mammoth. Groups of boys and girls were assigned separate condos, each with a same-sex chaperone. Priests, lay teachers, and parents volunteered, and picked the boys and girls they felt most comfortable chaperoning. Father John D'Agostino chose David and Chris and six other boys.

It had been arranged so that on one night, a condo group of boys would prepare dinner for a condo group of girls. The next night the girls would then cook dinner for the boys. Father John delighted in doing most of the work for his group of boys, allowing them to spend most of the day skiing. However, he always arranged to have at least one day free so that he could ski. Students were often surprised to learn that he was an expert skier. While in college he had given serious thought to training and then making a bid for the USA Olympic ski team. However, his life had gone in a different direction, and after four years of college, he had entered the seminary. Eventually, he had earned a master's degree in psychology and a doctorate degree in philosophy. His first assignment as a teacher and counselor had been to Sacred Heart High School.

Originally, he was to teach advanced-placement mathematics classes. Recently, he had been given the additional responsibility of teaching religion and philosophy classes to juniors and seniors. In the past, most Sacred Heart students had dreaded these classes. Father Jerome, who would read from his notes for the entire hour and never answer questions, had taught them for more than ten years. His reading lists remained the same, and were nothing more than the Catholic Catechism, parts of the New Testament and Durant's *Introduction to World Philosophers*.

In contrast, Father John was known to be a demanding teacher but inspirational. His reading list included parts of the Torah, the New Testament and the Koran. He required his students to read original texts such as Kierkegaard's *Fear and Trembling* and Camus's *The Stranger*. Also included were Schelling, Sartre, Nietzsche, Kafka, Heidegger, St. Thomas Aquinas, St. Augustine, and others. He did not give tests, but assigned four papers per semester. One was an original thought paper, one was focused on philosophers and philosophical questions, one was on religious questions with reference to the Bible and the Koran, and the final for each of the two semesters was a paper integrating the semester's work. He had students standing in line to be assigned to his classes.

Besides being the most demanding, thought-provoking, and difficult class at SHHS, it was also the most controversial. Diane had been excited about Chris's enrollment into this advanced-placement class. David's parents, especially Paul, had had great reservations. Perhaps the only reason he had not stopped David from enrolling was that Father John was one of the few priests who allowed deacons, including Paul Jarrett, to participate as much as they did in the service of the Mass.

After everyone was settled into the condos, the group headed to the Mogul Restaurant for dinner. They were known to have a great salad bar and good food at reasonable prices. After dinner everyone returned to the condos. Father John gave each of the boys a room and bed assignment. He then posted a bathroom schedule and various house chores. David and Chris were assigned to one room. They had twin beds, but their bathroom was common to the condo. Peter, Gary, Bill, and Jason were assigned to another room with bunk beds, but they had their own large bathroom and a television in their room. Two other boys were assigned the living room couches with the stereo, the television, and the fireplace, and Father John took the master bedroom for himself. Everyone was happy.

The first day Chris, David, and Peter prepared breakfast, and Bill and Gary cleaned up the mess. Then Chris and David headed for the ski lodge, leaving Peter behind to wait for Julie. Chris was wearing the new ski suit Richard had bought him for Christmas.

"You look good in red," David said. "It matches your personality." It was a one-piece bright red North Face ski suit with black markings.

"Oh, and how is that?"

"Hot, hot, hot," David said, laughing. David was wearing a pair of black North Face bib overall ski pants and a bright yellow waist-length jacket. "It's so hard sleeping in the same room as you and not touching you."

"We can't. It's not safe. Someone will hear us."

"Hear you, you mean."

"Shut up," Chris said, smiling.

"I know, but it's driving me nuts. I spent the whole night horned up."

"Shhh."

"Damn, I feel something moving down there."

"Shut up," Chris laughed, as he pushed David.

They carried their skis and boots up to Canyon Lodge and rented a locker. After they bought lift tickets, they met up with several other

Lies That Bind

students and made their way to one of the ski lifts. David was particularly excited about the day. Skiing was his favorite sport.

It was early. The two quickly made their way to the head of the lift line and started up the hill. David asked, "Are you going to go on the gondola today?" as he made himself comfortable on the lift.

"And ski the cornice?" Chris asked. The cornice was at the very top of Mammoth Mountain, where there were mostly double-black-diamond runs, the most difficult.

"Yeah, you can do it," David said with a smile.

"I know I can, but I want to take it easy today."

David handed Chris his ski poles, "Okay, cool."

"You don't have to hang with me," Chris said. "I'll ski with Gary and Bill and Carol and Julie. Julie said she was going to ski on this side of the mountain most of the day."

"Why don't you and Julie lose everyone else and make your way over to the Main Lodge for lunch?" David said, as he removed his gloves. "We can meet up there. I'll tell Peter. Then I'll ski the afternoon with you." David found his tube of sun block and began to apply it to his face.

"Okay, are you going to take off now?" Chris asked.

"No, I'll take a first run with you. We'll go down One Chance and Viva," David said, trying to hide his smile.

"Fuck you, those are black diamonds," Chris said, as he poked David in the side. David began to laugh. "I'm going down Avalanche, then Spring Canyon to the bottom."

"That's cool, I'll go with you. After lunch let's just you and me ski the afternoon, okay? Let's lose everyone else. Okay?" David asked, putting his gloves on and taking back his poles from Chris.

"Okay, with whom are you skiing the cornice?"

Giving the word "whom" a special emphasis, David laughingly said, "With whom am I skiing? I am skiing with Andrew, Peter, Megan, and Jessica, that's whom. I'm meeting them at nine-thirty at the gondola."

"Asshole. When do you want to meet for lunch?" Chris asked, shaking his head.

"Twelve-thirty, you should come up to the cornice, really. I'll help you down the hard parts," David said with a smile.

"You just love thinking you can ski better than me."

David broke out into laughter and said, "No, well, yeah. And what do you mean thinking I can, I know I can ski better than you."

"I know you can, too, but when you ski with me you never give me shit or laugh or anything. It's just when we're not skiing that you tease me. Then the thought that you're better gives you a hard on. Right?"

Again David laughed and said, "Yeah, you're right, I do love it."

"Asshole," Chris said, shaking his head.

"Sorry. Look, you do everything better than me. Everything. So, it's just so exciting to be able to be better at something," David said, in a very animated way.

"You know, if you were such an asshole about it when we were skiing, I wouldn't ski with you."

David responded, "Yeah, but that would be mean. It's more that I like reminding you." David's smile filled most of what you could see of his face under his black ski cap and goggles.

"Yeah well, you're still an asshole. I don't do it to you."

"Well, that's because you're better than me at everything. Can you think of anything else that I'm better at?" David asked seriously.

"Yeah, sure. Your drawings."

"No, that doesn't count. You don't draw. Like I don't play guitar. Something that we both do, that I do better than you."

Chris thought for a second and then said with a smile, "Yes, I can."

"What?" David asked, with an expression of disbelief.

"You give a better blow job," Chris said, as he broke out into laughter, and pointed both his index fingers at David.

David's mouth fell open, and then he started to laugh. "Is that bad or good?" he asked.

"I think it's great," Chris said through his laughter.

David had not seen Chris laugh this hard in a long time, and he was enjoying it. David was usually quiet and withdrawn when he was in the company of his friends. Long ago, he had realized that Chris's friendship was important to him. He felt calmer, more grounded, or perhaps safer in the world when he was with Chris. However, he was just becoming aware that he was able to have the same effect on Chris. This awareness, and the feelings it brought, were new to him, and he both liked and feared what he was feeling.

"Now who's the asshole?" David asked, smiling and shaking his head.

"What? Why? I just gave you something else to be proud of." Chris lifted his goggles to wipe the tears of laughter from his eyes.

"You're funny," David said, smiling. "You don't do so bad yourself, you know." He hesitated. "I can't believe you didn't bring the condoms."

Lies That Bind

Chris turned his head, looked at David, and shrugged. "You know we really don't have to use them," David pleaded. "Can't we just forget them?"

"No. Not until I get retested. You know what they said."

"Come on, Chris. You said she said she tested negative. And you said you always used condoms, anyway."

"Not for oral sex we didn't," Chris reminded him. "You *know* you're negative. Your test results cover you because you haven't done anything with anyone since..."

"Three years ago," David said, not wanting to be reminded of Derek. Chris and David were having oral sex, but Chris refused the exchange of fluids until they both were sure they were HIV negative. Unlike David, though, Chris had not yet been willing to allow himself to be anally penetrated, even with a condom. "After I get tested again. It has to be six months. Besides, we can't do that here. Someone will hear us."

"No, someone will hear *you*," David said, smiling. "Then, no more condoms, right? No more worry about oral sex and..."

Chris interrupted, "As long as we agree that if we ever do it with someone else we promise to tell the other."

David felt his stomach sinking. His head fell forward; his mouth fell into a frown. The thought of Chris sharing himself with someone else scared him.

"What?" Chris asked, nudging David. David looked away. "What? David, it's something we have to talk about if we're not going to use condoms."

"I guess. But," he hesitated. "Are you going to?"

"No. But we have to talk about it. We just can't assume."

"I know," David agreed. "Chris, I would never do anything with someone if we are..." he stopped, searching for the right and least threatening word, "together." He did not want to move beyond where he felt Chris could go.

"Together?"

"Whatever you call it. I promise that if I do anything with someone else I'll tell you. Okay?"

"Okay. And I promise that if I do anything I'll tell you." Chris waited for David to respond. "David, I don't want to do anything with anyone else. Really," he said, touching David on the arm.

David looked back at him and smiled. "I know. I guess I'm happy you think I give such good head." They both started laughing again.

When they reached the top of the lift, David smiled and said, "Let's ski to the bottom."

The slopes had been groomed the night before and the runs were virgin. David and Chris decided not to wait for the others, and started down the mountain. The sun was bright, the temperature was close to twenty-five degrees, and it was, as David yelled to Chris, "Awesome!"

David typically skied ahead of Chris. He hardly moved on his skis. Chris watched him simply dig in an edge and start his turn. David always said he loved the experience of skiing. It felt competitive, but in the way he loved. He was competing against himself. The challenge he set was to improve himself. When he skied with others, he skied with them. When he skied with Chris, it was with a great deal of patience.

Skiing felt freeing to David. It was a way to escape what he thought of as the limitations of his body. Whatever failings, real or perceived, fears, disappointments, regrets that weighed on him, anxieties that threatened to overwhelm his mind were all left at the top of the mountain. David stepped out of the world and became one with his body. In the past, when he had surrendered himself to the mountain, he felt more at peace with himself than at any other time. Now, giving himself over to Chris in their teasing, banter, and lovemaking brought the same kind of comfort.

David thought of skiing as a metaphor whose meaning was now changing. Previously, it had been something he did solely for himself. It was the one thing he did that was not at the demand of another, or to satisfy or prove something to someone else. It was as he experienced sex; alone, a private experience.

Now, David explained to Chris, skiing is like great sex. You start by knowing where you are going, and the goal is always the same, but getting there is always different. You set your edges and let the skis take you. The hill has something to do with where you go and how you get there. The hill, your skis, and you come together in some unplanned way to move you to the next unknown turn. It all happens in the moment. There are thrills, excitement, pleasure, and surprises ahead, and each time it is something new. Even though you've been down this same run many times before, if you just let go, it will be a new and wild experience.

David parallel-skied with the ease of an expert. Chris fought to keep up, and fought to stay in control. David explained to him that skiing was simply a controlled fall, a concept that remained completely foreign to Chris. Chris fought against the downward pull of the mountain. Letting go was a sign of weakness, a prelude to danger. For Chris, not being in full control was courting disaster. But Chris was also feeling changed by David, and it scared him. It was in their lovemaking that he noticed it. He knew it grew out of his feelings of passion, when for a brief moment he would give in to David the way that David gave in to the mountain. Chris, like David, had worked hard to escape the limitations of his body, but, unlike David, he had not found it led to being one with it.

They skied from the top of Avalanche to Canyon Lodge without stopping. When they reached the bottom, David waved to Chris and started up the lift with Peter to meet with Adam and the others at the gondola. Chris found Julie and headed to Chair Sixteen, to the top of Avalanche.

"How is it up there?" Julie asked.

"Great, we took Avalanche, the snow is great. It was just groomed last night."

"You guys are lucky to have Father John," Julie said. "We have Derek's mom."

"What's she like?"

"I guess she's like Derek. Your parents didn't come this year?" Julie asked. "Your mom was our chaperone last year. She was great."

"Richard couldn't make it. We're going later in the season."

"Peter said you and David are sharing a room."

"Yeah. Father John assigned it that way." Chris seemed defensive.

"Don't tell him, but since he and Jeanine broke up, a couple of the girls on this trip have been talking about trying to hook up with him. Then there are the others, who are trying to catch your eye," Julie explained. Then she smiled and nudged Chris and said, "Are you and he available?"

"Are you asking me out?" Chris asked, nudging Julie, knowing that Peter and Julie were planning their engagement for this summer.

"You are such a flirt," Julie said.

Chris smiled. "David told me that Peter was going up to the cornice?"

"Yeah, with Adam and the rest of them. I told Peter I'd ski with you. He said, 'good choice.'"

"Peter's cool," Chris said, nodding his head. "He's a great friend."

"I think so." Julie smiled. "He gets weird sometimes, withdrawn, but he's wonderful."

"I know what you mean. But I guess we all do."

Julie agreed and added, "He has a temper, too. Sometimes it scares me, I mean he's never done anything, but he can go off."

"Yeah, I suppose, but not more than a lot of guys."

"You mean like yours. I hear you have one, too."

Chris shrugged. He was surprised to hear that she thought of him as having a temper. "Who told you I have a temper?"

Julie laughed. "Don't worry about it. Everyone loves you."

"Well, I really like Peter. I guess it's weird that he and I are going to be co-captains of the baseball team. I'm not sure it's because they love us as much as because they worry we'd kick their ass," Chris said, laughing. He liked the idea of being thought of as likable tough guys. "Peter is cool."

"He thinks you are, too. You and David are pretty tight, aren't you?"

"What do you mean?" Chris asked.

Julie explained, "He's so different from you. He never gets angry. If I had parents who treated me the way his do I'd be beating the shit out of everyone." Chris nodded. "Did you know that I had a crush on him before I was with Peter?"

"Really? No, I didn't know that."

"Yeah. But he said he just wanted to be friends." She sat silently. "You know a lot of guys keep their distance from him, they don't know what to make of him, but you just hang in there. It's cool, I love David a lot."

Chris nodded as anxiety began to grip his stomach. He calmly tried to explain, "I was pretty down when I moved here from New York and went to school at Saint Patrick's." At the same time he spoke, his stomach churned. *I wonder what she meant by that.* "David always included me in everything. Like skiing." Chris's mind started to race, *Guys don't know what to make of David.* "He was just always reaching out, even when I'd tell him to go away." *I wonder if they wonder what to make of David and me.* "So, I think of his down times as just part of who he is." Chris smiled as his anxiety continued to grow.

"You're such a loyal friend. People know that about you, Chris," Julie said. Chris tried concentrating on the beautiful view of the Sierras. "You know, Peter and David used to be really good friends when we were in elementary school. Their parents were pretty good friends, too. Then Peter's parents got a divorce, and Mr. Jarrett wouldn't have anything to do with either of them, and stopped David from hanging around with Peter. I mean, Peter and David still stayed friends, but I guess things weren't the same."

"Really, I didn't know that," Chris said, feeling calmer.

"Yeah. Did you know that they used to live next door to me? I guess it was about eight or nine years ago. My parents used to know them, too, but my mom really didn't like Mr. Jarrett. When they had their third kid they moved to a bigger house. Where they live now. My mom was glad to see them go, but she loves David. David always came over to our house to visit, he still does." Julie turned and whispered as though she was telling some dark secret. "My mom used to say she wanted to adopt him. I think she'd marry him if she could," Julie laughed.

"My mom feels the same way. Probably a lot of parents do."

"You know, Cathy hates David," Julie said laughingly.

"Really? Why are you laughing?"

"I hate that air-head bitch. She's such a phony, and she's telling everyone that David broke you two up, and that he's gay."

"That's just not true. I broke us up," Chris said. Now, he was feeling trapped on the lift. His anxiety began to feel uncontrollable. He feared that it would soon betray him. The ground seemed to be getting further away. The end of the lift seemed nowhere in sight. He thought that there would be a day when other people knew he was gay, but he never imagined how that day would come to pass. He began to break out into a sweat. He was feeling claustrophobic.

"You're not going to go the rest of the year without a girlfriend, are you?" Julie asked. "You're our school president, you'll probably be prom king. You can't go alone."

"Actually, I think I am. You know, I'm going to Columbia," Chris said as though that explained everything.

"Yes. That's so exciting. They took you on early acceptance. And David applied to Columbia and NYU, too."

"He's almost guaranteed NYU, but we think it would be cool if we both went to Columbia. If he goes to Columbia we might live in the dorms as roommates. If he goes to NYU then we'll get an apartment. Columbia has a great school of architecture." He heard himself rambling. Then, changing the subject he said, "I heard Peter got early acceptance to Berkeley."

"Yeah. I'm hoping to get in, too. If I don't, he's going to transfer his acceptance to whatever UC campus I'm accepted to." There was a long silence. Chris was desperate to reach the top of the lift. "You're a sweetheart, Chris. David is lucky to have you."

Chris was beginning to get queasy, but felt a wave of relief as they reached the top of the lift.

Later that morning they met up with David and Peter, and the four of them had lunch. The others were still on the mountain. When Julie asked David and Chris to join her and Peter for the rest of the afternoon, David tried to explain that Chris and he were going off alone. Chris agreed that they should ski with Peter and Julie. Chris was sure Julie had guessed what was going on between them. It weighed heavily on his mind all afternoon. Each time David moved toward him, Chris pulled away.

Remarkably, the weather on their second day of skiing was better than the first. It snowed during the evening, but cleared at around eight that morning, just in time for them to head for Canyon Lodge. It seemed that half the people in line for lift tickets were Sacred Heart students. Chris even noticed some boys and girls that he thought were Sacred Heart Middle School students.

Julie and Peter met up with Chris and David in the lift ticket line, and asked what their plans were for the day. Julie was going to ski with "the girls," but she wanted to get together for lunch. Peter was heading out to the other side of the mountain and David agreed to accompany him, but this time Chris promised David that they would ski alone in the afternoon. Chris was going to ski with Kyle and Gary, two guys from the baseball team. After skiing most of the morning with them, he took off and headed toward Chair Sixteen. When he moved to the front of the line another skier joined him. As he made himself comfortable on the lift, and put his poles under his right leg so he could have his hands free to adjust his goggles and cap, the skier sitting next to him started a conversation.

"Hey, I didn't see you yesterday. Where did you ski?" It was Jack Payden. He put his hand on Chris's upper thigh.

"Get your hand off my leg," Chris said, pushing his hand away.

"Relax."

"Look, I don't have to relax," Chris said.

"Sorry," Jack said. "How have you been doing?"

"With what?"

"Skiing. How have you been doing?" Jack asked seductively.

"Fine," Chris said. As far as Chris could remember this was one of two or three times since that night that in the tent that Chris had been stuck alone with Jack.

"You up here with Derek, David, and Peter?"

"Along with others. Yeah."

"They're good skiers. They've been skiing for years. I used to ski with them when they were in middle school."

"Who are you up here with?" Chris asked. He felt himself getting angrier. Pressure was building in his jaw muscles, and his teeth were clenched.

"Bunch of kids from the middle school. Eighth graders." Jack said, as he turned to face Chris.

Lies That Bind

"Your favorite age, isn't it?" Chris said. Silence. Chris tried to gauge the distance to the end of the lift.

"You're still a little shit, aren't you?"

Chris's stomach tightened as he realized what had just happened. "Just how many kids have you diddled with, Jack?" Chris asked contemptuously.

"Diddled with? Just you, Chris."

"Somehow I doubt that." Chris's face burned with emotion. "I bet I can name the guys in my class that you diddled." Chris could hardly believe what was suddenly becoming clear to him.

"Yeah, and how many of them have you had?" Again there was that painful silence. Again, Jack spoke. "You wanted it, you still do, so drop the attitude." Jack leaned in toward Chris. "You were easy, Chris, you were almost too easy," he whispered, sitting so that he was able to stare at the side of Chris's head. He reached over and put his arm around Chris's shoulder. "It takes a lot of work to get in a boys pants. Well, except when he wants it. You wanted it."

"You bastard. I trusted you." Chris's heart was pounding and his grip around his ski poles tightened. He was grinding his teeth. "Take your arm down or I'll break it," Chris said, turning to face Jack as he spoke through his teeth. Jack removed his arm from around Chris's shoulder and just laughed. "What the fuck do you mean 'I was easy?'" Chris demanded.

"You wanted it. You never even blinked. I was always surprised you didn't come back for more. I would have bet you would have."

"Do they usually, *Jack*?"

"I just figured you must have found it some place else. Maybe your friend Jarrett," Jack said, in a calm and knowing tone. "I could see that David was always hot for you. But you know that, don't you, Chris?"

"Leave him out of this," Chris said, trying to control his anger.

"He's got a pretty crazy father, doesn't he?"

"It's a long way down, Jack. You fuck with me or David and you'll take a fall." They were turned to face each other. Both of their faces were frozen as they spoke.

"Don't threaten me, you little shit. Christopher Bellesano. Star baseball player," Jack said, moving his hand as if he was reading a newspaper headline. "Cocksucker." He laughed, then with a sneer he said, "If you had the nuts to say anything you would have. You got what you wanted."

"Yeah, and you didn't, if I remember correctly," Chris said with hatred.

"Who the fuck do you think would listen to you after all this time."

"Okay, look," Chris said, giving Jack a punch to his arm. "Let me put it to you simply. I have a grandfather who is Sicilian," Chris lied, "and he has friends. You know what I mean? You stupid fuck." Chris's voice was quaking. "If you think I would be stupid enough to get into it with you at school, you're stupider than you are perverted. All I'd have to do is tell my grandfather that you did me when I was twelve. And what do you think he'd do? He'd make a few calls to those friends of his and they'd pay you a visit." Chris's growled with rage. "You fuck with me, or you fuck with David, and I'll make the call and that's no threat, it is a promise." Chris had come to love that line. "It is a fucking promise, you bastard," Chris shouted, poking his finger into Jack's arm over and over again as he shouted.

"Okay. So let's just back up here and calm the fuck down."

"Stay out of my face, and stay away from David. I swear Jack, you fuck with either of us and I'll take you down. You bastard." Chris shouted and pushed at Jack. Chris thought that if he could punch Jack in the face, he would.

"I'm sorry, really. Let's just forget we met today. Hey, is that David over there waving?" Jack said, as they neared the top of the lift.

"Just go away, Jack. Just go the fuck away." When Chris and Jack reached the top of the lift they skied off in different directions.

"Is that Jack Payden?" David asked.

"Yeah." Chris was shaking. He had successfully avoided Jack for years. Whenever he had had the misfortune to be left alone with Jack, Peter always seemed to show up. During that time, Peter had hung close by and occupied Chris's space and time, as if he was protecting him.

When Chris had entered Sacred Heart, and was qualifying for Eagle Scouts, there had been several occasions when he had to interact with Jack, but there had always been someone around, and neither had dared make any reference to what happened. It wasn't until today that Chris realized how angry he was at Jack. Prior to this meeting, his anger had always been directed at himself. After all, as Father O'Brien had said, he must have wanted it to happen. Then it was easy to assume that not only had he wanted it to happen, but that he had made it happen. In Chris's mind, Jack had been the victim of Chris's desire. Hearing what Jack had to say, and realizing that Jack had had sex with other kids, gave his anger a new direction.

He skied with David, but ignored him. When they arrived at the main lodge and sat down for lunch, David realized what a bad mood Chris was

Lies That Bind

in. When he asked what was bothering him, Chris asked to be left alone for a few minutes. "Can we just sit here and eat lunch and not speak? I just need to be quiet for a few more minutes."

"Sure, whatever you need." David said, apologetically. Neither of them said a word throughout lunch. David was good at giving Chris what he needed; especially, when he looked so angry.

There were others, I never thought he'd done it with others. Chris stared down at his lunch, which consisted of a hamburger, fries, and a coke that David had bought for him while he held their places at the table. *Damn, and I bet he did it to Derek that night he moved Derek into his tent.* Chris looked over at David, who glanced back. *Fuck, I bet he did it to David, too. Shit, did it to David, did it to Derek, he did it* to *me, not with me. Why didn't I ever think he did it to anyone else?* Chris began to feel himself breaking into a sweat as he suffered through the beginnings of a downward spiral. *Why didn't I ever realize that this was done* to *me? Why did I think that I made it happen? He's a child molester.* His head began to swim and each bite of his lunch began to weigh heavily in his stomach. *If he is a fucking child molester, then I was molested.* He looked up at David and wondered if he was also a victim. The thought of being a victim began to frighten him, but he did not know why. He noticed his hand trembling and knew what was about to happen. He thought of the movie *Alien*, when everyone was sitting around the table and the alien that had been incubating in Executive Officer Kane burst from his chest. That was what he was feeling like.

"David, stay here, I have to go to the bathroom. Wait here for me," Chris said.

"Are you okay? You don't look good," David said. "You're white."

"No shit, I was born that way. It's something I ate. Wait here."

Chris went to the men's room. He knew how to stop the saliva from flowing. He'd done this before. He put his index finger deep into his throat and vomited. Five minutes later he rejoined David at the lunch table and said he was fine.

"Whatever was bothering me I just threw up. I feel fine. It must have been something I ate." And, miraculously, he did feel fine. All that was bothering him was vomited out. "I just need something to drink, something to get rid of the taste in my mouth," Chris said, as he drank down the rest of his coke.

When David was finished with his lunch they both made their way through the crowd of people standing around waiting to find a place to sit for lunch. As they put on their skis David said, "Just tell me if I did something wrong."

"You didn't do anything wrong. You did everything right," Chris said, putting his hand on the top of David's head and shaking it. "Let's ski." Chris pushed off and skied toward the lift.

David caught up with him and said, "Come up to the cornice with me." Chris turned and stared at him for a moment and then said, "Okay."

"Really, just like that. I thought you'd say no."

"You'll take it easy, won't you?"

"Of course." They skied out of line for the chair lift that would take them up to the top of Broadway, and started over toward the gondolas. The first gondola went to mid-mountain. There they would have to take another gondola that would carry them to the top of the mountain. "Are you nervous?" David asked as they removed their skis and joined the line for the gondola.

"Yeah, last year when I went up there I almost got blown off the top of the mountain, and it was tough going."

"You'll do fine. The weather is great. And there isn't much wind up there today. And the snow is great, too."

The gondolas usually held four people comfortably, but David had a plan. "Watch this, follow me. We'll get a gondola for ourselves, just follow me." When David got to the front of the line he dropped his skis and poles on the ground and then pushed Chris ahead of himself. Chris then put his skis in the brackets on the gondola door and jumped in as it continued through the station. David blocked the line until the gondola was almost at the end of the walkway and then threw his skis in the rack and jumped in the gondola. The group behind him opted for the next gondola.

"Smooth," Chris said with a smile, as David sat down next to him.

"I've been skiing here for years." David reached over and poked Chris in the side and said, "Now we can make out." He was only half kidding. David had learned that one way to help Chris out of one of his bad moods was to tease him. And when they were in public, one part of that teasing was to poke and push at him. This was all new to David. Before his trip to New York, touching people had always been difficult.

"You seem in a little better mood now. Are you sure I didn't do something wrong?" David asked, touching Chris's leg. Chris noticed that when he and David were alone, David nervously made efforts to be more demonstrative. When they rode in the car, David would put his hand on

Lies That Bind

Chris's leg. The first time he did Chris noticed how tentative David was. He decided not to comment, but continued talking, and then decided to put his hand on top of David's.

"Just because I am in a bad mood doesn't mean that you fucked up," Chris answered.

"Did something happen with Jack?"

"What do you mean?"

"Well, you two rode up together and I know he saw me, and he just skied off, and you looked pretty upset from then on."

"David, I really don't want to talk about Jack," Chris answered, as he took off his gloves and unzipped his jacket.

"Okay, sorry." They sat silently for a while. David stared at Chris. Being in love with Chris scared him. Although their passion for each other was obvious, neither of them ever talked about being in love. "What are you thinking about?" David asked.

"Father John," Chris answered.

"What about him?"

"I don't know. He's just a great guy."

"You mean priest," David said.

"Same thing. I was thinking that it's too bad he's a priest."

"Why?"

"Don't you think he'd be such a great dad to have?"

"Wow, I've never thought about that."

Chris turned a looked at David. "Imagine what your life would be like if he were your dad."

David looked stunned. "Wow. My life would be so different."

They arrived at mid-mountain. They made their way onto the next gondola, which they did not have to share with anyone else. They sat silently for a time, staring at the scenery.

David asked nervously, "You think that Father John ever, I mean you talk to him about a lot of stuff, but, well, have you ever mentioned anything?"

"About us, you mean?"

"Yeah, I mean he is my confessor, too, and, well, I've never…but sometimes I think he wonders, but then I don't know."

"I've told him about my feelings and well…yes, I told him, I told him about me and Cathy, but I never mentioned her name, and then, well," Chris hesitated, "I told him about us but I never mention your name either. So, yeah, he knows, but he doesn't know that it's you."

""Shit, Sano." Although others had tried, David was the only person Chris allowed to cut his name in two and call him Sano. "You told him that you're having sex with a guy? What did he say?" David asked nervously. He looked panicked.

"Well, he didn't throw any stones."

"What did he say?"

"Nothing, really. He just asked some questions and stuff."

"Questions? Like what?"

"Is this guy your age? Are you being safe? Other stuff like that."

"Oh wow, how can I look him in the eyes?"

"I shouldn't have told you," Chris said with some annoyance.

"I just think I'm going to freak when I see him tonight."

Chris shrugged his shoulders and said, "Well, then he'll know it's you for sure won't he? Look David, I think you could talk to him. You should talk to him. You should talk to someone."

"I do talk to him about some stuff. Besides, I have you to talk to."

"Yeah, but besides me. I'm glad I decided to trust him." Chris looked out the window of the gondola, admiring the view. He realized how much he had relaxed since his conversation with Jack. He looked at David, and wondered if Jack had molested him too. He squeezed David's hand.

"You're the only person I trust," David admitted.

"There you go. In September you didn't trust me, and I bet there are still things you hold to yourself, and that's okay. I don't tell you everything."

As they arrived at the top of the mountain and exited the gondola, David was still asking Chris what he wasn't telling him. Chris just laughed. He liked teasing David.

They skied the cornice, which was rated "expert only." Eventually, David convinced Chris to try a run called Climax, and then Upper Dry Creek, which were both double black diamonds. Finally, Chris had had enough, and they headed back toward Canyon Lodge. They took the long way back. They headed down to the bottom of the mountain, and then they took a chair lift up to mid-mountain and skied down again, each time heading closer to Canyon Lodge. And each time they took another lift, they were able to sit alone together, so that their conversations could continue. This was proving to be the only time they had alone.

"You did great up there. How did it feel?" David asked.

"It felt good. I'd say I was out of control only half of the time," Chris said, smiling.

Lies That Bind

"Really, you looked confident, but then you always look confident," David said.

"Yeah, I felt relaxed."

"I don't want you to get to be too good," David said, grabbing Chris. leg. "So what did Jack want?" David's curiosity was being fueled by Chris's refusal to talk about what had put him in such a bad mood.

"David, just leave it alone. I really don't know what the fuck he wanted and I don't care," Chris said, as he turned and looked away.

"I had a talk with Derek. I told him to look for someone else to work the exams for him after the finals," David said.

"What did he say?" Chris asked, turning to look at David's face.

"He said he didn't want to take any chances by asking someone else."

"Think he'll cut you off if you don't help him?" This was the first time since the night at David's house that either of them had mentioned anything about David's drug use.

"I stopped," David said, looking at Chris and nudging him with his shoulder.

"Really, when?" Chris was surprised.

"The night you broke into my backyard and made me your boyfriend."

"Really? I didn't know that," Chris said, as he poked at David. "And it's girlfriend," Chris added and started to laugh.

"I wanted to see if I could do it before I told you, girlfriend."

"Was it tough?"

"The tough part was wondering if I could, doing it wasn't that tough."

"What do you do when you can't sleep?"

"I've been sleeping a lot better lately, but when I can't, I write. At first it was hard, really hard. I actually went outside and sat with the bowl in my hand, but then I'd go back in and write."

"Where did you get the idea to write?"

"Father John." David said.

"Really. So you do talk to him."

"Well, yeah, about that. I mean I told him that I was smoking and that I wanted to stop, so we talked about it." Chris was surprised to see that David began to cry.

"Hey, what's wrong? David?"

"I don't know. I've never talked to anyone about stuff. I've always been too afraid. It felt easier after, well…" David continued to cry.

"David, what's wrong?"

"Nothing. Well, I mean I've talked to him before, but because I had to, you know, in confession. I talked to him about my dad and stuff. But after that night with you, I wanted to stop smoking." Chris reached over and put his arm around David and patted his shoulder. "So, I went to his office and, well, I don't know why, I just felt like it was something I didn't want to do anymore. So, I told him about it. I was really scared. I thought I was going to throw up. But, after I had told you I guess I wasn't too scared to tell him. I was shocked when it was all over. Shocked that I was able to tell him and shocked that he was so helpful. He even said that I might not be able to stop for a while, that I should give it time. I mean he was so Father John about it, you know?" Chris knew exactly what David meant. Father John always had this way of being warm, concerned, strong, and trustworthy. "He said I should set a goal of two or three months. I figured that would work. So I decided to stop for a week first and then smoke and then stop for two weeks. You know, ease off. But when the week was over I decided that I wasn't going to get high anymore." David turned to Chris and smiled, but there were still tears in his eyes.

"He suggested that I find something else to do. I thought of my drawing, and he said that I should try something new, something challenging. Writing is something I've always wanted to do, but felt like I couldn't. So he thought that was a good idea," David said, wiping his running nose with his glove.

"That is so cool. I mean, that you talked to him."

"Yeah, but I can't believe you talk to him about sex," David said, shaking his head.

"He didn't get on my case. What do you write?"

"Poems, bad poems. Stories. Stuff about my feelings."

"Poems about me?" Chris asked with a smile, as he reached over and shook David by the shoulder.

"Well, of course. But I don't mention your name," David said, smiling and shrugging his shoulders. "And other things."

"Can I read some of what you've written?"

David hesitated. "Sure, when I can hear you play your guitar and sing," he said, laughing.

Chris laughed too, and then hit David on the back of the head. "Smart-ass. So I get to read your poems about me when we get to New York."

"Okay, when we get to New York."

Soon they were mid-mountain again and skiing down Stump Alley to the Mill Café, where they decided to stop and use the bathroom.

Lies That Bind

"Let's get a candy bar," David said. "My treat."

"Okay, Sneakers. And get some water, too. I'll find us a table outside."

It took a while for David to return, but when he did he was carrying a large order of French fries, two Snickers candy bars, and two bottles of water. Chris smiled. French fries were his favorite non-Italian food. As they began eating the fries, Chris noticed that David was being quiet. "What?" David shrugged. "Okay, what is it?"

"No, I was just thinking about something while I was in line." Chris stared at him. "When did you think you might be gay, or know that you were?"

"What do you mean?"

"Well, when did you first understand that you were different from everyone else? You know."

Chris continued to stare at David and then sighed. "I guess I was about nine or ten, maybe. I mean, I knew I was a sissy before that, but I didn't know that it had to do with being gay."

"What do you mean, you knew you were a sissy?"

"My dad always called me a sissy."

"No way. You weren't a sissy," David said.

"I was a skinny kid who cried a lot and who was scared a lot, and he said I was a sissy."

"You a sissy? Damn. It's hard to imagine."

"Yeah, well, imagine it. He used to say it a lot. But, I never thought it meant being gay."

"So, when did you know?"

"My friend Larry told me that a friend of ours would show us her private parts," Chris said, "if we would show her ours. He said we could go to her house and take our clothes off and look and touch each other's private parts. I knew we weren't supposed to do it, but it sounded exciting, so I said okay. We went to her house and we took our clothes off. We took turns lying on the floor. The girl went first. Larry and I looked, and she let us touch her there. I noticed that Larry had a stiffy. I didn't. Larry went next. When he lay down, she and I looked at his erect penis. First she touched it, and then I did. When I touched it, my penis got hard. I remember that when I lay down all I could think about was that Larry was going to touch my dick and that I was so excited that he was looking at it."

"Wow. So then you knew?"

"Not really. I mean I didn't know until maybe a month later when I heard someone talking about hating fags and queers, and calling then

226

cocksuckers. I remember hearing that and then all of a sudden it all came together. I remember this sick feeling in my stomach. Me, the sissy-boy, excited by Larry's penis and wanting to see it and touch it again, and wanting him to touch mine. I knew they were talking about me. That was the first time I knew why my dad hated me so much, too."

"Man, that's so fucked up," David said, shaking his head.

"When did you know?"

"When did I think I was, or when did I know I was?" David asked.

"Both."

"I guess kind of the same as you, except maybe younger."

"What happened?"

"Peter and I were friends in first grade. We used to sleep over at each other's houses. One time when I was at his house, his mom told us to take a shower. I got in and then he got in after me. It was like nothing to him. I remember I couldn't stop looking at his penis. I remember I wanted to touch it. After that, I always wanted to sleep over at his house and I wanted to take a shower with him. I guess, looking back, I started thinking then that I might be. But I didn't know until later."

"When?"

"Don't make fun of me, okay?"

"I won't."

"The summer we started hanging out. You know, when we did that work for Father John before we started high school. I really knew then. I had the biggest crush on you. I loved swimming naked with you, but I was always so scared I would bone up." Chris laughed. "Maybe it was good that I was so nervous."

"Why?"

"You can't get wood if you're anxious. Right?" David said, laughing.

"I guess you're not anxious anymore," Chris said, smiling. "You know, I was attracted to you, too."

"Now I guess I figured you might have been, but then I never thought you were. I was sure if you knew you'd never be my friend."

Chris had had all he could tolerate of admitting to his feelings. "Are you done? I don't want to get back too later."

"Yeah, let's go."

After they put on their skis they headed for Goldrush, which brought them up again to mid-mountain, but closer to Canyon Lodge.

"Can I ask you something personal?" David asked once they were comfortable on the lift.

Lies That Bind

"Another question? What's with you today?" Chris asked, poking David. David shrugged and turned away, looking dejected. "Go ahead and ask, but I might not answer."

"It's about you and your father. I thought of it when you talked about him calling you a sissy."

Chris took a long look at David and then asked, "What about him?"

"Well, I remember that sometime last spring you bought him a birthday present. I remember we went to the mall and bought him a shirt."

"Yeah, so what?"

"You bought him a Christmas gift, too. Right? Well, I was wondering if you ever hear from him? Does he ever send you a gift? You never say." David could see that Chris was getting annoyed.

"He never writes, and no, he doesn't send gifts."

"That's what I thought. So why do you send gifts?"

Chris looked away. Neither of them spoke, then Chris looked at David and sighed. "My mom and my grandparents believe that it is important that I show him respect. When I send my grandparents my school pictures each year, my grandmother always calls and tells me that I'm beautiful." David interrupted with a laugh, and Chris gave him the finger. "And then she asks if I sent my father pictures."

"Do you?" David asked.

"Yeah. Why are you asking?" Chris was now clearly annoyed.

"Does it bother you that he doesn't send you anything? How do you even know he's alive?"

"I just don't think about it." Chris shook his head. "No, he never writes, so there's really no way to know. I guess he could be dead, and his wife could be giving the stuff to someone. But it never comes back, so someone is getting it."

"Are you going to send him an invitation to your graduation?"

"I hadn't thought about it. I don't think he'd ever come." Chris did not want to be talking about Frank. "Why are you asking all this?"

"Just thinking about when I leave. I would want to see my mom and brothers and know how they are doing, but I don't think I would care if I ever saw my father again. Sometimes the idea of never having to deal with him again seems so wonderful, and then sometimes it seems really sad." David continued to look at Chris, who continued to look away.

"I just send him stuff. I write him letters and tell him what I'm doing and how things are going for me. I mail them and then forget it," Chris said, looking away.

"Yeah, but how does it make you feel inside?" David asked. Chris did not answer. David pressed on, "Do you ever think about him when you play your guitar?"

Chris turned and looked at David and said, "I don't want to talk about this anymore."

"Okay," David said defensively. They sat for a while in silence. David was feeling guilty about upsetting Chris. "I can't believe it's going to happen. Chris, I am so excited, sometimes I can't sleep because I get so excited."

"About what?" Chris was still annoyed.

"Us being roommates and living in New York. I used to not be able to sleep because I was anxious. Sometimes I'm still anxious, but sometimes I'm just so happy and..." David's voice began to crack, and Chris turned to look at him. "...excited that I don't know what to do. Chris, I don't want to be beaten anymore. I don't want to be scared, either."

Chris reached over, pulling David closer to him. "It's going to be great. I get excited thinking about it, too." They sat there silently for a few minutes and watched as they moved closer to the top of the mountain.

David started laughing and said, "I have a woody."

"You always have a boner, dude."

"I can't help it. When you touch me and stuff I just get so turned on."

"Damn, now I'm getting one, too," Chris said, laughing.

After getting off the lift, David skied over to Chris and shouted, "Can you ski with a woody?"

"Shut up," Chris said, pushing him away and looking around to see if anyone heard.

"I've never skied with a boner. Let's go," David said, laughing.

"You're on," Chris said, as he started down the hill.

David caught up to him and shouted, "Don't fall and break anything."

* * * * *

"Chris, yesterday you said that you didn't see yourself as a victim in what happened to you, but today you tell me about an otherwise wonderful weekend when it did occur to you that you had been victimized."

Chris nodded and said, "Yeah, but then I realized that I hadn't been."

I was about to challenge him, but I noticed that there had been a noticeable change in his demeanor, and rather than make a point, I decided to go where he wanted. "Tell me more."

"You said I could disagree with you, that I don't have to make your opinion of me my opinion of me. Right?" Chris asked.

Lies That Bind

I wanted to smile, but at the same time I did want him to understand the seriousness of what had happened to him. Perhaps his denial, for the time being, was more important than my making a point.

Chris asked, "Can I explain how I see it?"

"Of course, please," I said.

"If he was able to get inside me, then I think I would say he victimized me. But he didn't. If he did, it would have been different. It would have been like when my father talked me onto the slide. I really didn't want to go down the slide or be in the pool with him, but I gave in to him. That's when I was a victim. If I had let Jack do what he wanted even though I didn't want him to do it, then I would have been victimized."

"So then, how do you understand what happened to you?"

Chris sighed, "I guess, well, I mean, I don't know how to say it."

"Just say whatever comes to mind. Think out loud. You can change it later."

"I just get so confused with it all." Chris's head hung down to his chest. He sighed. "I thought about having sex with a guy before this happened with Jack. I thought about it a lot." He sat back and pushed his hair out of his eyes. "I think I might have even thought about Jack." He shrugged and glanced at me. "So I was wanting to have sex."

"That's not unusual for an adolescent. You know that, don't you?" I asked, trying to calm his anxieties.

"With a guy?" he barked.

"With someone that they are attracted to."

"When it first started with him I was surprised, curious." His hands moved as his voice began to betray his anger. His hand gestures seemed to signal his meaning and moved toward his genitals as he said, "Excited, I mean, I was hard." He dropped his head again. "I had never touched anyone like that before. No one had ever touched me like that." He frowned and shook his head.

"What? Tell me."

"It sounds so lame."

"What does?"

"It was the first time, and I will always remember it because it was the first time, and I hate it. That sounds so stupid to me."

"Your first time should be a positive experience." I knew I was pushing him. Clearly this was a point of tension. "Instead, you are marked with an assault." He shook his head. I could see his jaw was clenched. "If this is going to be a conversation, Chris, you are going to have to respond. If you can."

He glared at me. "It wasn't an assault. I started it. Yeah, I wanted it to stop, and yeah, I wish I hadn't started it, but I did. I let it go on, and then when I didn't want to do anything more," his hand moved more freely as his anger filled his body, "and I knew how to stop it."

"And you did stop it."

"Exactly!" Chris said. "See what I mean? I mean, we jerked each other off. Then when I woke up and he was sucking me I didn't want it, but I didn't stop it. I was hard and…"

"And it felt good."

"Exactly. And it felt good. Then I had to do it to him and I didn't want to, but I just couldn't say no. Then, the next morning, finally I did say no."

"When you were going to be penetrated." He nodded. I could see his anger boiling under his skin. It radiated.

"I wasn't a victim. I did it even though I didn't want to do it. He didn't make me do anything. He stopped when I said stop. So…"

"Is all this anger at yourself?"

"I hate him, but I don't know why. So, yes. I am angry at me."

"You're looking like you want to scream." He turned his head and stared at me. His eyes were piercing, his jaw muscles were bulging. Then the life seemed to drain from his body. His shoulders slumped. "What happened?" I asked.

He shook his head and sighed, "It's all my fault."

"Chris, do you get that he betrayed your trust?"

He shrugged. "I just don't think you understand what I am saying."

"Okay, well, let me run through this and you tell me where I'm wrong." I summarized all that happened to him with Jack, focusing on the action.

He listened to me attentively and nodded. "Right, I did know how to stop him, you see? It isn't that I didn't know how to stop him, it's that I was too afraid to stop him. I was being a coward."

"But Chris, you really didn't stop him."

"Yes, I did!"

"Chris, he forced you into oral sex. Didn't he?" Chris stared. His face was bright red. "What are you feeling?"

"Like I want to hit something."
"Something or someone?"
"I'm just angry."
"You gave in to him after he agreed not to penetrate you. My guess is that you did it out of guilt, embarrassment, shame, fear, a desire to have it end. Anything other than a desire to be sexually involved with Jack," I said calmly, though my jaw muscles ached from tension.
"I did it because I was scared. I didn't want him to be angry at me. That's what I was afraid of. I wanted him to like me." He sighed. "I did it because I wanted friends."
"You know Jack seduced you. My guess is that he was not asleep and you were. My guess is that he set you up to believe you were the initiator. Later, when the emotional and psychological backlash occurred, you became numb, that is until you talked to Father O'Brien."
"Yeah, then the storm. Maybe if I had never talked to him I would have been numb forever."
"Perhaps. But I doubt it. Besides, that would have been no solution either. Numbness isn't a way to live your life. How can you love if you're numb? You know, often, when people are sexually abused and go numb, they love the people they don't have sex with, and are numb or angry with the people they have sex with."
"Sounds fucked up."
We both sat silently for a while. I felt a need to provide him with some kind of metaphor to contain his experience. One in which he was neither the perpetrator or the victim. But I had been stuck here before. "Perhaps, the distinction is the difference between a rape and a date rape. I don't want to lose the fact that you were twelve years old here. In a date rape, often the person who is raped trusted, liked, was attracted to the rapist. The rapist knows that, takes advantage of those feelings and attacks."
He shook his head.
"What?" I asked.
"Girls are date raped. Not guys."
"That's an anxiety-producing metaphor, isn't it?" He continued to shake his head. "Tell me."
"I don't know," he snapped at me. "It's not like a date rape, that's all I know."
"What is it like?"

"I don't know!" he said, throwing up his hands.

"Perhaps that's something you can think about."

He slouched and sighed. "I've been thinking about it for over four years. No, for all my life. It's just the same thing over and over again." Of course it was. He had fit this all into his world view. "Yes, but in your stories you are often the perpetrator. Perhaps you can look at it differently. Find a different metaphor, a different view of things." He continued to stare at me, but his face seemed to relax.

He nodded. "Okay, I will."

I was becoming aware of the time, and I wanted to get to the letter.

Chapter Thirteen

I GLANCED AT THE letter Diane had given to me. Earlier, I had set it down on the desk. Chris noticed me looking at it.

"My father," he said, wincing.

"At this time, you still did not know about your father's death?" I asked.

"He hadn't died yet. He died in March." He sighed and glanced toward me. "I got that letter in May, when we returned from a weekend in Palm Springs."

"I see." He fell silent. He dropped his head and rested it in his left hand. I decided to wait and see where he would go. His hair hung over his hand. There was a slight curl to his hair that I had not noticed before.

His head went back as he pushed the hair from his face. He looked at me and stared. He looked sullen. "That's when things started to get really, really bad." Chris said, shaking his head. His mouth turned downward and his stare returned to the floor. "You don't understand how much I hate myself for being a coward."

The girls and boys I see in treatment often move me emotionally. I admire their ability to survive as they do. This boy was doing everything he could to win the love of those he loved, all because of a father who could not love him for who he was. How tragic it is that the rejection of one person can eclipse the love of others. How deep a wound Frank must have left on Chris's heart.

"You can read the letter if you want." Chris reached across the desk and pushed it toward me.

I did not take the letter. I decided that I wanted him to read it to me. "What I am really interested in hearing, before you read it to me, is your thoughts about the letter."

He met my eyes, but this time he looked annoyed. "It's just a letter. I mean, she told me that he had cancer and that he knew for a while, that he got better, and then got sick again and died."

"That's all?"

He sighed, "Well, no. She said he was proud of me and loved me, and that he wished we had made up. Just stuff like that." Chris's color became chalky.

"You received the letter in May?"

"After a trip to Palm Springs with Richard, my mom, and David." Again, Chris seemed to disappear. Both of us sat, I was staring at him; he was staring into space.

"Where are you, Chris?"

"Wishing I could do things over." He sighed again and looked at me. "With my father. With David."

"What happened?"

* * * * *

The ski week ended too quickly. The semester was over, and this time both Chris and David earned straight A's. Richard and Diane always rewarded Chris by taking him and David skiing, but this year David's father said that he could not go. They were all very disappointed, especially Chris and David, since Richard and Diane always had them stay in a room of their own. Since the start of their relationship they had rarely had a chance to spend the entire night with each other. All they had were stolen moments in the back seat of Diane's Suburban, or the occasional weekend morning or afternoon when both Richard and Diane would go to a movie or play golf together.

The one time they were able to spend nights together was the weekend before finals. In the past, David had spent nights at Chris's house, but there had to be a good reason. David convinced his father that he and Chris would spend the weekend studying. Diane assured Paul that neither of the boys would be allowed to leave the house except on Sunday to attend mass. They spent most of the weekend locked in Chris's room.

They studied for hours, and also took breaks, during which they would get naked and go at each other ravenously. That Friday night was the first time they actually slept in the same bed. Chris, who had never been comfortable with any kind of intimacy, was surprised at how comfortable he was lying naked in David's arms. When he fell asleep they were spooning, with David across Chris's back, but later that night Chris awoke with his head on David's chest and his arm around David's waist. David had both his arms around Chris. He stared at his door, reassuring himself that it was locked. Diane trusted him to the point of never disturbing his privacy. He knew that no girl would ever be allowed to study in his room with the door closed, never mind spending the night. A wave of guilt washed over him. He considered moving from David's chest, but instead he closed his eyes, and immediately fell back to sleep. Since that weekend they had not been able to spend a night together.

Lies That Bind

It was the end of April when Richard asked Diane if she would like to go to Palm Springs for a weekend to celebrate their fifth wedding anniversary. When they discussed what they might do with Chris, Diane did not want to leave him home alone. Possibly Chris might stay with a friend, or a friend could stay with him. When they talked to him, he said David was the only friend he would consider. But he did not want to stay at David's house because of his father. Diane knew that Paul would never allow David to stay with Chris without adult supervision. So Diane called Paul and asked if David could accompany them to Palm Springs so that Chris would have company while Richard and Diane played golf and tennis.

Diane could hear by the tone of Paul's voice that he wanted to say no, but Diane was persistent. Paul finally agreed if, and only if, both David and Chris promised to get schoolwork done and attend church services Sunday morning. Diane agreed.

Richard made it clear to Chris that he wanted to be alone with Diane for the weekend, and that he had plans for a special dinner for her on Saturday night. He explained to Chris that he and David could eat their meals at the hotel restaurant or order room service, and that they could spend their free time at the pool. He also told Chris that he and Diane would not be attending mass Sunday morning, and that the hotel would arrange a ride to a church for them. Chris happily agreed. He and David would have a weekend to themselves.

The drive to Palm Springs took two hours. It was a Friday afternoon, and although they left right after the boys arrived home from school, traffic was heavy. When they arrived at the Doral Palm Springs Resort, Richard checked in and gave Chris the key to his and David's room. Richard and Diane's room was a poolside suite with a mountain view that also looked out onto the golf course. Their room was on the third floor and on the other side of the hotel. Chris waved to Richard as they entered the elevator and said, with a smile, "See you Sunday afternoon."

David could feel his heart beating as they followed the bellman down the hall toward their room. After Chris tipped the bellman and locked the door, David said, "I'm first in the shower." Chris nodded.

Minutes later, Chris joined him in the shower. "We've never done it in the shower," he said, running his hands along David's chest.

After their shower they put on the white terrycloth robes the hotel supplied and ordered room service. Richard told them they could order what they wanted. They were starved. They ordered steaks, French fries, salads, and dessert.

"That was a great steak. How was yours?" Chris asked, pulling the covers off one of the beds.

"Delicious, the chocolate cake was wonderful. Your cheese cake was good, too," David said.

"Did you eat all of it? I was saving it for later," Chris said as he removed his robe and stood naked facing David.

"Nah, I just had to taste it, though." David felt his face warm as he watched Chris walk naked across the room, take a taste of his cheesecake, and then return to the bed. Seeing Chris naked was nothing new for David. He saw him nude every day in the showers at school. But now, especially since they had become lovers, David did his best never to look at Chris while in the showers. He was too afraid he would become aroused. Sitting here, alone with him, he allowed himself to stare, and as he expected, he became fully erect. "You have such a great body," he said, feeling his cheeks burning.

Chris laughed. "Shut up, and come over here and give me a back rub."

"Sure, but you'll owe me." David jumped up, removed his robe, and threw it over the chair. He knelt straddling Chris's waist and sat on his buttocks. He loved the feel of Chris's body.

"Oh, and what will I owe you?"

"I'll tell you when we get to New York."

Chris half-turned his head to look up at David and smiled. "I talked to my grandfather about us staying with him this summer until we find an apartment. He was really excited. He said my grandmother has been making up the room we stayed in so we'll have a comfortable place to stay. I told him that we wanted to live on the upper West side in Manhattan so that I can take the train to Columbia and you can take the train to NYU. I asked him if he'd co-sign a rental agreement for us, and he said yes." Chris loved the feel of David's hands on his back. As he realized how much he was enjoying his massage he remembered that it had not been long ago that he would not allow anyone to massage him.

David said, "I can't wait to go. My parents want me here until a week before school starts, but fuggeddaboudit. How was that? I've been practicing."

"Keep practicing," Chris said, smiling. He thought about David sitting naked on him and felt his penis moving against the sheets. He delighted in the feeling. "I talked to my grandfather about us working in one of his stores. He said that wouldn't be a problem. He said that he'd have to put you in where he's working though, because you have a lot to learn." Chris laughed, "But he said, 'I'll teach him good.'" Then a wave of sadness and anxiety washed over him. He knew his grandfather would reject them both if he knew of their relationship. "He likes you," Chris added.

Chris felt David's erection slide across his buttock as David moved so as to massage his lower back. Chris responded with his own full arousal, but his sadness lingered. At times he wished he had not asked David to come to New York. If they were in separate cities Chris would be safe, and would not have to worry about anyone finding out about them. They could meet once in a while, someplace where no one knew them. Then he could be free to live in New York and make everyone happy by having a girlfriend, or making believe he did. As much as Chris wanted David in New York, his living there was going to create conflicts that Chris did not yet know how he would deal with.

"I like them, too. I can't wait," David said, as he dug his thumbs into the small of Chris's back. "I am so excited."

Chris reach around and grabbed David's erection and said, "I can tell."

David pulled at Chris's left hip and told him to roll over. When Chris did, David smiled as he saw Chris's erection and said, "I thought so."

"Is my massage over?" Chris asked, as he moved his arms up and put his hands behind his head. David stayed seated on Chris's legs and began to rub his hands up and down Chris's chest, then along his stomach. "Your navel ring is so hot. I'm going to get one when we get to New York."

Chris sat up, grabbed David by the shoulders and pulled him down on top of him. "Lie still. Don't say or do anything for a few minutes."

David lay there, resting his head on Chris's shoulder. Chris put both his arms around him. Neither of them moved. Chris relaxed under the weight of David's body. He wondered how something he enjoyed so much could scare him as much as it did. He ran his fingers up and down David's back. He could feel David's erection pushing against him. He smiled to himself, thinking of the news he was about to give David.

Chris took a handful of David's hair, pulled his head back so that he could look at his face, and then started to kiss him. David arched his hips back and forth, rubbing himself against Chris's stomach. He moaned loudly. Chris held David's head in place as they locked their mouths together. David sucked at Chris's lower lip. Then he took Chris's head in his hand and turned it to the side. Chris moaned as David began to lick his ear, bite his ear lobe, and then run his tongue and teeth down the side of Chris's neck. *David, I'm all yours,* Chris confessed to himself.

The sensation of David's body, hands, and mouth caressing his body began to ease Chris's worries. The voices that always instructed him in the art of lovemaking had disappeared months ago. Instead, he was now able to be lost in his passion. David's hands no longer moved shyly, and his body was no longer tentative in satisfying their desires. Chris delighted in David's strength, and in the push of his taking control of their lovemaking. Previously, David had limited himself to following Chris's lead. Chris also took pleasure in David surrendering to him, and in the way David's body finally relaxed under his. But then there were times like this, when David's strength signaled his desire for Chris to be still and be the object of David's lust.

David gently drew his tongue over Chris's nose, across his eyelids, and down his cheek, his hand tightly holding a length of Chris's hair. Chris's breathing was steady and deep. David turned Chris's head to face him, and for a brief moment their eyes met. David then began his descent, pressing his tongue down the length of Chris's neck, then down his chest to his navel. Then he ran his tongue around Chris's pierced navel. Chris's breath quickened as David's warm mouth closed around his penis. Chris's heels dug into the mattress as his back arched in pleasure.

Chris lay there, his body floating in sensation. He moved his fingers through David's hair. Chris opened his eyes to watch. Their eyes met. Chris pulled at David, moving him so that they could kiss. Their tongues met. Chris moved toward David's neck and gently bit down.

The room was silent, except for the sound of their breathing and occasional moans. They had established an unspoken rule that on several occasions David had almost violated. Once they started making love, seldom did either of them speak, and afterward neither of them would ever speak of how they felt about what they did.

"David," Chris sighed. David looked at him surprised. "I was tested again. I got the results." David pulled back and smiled. "It's all okay. So, if you don't want to use condoms we don't have to." David was speechless. He sat up straddling Chris's legs. "You'd better get the lube, though," he said smiling.

David opened the nightstand drawer where he had put the condoms and lube when they unpacked. He popped the top of the bottle of lube, squirted some onto his hand and then tossed the bottle onto the other bed. He reached for Chris' penis to apply the lube.

"No," Chris said.

David looked at him, "I thought..."

Lies That Bind

"Put it on you," Chris said, smiling.

"Really? Are you sure?" I mean you've never..."

"Just be careful. Go slow. Okay?"

"Of course," he said. His voice echoed his nervousness. David began to apply the lube to his erection. A pulse of energy passed through his body as he touched himself. When he was done he stared at his gooey hand, not knowing what to do. Chris pointed to the top sheet.

"I think I'm the one who's supposed to be nervous," Chris said, smiling. David leaned over and kissed him. He moved and lay down on top of him. Chris raised his legs, pulling his knees up to his chest, and then wrapped them around David.

David moaned, "Oh fuck, Chris, I..."

"Shhhh," Chris interrupted. "No more talking."

David had always found these silences suffocating, but had been afraid to make himself vulnerable. Tonight he could no longer contain his feelings. He gently pushed. Slowly he applied pressure as he felt himself entering Chris. He felt the tension in Chris's body build as he anticipated pain. They stared into each other's eyes.

Chris smiled. "Go ahead, it's okay."

David slowly began rocking his hips back and forth. With each motion forward, he moved deeper into Chris. "You okay?"

"I'm good. Don't worry." He pulled David to him and kissed him passionately.

David slowly started thrusting again. His breathing was loud. He grabbed a fistful of Chris's hair and moved his head so he could have access to Chris's neck and ear. He put his tongue into Chris's ear as the pace of his thrusting increased. Chris moaned in pleasure. David whispered, "I love you." David looked into Chris's eyes. "I'm in love with you bad, Chris."

Chris froze. He looked shocked, confused, scared; he seemed to disappear. David waited, hoping Chris would say something. Chris said nothing. David withdrew from Chris and sat back on his knees. "I guess I shouldn't have said anything."

Chris began to lower his legs and said, "I'm not sure what to say." Chris swallowed hard, looking into David's eyes. He knew what he was supposed to say; what David wanted him to say. David looked hurt. "I guess I don't know what that means."

"You don't know what 'I love you' means? You tell people that you love them," David said.

"Well, sure. I tell my grandparents, my mother. But that's different." Chris said, as he pulled back and sat up against the headboard. "I mean, I love you like that. You're my best friend ever. I mean, look at the way we are with each other. I've never done this with anyone else."

"You've never had sex with a guy before in your life?" David asked, having fully guessed the answer. He knew that Chris would not lie to him.

"I didn't say that. I said I've never had sex with a guy like I do with you." Chris's voice signaled his anxiety. "David, I've never had sex with anyone like I have with you. Like I was just having with you. Never!" He hesitated, searching for the right thing to say. "It never felt like this before. I never felt like I do when we are together."

"So, what is that feeling? What do you call it?"

"Wonderful. Passionate. Hot. Comfortable. I guess, more than any of that, I feel happy. I don't know." Chris waited for him to respond, but David just stared into space. "David, I don't have words for feeling the way you do. I don't understand feelings." Chris reached out and tried to pull David toward him. "Don't be sad, please. I…" Chris caught himself. *Wow, I almost said I love you.* "… care about you a lot." Chris could feel his palms sweating. "I've never really told that to someone who isn't family. I've never told someone I've had sex with that I loved them. You know, that I was in love with them. I don't know what that means."

"I wish I had never said anything. I really fucked things up now. This always happens," David said woefully, as he pulled further away from Chris.

"Damn it, David, why do you always think that you fucked things up? And this has never happened."

"Not with us…"

"With who, then?"

"Forget it," David said, as he came close to tears.

"Look, you didn't fuck anything up," Chris said, reaching out to David.

"It will never be the same. You'll want to pull away," David said as he himself abruptly pulled away from Chris.

Chris was becoming impatient, "David, fuck you. I am not Derek, okay. And who else are we talking about?"

David turned so that he was facing away from Chris. Chris moved closer to him. "David, talk to me. See, you're the one who's pulling away, not me, and I hate it when people do this to me." Chris felt himself getting

Lies That Bind

angry. It was the one feeling that Chris knew well. Other feelings remained a blur. "David, who else?" Chris asked again, while he shook David by the shoulder.

David turned and pushed Chris away from him. "Fuck you, Chris. Damn, you're making me so fucking angry." Chris was shocked; he had never seen David angry with him. "Why is it that when you don't want to talk about something, I say 'okay' and drop it, but when I say forget it, you keep asking?" David got up from the bed, walked across the room, and sat down in one of the armchairs.

"David, who else?" David folded his arms across his chest. "You know you look pretty funny sitting there pouting in the nude. Somehow, it just doesn't look convincing."

David looked down at his nude body and just shook his head. "You already know."

"Jack," Chris said without equivocation. "David, come here or I am coming there. It isn't fair that you do this."

"Yeah. He said something on the lift, didn't he?" David got up and moved back to the bed. He sat next to Chris, facing him. "He did it to you, too, didn't he?" David asked carefully. He knew that Chris never talked about painful experiences.

"What happened?" Chris asked, putting his hand on David's back.

"Bullshit. You tell me. You had sex with him, too, didn't you?" David insisted.

"No, I didn't have sex with Jack, and neither did you. He molested me, and he molested you." It was much easier for Chris to see what had happened as a molestation when it was David rather than himself..

"Maybe he molested you, but I went back." David turned away from Chris.

"Yeah, so what does that mean? You sound like an idiot when you say shit like that. I guess you could say I went back, too," Chris said, challenging David.

"What do you mean?" David asked, glancing up at Chris.

"It happened on a camping trip. I stayed with him in his tent. It happened the first night, and then again the second night. Two nights. It didn't stop until I stopped him, so I guess you could say I went back the second night," Chris explained, "but then he wanted to fuck me and I wouldn't let him. So then he moved me out and moved Derek in."

David slowly dropped his head. "I said no, too, at first, but then I kept going back to his house. I guess it was after your camping trip, when I had him for a teacher in the eighth grade. I just wanted him to like me. I looked up to him so much. He was always so kind and understanding to me." David began to cry. "I didn't want him to fuck me, but if I didn't let him he wouldn't talk to me, so finally I said yes. The first time it hurt really, really bad and I said I wouldn't do it again. There was blood for three days." Tears ran down his face and rolled off his chin. This was the first time he had ever said the words out loud. Chris moved over and sat beside David. He reached over to wipe the tears away, but David pushed his hand away. "He told me not to come back. I knew he was doing it with Derek. I could tell. Derek used to go over to his house after school. I would follow him there."

David got up from the bed and started to pace. "So, I went back and said okay. Damn it, Chris, this is so sick. I can't believe that I'm telling you this," David said, sounding disgusted. "I told him that I loved him and that I wanted him to love me again, and that I would do anything he wanted to do." David threw up his hand. "Fuck, Chris. So, then he fucked me and then told me not to come back anymore. Imagine, a thirteen-year old kid thinking he's in love." David slammed his fist down hard on the bed and cried as he relived the humiliation and rejection. Then he looked up at Chris. "So, he may have molested you, but he didn't molest me."

"Fuck if he didn't," Chris shouted. "God, what a fucking prick he is! David, he molested you, and he fucked with your head, too. David, I am not going to tell you to go away."

"No, but you'll go away. I'm in love with you. And it isn't anything like with Jack. He didn't care about me, and I didn't care about him. I was so lonely and desperate for attention," David said as he again burst into tears. "I know you won't say you're in love with me, but I know you are. I can feel it. I just don't understand why you don't know it." Chris sat silently. David sighed, "Chris, I love the way I make you happy and the way you make me happy. It feels so good to watch you being protective of me, defending me, like now, talking about Jack. I love knowing that we're special to each other; and I love the way you share your family with me. The way you do things like helping me find a job in New York." David touched Chris's leg. "I get so excited about seeing you and being with you. I can't sleep at night thinking about us living in New York. You know, Julie talks to me about her relationship with Peter and how she feels about him, and all the time I'm thinking that I love you the way they love each other. Is that wrong?" Chris didn't answer. "I love making love with you." Again Chris didn't answer. After a long pause, David added, "I guess this is why we've never talked about any of this."

Chris felt his body tense, "You haven't said anything to her, to make her think anything. Have you?" he asked.

"No. No," David said, looking down and shaking his head.

"It sounds like you've given this a lot of thought." Chris rolled over onto his back and stared up at the ceiling. "I haven't." David looked at him. "Well, I have thought about it, but I haven't thought it through like you." David continued to stare at him as he stared at the ceiling. "I guess you're saying that you're gay and that you're okay with that." Chris glanced at David. His stomach was beginning to churn. "Do you care if anyone knows? If Julie knew?"

"I wouldn't mind if Julie knew. But that's because I know she'd never say anything, and she wouldn't get weird about it, either. And I don't think Peter would get weird about it. But, no, I don't want anyone to know, right now. As your mom says, 'my life as I know it would be over' if my parents knew now, or if it got out at school. But, once I get to college, I want everyone to know it." Chris remained silent.

Finally, David said, "Shit, I am so scared right now."

"Why?" Chris turned to look at David, and put his hand on his leg.

"You don't ever want anyone to know, do you? Did you want us to always be a secret? I mean, how would that work?"

"I never thought about it." Chris paused, then he turned to look toward the ceiling again. "I don't know what to say. I can't imagine people knowing that I'm bisexual." David stared at Chris. "Okay, that I'm gay. I can't imagine people knowing," Chris said angrily. "No, that's not true. I can imagine it. My mom would never talk to me again. My grandparents would disown me."

"That's bullshit and you know it," David argued. His tone of voice surprised him. He was not used to being angry or sounding harsh with anyone, especially Chris. In some odd way, it felt good. It also surprised him that Chris was not striking back in a rage, but rather, was listening and responding.

"No, I don't know that. What do you think your parents would do?" Chris asked.

"My dad would throw me out of the house. My mom would cry. When they do find out, they'll probably never want to see me again. But your mom is different." David moved closer to Chris. They made eye contact as David put his hand on Chris's chest. "Yeah, I think she'd be upset, but Chris, she and your grandparents would love you no matter what. God, Chris, how could you even doubt that? It's so obvious," David said, continuing to stare at Chris.

Chris just lay naked on the bed, shaking his head back and forth. "That's easy for you to say. You don't really know my granddad; he's tough. He wouldn't let my mom divorce my dad for years because the Church says it's bad. What do you think he'd say if I told him I was in love with you?"

"He'd probably ask you what that meant, and you wouldn't have an answer."

"Asshole," Chris said, sounding downcast. "David, please don't start being cruel."

"I'm sorry. You're right. But you have to understand something. I really do believe that the best thing a person can do is love another person. I don't want to live my life being ashamed of loving someone. I know there will be people who will hate me, like my father. But, those people just won't be part of my life. I just can't live hating myself for loving someone. Do you know what I mean?"

"Yes, I do."

"I guess we want different things. I really want to be happy about who I love and I want other people to be happy, too. Like everyone is so happy about Julie and Peter. You look at them and it all makes sense. You know, you kind of get this smile on your face. Well, I want my friends to smile, too."

"I want the same thing, David. But not everyone is going to smile."

"I know that. But, I don't give a shit about everyone. The people who will be in my life will smile. If they can't smile, then they won't be part of my life."

"I understand, really I do," Chris said looking down at his hands. He sighed. He was finally being forced to look at how he had been hoping life would work for him, and how dysfunctional, even though common, his dream was. He wanted to have it all. He wanted to have a good cover story, but live out his passions in secret.

"But, please, if you're going to end this, please still be my friend," David said, with tears welling in his eyes.

"Knock it off, David. I just haven't thought this through. I mean I think about us all the time. I look forward to seeing you, too. And I can't wait to get you alone. You know that. But I just never thought about what I feel, or what it all means." Chris rolled over on his side away from David. Neither he nor David said another word.

David sat watching Chris for a while, and then he lay down, moved closer, and put his arm around him. Chris took David's arm and held it close to his stomach, as David moved up tightly against him so their bodies were fully in contact, front to back. After a long while, David fell asleep. Chris could hear his breath quiver every once in a while. He had been crying. Chris tried to remember the last time he had cried.

Chris lay awake for most of the night. He felt an ache in his stomach that he thought was hunger. Then he realized it was fear. Fear, not of what David had said to him—he had known for a while that David was in love with him. He feared the truth of his own feelings. For the first time he understood himself more deeply, and it scared him. He did not only love David; he was in love with David. He used to tell himself that his crushes were lustful. He told himself that his lust was just sexual, and that he was really bisexual and could deny himself his homosexuality. The truth he was now so afraid to face was that he was in love with David the way Peter loved Julie. Although he knew it, he had never thought it. And the thought scared him. He knew that he was gay, but he did not know how to think of himself as gay, or more importantly, how others would think of him. He knew he both loved David and desired him sexually, but he could not imagine anyone else knowing. The chasm between his desires and how he thought of himself—or was it how others thought of him—felt insurmountable. Did he even have the vocabulary to name the feelings he had? He had long ago given up the naming of feelings. He could not imagine putting words to his sexuality.

He wanted to be with David. He realized his sex play with girls had been just that: play. The passion he felt for David in the last few months was only the physical and sexual manifestation of what he had been feeling since their friendship began. *And damn, David is right, I want to run and hide from him.* He felt as if David had opened a hole in the floor and invited him into it with him. He was drowning in anxieties. He thought that what was keeping him from spiraling and then "breaking free" was David's arm around him, which he held onto tightly. This was the first time he could remember fighting not to break free of his feelings. And he was allowing himself to use someone else's strength to do so.

The last time Chris looked at the clock it was four in the morning. David woke up at about eight, and listened to Chris, who was breathing deeply. Chris was lying on his back, and David had his head on Chris's chest, his arm around his waist. David wondered if he could get up and not awaken Chris. Slowly, he moved off Chris, who then rolled over and remained asleep.

At nine o'clock, David called room service. He ordered bacon and eggs and pancakes and a large glass of milk for each of them. Before the room service waiter arrived, David considered messing up the still undisturbed bed that was supposed to be his. He decided against it. He smiled as he thought about it being the first public statement he would make about his relationship with Chris, albeit to a stranger. When the room service waiter arrived, David asked him to be quiet, and pointed to Chris asleep in the bed. David noticed the waiter notice the undisturbed bed. They smiled at each other. After the waiter left, David served everything onto two plates, and then brought Chris's plate to the bed. He sat besides him and lightly bounced on the bed and blew the aroma of the food toward Chris's face.

Chris tried not to smile.

"Yum, bacon, eggs, pancakes. Yum," David said.

"I'm sorry about last night," Chris said.

"Forget it, I mean fuggedaboudit. Let's have a great day, and a great night. Get up. Let's have breakfast and then do it in the shower. That was fun."

"I was having this really weird dream," Chris said.

"When?"

"When you woke me up."

"What was it?

"I was riding a horse. It was daytime; the horse was this really beautiful strong white stallion. I think I was a general or something. I had a uniform on, but I couldn't tell what uniform, but I'm pretty sure it was a Civil War uniform. I couldn't tell what side I was on, but for some reason I think I was a Confederate general. Anyway, I know it was me on this horse, but I was watching me from someplace else. I had this sword in my right hand and I was holding the reins of the horse with my left hand. I was moving back and forth before the troops.

"Anyway, the horse reared up. I was supposed to be leading my troops into battle, but the horse went wild. I kept trying to get the horse under control but I couldn't. You know those movies where the horses go out of control and run wild and carry the stagecoach over the mountain's edge and into a ravine? Well that's what this was like. There was no way I could get this horse under control.

Lies That Bind

"Then the dream switched and it was nighttime. I was lying on the ground and everything was wet. I was soaked and there was this body pressing down on top of me. I turned my head and looked around and there were all these dead bodies around me. I guess I was feeling really scared. I don't think I could move my legs or anything. I started to try to move and then this guy on top of me said, 'Don't move, it isn't safe' So I just lay there. In this part of the dream I wasn't watching myself from afar anymore. I moved my head again and I thought I saw some of the other bodies moving. But again he said, 'Don't move.' He pressed down on me even harder. So I just lay there. Then I saw a guy get up and sneak off into the woods. Then another guy went off into the woods. I asked this guy what was going on and he said that they were joining together in the woods where it was safe. Eventually, everyone left, and it wasn't until then that he said to me that he thought that it was safe for us to go and join them, and that we were all joining together so we could all go home."

"Yeah, so what happened next?"

"I don't know. You woke me up."

"Who was the guy?" David asked.

"I don't know. I mean I never saw him. You know what was weird, too? I remember thinking in the dream that "Wow, all the men they say died in battles weren't really dead. They just played dead and then snuck away when no one was looking. They're all hiding until the war is over. Weird, huh?"

As Chris sat and ate his breakfast, he realized that room service had delivered their food and that the second bed had not been slept in. He looked at David and smiled and, shaking his head, said, "You're such an asshole."

"What?" David said smiling. "I'm sure he was gay."

"Oh, and I suppose you knew that before he got here. Or did you ask for a gay waiter?" David grinned and shrugged his shoulders.

David and Chris spent the day as if nothing had happened the night before. After their shower they went down to the pool and sat in the sun. The sun was warm. This was their first time in the sun this year. They spread sunscreen over each other's backs. After they swam and sunned for most of the afternoon, they showered again and then decided to walk into town for dinner. That night in bed, Chris again gave himself to David. This time neither of them said a word.

"Both of you boys look like you spent a lot of time in the sun," Diane said, as Richard loaded their luggage into the trunk of the car.

"So do you, Mrs. Patrona. You look great," David said. "You always look great, though."

"You are so sweet, David," Diane said.

"Yeah, you are so sweet, David," Chris said, mimicking Diane. Chris tried to mess up David's hair, but David pushed him away.

"Well it's true, your mom always looks so good. I mean, Mrs. Patrona, you are in great shape," David said, eyeing Diane up and down. Diane was wearing a white sleeveless cotton blouse, navy knee-length shorts and her tennis shoes. A whispered fragrance of roses followed her. "Mrs. Patrona, you smell great, too."

Both David and Chris were wearing tee shirts, shorts, and sandals. David's tee shirt had the word, "whatever" printed in green across the chest. Chris had bought it for him as a souvenir of their New York trip the summer before. Chris was wearing a tee shirt with the comic strip character Calvin on it. Above Calvin's head were the words, "Every day of my life I'm forced to add another name to the list of people who piss me off." It was his second-favorite tee shirt. Richard was wearing his usual polo shirt and khakis.

"Are you making a pass at my mother? Hey, Richard! David just made a pass at Mom."

"I heard him," Richard said as he joined them in the car.

"It wasn't a pass. I just think your wife is hot," David said with a smile. Everyone laughed as they buckled up for their long drive to Los Angeles. Richard glanced at David in the rear view mirror. He reached over and rubbed Diane's leg and said, "He's right."

"David, are you going to Shaun's Eagle Scout ceremony?" Diane asked, half turning in her seat to face him.

"Yeah, I guess so. My dad's the presenter, although I don't know why."

"Your dad is the presenter because he and Shaun's dad are good friends," Diane said, in full awareness of the intention of David's statement and his negative tone of voice. "Some people really like your dad." Richard glanced over at Diane and raised his eyebrows in disbelief.

"Whatever," David mumbled. "Are you going? It's tomorrow night, right?"

"David, don't you start with 'whatever'. And, yes it is tomorrow night. We are thinking about going. Chris was invited to take part. He helped Shaun with his service project. You remember, he did that big food drive at school and church."

"Oh yeah, sure, for the Meals on Wheels," David recalled.

Lies That Bind

"Yes, Chris helped him with all of that. He went to various restaurants and markets and talked them into donating their unused food on a regular basis. It really took a lot of work," Diane said, glancing over her shoulder at David.

"Chris helps everyone, he's such a good Eagle Scout," David said laughingly, as he poked Chris in the side. Chris closed his left fist slowly, so David could anticipate the strike, and then punched David on his right thigh. "Ouch! What?" David said with a grimace as he rubbed his leg. "You do help everyone."

"You're not laughing now," Chris said with an exaggerated smile.

"Chris, I heard that, you must have hurt him," Diane said.

"Yeah, Chris, you must have hurt me," David said, pointing at Chris.

"Don't bruise him, you guys have an important game this week. Wednesday, right?" Richard asked.

"Yeah, don't bruise me," David said, snickering at Chris. "Yes, Mr. Patrona, we have a game on Wednesday. Are you going to be able to make it?" Chris reached over and grabbed some skin on David's arm with his thumb and index finger and twisted. "Ouch!" David said.

"Chris, stop it, and act your age," Diane shouted. "Richard can't make it, but I'll be there," Diane said.

"Yeah, act your age," David said, smiling at Chris. "Mrs. Patrona, you really are looking good." Everyone laughed and Chris gave David the finger.

The drive home was pleasant. Diane and David talked throughout the ride. Chris sat and thought about how much his mother liked David, and how much that might change if she ever found out about them. They arrived home late that afternoon, and decided to have an early dinner before driving David home. It was unanimously decided that dinner would be take-out pizza: one Italian sausage and one pepperoni with extra cheese. David wished he never had to go home. He had the days counted until his graduation. His plan was to leave for New York very soon after, perhaps the next day.

Arriving home, Diane and David carried the pizzas into the kitchen. Chris and Richard carried in the luggage. Chris quietly said, "Hey, Richard, thanks for letting me bring David along for the weekend." Richard nodded, putting his hand on Chris's shoulder as they entered the kitchen.

Diane put plates and napkins on the table while David opened the boxes of pizza. "They smell so good. Pizza is my second-favorite Italian food," David said.

"Really, what's your first?" Diane asked.

"Anything you cook, Mrs. Patrona," David said grinning from ear to ear.

Chris said, "Oh man, can you ever pour it on." He wrestled David into a headlock while messing up his hair.

"Yeah, well, next time my mom makes spaghetti and meatballs I'll invite you over and you'll see what I mean."

As they finished the first pizza and were starting the second, Richard went to the living room. When he returned he was rifling through the mail. "Chris, there's something here for you," he said as he turned it over, looking for a return address.

"Who's it from?" Chris asked.

"I don't know. There's no return address, the postmark is the Bronx," Richard handed it to Chris.

"It isn't Grandma or Grandpa," Chris said, staring at the handwritten address.

"Open it," Diane said impatiently.

"Yeah, open it," David said with a mouthful of pizza.

Chris opened the envelope and unfolded the pages of the letter. In between the folds was a photograph. He stared at it as everyone around the table stared at him.

"What is it? Who is it from? Diane asked, leaning over trying to see the picture.

"Fuck, my father is dead," Chris said, staring at the picture. He glanced up at Diane, then again at the picture.

"What?" David said, as he moved toward Chris to see the picture.

"What do you mean he's dead? Who is that from?" Diane asked, pulling the letter from Chris's hand. She turned to the last page and said, "It's from Jean."

Richard asked, "Who is Jean?"

"Frank's wife," Diane said, reading the letter.

"Mom, it's my letter," Chris said, taking it from her and handing her the picture.

"I guess he died on March second, " Diane said, looking at the picture of the tombstone. "Why would she send you a picture of his headstone?" She handed the picture to Richard. "Read the letter, Chris. What does she say? Read it out loud."

David asked, "Chris, are you okay?" He couldn't take his eyes off Chris. He didn't know what he was looking for, but he was expecting something.

Lies That Bind

Diane asked, "Chris, are you okay?" as she reached over and touched his arm.

"Yeah, fine," Chris said, looking up from the letter.

"Chris, you can't be fine," Diane said. "Do you want me to read the letter to you?"

Chris shook his head no. Chris continued reading the letter, ignoring Diane's request.

"Chris, read it aloud," Diane demanded.

"She says he died of cancer, lung cancer. Wow, he knew he had it when I was still in New York. Fuck, he knew the last time I saw him, that time in the car." Chris said, looking up from the letter. Looking at Diane, he said, "He didn't tell me, Mom." Diane put her hand on his arm. "She says it was in remission and got bad again last October. She says he liked the pictures I sent him and that he wanted to write, but didn't." Chris continued to read to himself. Diane noticed an instant change in his demeanor as he continued reading. His eyes seemed to glaze over. His voice became flat.

"Chris, just read it out loud," Diane insisted. Her curiosity was to the point of turning to anger. "What else does she say?"

Chris was fixated on the letter, "Ah, well, that they went on vacation in January, and that he got sick again. They went back to New York and he died in March." Chris looked up from the letter and said in some confusion, "She says that he loved me. Why would she say that he loved me? He never acted that way."

"Your dad did love you, Chris," Diane assured him. "But he was a very troubled man. He couldn't just love you or anyone. He always seemed to have to hurt those he loved. He always seemed to have to drive people away.".

David was trying to gauge what was happening to Chris. "If she said he loved you, Chris, I bet he did. Like your mom says though, he probably just couldn't show it."

Chris pushed himself from the table. "Let's just forget about it. I mean, it doesn't really matter. He's dead now."

Diane said, "Chris, I don't like the way you deal with things like this. You can't just forget it. You worry me," she touched his arm again.

"Me, too," David added. "Chris, I'm your best friend and I've seen you do this before, and I agree with your mom. You don't deal well with stuff like this," David said, staring at him.

"David…" Chris said, turning and glaring at David.

"What?"

"Fuck you!" Chris growled, giving David the finger.

"Christopher," Diane shouted, swatting him on the arm. "He isn't the one you should be angry at." David looked away and sighed.

"I'm sorry, David," Chris said, continuing to look at him. "Really, I am," he said as he reached over and touched him. "Finish your pizza, then I am going to take you home."

David stared at his pizza. "I'm not hungry anymore."

"Okay, let's go then. I'll be right back, Mom." Chris found the keys to the Suburban and stepped outside.

Diane stopped David as he started to leave the kitchen. "David, I'm worried about him."

"Me, too."

"See if you can get him to talk to you. He's angry and he doesn't know it. But do me a favor—when he leaves you, call me and let me know so that I'll know he's on his way home. Tell him to come right home, that I'm waiting for him."

"Mrs. Patrona, thank you for the best weekend. Too bad this had to happen. No joke, I think you're awesome," David said as he hugged Diane and kissed her on the cheek."

"I love you, David. You know that, don't you?" she asked as she hugged him. "Talk to my son. I know he trusts you. He just won't open up to me."

"I know, and I love you, too, Mrs. Patrona, Chris doesn't open up much to me either. But I'm working on him. I really try to be there for him. He's always there for me, he's such a good friend, but , , , " Diane brushed her hand over David's face.

"David, let's go," Chris shouted from outside. He had the car started and loaded with David's luggage. As soon as David closed the car door, Chris started to back out of the driveway.

"I don't have to get right home. Let's go someplace and talk."

Chris pulled the car to the curb. "I want to read something to you and see if you remember any of this." Chris parked the Suburban, opened the letter, and looked for the part he wanted to read. "Here it is, listen to this:

"'*After he received your letter at Christmas, and with the recurrence of the cancer, he decided that he wanted to visit Los Angeles…*'"

"Yada yada yada," Chris said, as he skimmed the letter.

Lies That Bind

David asked with surprise, "They were here?"

Chris glanced at David and then back to the letter. He continued, "Yada yada yada…Here, here it is.

"'*Then we drove by your house. We passed it several times, until he parked across the street a couple of houses down. I looked at my watch and saw that it was nearly three o'clock. We sat there until almost four, when we saw you walking down the street with a friend of yours. The two of you looked so handsome in your school uniforms. I watched as your father's face lit up and tears came to his eyes. We sat there and watched you.*

"'*When you got to your house, both of you stood out front and talked and laughed. Several times you looked our way, but you never noticed us. Your father said over and over again that he though…*'"

"We'll skip this part."

"Chris, just read it," David said, sounding annoyed.

"Here it is.

Then you turned and went inside and your friend, a handsome blond boy, walked right past the car and looked in at your dad. They nodded to each other and then your friend went on his way.'

"That had to have been you, right? Do you remember any of that?" Chris asked, looking up at David.

"It's weird, I think I kind of do remember it. I mean when you were reading it I was thinking that I could picture it all." David was feeling anxious as he stared at Chris.

"I was thinking maybe she was making it up, but now I don't think so. I mean, I think I told him about you and stuff, and I think some of the pictures I sent were in front of my house. But, we always go to your house first and I would come home alone or you would come in to my house. So that doesn't make sense."

"Chris, I think I remember it. I remember going to Julie's. We were doing stuff for the class we were taking."

"Shit. You're right." Chris stared blankly into the street in front of him.

David said, "I think I do remember them sitting in the car. Damn."

"Okay. Well, that's all I wanted to know."

"Chris, why didn't he get out of the car? How fucking stupid, he was twenty yards from you."

Chris looked at David and stared, then said, "Maybe that's all he wanted to do. Maybe it would have been too hard for him to talk to me."

His anger was surfacing again. "Maybe he thought I'd start screaming at him again and he didn't want to get hurt again. I mean he was dying, damn it."

"Why are you getting angry at me, Sano? I didn't do anything." David was becoming frustrated with Chris always being able to make excuses for other people's behavior. "You know, maybe he was just being a fucking coward. So it was bad the last time he saw you." Chris recently had told David what had happened the last time he had seen his father. "If he really wanted to talk to you he could have taken the chance. Chris, he was dying and he just...damn it Chris, you really piss me off."

Calmly, Chris said, "Wow, I've never seen you get so angry. What is up with you? This is twice in one weekend."

"I don't know. I just think it's so fucked that we have fathers who are so mean. Chris, what he did was so nasty. I mean look at how great your grandparents and your mom are to both you and me. They're kind and nice to you, and so is Richard. I mean, really, Chris, you don't deserve bad treatment. Really, don't you see that?" David said, leaning toward Chris and touching his arm.

"Yeah, but I was really mean to him. Once I told him I didn't want him for a father anymore. I mean that's the worst thing a kid could say to his father."

"Fuck, Chris, maybe he deserved it," David said in exasperation. "Whatever. I'm not going to argue with you. Would you have been mean to him if he had come up to you that day?"

"No, probably not, but I don't know. I can be a real jerk sometimes."

"Shit, Chris, you aren't like that."

"Yeah, but he doesn't know that, or didn't know what I'm like. He just knows, knew I was this kid who screamed and yelled at him."

"Okay! Fine! But if he couldn't come up to you he could have written to you. Why leave it to his wife to write to you? Man, talk about not having the courage to face someone. Look, Chris, I know you're a real jerk most of the time," David smiled as Chris turned and looked at him in surprise. Chris slowly made a fist so that David could see what he was doing, but this time he did not strike out. "Fine, okay, take it out on me," David continued. "Why didn't he just write and say, Look asshole son of mine. I'm coming to see you and you better be nice to me because I am dying. No, he just sits back and does nothing. Don't you see that?"

Chris started the car and began to drive toward David's house. "Pull over and turn off the engine. I still want to talk to you."

Lies That Bind

"No, I'm going to drop you off and then I'm going to go. Really, I'm fine. I mean, there's nothing I can do about any of this, anyway."

* * * * *

Chris's voice was heavy with pain. "When I drove up to David's house, Paul, David's father, came out. I thought something was wrong, but I thought maybe he was just being his asshole self."

Time was getting short, so I said, "Chris, I was wanting to get to the letter and talk about it in great depth, your feelings about it. But, I have to tell you that I am really stuck on your dream."

"What dream?"

"The one with you on a horse."

"What about it, I mean it was just a stupid dream."

"One that your unconscious created. Dreams are the poetry of the unconscious, and this was one you chose to remember, and one you chose to share with me." Diane was right. His expressions were a window to his feelings. Clearly, he thought I was wasting his time. And perhaps I was. But now I was curious to see if he would hold to his feelings, or if he would decide to play with the dream, and what he would make of its meaning.

He glanced toward me. "Are you one of these Freudian guys?"

"Well, if you mean psychoanalyst, yes I am. But I am not a Freudian. There are all different kinds of psychoanalysts, and yes, dreams interest me." Now, although I was not sure why, I was hoping he would tell me to "fuggedaboudit," and say that he was not interested and did not want to play my analytic game.

"I guess, I mean, if you think it's important."

"You seem resistant. Can we talk about that?"

"Well, I've read about this stuff, you know, that dreams have all kinds of sex in them that you don't know about. You know about the unconscious and Oedipus and all that. But I really don't understand it all. I don't think I can do it."

"As I said, I am not Freudian, and I don't know that all dreams are about sex and Oedipus. And I don't know what this dream is about either. But it feels like a very powerful and important dream to me." He shrugged. "What just happened?"

"I was just thinking that you think that I'm smart, everyone does. And I guess I am book smart, because I read and remember things. But I don't think I'm creatively smart. I mean, I write. I am going to be an English and philosophy major at Columbia. I just don't think I'm very creative. More analytic than creative." He stopped and shrugged.

"And?"

"And, I think I'll sound stupid. I'll do it if you tell me what you think about the dream. Okay?"

"Okay." He was clearly being compliant, and doing what he thought would please me. He was also frightened about exposing what he thought to be his weaknesses. I saw his invitation to me to play in his dream with him as a need to reduce that anxiety, and marshal the support he needed in attempting something new.

"What do I do?"

"What is the first thing that comes to mind when you think back on the dream?"

"I was on a horse, a white horse," he said, closing his eyes.

"What does that mean to you?"

"I don't know."

"Just let your mind wander. Play with the words and the images."

"Well, white isn't a color. Well, actually it is. It's the color that reflects all other colors, or their wave lengths."

"Good, go on."

"White is for purity and innocence. I read that once. The white in our flag means innocent and pure." He became quiet, his eyes darted back and forth, he seemed deep in thought. "I read that when something is heated to very high temperatures it gets white hot."

"Go ahead."

He turned and looked at me. "It doesn't make sense. A hot horse." His eyes darted upward again.

"What was that?"

"I read this short story. A guy was angry, really angry; the author said something about white fury. Damn, that's weird. Fury is that horse. Fuck." He looked both amazed at his associations and anxious.

"What's going on?"

"My stomach feels weird."

"Tell me."

"I'm, like, riding my anger in this dream and I remember that at first it all seemed under my control. I mean the horse was doing what I wanted, but then the dream changed and I was completely out of control. I just knew that this horse was going to kill me if I didn't get it under control."

"Something like how your anger feels sometimes?"

Lies That Bind

"Wow. This is weird stuff." I couldn't help but smile. "So then I remember this thing about my uniform. I knew it was the Civil War and that I had on this Civil War uniform, and I was almost sure it was the Confederate uniform. But later in the dream I was sure I was wearing the Union uniform, you know when I was down on the ground after the battle."

"Okay, what do you want to do with all that?"

"Well," he said, "civil war. First there was one country, and then it was broken into two. A lot of people think it was over slavery, but I think it was mostly over those who believed in states rights versus those who believed in the power of the federal government."

"And how would that pertain to your struggle?" I asked.

"I don't know. What do you think?"

"Well, going with what you've said…the demands of society over the rights of the individual."

He nodded, "Oh, the conversation with David that night; about being gay and what would people think."

I added, "I think it is a battle you've been forced to fight since you were a child. Your father's will versus your inner life." He again looked deep in thought. "What are you thinking about?"

"I was thinking about what the word "confederate" means. It means a group of people aligned together. Allies."

"Yeah."

"Me, my mom, my grandparents, my cookie grandma, against my dad."

"Okay. Another direction we can take in a dream is that there are different parts of yourself represented in the dream. So perhaps the confederation might also be all the parts of you allied in battle. Perhaps your anger being that feeling that can best mobilize all those parts of yourself. But then your anger, the anger of an innocent, a child, which to a child can feel out of control…" I hesitated.

"That anger makes me lose the battle and almost kills me."

"Or it seems to you that it will."

"Wow," Chris said, seeming genuinely excited. I thought it a very positive sign that he was willing to explore his inner world, and that he could be in awe of what it might have to offer him. "Then the second part of the dream. It happens at night and after the battle, I guess. You know what's weird about this part of the dream?"

"What?"

"A lot of times when I have dreams I'm watching myself in the dream, but sometimes I'm me in the dream. In this dream, first I'm watching myself and then I'm me in the dream."

"What do you make of that?" I could see what it was about Chris that drew people in. When he was excited, curious, and filled with anticipation he became very engaging. His efforts included doing the work of drawing you into his process. His voice was animated, his body language was open, and his eye contact was steady. I now also understood the energy depression drained from him, when he withdrew into himself, when he emotionally closed down, when he "broke free," as he called it.

"Well, maybe the first part of the dream is me from a distance, like from my past. You said something about the innocent anger of a child. Maybe that part is me, then, and the other part of the dream is more like me now, or that night with David." He stared at the wall in silence again. I decided not to question him, but to wait.

"I think that guy lying on top of me telling me to wait until it is safe is me. I think it is the me from the first part of the dream. Is that possible?"

"It's your dream, anything is possible." I smiled.

He laughed. "Yeah, I think it was me."

"So, that child part of yourself is protecting you from dangers you cannot see?"

"Yeah. I mean it seems to me that the battle is over. And those other soldiers are heading into the woods to hide and join up together. I mean they think it is safe to go, but I am pretty much the last one up, because I listen to this guy, or me."

"Okay. So?"

"I like what you said before. I really do think they are all parts of me."

"That you thought were dead."

"Yeah, I guess. But they aren't dead."

"No, they aren't. They are all heading into the woods waiting for you to join up with them," I said.

"I told David that I didn't know what it meant to be in love with him."

"So, that might be one part of you." Chris's mouth turned downward. "What's happening?"

He shrugged. "I've never been in love, David is the first. I was always scared that I would never feel that." He shrugged again, pushed his hair off of his face. I could see tears in his eyes. "I was, I am in love with David." Again he seemed to get lost in thought. He looked like he might cry, but did not.

"Another part of you that you think is dead is the part of you that cries."

"Yeah. I mean I feel close, but it just dies."

"Exactly. Chris, we could spend weeks talking about this dream and all the meanings it might have. But I do want to get to the letter before we stop."

His eyes glanced back at the letter on my desk. "The letter. Wait. You said you would tell me what else you thought of."

"I did, didn't I? Okay, I want to stay close to your associations with one part and then I'll also give you my associations to another part of the dream that struck me."

"Cool. Go for it," Chris said eagerly.

I smiled. "Your first association to white was a non-color, but then you said it reflected all other colors." He continued to stare intensely at me. "So as an adjunct to all you've said I might add that the white is perhaps a reflection of all your unfelt or undifferentiated feelings. Energy that becomes…"

"So like white noise in sound—it becomes fury."

"I knew someone who had a great vocabulary for colors. He was an artist and understood colors far beyond anything I could imagine. However, he had very few words to describe or understand feelings. They were white noise." Again, I became aware of the time. "I believe all your feelings are compressed, or undifferentiated into white noise or white fury."

"I see," he said, nodding and staring into space.

"Tell me," I said.

"I was just thinking about the saliva, you know when it becomes too much. White noise in my stomach." He abruptly turned to me and said, "So what was the part that struck you?"

"Well, just a simple play on words. I was struck when you said—here I wrote it down—'the body was pressing down on me.' I thought that was an interesting way to describe what was happening."

Chris said, "Well, you know, he was lying on me, holding me down, like pushing me down."

"Oh sure, I understand, but I found it interesting that you used the word pressing. And my play on words went like this—repressing, compressing, suppressing, depressing—all words that I associate with darkness."

"Oh yeah, right. Wow." Silence. I waited. "My father."

"How so?"

"Oppressing."

"Exactly." He glanced at me and nodded. I said, "As I said, we could spend weeks on your dream. Have you written it down anywhere?"

"No," he shook his head, "but I will."

"I want to say this. I was hesitant about spending the time on your dream. I'm glad that we did, I think the time was productive. And, perhaps you are more creative than you allow yourself to realize. But now to the letter."

"Wow, I didn't think it would be interesting, but I am glad we did it." He looked as if he were blushing.

"What's happening?" I asked. He shook his head. "Try, if you can."

"I was thinking about something that Carl and I were talking about."

"What is that?"

He shrugged. "I don't know if it's okay to say."

"Okay, then I won't press you."

He glanced at me. "No, it's not like it's a secret. It was about you."

"I see."

"We were just saying you seemed like a nice guy who cares a lot." He took a deep breath, his chest quivered. I was about to take it further when he said, "The letter." He sighed. "I wish we had done the letter first and then the dream." I nodded. He reached across the desk and took the letter. For a moment he just stared at it, then he opened the envelope and handed me the picture of his father's headstone and began to read aloud.

"Dear Christopher,

"As you can see, your father died on March 2nd. He died of lung cancer. He first found out that he had cancer during that summer you left New York. He had his first treatment soon after you left for Los Angeles. Soon after that he had to have part of his lung removed.

"For a couple of years he was in remission, but last October they found a growth on his other lung. He was under treatment, but they told him that it didn't look good. They told him that it was progressing slowly, and that treatment might slow it even further, but as it turned out he only had six months to live.

Lies That Bind

"I wish I could explain to you how much your father loved you. Your letters, gifts, and pictures meant the world to him. Every picture you sent was framed and set out in our living room for him to show everyone who visited. I wish I could also convey to you how proud he was to hear of your acceptance to Columbia. Your letter brought him to tears. He so wanted there to be reconciliation between the two of you. I guess he saw your return as opening the door to re-establishing a relationship.

"Before he opened each one of your letters, he'd sit and stare at it. I know he was hoping that this would be the letter that would hold your apology. But that never happened, and each time he was disappointed. But he still took joy in hearing how you were doing.

"I know he wrote to you in his heart thousands of times, but he was a stubborn Italian and believed that he had to wait for you to come around, be a man and apologize. After he received your last letter, and with the recurrence of the cancer, he decided that he wanted to visit Los Angeles. I did not question him as to why; we just planned a vacation. We arrived in L.A. the first week of February and stayed at the Hilton at Universal City, up on the hill that overlooks Studio City. You live in a nice area.

"We rented a car and did some sightseeing. One day we drove all around your neighborhood and eventually found Sacred Heart High School. We slowly walked around the school and once when everyone was in their classes we entered one of the buildings. When the kids came out and went from one class to another, we walked to the fence and watched. I never said a word to him, but I know he was looking for you. Then we drove by your house. We passed it several times, until he parked across the street a couple of houses down. I looked at my watch and saw that it was nearly three o'clock. We sat there until almost four when we saw you walking down the street with a friend of yours. The two of you looked so handsome in your school uniforms. I watched as your father's face lit up and tears came to his eyes. We sat there and watched you.

"When you got to your house, both of you stood out front and talked and laughed. Several times you looked our way, but you never noticed us. Your father said over and over again that he thought you were so handsome. He kept saying, 'I can't believe what a handsome young man he is, he looks so strong and so happy.' Then you turned and went inside and your friend, a handsome blond boy, walked right past the car and looked in at your dad. They nodded to each other and then your friend went on his way.

"We sat there for a while. He stared at the house and then he said. 'He is so handsome and he is smart too. He does seem happy, doesn't he? Did you hear him laughing? He has a wonderful laugh.' We drove to the hotel and had dinner. He didn't say a word. I believe seeing you gave him some kind of peace. We were scheduled to go on to Las Vegas, but he decided that he wanted to see you play ball. He called your school and found out that in two days you had a game. They gave us directions to where you'd be playing, and that day we sat in the stands and watched. Christopher, your dad beamed with pride. On the way to the hotel he said that he thought it was the second happiest day of his life. The first was the day you were born.

"That night he told me that he was sure that once you moved back to New York, you'd come to your senses and apologize, and then you and he could be father and son again. The next morning as we left the restaurant, he collapsed. We got him back to New York, but it was all downhill from there.

"I am writing you this letter to put your heart at ease and to let you know that your father died a happy man. Before he died your dad told me to tell you that he loved you, and was proud of you, and that he forgave you. So, please don't punish yourself too much for never apologizing, or not finding the courage to face him. He knew it was just a matter of time. I only wish he could have lived long enough for that to have happened. Please always take comfort in knowing he loved you dearly.

"Your stepmother,
Jean

"P.S. The information as to where he is buried is on the back of the photo. I know when you come to New York you'll want to visit and lay flowers on his grave. You can find me there every Sunday morning after church at 10:15."

When Chris was finished reading the letter, I realized that my mouth was clenched tightly again. I sat there, afraid that my anger would show through my words. There was so much that I wanted to say. Each sentence seemed to start with the word "fuck." Chris looked at me and shrugged. I asked, "How are you feeling?"

"Like I really fucked up," he shook his head.

"That really isn't a feeling."

"Now you're sounding like David."

"I see. Chris, what is your body feeling like right now?"

"Tense, sweaty, hot. Angry, I guess."

"Angry?"

"Yeah, because I really fucked up." He sounded annoyed.

"How so?"

"I should never have gotten angry with him that day. He must have been really scared—you know to have cancer—and I got so angry at him."

Lies That Bind

"Chris, that was a very nasty letter, or maybe I should say angry letter that your stepmother wrote to you."

"How so?"

"He was the adult, the parent, not you. She is saying that you should have been the adult. He wronged you. If he wanted resolution, because he was dying, he had four years to reach out to you. Chris, he had the opportunity to re-establish a relationship with you. Instead he let the opportunity slip away. And it was his last chance, and he probably knew that."

"You really do sound just like David," Chris said. That stopped me in my tracks. Perhaps I was trying to make my anger at my parents into his anger at his father. "He said the same thing to me. I mean, I guess my father could have gotten out of the car, but I still say he might have thought that I might freak out and hurt his feelings."

Clearly, this was about my parents also. I added, "Or you might have embraced each other. She put that all on you. Chris, if you noticed him in the car what would you have done?" Chris's eyes filled with tears, he shook his head. "Chris, it's okay to cry." Again he shook his head and shrugged. I waited and then asked, "What would you have done?"

"I don't know," he snapped back.

"There's your anger again," I stated. Chris glanced at me. "It's okay to be angry also. All your feelings are okay, whatever they are, but it seems to me that anger is more available to you than your other feelings."

He shook his head and said, "I am not angry."

"Okay. We have to stop for today. I'll see you tomorrow. Okay?"

"Okay."

Chapter Fourteen

ON THE WAY HOME, a chill ran through me. I thought about how angry I had become when I heard that letter. Angry that Frank had refused his son the opportunity to heal deep wounds; that he would only allow reconciliation on his terms. Surely, it would have been painful for them both, but he owed his son that much. I was sure that if he had given Chris the chance he would have embraced his father with an open heart.

But, was not my mother, in her own way, reaching out to me? Wasn't she offering me a chance at healing? A battle was going on between my head and my heart. I refused to reconsider. It was not the same, I decided. *What did I say to Chris? Something about... fuck it. It isn't the same thing.* I was adamant in my refusal.

Damn, I hate this. Once again, Karen was right. Many times she had said, "You are most changed by those patients whom you most change. Change is a two-way street."

When I arrived home there was a message on my machine. It was from Janet: the call I was dreading. I knew what was coming, and I was not feeling as strong in my resolve as I had been this morning. I started practicing compromises. I wondered if my sister Claire had told her that she had talked with me about my mother's offer. I decided she probably had not—Claire was a coward.

Surely, I could hold my own in this. But how could I if I was already wavering? Janet was tough. Janet the lawyer; Janet my older sister. She and I were nearer in age than she and Claire, but it was not the age difference. Claire always tried to drive a wedge between us, but that only made us better friends.

I loved my sister Janet, but she could be very difficult. I had always said that she was stubborn, but she had informed me that stubborn people are misunderstood. She said that they are actually people of superior intellect who have given a certain problem a great deal of thought and then, having come up with the most appropriate conclusion, find it unnecessary to change their mind. How could I argue with that? Because, of course, she had given stubbornness a great deal of thought with her "superior intellect"—case closed.

Lies That Bind

I was dreading this telephone call. It did not surprise me that Steve, someone I valued as a friend, had fallen in love with my sister. But I was surprised that Janet had agreed to marry anyone. She had always been so furiously independent. Also, it had not surprised me when Steve asked me to be his best man. However, carried away in the excitement of the moment, I had not thought my answer through, as Janet might have, when I said yes. Since then I had decided it would probably be for the best if I were not his best man. Still, if I reconsidered, compromised on that point, perhaps Janet would back down with regard to my mother.

I poured a cup of coffee and called her. Did I say that I take it black?—they say it grows hair on your chest—do you ever wonder just who *they* are—anyway, no hair yet.

"Hi, Sis. How are you?"

"Okay. How are you?"

"Good. I got your message," I said.

"I have all kinds of news you should hear." *Right to the point.*

"What's up?" I asked.

"How is the packing going?"

"Good. I'm about half done. I can't believe the crap I've collected in two years."

"Steve is excited that you're moving back here. He asked me if I would mind if you and he did one of those outback week vacations next spring."

"I know, he mentioned it. Bicycling in Italy."

"Bobby, please go with him. I can't think of anything I'd rather avoid more than spending a week on a bicycle."

I laughed, "It actually sounds like fun. I've gotten so butch living here in California." *Small talk from my sister; she's gearing up. Shit, this is going to be the call from hell.*

"I thought I'd meet up with you guys after your trek, and then he and I would take off and go to Rome for a week. I want to stay at the Grand Hotel de la Minerve. I hear it's beautiful and one of the best hotels in Italy. It's in central Rome and near the Piazza Navona, and the Spanish Steps; which means I can shop all day and dine all night."

"It sound like your kind of vacation," I hesitated. "So, you didn't answer me. What's up?"

"I talked to Claire this morning. She called you, didn't she?"

"I don't remember who called who," I lied.

"Who called whom, and bullshit. Bobby, if we're going to have a conversation, I refused to be lied to."

"Does it really matter, Jan?" *Stupid question.*

"Yes."

Yeah, I know. What is it they say in court? It goes to credibility, Your Honor. "She called."

"What did she tell you?"

"She said that...*Here we go*...Mom and Dad decided that if I'm Steve's best man that they would not only not come to the wedding, but that they would ask other people in the family not to come. They said that it was okay, however, for me to be in the church."

"Actually, that was Dad who said that, not Mom," Janet said.

"Mom never says anything. She's the obedient, dutiful wife," I said sarcastically.

"And?"

My sister the lawyer had been born when Claire was four. Claire had not been happy with a new sister. Stories abounded. Once, while my mother was changing Janet's diaper, Claire had convinced my mother to allow her to watch. She sat Claire at the edge of the changing table and when she reached for a diaper, Claire shoved Janet off the table. I guess it was downhill from there. On Janet's first birthday Claire tipped Janet's high chair over, sending Janet face first onto the floor. Claire explained that Janet wanted to get down. We joked that Claire must have known when Janet was old enough she'd torture Claire. The way Claire now explained it was that she was just getting even while she had the chance. When I was growing up Claire never had a chance to pull that with me. First, my parents were prepared. Second, Janet was my protector. So Claire became the body healer, Janet the litigator, and me, well...

"Claire said that if I come to the reception Mom and Dad would leave." The silence on the phone was deafening. "Janet?"

"Bobby, don't do it," she said. The anger that I thought I had been hearing in her voice, masked with superficial chitchat, was now passionate, as was usually the case with Janet. Nothing with her was ever half felt.

"I can't let this happen. Tell Steve I don't need to be his best man. I really am flattered, but..."

"Fuck you, Bobby, you tell him."

"You're right, I should tell him."

"Who comes to the wedding isn't your decision to make."

"I know. It's your wedding, Sis. I'll be there, just not up at the altar. Be reasonable."

"And the reception?" Her voice was seething.

Lies That Bind

"I'll be at the church, that's what matters."

"Damn it, Bobby, when are you going to grow up?" *The attack is on.* If I were there she would be pacing with her hands on her hips.

"What does that mean?"

"Stand up for yourself. Stop being the perfect martyr."

Okay, that was a good one, but below the belt. "Janet, that's not fair, and now I'm getting pissed," Janet was both the person I felt closest to and the person with whom I could get the angriest. "I'm not your little brother anymore, and I prefer to be called Robert."

"Then act like a Robert." She was practiced at this. "First of all, this is not your wedding, it is Steve's and my wedding. You don't get to say who comes and who doesn't, and neither do Mom and Dad. Steve and I are paying for the wedding, and it's our wedding."

"I know that, but…"

"But shit. And don't interrupt me."

Wait a minute—didn't she just interrupt me?

"Steve and I decide who is invited and who is not. If you don't want to be in the wedding, then don't be. If you don't want to come to the reception, then don't. But you should know this: I told Mom and Dad that they are not receiving an invitation. I told them that they did not speak for the rest of the family, but if they wanted to boycott the wedding, they could. Whether you are best man or not, Mom and Dad are not invited." I started to speak, but Janet cut me off again. "Wait, Robert. I am not done. I don't want a lecture from you about this. Believe me, your opinion on all of this is not welcome."

Did I say that she isn't into soft talking anyone? "Damn it, Sis. It's supposed to be the happiest day of your life."

"Bobby, I love you. I adore you. Steve loves you, he doesn't give a damn if Mom and Dad are there, or anyone else from the family, especially Claire. But he would be so hurt if you turned him down."

"Sis. I…"

"Bobby, you can't undo what Mom and Dad did. And this isn't the first time they've done this. So Claire has a stake in me backing down."

"What do you mean?"

"Bobby, for a psychologist…"

"Don't do that." I hated it when people thought that I spent all my time figuring out the different dynamics in everyone's relationships. Like I was the Dr. Freud of the Mitchell family and when I wasn't, then I was Dr. Clouseau.

"Okay. Mom and Dad broke up Claire and Michael, because he was Jewish."

"I didn't know that."

"Really!" she sounded surprised. "Well, I guess you were away at college. You remember how madly in love she was with him; Dad wouldn't have any of it. When Claire told them that Michael wanted to raise their children Jewish, Dad forbade the marriage. He said he would have nothing to do with her or their children. Claire finally broke it off with Michael. She married Roger, who loves her and who is wonderful to her, but she has no love for him. She's told me her life is empty, three kids with him and she has no feelings for him at all."

I really did love Claire, but there was something so pathetic about her. Personally, I thought she was a carbon copy of my mother, and her career was a carbon copy of my father's. I often wondered if she had any idea who she was. "I didn't know that. Why does she stay with him?"

"He's a fabulous father to the kids, and a good husband."

"Yeah, but…"

"So, now look at what else she has to deal with besides a loveless marriage. You come out and stand up to Mom and Dad. You accept their rejection as the price for doing what is best for you, she didn't."

"I couldn't…"

"Cut the crap, there are a lot of gay men who get married and have boyfriends on the side. You know James in my office?"

"I don't think so."

"Well anyway, he's married, three kids, and is having an affair with another married guy in the firm. You could have done something like that."

"No, I couldn't."

"Now, Dad is doing it again. Don't you think Claire has an interest in seeing me give in to his demands? And, it gets worse."

"Is that possible?" *Damn, do I really want to move back to New York? And if I were nuts enough to agree to see my mother, wouldn't I get pulled into all this shit again?*

"She's supposed to be in the wedding."

"That's right. Oh fuck, what is she going to do?" *Damn, poor Claire.* "She hates getting caught in the middle."

"Well, she knew I told Mom and Dad they weren't invited. She knew that Steve and I had the discussion long ago about how we were going to handle this. If you come, she has to either go against Mom and Dad's wishes and be in the wedding, or…"

Lies That Bind

"Poor Claire," I said laughing. "This is why she tried to kill you when you were a baby."

Janet laughed. "If she backs out, she's history with me."

"Damn. Stuck between you and Mom and Dad," I said.

"I have another favor to ask you. I want you to walk me down the aisle."

"Oh fuck, Janet, think about what you're doing."

"No, Bobby. Think about what Dad is doing. Dad won't walk me down the aisle because Steve wants you as his best man. That is sick, Bobby."

"But how can I take Dad's place?"

"You are not taking his place. You are walking me down the aisle. Don't turn me down, please."

"God, Janet, what are you doing, making a political statement?"

"Bobby, why won't you let people love you, and why do you love those people who can't?"

"Jan, I don't. Well, I do love them, they are my parents, but damn, if it weren't for me, your wedding would be perfect."

"Damn, that makes you pretty powerful, fucking up my wedding all by yourself." *Smart-ass, those are my lines.* "Bobby, do you remember the last thing that Dad said to you?"

"Of course I do. I should have been aborted. How does someone forget that?"

"Do you think you should have been?"

"Of course not."

"Then why do you act like it?"

"Jan, you are really being a bitch today." *This had to be Steve's coaching her.*

"Bobby, don't you see how you are always aborting yourself? The holidays I wanted to spend with you that you turned me down, and that you spent alone. Think about it. You keep making yourself a non-person. Bobby, you're my baby brother, a wonderful human being, the future godfather to all our children. Stop playing the part they've assigned to you."

"Damn, Sis, where are you getting this from?"

"If Steve finds out you were thinking about not being his best man, he'll have you committed someplace. How many times do I have to say this, Bobby? Stop making other peoples opinions of you, your opinion of you. Stop living your life as others would have you live it. Life is too fucking short."

I just heard myself say that to Chris. But, of course, far more eloquently and much more compassionately. "I know you're right, but it's hard, Jan."

"I know it seems that way, Bobby, but it's easier than the way you've been living your life. So many people love you. Let that be your focus for a while."

"Whatever." *Yeah, I had recently picked that up working on the wards. And they were right. It did have a great dismissive ring to it.*

"So you are walking me down the aisle?"

"Damn, Jan. Are you sure?"

"Very sure. Oh Bobby, I'm so excited. I didn't want to walk down the aisle alone. Dad would have been my first choice, but you're a great second choice. And I'm not going to tell Steve that you were actually thinking about not being his best man."

"Okay." I couldn't believe it, but I was doing my best to choke back my tears. She would never really know what the strength of her love meant to me. I could tell her I loved her, and I'd do anything for her, but she would never really get it.

"Bobby, someday I really do hope you'll take down those walls and let in the love that so many people have for you." There was a silence, a long silence. "Okay, now for news you will not believe. Are you sitting?"

"Can't we skip this? Claire told me. Mom wants a meeting."

"I am going to strangle her. I told her not to tell you." I almost laughed; I guessed I did like getting Claire into hot water. She had told me not to tell Janet that she told me. "Well, she didn't give me the details, just that Mom wanted a meeting."

"Okay, well listen. It's in the details. Are you sitting?"

I loved her dramatics. She loved life and was full of it. "Actually, I'm lying down on the couch and I've already made up my mind. It's no, and you are not going to win this one."

"Fine, but just listen, and whatever you decide, I won't argue with you."

"Right. Like I believe you," I said. "Get on with it."

"Mom called me and asked if she could meet me for lunch. So we met at the New York Athletic Club. I was sure this was a pleading for reconsideration about the wedding plans." Her voice was full of energy.

"Yeah," I said, smiling, seeing her enthusiasm in my mind's eye.

"So we order martinis and salads. She is making small talk—God, I hate that crap—but I'm ready for her. She puts down one martini and orders another and is half done with that one when in the middle of a sentence she breaks down crying. I mean a napkin-over-the-face, gasping-air kind of crying."

Lies That Bind

I was surprised. "At the club?" I asked, my mouth falling open. "Damn, they know her there."

Janet went on, "I sit there ready to take her apart. I am thinking this is the most manipulative bullshit and it isn't going to work." Janet was on a roll. I could see the picture, my mother in her uptown-conservative-but-frumpy summer wear and Janet mostly in black.

"It would work with Claire, but I can't believe she thought it would…"

"It would work with you, too, Bobby," she quickly snapped back.

Good one. "Bitch!" Janet never let one get by. She was what we call New York real.

She continued, "Just shut up and listen. So I'm waiting for her to stop. She calms down, tries to speak, and starts all over again. She gets up and goes to the ladies' room. I just sat there, but then I started feeling sorry for her."

"Softy."

"Kiss my ass," she shot back. "So I went in and she's sitting there. She looked up at me and said…Bobby, are you sitting?"

"Go for it."

"'When will he be here?'" Janet said.

"Me?"

"Mom asked, 'When is he getting to New York?' Bobby, I had to sit down. She started crying again. I told her at the end of the July. She asked me if you were badly hurt by Adam."

"What? You're bullshitting me. She knew his name?"

"I swear it. She cried like I've never seen her cry. Bobby, I started to cry, too. She kept saying, tell me about him, tell me how he is, do you have a picture? Bobby, it was like this was all just bursting out of her."

"Damn, Janet. Where did she get Adam's name from?"

"I asked Claire if she had talked to Mom about you and she said no. So, all I can think is that I talk to cousin Pat. She's always asking about you, always. She must tell her mother. Bobby, she knew everything. She knew you lived by the beach and that you're coming back to a job at John Jay College, everything."

"Damn. I guess I am surprised."

"I think she's coming to the wedding without Dad."

"No. You think?"

"She asked me if I thought you could ever forgive her."

"Really? What did you say?"

"I told her I thought she knew the answer. I said, 'Mom, Bobby is still Bobby, you know he will'. She started crying again and nodding her head. Bobby, how often do you see me cry? I was crying." I could hear Janet choking up as she said, "You know Bobby, as much as Mom drives me nuts, I really do love her."

"I know, Janet," I said. The thought of Janet being touched by all this finally got to me; my eyes filled with tears.

"She asked me to ask you if you would be willing to see her when you got back. But, she said she didn't know if she could tell Dad. So I'm supposed to ask you if you'd see her so she can apologize, and if you would be willing to rebuild your relationship with her, even if she couldn't tell Dad." I sat up as tears rolled down my face. "Bobby?"

"I told Claire that I wouldn't see her."

"Bobby, don't be pigheaded like Dad,"—another one—"I really think you should see her." There was a long silence. My head said to say no. I wanted to punish her. I wanted to hold firm, to be angry. Oddly, I thought of Anthony Dinato, and then Chris and Frank Bellesano. I could picture Frank sitting in his car refusing to take the risk to allow reconciliation. *Damn, was I being as much of an ass as Frank?*

"Damn it, Janet. You said you wouldn't pressure me."

"Sorry. You're right. Mom does deserve what she gets." Janet said matter-of-factly.

"I see, so this is your attempt at reverse psychology. Remember who you're talking to," I snapped at her.

"To whom." Neither of us spoke. "So what should I tell her?" Janet asked patiently.

"Tell her that I'd love to see her," I said, as tears rolled down my face.

"She said she's missed you so much, and that she'll do anything to make up to you what she's done to you."

"Tell Mom I've missed her, and that she doesn't have to tell Dad. I am not going to make my relationship with her conditional on how she lives her life."

"Oh wow, good one, Bobby. I'm going to write that one down."

"Jan, tell her she doesn't have to apologize either."

"Bobby, let her say what she wants to say to you. I think it will be painful for both of you, but I think it will clear things up and bring you together. That's what you both want, and that's what I want, too."

"You're right. Do me a favor, Jan."

Lies That Bind

"Sure."

"When we hang up, call Mom. Tell her I miss her and that we will meet someplace whenever she wants, but not at the Athletic Club. Actually, I know a place in the Bronx, a Jewish deli, where it's private."

"That place on Pelham Parkway?"

"Yeah."

"Robert—you'll always be Bobby to me—Robert, did I tell you that I love you recently?"

"Yeah." And then from the depths of my gut came a sadness churning through my chest, and then I heard myself sobbing.

"Ah, Bobby, I wish I was there." And then I heard Janet sniffing.

"Jan, I've hated being an orphan."

"Oh, Bobby." Now we were both crying.

Then I started laughing. "Damn it, Janet, I don't know why I'm laughing. I guess I just feel relieved." She started to laugh too.

"I love you, Sis, and Steve, too."

"When will you be in New York?" she asked, as she blew her nose.

"I'm thinking that I'll be there in about three weeks, mid-July. The apartment will be mine August first."

"You can stay with us if you want."

"I was hoping I could do that." We were both composing ourselves.

"Okay, I've got to go."

"Oh, Jan! I've got a date."

"With whom? When? Where?"

"He's a friend of Barbara's. They're moving back to the city next year. I can't wait for you to meet them. Anyway, he's a guy who lives on the upper West side. Josh Rosen. He's a photographer and a professor at The New School. He sounds really nice, warm, sincere, funny, and pretty aware of himself."

"Good for you. Great. Bring him to the wedding."

"One thing at a time," I said.

"You're right. See, I let you win one." We laughed. "Talk to you in a couple of days."

"Sounds good."

"I love you, Robert." She hung up.

My sister Janet. Where does she get it from?

Part Four: Monday

Chapter Fifteen

"Good morning, Karen," I said, as I entered her office.

"Good morning, come in." She was conservatively dressed in a navy blue suit. Everything about her, her posture, her dress, her tone of voice and mannerisms, always carried an air of confidence and professionalism. I explained all that I had learned from Chris since I had last seen her.

"You have to read this letter, Karen. I put a copy of it in his chart."

"I read it. Passive-aggressive bitch. He's a kid. What could have possessed her to write such a letter? And for him to come three thousand miles and not reach out to his son, and then for her to tell the kid," she said shaking her head.

"Well, maybe he didn't want to disrupt Chris's life. Or maybe it was just too emotionally charged for him, besides…" I stopped, *where did that come from*, I wondered.

"Bobby!" she snapped at me. "Who was it that said, 'I hate the victim that respects his executioner?'"

"Sartre," I answered. "You knew that—as a matter of fact, you were the one who told me he said it."

Karen smiled. "Forgiving your father—sorry, I meant to say his father—" she said, looking as sly as a fox, "will come in time, but respecting him is a mistake."

"Actually, this is about my mother, her wanting to meet with me. After I talked to my sister Janet I decided that I would meet with her."

"Good for you, Bobby."

"I guess what I said before, about Frank, maybe I was just wanting to…"

"Bobby, just let it happen. Don't rush the process, don't make excuses for what she did, but be open to forgiving her."

I nodded. "Anyway, we did some interesting dream work."

"What do you mean?" Karen asked.

I explained Chris's dream to Karen. I told her of my first impressions of his being hesitant, fearful and resistant. I mentioned my concerns that he was at first overly compliant, but said I thought that he was nonetheless able to take great interest in what we were doing. I also confessed that, although it was very unusual for me to take a patient in a direction that I thought was interesting, rather than just following their lead, I thought he benefited from it. As I was finishing what I could remember from our session, I began to realize that I was rambling nervously. I could see that not only was Karen listening to me, she was also listening to her analytic/supervisor voice. "Just say it, Karen. What did I do?"

"There was a reenactment going on."

"Shit, what did I do?"

"Nothing bad. Listen, you know how I look at transference. There must be reenactments for healing to occur for this boy. He has consistently given himself over to the agenda of others. Given himself over to what others wanted from him; his father over and over again; Jack in the car, getting him to open up and then in the tent; then that son-of-a-bitch priest in the confessional."

"Damn it. Damn. I did exactly that. Damn. I asked him to play with the dream—my agenda; and he did."

"Bobby. His therapy is going to come in those reenactments. Do you realize the trust he is placing in you? He has opened the door to the most damaged part of himself."

"You're being kind. I fucked up."

"Bobby, do you know me to worry about the feelings of the therapists I supervise over the welfare of the patients on this ward?"

"No."

"If I thought you fucked up, I would tell you. You come to this from your heart, and then use your head. You don't come from just your head. I know that, and I think Chris senses that.

"I have no doubt that he could have shut you down cold if he didn't want to work with you. And, my guess, if he had made a move to stop the play, you would have stopped."

"Okay." My stomach felt unsettled. "Anyway, Chris's boyfriend David was also molested by this same guy, Jack." I couldn't help but continue beating myself up about what I had done. Oddly, I knew she was right, and I also knew she wouldn't spare my feelings; she hadn't in the past. But, given the opportunity, I had to at least suffer through this for a while longer.

"I saw your notes."

"I want him to meet with the police first."

"Why?"

Lies That Bind

I explained my reasoning and also reminded her that I wanted to meet with Chris first, then with Carl. "I'm hoping to get Chris out of here late this afternoon. I'll see him again after lunch with his family and then, if things work out, I want to release him."

"I wouldn't bring in everyone at first. Just his mother, then the grandparents."

"Actually, I was thinking of his grandfather. He's the father figure, and there is a lot of pain I'd like to get to. You know, with all his father stuff. I think that's where I can make the largest impact."

"Whatever you think is best. I trust your instincts. I'll send the authorities in to interview this other boy. Is he here?"

"Yes, he's in the lobby with Mrs. Patrona."

"Have you thought about recommendations for treatment?"

"Yes. I called Dr. Aston at NYU postdoc. I'm going to give Chris his name and number. I'm sure Dr. Aston will be able to refer Chris to someone who will be helpful."

"What about you?"

"What?"

"You'll be in New York. You're opening a practice, aren't you?"

"Yes, but I don't know how ethical that would be."

"I don't see a real problem with it. Do this. Have him see Dr. Aston for referrals, and when Dr. Aston gives him the names of two or three therapists Chris might call, have him give Chris your name also. Then Chris can decide if his experience with you here is something he values and sees you as someone who can help him."

"I guess I could do that. I won't say anything to Chris about it now, though."

"Good. See me later today."

While I was sitting in the nurses' station, a call came in that the police would be in at ten o'clock. to interview Chris. I informed them that David Jarrett was waiting to be interviewed also, and that they should interview him first. I promised that Chris would be free to be interviewed by ten-thirty. "Nurse Ortiz, could you bring Mr. Bellesano to treatment room four?"

Chris looked both exhausted and agitated. "How did you do last night?" I asked.

"It's hard to sleep around here," he said as he sat down, again not looking at me.

"You didn't sleep?"

"On and off. I guess I was thinking a lot."

"About your father?"

"Yeah, about what we talked about, but mostly about David."

"What about him?"

"Where he is. If he still hates me." His eyes filled with tears, and his voice became strained. This was the closest I had seen him come to expressing his emotions.

"Chris, I want to tell you again that it's okay to cry."

"I don't cry."

"I see, that 'sissies-cry' stuff."

"No, I wish I could sometimes, but when I get close, it all stops automatically. It just disappears."

"Or it turns to anger."

"Yeah, I guess, that too."

"Why do you think David hates you?"

"When I took him home after I got the letter, I fucked up. I should have known something was wrong. I did know something was wrong. But David was right. I'm really just a coward."

"David called you a coward?"

"Yes."

* * * * *

"Your dad just came outside," Chris said, pointing to the front door of David's house.

"Ignore him. Talk about sadistic assholes," David said, waving his hand toward Paul and giving him a phony grin.

"Chris, I'm scared for you. I'm scared of what this is doing to you. I'm sad because your dad died."

"You didn't even know him," Chris said, watching Paul Jarrett standing in the doorway of his house.

"Sad for you," David said. "No matter how big a prick he was, he was your dad. Like that shit there," he said pointing to Paul. "He's my dad. I hate him," David said with a growl. "But I'd be sad if I found out he had died. Especially since I still hate him."

Chris gave David a look of disbelief. "You're always too emotional. You're always crying or tearing up or something, and now you're getting angry for no reason at all," Chris said, dismissively.

"And I'm angry about that letter, and I'm getting angry at you, too."

"That's three times now in one weekend. I can't remember you ever getting angry at me," Chris said, as he continued to watch Paul.

Lies That Bind

"David, I think your dad is waiting for you. What is he hitting his leg with?"

"Shit, he has the belt."

"What time were you supposed to be home?"

"I'm early. I told him I'd be here after dinner. God, what is his problem?" David said, exasperated.

"Your dad scares me. I think he's insane. Here he comes," Chris said, giving David a quick rub on the leg. "Let's get your stuff out of the back."

As Chris opened the hatchback of the Suburban and David reached in for his bag and backpack, he said to Chris, "Listen, if you need to talk to me tonight, come over. I'll leave my window open."

Chris closed the hatchback as Paul joined them. "Hi, Mr. Jarrett."

"Dad, Chris just found out that his father died."

"Richard?" Paul asked, staring at David as David picked up his backpack and suitcase.

"No, my father in New York," Chris answered. Paul looked at Chris, and then back toward David. As David took a step toward Paul, he asked, "What's wrong?" with a tone of disgust in his voice. Paul grabbed at David with such hatred in his eyes it scared Chris. He yanked his son so hard that David dropped his suitcase and lost his footing. "God damn it, what's wrong?" David mumbled, and with that, Paul began to whip him across his bare legs with the belt.

"Hey, what is your problem?" Chris shouted, instantly enraged.

"Get in the house," Paul ordered David. "Now!"

David turned to Chris, eyes downcast, and said, "I'd better get inside," as he shrugged his shoulders and shook his head. Paul took that opportunity to whip David across the arm. David winced and started to walk away. Chris stared at Paul and the older man stared at Chris. Neither of them budged.

"Be gone. He isn't allowed to have friends anymore, and that includes you."

"Be gone, my ass. You know you're a real nut case. And you don't decide who I have as a friend," Chris said, feeling heat running through his body.

"Watch your language, my son," Paul said, taking the other end of the belt in his other hand.

"First of all, I am not your son. Second, don't even think you can threaten me." *Go ahead, you bastard, swing that belt at me. I wish you would.* "I'm not afraid of you," Chris said, never taking his eyes off of Paul.

Paul shouted, "I never liked you. Get out of here." He slapped the belt against his own leg.

Chris didn't move. His face burned with anger. His jaws locked tight, and he found that his hands were tightly fisted. "I never liked you, either." *Go ahead asshole; please swing that belt at me. I'll flatten you right here and now. Then I'll take that belt and shove it up your ass.*

"Get off my property."

"David is my friend and he'll always be my friend, so you can eat shit and die, old man." *And when you die you can visit my father in hell.* "You're a scared little man, with an ugly heart and a black soul. All you do is cause people pain."

Paul turned and walked up his walkway. As he was halfway to his doorway he turned and said, "You won't want to be his friend for long." Then he walked into his house and slammed the door.

Chris opened the car door and sat behind the wheel. *What the fuck does that mean? Damn you, you dumb bastard. Damn you!* he thought, as he slammed his fist against the steering wheel over and over. He looked into the Jarrett house from his car; everything seemed quiet. Then he noticed Paul staring back at him from the living room window.

Chris started the car and backed out of the driveway. *What was that supposed to mean, I won't want to be his friend for long?* He was sure David was in trouble. *But why?* When he arrived at home Diane was surprised to see him. She explained that David was supposed to call her, and that he never had. Chris described what happened at the Jarrett house. Now, they both began to worry.

"I'm going to call there and ask for David," Chris insisted. "I just have to know if he is okay."

"No, let me," Diane insisted. "If you call he'll just start with you again. What do you think he meant?"

"I have no idea," Chris said, but he did. He was beginning to wonder if David's father knew about them. But if he did, Chris reasoned, he wouldn't have said what he had. Chris thought Paul would have said something much more caustic. "What reason are you going to give for calling?" Chris asked.

"I don't know. Maybe, I can say that I need David to drive me tomorrow night. I'll say it's something about tomorrow night." Diane dialed the phone, and Paul answered.

"Hi Paul, I want to thank you for letting David accompany us this weekend. Richard and I really enjoyed having him along. He's a good

Lies That Bind

boy." Diane waited. "Paul, are you there? ...I was wondering if I could talk to David about tomorrow night... Why not?" Diane asked. "Paul, is he there?" Diane stared at Chris while she looked disturbed and shook her head and rolled her eyes. "I might need a ride over to the ceremony tomorrow night. I know you're going early, and so is Chris." Again she rolled her eyes as she stared at Chris. "He's not going? But he told me earlier that he was...Paul...Paul are you there?" Diane pulled the phone from her ear and stared into the receiver and shouted, "*Stu faccima!*"

"Mom, David's in trouble. Big trouble, I just know it."

"There's nothing we can do now, honey. He'll be okay. God, what an asshole that man is," Diane shouted. "God, please let that boy be okay," Diane mumbled as she glanced up toward the ceiling.

Chris went to his room and paced. He read the letter several times, and then he thought about David. When he thought about Paul his body tensed with anger. When he thought of David, his stomach churned. At midnight, he wrote a note for Diane and left it on his pillow. After he lowered himself into the Jarretts' yard he looked toward David's room. The window was closed.

Chris made his way across the yard toward David's window. He slowly and very quietly moved himself along the back of the house. When he was near David's window he stood silently with his back pressed against the wall. David's room was dark, but Chris waited, staring away from the streetlight so that his eyes would adjust to the dark. Then he turned and stared into David's room. The room looked like a tornado had hit it. He looked at the corner of the room where David's bed should be. There he saw a mattress on the floor, and there was David, curled up in a ball, naked. Chris lightly tapped on the window. "David," Chris whispered, and then tapped again. Each time Chris turned and looked toward Paul's bedroom window.

David rolled over and stared at the window, and then noticed Chris waving. David moved painfully toward the window and opened it just slightly. "Go away, Chris, please."

"No, let me in," Chris said as he pushed the window open. "I'm coming in."

"Shhhh, I think he's still up," David said, pointing to the bedroom door.

Chris slowly pulled himself in through the window. "Oh my God, what happened to your room?" Chris asked, noticing that everything David owned had been thrown all over the room.

"He found my journal with my poems. He knows I'm gay," David said.

"Oh, shit. What did he do?" Chris said.

"We've got to whisper, really, I think he might be in the living room. He's locked me in my room. He put a padlock on the outside of my door so he could lock me in at night and lock me out during the day. I'm not allowed in my room except to get clothes and to sleep. When we go to sleep I have to be locked in my room."

"Oh my God, David, you've got red marks all over you." Then Chris noticed strap marks on the back of David's thighs and buttocks. "David, there's blood on your leg." Chris felt heat rush through his neck and face.

"It's weird, Chris. When he came into the house he made me undress in front of my mom. My brothers were in their rooms. That's really the worst part. I haven't had to do that for a long time. It's so humiliating. I told him I wouldn't and he tore my tee shirt off me and started to hit me on my back with his belt. I thought about you wanting to hit your dad that time you told me about, but I decided just to get naked. Then he started hitting me on the legs and the butt with his belt. I still didn't know why. I kept asking, but he wouldn't say. Then he told me to go to my room."

"Damn him David, I want to kick his ass."

"Forget it, Chris. I've been thinking, I'll be gone in forty-five days," David said.

"Why is your mattress on the floor?" Chris asked, circling David and looking more closely at the marks on his body. Chris's hands were shaking.

"He took my bed. All I'm allowed to have is the mattress. He's afraid I am going to hide stuff again. He told me I had to fold all my clothes and pile them on the floor."

"As soon as I saw my room I knew he knew. He followed me into my room. He told me that he knew I was homosexual. He started beating me with the belt again. He was screaming at me about something. I mean, it was like he was crazy. I don't completely remember what he was saying. I think I was kind of blanking out by then. I just kept trying to figure out how many more days until we'd be gone. I mean it was all hurting pretty bad, but I didn't care anymore. I just kept thinking of you and me living in New York." David's voice cracked with sadness. "Do you think I'm going crazy?"

"What?"

Lies That Bind

"It was weird, Chris. He was hitting me and I mean I could feel the pain and all, but I was trying to remember today's date and how many days there are until graduation. I kept thinking of us on the plane in forty-five days."

"Well, if you're crazy, then so am I."

"Shhhh." They both listened. They heard nothing. David moved closer to Chris and whispered, "Then he started to ask me questions. I'm not sure I heard all of them but he asked me if I had ever had sex with a guy, and I said no. Then he asked me if I had ever had sex with a girl, and I said no." He paused and then jokingly added, "Maybe I should have said yes. He asked me how many more of my friends knew that I was gay. I told him that no one knew. Then he asked me if I had ever touched my brothers."

"Oh David, he's such an asshole. I swear, David, he's psychotic."

"Yeah, I think he must be. I couldn't believe he was asking me if I'd molested my brothers. He had me pinned naked against the wall here in my room. Then he asked me again. I started to get really angry. I mean, he thinks I would molest my brothers."

"Why would he ever think of something like that?" Chris asked.

"I started to try to push him away, and then I called him a sick fuck."

"Oh shit, I mean he is, but…what did he do?"

"He brought his leg up and kneed me in the balls really hard. I fell on the floor and then tried to get up to get to the bathroom, but I didn't make it. I threw up all that good pizza." David laughed painfully.

"Always a joke. You have to make everything into a joke, don't you?" Chris said.

He watched as David walked toward his bed, doubled over and holding his hand against his lower stomach."

"He's nuts. Molest your brothers?" Chris repeated in disbelief.

"Shhhh, shit, someone is coming. Get in the closet," David whispered. Chris closed the closet door and David lay down on the bed. Seconds later Paul unlocked the padlock on David's door and looked in.

"Did I hear something?" Paul asked as he turned on the light.

"No, well, maybe you heard me praying."

"You'd better pray, you disgust me." Paul turned the light off, closed the door and padlocked it. Chris opened the closet door as they both listened to Paul's footsteps move down the hall.

"You can come out of the closet," David whispered and then laughed.

"David, you are such an asshole, I swear. This is no time for jokes. This is bad."

David whispered, "I'm just going to play along. It's only forty-five more days. I have to get through graduation. He said I can't go to New York this summer, and that I can't go to NYU ever, but I don't think there's anything he can do to stop me. My trust kicks in when I turn eighteen in July. I'll need to work for extra money, but I can still go to NYU and live with you like we planned. It will all work out, just forty-five more days. Do you think we can leave right after graduation?"

"Yeah, sure."

David winced and moaned as he moved on the mattress. "He's going to make me go to therapy with some Catholic guy who cures gays. Some Doctor Nicolas or something. He found the journal Friday night after I left, and by Saturday afternoon he had this guy on the phone. I'm supposed to see him tomorrow."

"He's going to cure you in forty-five days?" Chris asked quietly.

"No, no, I'm supposed to stay here until I am cured. The doctor told him that if I've never had sex with a guy there was a good chance I could be cured, or at least a much higher probability of success. But, if I've had sex with a guy, and if I liked it, then it will take a lot longer."

"Well, then, it's going to take him forever to cure you," Chris said, and David laughed.

When he laughed he grabbed his groin and said, "Don't make me laugh, it hurts.

"I told him that I really want to be cured. I think that settled him down. He made me promise that I wouldn't have sex with a guy. I promised him, but in my head I said for only forty-five days. Do you think we can wait forty-five days?"

Chris ignored David's question. He moved next to David on the mattress, put his arm around him and then slowly pulled himself close to him. He thought of saying that he loved him, but he noticed that David's body was beginning to shake. David rolled to his side and pushed the pillow over his face as he lay there and sobbed. Chris wanted to hold him, but did not know where to touch him. He tentatively moved closer. David reached around, took Chris's arm, and pulled himself tight against Chris's body. "I'm so scared," David said through his sobs. "I think I'd go crazy if it wasn't for you and your family." Chris held him tightly as David continued to cry silently.

When David stopped crying and settled down, Chris said, "David, this is so fucked. You've got to hate him."

"Chris, I just want to get away."

Lies That Bind

"Why do you think he decided to search your room?"

"I don't know."

"It's weird that he asked you how many more of your friends know you're gay. Why would he think any of your friends knew? And if he thought your friends knew, why wouldn't he think that I knew?"

Chris lay there holding David most of the night. David talked about living in New York City and working in the Bronx at Mr. Dinato's store. They wondered where they would find an apartment, and talked about how wonderful it was going to be living together. David thought he might focus on art classes, but also major in architecture. As they whispered, David seemed to relax, to feel hopeful and safe. Chris thought about causing Paul pain.

The next day after baseball practice, Chris arrived home to find his dinner waiting. Richard had decided to accompany Chris and Diane to the ceremony. They were dressing for the Eagle Scout ceremony while Chris rushed through his dinner. After dinner he reluctantly dressed in his Eagle Scout uniform. He was dreading seeing Paul at the meeting. Diane and Richard had a cocktail in the backyard as they waited for Chris, who was delaying as much as possible. He hoped that they would not arrive long before the beginning of the ceremony.

As Richard backed the car out of the driveway, Diane asked, "How was David today?"

Chris said, "He wasn't in school," looking out the backseat window.

"Really?" Diane was surprised. "Chris, I'm worried about him."

"Me, too."

"And Paul said David isn't going to be there tonight, either."

"I know," Chris said.

As Chris had hoped, they arrived only a few minutes before the ceremony began. Diane and Richard found seats as Chris walked to the front of the auditorium and joined the other participants.

The ceremony began with Shaun Rolland's two older brothers, who were also Eagle Scouts, escorting Shaun to the front of the auditorium. As Shaun turned and faced the audience, the lights dimmed. Paul walked up to the microphone and asked everyone to bow their heads in a moment of prayer. After the prayer, he led the crowd in the Pledge of Allegiance.

"Presentation of the Eagle Award is a serious matter," Paul Jarrett read from note cards. "This award is the culmination of Shaun Rolland's efforts for many years. I want to point out that this award is made possible with the assistance of those with the candidate tonight. His

Thomas Domenici

Scoutmaster Jack Payden, troop leaders, his fellow Scouts, especially Christopher Bellesano, his parents, brothers, friends, and members of the local community, have all been significant in Shaun's advancement."

Chris found it both ironic and outrageous that two of the people he hated most were standing with him honoring Shaun. He wondered just how influential Jack had been. Chris blushed with anger at the thought that Jack had had his way with Shaun. All this pomp and ceremony covering another boy's journey into young adulthood. A journey scarred with seduction, confusion, and pain.

"Shaun Rolland," Paul continued, "has distinguished himself through active service in scouting. He is trained and practiced in leadership abilities, and the character gained through the guidance of his mentor Jack Payden marks him. Shaun's commitment to citizenship and religious beliefs, the backbone of Eagle Scouts, was gained through the guidance of Christopher Bellesano, who will assist in the ceremony."

Shaun's brothers then moved to center stage and took turns reading the Eagle Scout Charge. Vance began, "The appeal of the majestic eagle has been felt by individuals from prehistoric times to the present day. To the Egyptians, the eagle was the messenger to the gods and the sun, a symbol of eternal life. To the Romans, he was the carrier of Jupiter's thunderbolts and a sign of power. To the American Indians, he stood as the incentive to valor and the pledge of victory. For us today, the eagle is a living symbol of courageous and freedom-aspiring Americans. When the badge of rank for Eagle Scouts was designed in 1912, a small silver eagle was suspended from a tricolor ribbon of red, white, and blue. It remains so today."

Al Rolland followed: "The foremost responsibility of an Eagle Scout is to live with honor. To an Eagle Scout, honor is the foundation of all character. He knows that "A Scout is trustworthy" is the very first point of the Scout Law for good reason. May the white of the Eagle badge remind you to always live with honor." He continued, "The second obligation of an Eagle Scout is loyalty. A Scout is true to his family, Scout leaders…" Continuing, Vance read the third and fourth charges: to be courageous and cheerful. Al finished with the fifth and final responsibility: service.

Mr. and Mrs. Rolland were then escorted to the front of the auditorium. Chris stood and joined Shaun at center stage. Chris read, "Your conduct along the trail has been excellent. You have rededicated yourself to the principles of scouting, but one more thing is important: your future.

Lies That Bind

"As an Eagle Scout, you become a guide to other Scouts of lower rank. You become an example in your community." *Jack, an example of what?* Chris wondered. "Remember that your actions are now a little more conspicuous, and people will expect more of you." *Action like beating your son half to death.* "To falter in your responsibility would not only reflect upon you, but your fellow Eagles and all scouting." *Does that responsibility include stopping Jack, an Eagle Scout child molester?* "The torch you carry is not only yours, but ours also." *I wonder just what you're really carrying. I am sorry, Shaun, I should have stopped him. I just never thought...* "Shaun Rolland, I challenge you to enter this Eagle brotherhood, holding ever before you, without reservation, the ideals of honor and service. By the repetition of the Eagle Scout Promise before your fellow member, you will become an Eagle Scout. Through the words you use..." Chris read the words before him, but felt himself pulling away. He felt waves of heat passing through his body as he read on. He thought of Paul and his violence against David, and his face flushed. It suddenly occurred to him that if he had never seduced David maybe this would never have happened. He thought of Jack and his hobby of molesting boys, and sweat ran down his back. He thought of the boys he had failed, those who were molested after him and those soon to be molested by Jack, and his stomach churned as he chided himself for his inaction. He thought of how he had failed as a son. Owing his father an apology rang true to him. His failures began to weigh heavily on him, and rage filled his body.

Chris continued, "Scouts, parents, and guests, please stand. Shaun Rolland, please repeat after me: I reaffirm my allegiance..." Chris wondered if David was okay. He thought he might sneak out again tonight and make his way into David's room. He knew he was taking a chance, mostly at David's expense, but he was worried.

The rest of the service proceeded as expected. Shaun was an Eagle Scout and his parents were proud. Three sons who were Eagle Scouts, one son graduated from Sacred Heart High School, and two sons to follow. Three sons, good citizens dedicated to service. They thanked Paul Jarrett for his part in helping Shaun, and Jack for his taking special interest in all three of their sons.

The ceremony usually ended with the Scout saying a few words to the audience, but Paul asked that, when Shaun was finished, he be allowed to address the group.

"Ladies and gentleman," Paul said into the microphone, "Eagles, Shaun, I know this is a very important time for you and your family. I want to thank you for asking me to officiate at your Eagle Scout ceremony. It made me proud."

"I asked to speak now, however, for another reason." Chris, who was looking down at the stage floor, slowly raised his eyes and looked toward Paul. "I speak to you tonight with a heavy heart." *Oh my God, he isn't going to do this.* "I want to ask you to pray for my family, and especially for my son David. *Oh shit, don't do this.* Chris swallowed hard as his heart began to pound in his chest. "It has come to our awareness that David is a homosexual." *You stupid fuck, everyone at school will know within an hour. You stupid fuck.* All Chris could feel was rage. He thought about jumping up and calling Paul a liar or telling everyone that he beat David, or that Jack was a child molester. He had to do something to stop what was happening. He looked out at Diane, who was staring up at him. People in the audience began to rustle in their seats as they listened to Paul. He could hear gasps, moans, groans, and even laughter as Paul continued.

"As you know, this is inconsistent with the values and traditions of being an Eagle Scout. Therefore, I feel it is my duty to inform you, and to resign David from the Scouts. I have here his uniform, which he will no longer wear." Chris stared at Diane as she continued to stare back at him.

"Today, David met with a wonderful doctor who assures me that David can be cured of this terrible disease. He said that in David's case cure is almost a guarantee. I will say that David is eager to rid himself of this terrible affliction, and has never acted upon his impulses. However, it is important that we pray for him." Paul asked that the audience bow their heads and pray for David in silence. Then he smiled, as though nothing had happened, and congratulated Shaun and the Rollands for raising three fine boys.

As Chris left the stage and made his way to Diane and Richard, Chris saw Jack arguing with Paul. He heard Paul say, "I told you never to talk to me. Isn't it bad enough I have to see you?" Then he heard Jack say, "Taylor, listen to me," as Paul pushed him away.

Why did Jack call Paul, "Taylor?" Chris wondered. Suddenly, Paul reached out and grabbed at Chris. "Did you know that David was a homosexual?" Paul asked, tightly gripping Chris's arm.

Chris looked at Jack, and then at Paul's hand on his arm. Chris, eyes slowly drifting upwards to meet Paul's, spoke, saying each word slowly and purposefully. "Take your hand off of me." He then looked toward Jack, who backed off and walked away from them both.

Lies That Bind

Paul stared at Chris and tightened his grip. "I want you to stay away from my son. He is not going to New York with you. We will enroll him in a college here, he will live at home until I feel comfortable that he is no longer homosexual."

Turning his glare back toward Paul, who was still gripping his arm, Chris said, "Take your hand off my arm, old man, or I will break it." Chris grabbed Paul's wrist and started to apply pressure to it. Paul showed surprise at the strength of Chris's grip. Trying not to wince, he let go of Chris's arm, but Chris did not let go of Paul's wrist. Paul grimaced as Chris began to squeeze and turn Paul's arm, so that his elbow turned upward toward his chest. "You are a sadistic bastard, old man, but don't you ever think that what David allows you to get away with you can try with me. You may be bigger than me, but I'll hurt you bad," Chris said, finally letting go of Paul's wrist. Chris then poked his finger into Paul's chest, and never breaking eye contact said, "If you ever put your hands on me again, I'll wipe the floor with your face." Then turned and walked away.

"What was that about?" Richard asked.

"He just told me to stay away from David," Chris said, as he quickly walked toward the door of the auditorium.

"Did you know about any of this?" Diane asked.

"Why would I know?" Chris answered.

"Because he was your best friend," Richard said, putting his jacket on.

Chris said, glaring at Richard, "Was? What's with the 'was?' He's still my best friend."

"He never said anything to you about…?" Diane hesitated.

"Did he ever tell me he was a homosexual? Is that what you want to know? No, he didn't." Chris stared at the ground as he walked.

"I'm shocked. I would never have guessed," Diane mumbled, while shaking her head.

Richard would not back off. "You must have suspected something. The two of you were inseparable. You just spent the weekend with him in a motel room. How could you not know?"

"Fuck off, Richard," Chris growled.

Diane waved at Richard, trying to get him to back off. "Did he ever try anything or suggest you two do anything like that?" Diane asked.

"Why are you asking me this? I said I didn't know."

"I'm really surprised, he always seemed so, so…" Diane fumbled for words.

"So what, Mom?" Chris asked, now turning his anger on her.

"I don't know. Heterosexual." Diane said, as they left the auditorium.

"You mean not gay, right?"

"Yeah, I guess. Good thing you found out before you moved in together. I wonder if we can still get you into the dorms."

"Just leave it alone, Mom."

"Well, I mean, you can't live with him. I mean in a studio apartment you'd be…"

"Yeah, what? I'd be what, Mom?"

"Uncomfortable," Diane said, as they waited for Richard to unlock the car doors.

"David has been my best friend for four years. I've never felt uncomfortable around him before. Why the fuck would I feel uncomfortable around him now?" Chris shouted.

"Christopher," Diane shouted back, "I know you're upset, but don't you dare use that language or that tone with me." And then in a calmer tone she said, "Anyway, it doesn't sound like he's going to New York."

"I'll live with Grandma and Grandpa until I get an apartment. Until I get to know people and find someone that I want to live with. But I am not going into the dorms."

"This must be a real disappointment to you," Diane said, as Richard started the car.

"Disappointment that he's gay?" Chris asked.

"Well that, and you were looking forward to living with him. Don't get me wrong Chris, I like David, he's a sweetheart, but…"

"You keep tripping over it, Mom." Diane could again hear the anger in his voice.

"I have nothing against gay people. There are gay people in my family, and I love them dearly."

"Who are they? I know everyone; they're my family, too. Who?"

"Never mind. I just think it's better if you find someone else to live with."

"Afraid it will rub off?" Chris asked caustically.

"Chris, stop it, I am not worried about you being gay." Diane hesitated. "Or should I be?"

"Pretty slick, Mom. I was waiting for that one."

"No, I mean I know you're not gay."

"Pretty slick, Chris. You didn't answer your mother. Should she be worried?" Richard chimed in.

"Fuck you," Chris barked.

"Christopher," Diane shouted, and again turned to wave Richard off.

Lies That Bind

Chris could not stop. He had to strike out at someone. The pace of his words was slow and the tone in his voice was harsh, "Richard, remember one thing. You are only married to my mother. You are not family, you are an in-law, a step, you are a stranger, you know. You are not blood…"

"Okay, Chris," Diane said calmly. "Enough, please. Richard, back off."

Everyone remained quiet for the rest of the drive home. Chris was feeling lost. Nothing seemed settled anymore. He wanted to sneak into David's bedroom, but he feared getting caught. He was sick with worry that everyone would think he was gay.

* * * * *

"Taylor," I said. Chris stared at me. I ran through my memory banks. Was I making this up or was I remembering something? "Taylor." Chris continued to stare.

"That's right, Taylor," he said, waiting.

He was about to speak when I said, "Zachary Taylor Payden. Andrew Jackson Payden. Paul is Jack's brother," I said feeling queasy. "He knew David was his nephew."

"For sure. He said that he had found Paul and met with him when he moved to L.A." His eyes welled up with tears.

"Did you ever tell David who Jack is?" The queasiness was turning to anger.

He spoke as he shook his head. "I didn't even remember that Jack had told me until after David disappeared."

Chapter Sixteen

"DAVID DISAPPEARED?" I ASKED. "What do you mean, disappeared?"
"I haven't seen David since then. I think he went and stayed with an aunt he told me about, but I can't remember where that is."

* * * * *

David did not attend school on Tuesday or Wednesday, nor did he show up for the baseball game Wednesday afternoon. Everyone was off their game, resulting in a loss to a team they should have beaten. It was their first defeat of the year.

Thursday morning was David's first day back at school, and the first time he had had a chance to speak to Chris alone since Sunday night. As they walked to their first class, physics with Father Anthony, David told Chris about his second appointment with Doctor Nicholas, and that his playing the part of a wanting-to-be-cured homosexual was working. It had to work, at least until graduation; "forty-one days and counting," David reminded Chris. Then his plan was to leave Los Angeles with Chris. Chris listened and wondered when David would talk about what had happened Monday night, but he never did. During their physics class it occurred to Chris that Paul had not told David that he had "outed" him on Monday night. Chris found it impossible to concentrate on what Father Anthony was saying; his mind was lost in worry about what might happen at school that day. Paul had to know that someone was going to call David out for being gay. Chris was afraid that if that were to happen, David would be caught off guard and humiliated. Chris then realized that was exactly what Paul wanted to have happen. Paul had not only "outed" his son, but had also left it for David to find out that everyone knew he was gay.

Chris continually glanced at David. For all that was going on in his life, David seemed okay. But David always seemed okay, especially when Chris was around. Chris could not decide what to do, when or how he should tell David, but he knew he did not want anyone else to tell him. He decided to tell Peter and Julie that David did not know, and that he would tell him after school that day. This would give David the evening

Lies That Bind

for a meltdown. Chris did not let David out of his sight the entire day. He knew no one would say anything as long as he was with him. Every time they were alone, Chris labored over whether or not he should tell David, but each time he decided it would be best to tell him on their way home. He knew David would react badly.

Their last class for the day was physical education, baseball. The team practiced, but again everyone seemed distracted. The coach kept everyone later than was normal and worked everyone harder than usual. Finally the coach ordered, "Everyone head to the showers. Chris, Peter, and David wait here." As the boys ran over to the coach he said to David, "You missed an important game yesterday and you looked like shit in practice today. I've been noticing a slow but consistent decline in your concentration and your physical conditioning. Anyway, I think it might be best if you think about sitting out the rest of the year. Maybe even step off the team."

"He's fine," Chris interrupted. "He's not going anywhere. He had some kind of flu, but he's fine. He'll be fine for the next game. I guarantee it."

David was surprised. "Coach, I think I'll be fine. I'd really like to play."

"He also pulled a groin muscle, but he's okay," Chris said. He would not take his eyes off the coach.

"David, you don't seem fine to me," Coach Fraser said looking at Chris.

"Coach, I'm really okay," David said, watching Chris and the coach staring at each other.

"Okay, look, David, give me two laps, and let me see your best. Then head into the showers."

"Look, you guys," Coach Fraser said to Chris and Peter, as David started to run his laps, "you're the captain and the co-captain of the team. The guys don't want David on the team. You can't blame them. It's all over the school that he's gay and, well, almost all of them have come to me since yesterday and said they want him off the team."

"I don't want him off the team," Peter said, with his arms crossed over his chest, as he stared down at his feet.

"So why don't you throw him off the team?" Chris asked, knowing full well that the coach could not throw a guy off the team because he was gay. "Why are you talking to us?"

"Well, I can't exactly do that. But if you both pull him because he's not playing well…"

"Forget it," Chris interrupted.

"Look, the team is not going to play well with him on it," Coach Fraser insisted.

"Anyone who doesn't play gets bumped," Peter said.

"Well, that might be most of the team. Look, guys, I know he's your friend," the coach said, as he looked over at David completing his first lap, "but I'm asking you to make an adult decision here. You've got to think of the team above the individual. Your loyalty has to be to the team, not your friend."

Chris continued to stare at the coach as he said, "The team will play with him on it, and any player that doesn't want to play can choose not to play." Chris could feel his anger brewing, but he knew he had to be careful with the coach. He also knew the coach needed him on the team to get to the playoffs.

"Chris, you were picked team captain, not each guy's friend. You have to think of the team," the coach insisted.

"I agree with Chris," Peter joined in, "This really sucks. I'm not surprised by some of the guys on the team, but you surprise me, Coach."

"I have nothing against gay people, but I want us to at least get to the city playoffs. I think we can make state, but I think this team will fold with David playing."

"You know what, Coach, if you kicked some ass," Peter suggested, "they'd play just fine, but I think they know they have a sympathetic ear."

"Cut the crap, Cartola. Go take a shower, Jarrett," the coach shouted to David. "You still look to me like you're hurting."

Chris whispered, "That's bullshit, Coach, and besides, he'll be fine by the next game." His voice strained against his anger.

"Coach," Peter said again looking at the ground, "I say he plays."

"You guys might get voted out. They thought this might happen and they are talking about Derek as the new captain."

Chris laughed, "No problem." Chris stepped back, bent over and put his hands on his knees. "Derek," Chris hissed shaking his head. Chris was thinking of ways to hurt Derek.

"Okay," said the coach, "then I guess that will be it. Jarrett goes, but I really didn't want it to happen this way. You've been a good captain."

Chris straightened up. "No problem, Coach," Chris said smiling caustically, "and you'd better find someone else to play first base. David goes and I am going to be very injured the rest of the season."

"You don't want to do that, Chris." His voiced strained with anger. "You fuck with me and I'll fail your ass."

Peter said to the coach, "You'd better find another third baseman too, Coach. I'm feeling injured, too."

Lies That Bind

"You guys, don't fuck with me. I swear you don't want to fuck with me," he warned, taking a step toward Chris, who in turn took a step toward the coach.

"Coach, just leave it alone. They'll play," Peter said. "I promise you."

"Derek is the new team captain. I want the both of you to run a mile. You two better think hard about not playing."

Peter and Chris started to run around the track. They watched as the coach talked to Derek at the front of the gym. Chris told Peter that he didn't have to drop off the team in support of what Chris was doing. Peter assured him that he was doing it for David, and besides, failing physical education at this point meant nothing to him. Julie had been accepted to Berkeley and he could explain what happened if the college officials ever questioned him. "And besides," Peter said, "I have more than enough credits to graduate."

After finishing a half-mile they agreed to head to the shower. The coach had gone into his office, but Derek was waiting outside the gym.

"Guys, this wasn't my idea," Derek announced as they approached. "I think it sucks, but I think it's best for the team."

"Fuck you," Chris said angrily, as he moved quickly toward Derek. Peter grabbed Chris by the arm. "I'm going to kick your ass, you prick," Chris shouted.

"Chris, ignore him," Peter insisted, pushing Chris toward the locker room door. "Let's just go and take a shower."

"Wait. Wait, you guys, let's talk. Maybe we can work this out," Derek pleaded.

Peter tried to cool things down. "Okay, Derek. Just how are we going to do that?"

"Chris, maybe David doesn't want to play. I mean, maybe he just would rather sit the rest of the season out."

"And why would he want to do that?" Peter asked, still holding onto Chris's arm.

"For the team. The coach will give him an A. He'll letter him again in varsity. I think once David knows how the team feels, I think he won't want to play. I think he'll do the right thing."

"The right thing," Chris said, glaring at Derek.

"Everyone knows, everyone. Guys on other teams know," Derek said, sheepishly. "And that isn't my fault. His dad told everyone. You were there, Chris. He must have wanted everyone to know."

"David doesn't know what his father did," Peter said, looking at Derek. Chris said calmly, "He is going to freak when he finds out that everyone knows."

"Wow, he didn't tell him. Oh shit, that really sucks," Derek replied. "Why didn't you tell him?" he asked Chris. "I mean, you're his best friend."

"He wasn't at school until today. I wanted to tell him, but I just couldn't. I couldn't," Chris said, shaking his head. "I will later. On the way home," Chris said, with a great deal of apprehension.

"Shit, you'd think his father would have told him," Derek said to Chris. "What a bastard. Someone tells you that your son is gay and then you tell everyone. Why would he do something like that to his own son?" Chris turned and glared again at Derek.

"Chris, you've got to tell him," Peter said. "I would, but really, Chris, you should."

Chris stared at Derek, "I guess, but it's going to be bad. Derek, if David is off the team I'm gone. I don't care if he's thrown off or if he decides to leave. He goes and I go."

Derek pleaded, "You can't do that. The team needs you. Chris, that just isn't fair."

"Fuck you with fair," Chris said, as he continued to stare at Derek.

"Same for me, dude," Peter said, holding onto Chris.

"Guys, but listen. Maybe after he finds out what his dad did, he'll quit. I mean, maybe he won't want to embarrass the team by playing. What do you call it? Oh yeah, 'team cohesiveness,'" Derek said with a smirk. "Isn't that it, Don Bellesano?"

Chris glared at Derek. "You are such an asshole, Derek. You'd better just get out of my face. It is taking every bit of control I have not to beat the shit out of you right here and now. As a matter of fact, fuck it, I am going to beat the shit out of you," Chris growled, lunging at Derek again. Peter held Chris back by leaning into his chest and holding onto his arms.

"And why would he be embarrassing the team by playing?" Peter asked Derek.

"Derek, let's go if you want a ride," Gary called out as he exited the gym with three other players. Derek turned and started to walk away.

"Derek," Chris called out. "You said something before."

"What?" Derek called out, now walking backward facing Chris.

"You said that someone told Paul that David was gay," Chris said as he began to walk toward Derek.

Lies That Bind

"I did?" Derek said, shrugging his shoulders.

"Derek, come here." Peter could see that although Chris sounded calm, his neck was bright red.

Derek turned and began to walk faster. "Guys, I've got to go or I'll miss my ride."

Chris called out again, "Derek." Peter grabbed hold of Chris. "Derek, I made a promise to you. Do you remember?"

"Fuck you, too, Bellesano," Derek yelled back, laughing and giving Chris the finger. "Now who has the coach's ear?"

"You're dead meat, Derek, dead meat!" Chris screamed.

Peter asked, "What the fuck is that about?"

"That fuck told David's father. I know he did," Chris snapped back.

"Are you sure?" Peter said, letting go of Chris.

"David didn't know why his father searched his room. He hadn't done it before. Derek said someone told Paul."

"Damn, why would he do that?"

Chris shook his head. "That's too long a story. Fuck him, I swear I'm going to kick his ass," he replied.

Chris's, Peter's, and David's lockers were all in the same area of the locker room. On his way to his locker, Peter stopped to use the bathroom. When he returned to his locker Chris was naked and sitting on the bench in between the rows of lockers.

"Do you want me there when you tell him?" Peter asked as he began to undress.

"Shit." Chris thought for a moment while he stared at the floor. "I guess not. Where is he? Did you see him come out of the gym?" He felt afraid. Afraid of how badly David was going to feel, knowing that everyone knew he was gay.

"No, he's probably in the showers. Check his locker and see if his stuff is still in it," Peter replied, pointing to David's locker.

"Yeah, it's all here," Chris said, opening David's unlocked locker. Chris sat staring at Peter. "I know he called Paul. That fuck."

"Did you ever think David was gay?" Peter asked Chris.

Chris just shrugged his shoulders. "Does it make a difference to you? I mean, I know you don't want him off the team and that you're his friend, but I mean, well, you know, if he's in the shower?" Chris asked sheepishly.

"You mean being naked in the shower with him? Nah, it doesn't matter to me."

"Wouldn't you worry he was thinking about you sexually?" Chris asked, looking at the floor.

"Are you worried?" Peter asked, sounding annoyed. "Chris, he's your best friend. Doesn't that count for anything?"

"Yes, of course. Really, it's fine with me. But I know it bothers some guys."

"That's so stupid. First, I would have to be pretty full of myself to think he'd find me attractive. And second, if he did, the only reason I would be afraid is if I didn't know what I would say if he propositioned me. And I know what I'd say."

Chris smiled and nodded. "What would you say?"

"I'd say no, Julie would kick my ass if I did anything with anyone," Peter said smiling.

Chris laughed, "You're right, she would."

"I mean, if you know you don't want sex with a guy, what do you care if some guy finds you attractive? Anyway, I've been David's friend since we were in first grade. Actually, I kind of thought he might be gay. I mean, I don't know if I'm remembering things now because I know, but anyway, I really like David. And I hate his dad and I think this is all a bunch of shit," Peter said, putting his gym clothes into his locker. "But I really think you have to be the one to tell him. Can you imagine his dad doing that and not telling him? What would he feel like if someone who wasn't a friend came up to him and told him and made fun of him? God, the humiliation."

"Well, that *is* why his dad didn't tell him. He is such a prick." Chris felt queasy. "I'll tell him on the way home. Fuck!" Chris whispered as they walked toward the shower.

They could hear a shower running as they approached the shower room. Chris stopped on his way to the shower to go to the bathroom. As he stood at the urinal just the other side of the wall from the showers he heard Peter shout, "Oh fuck, David! Chris, Chris, come here!"

Entering the shower Chris saw Peter, naked on his knees, bending over David, who was lying on the floor of the shower. A cotton tee shirt was pulled over his head and one leg from a pair of panty hose was tied over his mouth. Another pair was used to tie his arms and legs. Chris froze as he felt the blood draining from his head. Peter kept saying, "Oh fuck, David! Oh fuck," as he tried to untie the gag from around David's mouth. "Oh fuck, David. Chris come here and help me. Oh fuck," Peter went on, his voice quivering. As he continued to struggle with the knots, Chris knelt down and tore open the tee shirt that covered David's face. David's eyes seemed to be swimming in his head, but as he made eye contact with Chris a calm settled over him, and he began to cry. "Damn it, Chris, help me!" Peter shouted.

Peter was finally able to untie the pantyhose that were gagging David, while Chris wrestled with the knots that tied David's feet. When he was able to free his feet, and Peter was able to uncover all of his face, Chris turned David on his side so that he could untie his hands. David said nothing. He was half lying on his back, which made it very difficult for Chris to untie his hands. Each time they tried to move him onto his side so they could see behind him, David used his feet to push himself onto his back.

"Peter, turn off the shower. These knots are tight, I can't see, either." Peter turned off the shower and then decided to help Chris roll David further onto his stomach and hold him there. As Chris focused on the knots he noticed that blood was running on the shower floor. "Peter, blood," he whispered.

"Shit, where is it coming from?" Peter asked as he continued to roll David over onto his stomach. But David kept trying to roll back onto his back. "David, stop it. We have to untie you." Chris froze again. Then he looked at Peter and said, "There's something in him."

"What, where?" Peter asked, holding onto David's right hip, and he leaned over to see what Chris was pointing at. Peter's eyes filled with tears.

"There's something sticking out of his butt!" Chris said in horror.

"Please untie my hands and go away. Please," David said, crying. "Please just leave and let me take it out."

Peter fell back and sat on the shower room floor. He felt himself getting nauseous. Chris continued trying to get David's hands free. When he had untied the last knot, David again pleaded with them to leave. Both Peter and Chris refused. David reached around and began to slowly remove the hard rubber rod from his anus; it was at least two inches in diameter. "Please leave me alone," David pleaded. Chris watched as David pulled at the rod and more blood ran down David's buttock.

"Oh my God, it's a rubber penis," Chris said. "It's a rubber penis and the head is still inside," Chris whispered to Peter. David lay there crying. The pain was excruciating.

"Let's call the coach," Peter said to Chris.

"No. Go away, I'll do it. Please go away," David said through his tears.

"No, you need help. You're bleeding," Chris insisted.

"Please don't call anyone. Please, I don't want anyone to know. If you tell the coach everyone will know."

"Okay," Chris said, "but it has to come out. And you're really bleeding." Chris stared at Peter. Peter then sat up.

"Do you want me to do it?" Chris asked in his eerily calm voice.

"Yes, please. I can't," David said, his body going limp.

"It's going to really hurt," Chris said, leaning over David and looking into his eyes.

David turned his head, looking back at Chris, and nodded and said, "Just do it, it won't hurt any more than when they shoved it in."

Chris grabbed onto the dildo with his right hand and held David's hip with his left hand. "Turn it, you know turn it around as you take it out. That might help," Peter suggested. "Wait, Chris." Peter grabbed Chris's arm. "David, pull your knees up and push like you are going to take a shit. That might help, too," Peter said, pushing at David's legs.

"Push," Chris said, as he began to turn the dildo and pull on it. They both watched as David's legs shook from the pain as he muffled his groans in the wet tee shirt. When Chris was finally able to remove the dildo, he and Peter watched as more blood ran onto the shower room floor.

"Who did this to you?" Chris asked in an emotionless tone.

"I don't know. It was empty when I came in here and then someone put this over my face. No one said a word. They tied me up."

"The only guys here were guys from the team," Chris said. Peter looked at Chris, hearing the anger in his voice. Chris still had the dildo in his hand, although he did not seem to realize it. He sat there staring at Peter as Peter nodded in agreement.

"Why would they do this? It can't be them," David insisted. He rolled onto his knees.

"You're bleeding, David. You should go to a hospital," Peter said, as he sat down on the shower floor in front of David.

David reached around and touched himself and then looked at his hand. "It will stop. I'll be okay. Chris, please help me get home. Peter, I'll be okay, really. Please, I don't want anyone to know." David stood slowly. Peter and Chris stood behind him and noticed blood running down his legs. "Why would guys on our team do this?"

Both Chris and Peter helped David get to his locker. He asked Peter to get him some toilet paper to put in between his buttocks so that he wouldn't get blood on his clothes. Chris dried David off as David stood

Lies That Bind

and held onto his locker door for balance. After David put the handful of toilet paper against his bleeding anus, Chris helped him into his underwear. Both Chris and Peter then helped him get dressed. Peter felt sick watching David; he fought not to cry. Chris was in a rage.

They decided that David should not walk home. Peter would run home, get his mom's car, return to school, and drive them home. It was during that time that Chris told David what his father had done on Monday night. David turned ashen as a look of fear froze his face.

"I can't ever come back here," David said, talking into the air.

"You have to, you have to finish school so you can graduate and go to NYU in September."

"Oh my God, everyone on the team knows. That's why they did this, isn't it?" David asked, still in shock. "Oh my God, I can't come back."

"David, it's only one more month, four fucking weeks, David," Chris pleaded. "Then you're free from all this. You have to finish school."

David's eyes darted around the locker room as he heard someone coming through the outer doors. "Oh God, Chris, I'm scared."

It was Peter entering the locker room. When he made his way through the rows of lockers, David looked up at Peter and then turned away and covered his face. "It's cool, David," Peter said, "You're my buddy, dude, for as long as I can remember." Peter walked over and put his arms around David. "I'm serious, dude. Come on, don't turn away."

"Oh shit. Everyone knew today, didn't they?" David asked. "Oh my God, how could you let me walk around all day thinking they didn't know?" David shouted at Chris.

Chris answered, "David, so they know. So no one did anything." He tried to make eye contact with him.

"Oh no?" David shouted, "what do you call what just happened?"

"I mean during the day. No one said anything."

"That's why you were with me all day, isn't it? You were guarding me. Oh, shit."

Chris reached for David's arm. "David, I was going to tell you. I didn't know your father didn't tell you. When I figured out you didn't know, well…"

"Oh man, what a fucking prick he is. He does this on Monday and never tells me. God, he pisses me off so bad. I hate him," David said, punching his locker door. "Take me home, Peter."

"Calm down, David," Peter whispered. "The coaches are still here."

"No, let him be angry," Chris said to Peter. "No, we are not taking you home yet," he said to David.

"Fuck the both of you. I'll walk," David said, picking up his backpack.

Chris grabbed at David. "David. Stop. Look, be angry, but don't go off on your father. He'll kick your ass,"

Trying to reason with David, Peter said, "David, you have to live with him."

David turned and looked at Chris and calmly said, "I can't believe you didn't tell me. You had three days to tell me."

"I didn't know you didn't know," Chris pleaded.

David shouted, "Why didn't I hear from you? Why didn't you come crawling through my window at two in the morning like you usually do?" Peter turned and looked at Chris.

"Cool it, David," Chris insisted. "Enough."

"Fuck you, you coward. Sure, it's okay for me to walk around school with everyone knowing that I'm gay, but…"

"Shut up, David," Chris interrupted as he grabbed his arm again.

"You don't want anyone to know that you are, do you?" David shouted, as he pulled free from Chris's grip. "I can't believe you tell me it's fine to come to school, no one will say or do anything. Fuck you. I can't believe you're such a fucking coward. I hate you, too!"

"David," Chris said with a sigh, as he glanced from David to Peter.

"I loved you, but all you wanted was sex. When it got tough, you hid, didn't you? If you had told me, none of this would have happened," David shouted. "Coward! You fuckin' coward. I guess it runs in your blood, doesn't it?" David shouted as he stormed away.

Chris sat down on the bench between the lockers and stared at the floor with his elbows on his knees and his head resting in his hands. Peter stood there silently. When Chris glanced up at Peter, Peter asked, "You two have been lovers?"

"Yes," Chris said with a sigh.

"How long?"

"Thanksgiving, six months," Chris said, looking back down toward the floor.

Peter sat down next to Chris on the bench and put his hand on his shoulder. "Look, Chris, you know this is all cool with me. I guess I wish you had told Julie and me. I mean you guys could have told us if you wanted to, but I understand."

Lies That Bind

Chris sat silently and just shook his head. "Fuck, I can't believe all this happened. Peter, I never knew anything like this would have happened."

"I would have done the same thing you did." Peter put his arm around Chris's shoulder and said, "Dude, I won't tell anyone about you and David. Don't sweat it, okay?"

"Thanks, Peter. Thanks."

"Well, I have to tell Julie. I mean we really don't have any secrets," Peter said, knowing that he did indeed have secrets. "And, besides, she and David are really good friends and she would never tell anyone. You know that."

"Yeah, I understand. Peter, if people find out, then my mom will find out and…"

"She and I won't tell anyone," Peter assured Chris. "I promise. And my promises are as good as yours." Chris's thoughts turned to Derek.

* * * * *

"You think Derek called David's father and told him? I asked.

"I'm sure he did. I just wish I could have explained it all to David. I know he hates me."

Chapter Seventeen

"How did you find out that he ran away?" I asked, trying to sort out my feelings.

"I talked to his brother, and he said that David was in his room that Thursday night, and Friday morning when they unlocked his door he was gone."

I felt my face warm. I wondered if I should tell Chris that David was at the hospital, but then I also knew that David was planning to leave. Perhaps David did not want to see Chris. But then why was he here? Maybe just to report Jack.

"He must be at his aunt's. At least I hope so. She hates his dad, and maybe he went there." Another deep breath and a shrug. For the first time he truly did look fragile; done in by his yet-so-very-young life.

He looked like he was in a great deal of pain. He took another deep breath and shrugged again. I felt uncomfortable knowing that David was in the building, but I decided that Diane would surely tell Chris all that he needed to know in due time. "So you found out your dad passed away and you lost David all in five days' time."

"All I could feel was anger. I wanted to get even with everyone, and I did. But it all came crashing down at graduation."

"This last Thursday?"

"Yeah."

* * * * *

"Welcome Cardinal O'Rourke, Monsieur Ruiz, fellow faculty members, parents, family, and friends of this year's graduating class. It has been a great honor for me to be the graduating class's faculty advisor," Father John D'Agostino announced to the crowd seated in the Sacred Heart High School auditorium. "I was introduced to these young women and men on a Wednesday morning, four years ago, in this very auditorium. Then younger, wide-eyed, eager, anxious, but determined; now older, wearied, a bit wiser, but still anxious and determined, I am here to tell you that, even though it was touch and go a couple of times, I made it.

Lies That Bind

"I have been teaching at Sacred Heart High School for twelve years. Four years ago I was given my first opportunity to be a class advisor. I must admit that I was both excited and intimidated. As I had imagined, this has been a very interesting four years. Actually, it has been a incredible experience, with a group of extraordinary girls and boys. I have gathered memories that I will treasure all my life." The audience of students cheered and applauded with great enthusiasm. When Chris rose to his feet the entire class stood up and started cheering. Someone in the first row started to whoop loud enough so that eventually most of the boys in the crowd joined in with him.

"Thank you," Father D'Agostino said, with a smile, as a blush betrayed his embarrassment. "Please know that the feeling is mutual. Getting to know all of you has been very meaningful. Besides our many academic endeavors, there was time to play. Winter ski trips and trying to keep some sixty odd boys and girls under control for five days was…"

Chris sat staring into the crowd. This was the last place he wanted to be. How could his friendship with David have gone from where it was in January at Mammoth to where it was now? *How could I have fucked up so badly? How is it that everyone I love I destroy?*

"One of the greatest pleasures I have had during this last year was working closely with your student body president, Christopher, sorry, Chris Bellesano. I met Chris four years ago when he promised me that he would do the best he could academically. He was a reserved boy who spoke in three-word sentences and was too shy to make eye contact. Hard to imagine, isn't it?" The crowd laughed, and again the boys in the front row whooped. "Well, as you all know, Chris prides himself on keeping his promises: he is one of our four valedictorians, he lettered in varsity baseball for two years, and you selected him as your president. When I asked him if he wanted to address you as one of our valedictorians or as student body president he said that he was most proud of being selected president. He said the academics were easy, and that winning your respect and support was his greatest accomplishment.

"Cardinal O'Rourke, Monsignor Ruiz, fellow faculty…"

Chris sat on the stage waiting to be introduced by Father John, but he was not hearing what the priest was saying. *You don't deserve anyone's respect and support. When it came time for you to support your best friend you failed him. You were more worried about what everyone else would think than about what might happen to him. And now what do you have? Nothing. He loved you and you put his life in danger. Now he's gone.* Chris's demons had been tormenting him relentlessly since he had last seen David on the day that David was raped. His nights were sleepless.

Chris, not remembering his walk to the podium, found himself standing before an applauding audience. As he began to speak, it occurred to him that his voice sounded odd, as though it were someone else's. "First, I want to give a very special thanks to a man who I have come to respect, trust, and admire: Father D'Agostino." Again, everyone rose to their feet and cheered. Chris walked across the stage and reached out to shake the hand of the now standing priest. As they shook hands, Chris pulled the priest to him and they hugged. Father John noticed that Chris's hand was cold and wet with sweat, and that he seemed to be trembling.

Chris returned to the podium and said, "You heard his story as to our first meeting. What I remember is somewhat different. What I remember is being assigned a half a semester's worth of algebra to finish in five weeks of my summer vacation…" Chris saw the words on the cards and could hear himself reading them, but his thoughts were elsewhere. *That's when you first got to know David. He befriended you and all you could do was reduce him to a sexual play toy, just like you did with everyone else who loved you. No, that's not true, I loved him. I just didn't know it. Is that why you hurt him the way you did?* His demons were relentless. "When I wrote my first essay in Father Renaldo's class—"What I did over my summer vacation"— I simply wrote that I met with Father John and spent the summer doing algebra…" His demons kept hammering away at him. *Here you are graduating and David had to run away to free himself from the hell that you did nothing to save him from. If it had been the other way around he would have sacrificed everything for you.* "…and then more algebra. Father John was not only our faculty advisor, he was for many of us our toughest teacher, a relentless mentor, an unruffled confessor, guide, ski instructor, and trusted friend. Oh, yeah, and he can cook one mean pepperoni pizza.

"This last January our class went to Mammoth Mountain…" Chris said as he read on. Everything seemed to remind him of better times, of times with David. *David and I went to Mammoth. Where are you? You were right, I was a coward. I've always been a coward. I was only thinking of myself and you got the worst of it.* Chris began to feel a surreal feeling coming over him as he continued reading, "Father John, as the representative of our class, I have the honor of presenting you a gift that is going to be modeled for you by my step-dad, Richard Patrona." Richard walked onto the stage from one of the wings. He was dressed in a new North Face ski suit

Lies That Bind

and was carrying an envelope. Richard handed the envelope to Father John. "Father John, oh, and by the way, we did get permission from Monsignor Ruiz, in the envelope is a gift certificate for a new pair of skis, bindings, and boots from the Sports Chalet. They said that you should come in at the beginning of next season and they will fit you with all new equipment." The graduates again rose to their feet and cheered as they applauded. Someone shouted, "We love you, Father John," and the whooping began again.

Father John smiled when he saw his new ski suit. It was all black with white markings. "Thank you all very much," he said from his seat. "Thank you, you've all touched me deeply." He made a fist with his right hand and thumped the left side of his chest.

Chris walked over to the priest and hugged him again. "Thank you, Father, lately you've been my rock," Chris whispered. Father John smiled at first, and then wondered what Chris might have meant. He noticed that Chris seemed especially distressed.

"Now I would like to thank all the faculty at Sacred Heart. I know we put you through," he hesitated and then said, "the mill. I heard one of our teachers say that our class was both the brightest and the most trying in years. Our class, in an effort to say thank you, has arranged to have the patio outside the faculty lounge re-landscaped with rose and other flowering bushes. The work will begin on Monday." Again the students cheered.

"Lastly, but not at all least, we want to thank our families. We want to thank you for being here today." Thoughts of his father had also been haunting him. He had been reliving the last time he had seen Frank, and with each foray into the past, his father was more the victim and he was more the perpetrator. Now that he had successfully rescued his father from his hatred all he could do was surrender to his demons. *I wonder if he is here today. You know you should have apologized to him. You knew all along that he wanted an apology. I shouldn't have yelled at him. How could I have yelled at him when he knew he had cancer?* Sweat began to gather around his upper lip as he continued to read what now seemed to be unfamiliar words to him. "We want to thank you for your guidance, understanding and patience. Oh yes, and we want to thank you for all your support, especially your financial support..." *I was too much of a coward to apologize. Dad, I am sorry for causing the divorce and for what I said. Please, Dad...*

Chris found himself fighting to stay steady on his feet as he continued. "...which leads me to the fact that over ninety-six percent of our graduating class will be needing continued financial support as we attend college. So as they say, Mom, Dad, it ain't over yet." Chris watched his body in action. He glanced down at his note cards and read what was written there. Then he looked up and looked at the audience, just as he had practiced. But it all felt robot-like to him.

"Thirty-six of us are going to be attending colleges out of state. Students from this year's graduating class will be attending such colleges as Columbia, Harvard, Yale, Princeton, Duke, Penn State, and Boston College—some people never learn—and Juilliard—good going Andrew—Cindy is going to the Air Force Academy and Sharon is going to the Naval Academy—you go girls. Others will be attending the universities of Hawaii, Texas, Colorado, and Wisconsin. Two of our graduates will be going to Father John's alma mater, Notre Dame. Oh, and did I mention Columbia University?"

Chris found himself glancing out into the crowd looking for David. *I told you to take the time to graduate. If you had, we'd be on our way. How could he, after what happened to him? Something you could have prevented. It was all your fault. You were just so scared to have him at school when he found out. Afraid he'd lose it like he did. So you protected yourself and he was raped.* Then he remembered that David would not be there.

"Others will be attending college here in California. We have classmates who will be attending UC Berkeley, Santa Cruz, and Santa Barbara. Bill, Steve, Bobby, and Jim have extended a standing invitation to party on any weekend. Sharon and Carol said they are not going to party at UCSB—right! Oh, did I tell you that the guys will not be living in the dorms, they have an apartment on—Steve, where is your apartment? " Steve yelled up from the audience, "on Trigo." Chris continued, "You can catch them later for the exact address." Steve gave another whoop. *We could have had an apartment. A studio. I'm sorry. Sorry? You'd do the same thing if you had it to do over again. You're just a coward, just like he said. No backbone. You think you loved him, but you can't love anyone. All that matters to you is looking good. Mr. Popular. Mr. Class President. Mr. Jock. Mr. All-I-Want-is-to-be-Popular.* "...UCLA and Irvine, Harvey Mudd College, and there are those who will be attending various California State Colleges. Some of our classmates have decided to join the military. Good luck to you and God speed. Some of our classmates have been smart and lucky enough to find jobs." Chris wondered why he did not include those who were not here. *Then there are those who never made it to graduation. They can thank you for that too. And you did that behind*

Lies That Bind

everyone's backs, too. David was right. You are a coward. You didn't want to take the chance that anyone would disapprove. If people really knew you and all you've done, all they could do is disapprove.

"We started this journey four years ago with great expectations and high anxiety. Those expectations and anxieties are still with us. For some of us this last year was long and difficult..." As he drifted from the sound of his voice to his demons and then back to the sound of his voice again, the differentiation between the two began to fade. *More difficult for some of us than others, but you had a hand in most all of it.* "...but I believe that our experience here at Sacred Heart High has prepared us for a future filled with many challenges and great opportunities.

"Who will forget the day that Chad ate the three-dozen hot dogs at the class picnic? And that included the buns. Or the day that John was so nervous taking a chemistry exam he threw up? And where did John throw up? In his—" Chris pointed to the audience, and they yelled back, "backpack!"

Someone else yelled up from the audience, "It could have been worse. I was sitting in front of him." Everyone in the auditorium laughed as John stood up and took a bow.

Chris listened as the voice he heard, the voice he thought must be his, repeated the words that were on his note cards. "Of course, we will never forget the day at the senior class picnic that Cathy..." *They all laugh; you're the man, their president, the stud, the liar, the coward, and the queer...* Chris recognized the familiar sensation that he had come to call "breaking free," and was now only watching what was happening. He could hear his voice clearly, but now, more than before, he thought it sounded outside him. The sensation was one of a dream, where he was both the person in the dream and the person watching the dream.

The crowd yelled, "swimming pool," and this time Cathy rose to her feet and took her bow.

But then, as in a dream, he was no longer watching himself in action; he was now the actor in the dream. Instead of watching himself tremble he could feel his body trembling as he began to mouth words that were not on his cards. "How about the day the police showed up and searched Derek's locker, and what did they find?" Chris pointed to the audience as a groan moved through the crowd. "Come on, you know they found—" Chris waited, but no one answered. "They found drugs! Yes, I was the one who informed the police that he was selling drugs," Chris said, now fully aware of the fact that he and his voice were one and the same, and that he was no longer reading words from his cards. "Revenge is all it was. I knew for a year that he was selling and did nothing, but after he called Paul Jarrett and told him that his son David was gay I knew how I could get him, and I did." A calm seemed to fall over him. His tone of voice had conviction and focus. "I told him I would nail him if he screwed with David.

"And I was also the one who told Father Anthony that some of our classmates had his exams. I told Father Anthony that they would show up at the final with a copy of the exam. I never said who they were, but I knew they'd get caught. They were in on David's rape." Chris was fully aware of the unrest that was moving, not only through the crowd, but also on the stage. "Derek knew it was going on. He kept Peter and me occupied until they were done with David. Yes, the rumors that David was raped are true, and the guys involved are not graduating today."

"Chris, Chris, sit down," Father John said.

"I loved David. I did," Chris said to the priest, and to everyone in the auditorium.

"I know you did, Chris," Father John assured him.

"No, you don't understand. I mean I was in love with him. He was my boyfriend, and it was my fault he was raped," Chris insisted.

"I know you were, Chris. Chris, please sit down," Father John said, grabbing onto Chris as Chris's knees collapsed under him and once again he began to shake violently.

"Chris. Chris." Father John called to him.

* * * * *

"Can you tell me what happened to me?" Chris asked me.

The picture of Chris sliding down that slide into no one's arms had never left me. I was hoping this time he might feel not only caught but held. Here was my invitation to reach out and help him get his head above water. "I will try. I want to help you understand all the things that went on, to help you make sense of it," I said. "You've been through a great deal, and in such a short time. The amount of trauma that you've experienced wouldn't happen to most people in their entire lives. But, then again, there are those who have experienced a great deal more.

"First let me say this. Making our way through childhood is difficult at best. Many children will experience varying degrees of trauma to which they will have varying degrees of emotional, cognitive, and physical reactions." I had given this speech before. As I spoke, I tried to put together all that I wanted to say to him. I had gathered most of my thoughts, and had made notes the night before. I knew there would be

Lies That Bind

nothing therapeutic in my long-winded explanation. Well, nothing that would change the way he dealt with people or his emotions. For that, he was going to need long-term therapy. But my hope was that, at least, I could let him know he was understood; that he was not crazy, and that he could, if he desired, make different choices. At this point, perhaps hope for that was therapy enough.

"These reactions are all normal, but they are often hard for children to make sense of. If they're lucky, the adults around them will help them understand, make sense of what is happening to them, and why they are responding the way they are. So, even though the world is painful at that moment, it all makes sense to them. And then, hopefully, they can move on. They will have learned to trust themselves and those around them.

"Let me give you an example. Let's take your being bitten by the stray dog and then having to undergo two weeks of rabies shots. Clearly, this was a traumatic event. At the very least you were hurt and frightened. Okay, so the external world felt like a very unsafe place to you. You had just been attacked, and then you had to undergo painful treatment. You had very powerful and confusing feelings, so your internal world felt chaotic and overwhelming. If your father had encouraged you to express those feelings, and then helped you to understand and accept them, he would have helped you make sense of your internal world. Your father would have held you both physically and emotionally. Your father would have helped you to find safety in the world again by making sense of it for you. You would have learned that the world might be scary, but your world, with your father in it, could again be a safe place, and your internal world, though painful, was not crazy. So there is trauma, but no abuse.

"But what did your father do? He forbade emotional expression and, worse, ridiculed you for your feelings. You learned that not only was the outside world not safe, but your internal world couldn't be trusted. Now, not only was your internal world chaotic, but it was overwhelming and dangerous. My guess is you came to believe that your feelings were so powerful they could cause the chaos that was going on around you. You came to believe your emotions were inappropriate, destructive, and too powerful for the adults around you. Okay so far?"

"Yes."

I glanced at my notes, "As in most of what you've told me, you did what you had to do to survive not only the trauma, but also your father's abusive demands on you." Again, I glanced at my notes. "The lying. Your father lied to your mother, to your grandfather, to save his ass. He lied about where he was when the dog bit you. He lied to escape responsibility for who he was and what he did. Then you lied for him, to calm your mother, to stop their fighting, to end the conflict. You found that lying could bring an end to conflict, and that it could control people.

"Your father demanded another lie. He demanded that you lie about your internal world; a tall order for a four- or five-year-old. Well, your psyche found a way to accomplish this. Your desire to please your father was so strong," I said, feeling my throat tightening, "you went into a trance state. Or, what you did in your mind was to try to save the stability of your external world by sacrificing your internal world. What was clearly a traumatic event became an abusive one. You had to keep all the very disorganizing feelings you were experiencing to yourself, and as a result you became psychically overwhelmed. Overwhelmed by terror and helplessness.

"You held everything together by going numb and becoming 'the man' your father demanded you be, so as to win his love. You found a way to psychically escape your internal world when there was no way to physically escape your external world. You call it 'breaking free.' Are we okay so far?"

"Yeah."

"I believe most of the interactions with your father that you've talked to me about are basically a mere repetition of those events. For example, the incident in the pool. Many children are frightened when they learn to swim. I'd say it's a healthy fear. Your father could have sat you down and explained that he's been afraid in his life and that he understood. He was in Vietnam, he must have known fear. He could have patiently taught you to swim. At the end of the day he might have encouraged you to face your fear and try the slide, and when you did he could have immediately pulled you to the surface. More than learning to swim, he would have been teaching you to trust him. He accomplished just the opposite."

I paused, and we both took in a deep breath. "Then your exchange in the car after your day at the pool. Once again the power of your words, or so you came to believe, destroyed your mother's marriage." Chris nodded his head. "Their marriage was over before you were born, but you were left to believe, again, that the truth of your feelings could destroy, cause chaos and pain. Chris, you were a child and they were words, yes, harsh words, but only words.

"So again you learned that your inner truth could create havoc. Denying the truth of who you were for others and who you were for yourself was a far more successful coping mechanism than truth-telling.

Lies That Bind

However, when one becomes a young adult, enters the world of intimate relationships, what worked as a child sometimes stops working. That very same denial of your internal self that worked so well in the past became the lies that bind you today. Something had to give. But I'll get back to that.

"Now, to your being molested."

"Oh, I have something I want to tell you," Chris said, with enthusiasm.

"Let me finish what's on my mind first. I've been giving a lot of serious thought to what you said about being victimized versus what happened with you. You are right. I want to say that what you suffered was different than if you had been taken unwillingly. But, I look at all molestations as having a victim and a perpetrator. You do see that when an adult takes a vulnerable adolescent and uses him, even if he is a willing participant, the adolescent is still being victimized. Perhaps even more so, in that, as you described, the boy grows to blame himself and loses trust in himself. I believe that on the one hand the boy sees what happened as feeling good physically, but on the other hand causing pain psychologically. That conflict is internalized and anger, depression, drug use, et cetera result."

"So, in your short life you were emotionally, physically, and sexually violated. And that is why, I believe, you would do all you could to evacuate most, if not all, subjective experiences in an effort to escape the emotional pain you were experiencing. I want to quote you here: 'Feelings are being out of control, and being out of control feels like I am going to die.' Are we still okay?"

"Yes," Chris said, as he nodded.

"What has happened is that two very different forces shaped your personality. On the one hand, you had the influence of your father and people like him, and on the other you had your mother and grandparents and people like them. The good news is that you had a loving mother and grandparents. The bad news is that they did not understand all that was happening to you and how to properly deal with your father. My guess is that prior to that smack in the back seat of the car, you knew how to use your mother and your grandparents for support. When your father said that he did not want you for a son…"

"He didn't say that. What he said exactly, and I remember it, was that he didn't want a sissy for a son."

"And he thought of you as a sissy. Didn't he?"

"Yes, but I could change that. That's what he was saying, but…"

"Chris, what you did was call on your grandfather. You figuratively jumped into his lap and said, 'if you don't want me, he does.' But I believe that later you decided your spontaneous response, your close connection to your grandfather, had destroyed your family. I believe it might have been at that point when you completely closed yourself off from allowing the intimacy you had with them. You never stopped loving them, but you no longer saw them as a usable or appropriate support system. Perhaps it was guilt, I don't know.

"There is something more I want to address. Then we'll get to what you wanted to say. We all have a public self and a private self. Typically, our public self is just that. The self we show to the world. Our private self we usually only share with people we trust. You have a public self which is accomplished, athletic, gifted, loved, and admired; rewarded by your mother and grandparents. But all that admiration stays attached to your public self. Then there is this other part of you, the private self, which in your case holds all those feelings of self-hate, inadequacy, guilt, and shame. It is a place from which your father still talks to you. Unfortunately, his voice did not die when he did; I'd say it might have even come more to life. He lives where those persecuting voices come from. In your case, there is a large chasm between the various parts of yourself. And there are structures that help keep those sides apart.

Chris nodded.

"As I said, we all have public and private parts to ourselves. Hopefully, however, we have bridges from one to the other; ways of making our private self public when we want to. Most people spend their entire life building those bridges. Then there can be a steady flow of traffic from one side to the other, each side supplying the other side with what it needs to function more productively in the world.

"If our private self is chaotic and filled with self-loathing and we don't allow bridges to be built to the outer world, then life can be torturous, chaotic, and lonely. When there is a great deal of energy going into keeping the private self private, bridges that are built from the public self to this hated private self begin to feel threatening rather than comforting. Eventually, connections between these parts of ourselves have to be destroyed; people who want to know that private self are pushed away. So we develop ways to keep connections from being built; we look for the perfect lover, who of course does not exist. Or, the grass is always greener on the other side. No accomplishment is ever enough. There is always something better, and someone else has it. Or what if I commit to this person and someone better comes along? All that shit.

Lies That Bind

Or the one I think you use, perhaps, is that I don't know what it means to love someone."

Again, Chris nodded his head.

"So your trouble sleeping, your hypervigilance, your irritability, your depression, your emotional numbness, your minimization of the responsibility that others have in a given situation, your willingness to understand others and forgive them but blame yourself, and a lot of other tricks that you play on yourself, are the work your psyche does to keep all of this functioning. And there are many, many more of these tricks that we play on ourselves. By the way, we all do this to some degree or another. Anything to keep alive the contempt we feel for that private self, and to keep away anyone that might get too close."

"You mean like the voices, or as David called them, 'the night demons?' " Chris asked.

"Yes, exactly. Think of your demons as slowly but efficiently dismantling any bridge that is built across that chasm. They call you coward, mean and sadistic, stupid, insane, vengeful. I am sure I've left something out. Anyway, the cacophony of accusatory voices assures you that there is no way out, to free yourself of the loneliness, the depression, the anger. Any road, any action on your part, will lead to death."

Chris nodded, "Like that dream I told you about, where I am trying to get out of the canyon and every path leads to me dying."

"Exactly." Chris nodded and then turned to stare at the wall.

"What are you thinking about?" I asked.

"I guess the time I teased David when my mother saw him naked. I was sure he hated me. I mean, I knew he did and I knew he'd never be my friend, and then he showed up the next day and wanted to be my best friend," his voice sounded pained.

"Exactly," I said nodding. "You're sad?"

"Just feeling sorry for myself, I guess. Sorry," Chris said, glancing down at his feet.

"Why do you apologize?"

"I don't know, I guess it's weak to feel sorry for yourself," Chris said shrugging, then pushing the hair from his face.

"Oh, yes. There's another. Weak. I forgot that one. I wonder if your sadness might be about the fact that we are talking about very painful memories of trauma and abuse; real events in your life. Also, might there be relief at feeling understood in some small way?"

Chris's eyes filled with tears as he nodded and said, "I guess."

"What has also happened is that you compartmentalized different parts of yourself. Some parts of yourself are tucked away in your public self, some are private; some you take delight in, some you despise. Let me give you an example: your singing and guitar playing. I believe it has remained private because you use it to soothe yourself."

Chris interrupted, "Quiet the voices."

"Exactly. You fear if it were public it would lose its soothing ability. Very little that is part of your public self soothes your private self. I believe the only people you share it with are those who also soothe you. Again, it has a place and there it stays.

"You are exceptionally bright. That is part of your public self. Privately, you think of yourself as stupid, naïve. Let me quote you: 'Why can't I figure out what it is that I do that drives people away?' Your accomplishments, your many friends who are part of your public self, are not able to make their way across the chasm and contradict the private view of yourself as stupid and bad.

"It's the same with your homosexuality. You've kept that hidden. I understand that you would be criticized by your peers and shamed by society, but it is a part of you. A part of you that gives you both pleasure and pain. You've allowed yourself your homosexual fantasies, and, lately, gratification with David, but you also punish yourself; berate yourself. What I'm saying is that the process is the same but the content is different. Or, to put it in your words, 'the music is the same, but the lyrics are different.'"

Chris looked up at me, and his eyes welled up as he said, "Thank you."

"Tell me what is happening."

Chris shrugged and said, "You listened to what I said and you remember it. I don't know why that makes me sad." I was not sure, but I thought that was the first time I heard Chris verbally acknowledge feeling sad in the present.

"Well, perhaps it is that for me to understand you, I have to listen, remember, and communicate that to you. And perhaps it is about all the times, as a child, you so desperately wanted that, but found it was not there for you. Maybe you gave up hope that it would ever be there for you. Perhaps it is the beginnings of a bridge.

"Remember the night in Palm Springs after David confronted you? He went to sleep with his arm around you." Chris nodded. "You held onto him. You said it helped you not to spiral into anxiety and then break free."

"Yeah."

Lies That Bind

"Understanding words from another can do that. Self-understanding can do that. The bridges between our various selves can do that. You did that for David."

"How?"

"Remember the night he was beaten after his father found out he was gay?"

"Yes."

"Actually, it happened twice. Once when he was being beaten and he called on you, in his mind, to help him through his pain and fear. To make it through that he used his future relationship with you—'forty-five more days' is what he said. Then you showed up. You and he talked. He joked. In a situation like that I'd say that was a pretty good sign that he was frightened, and for good reason. All that time he isn't very emotional. Not typical for him. He's in survival mode. Then you put your arm around him and what happened? He began to weep. You opened the door to his inner world. A world he trusted you to be in."

Chris suddenly dropped his head. "What?" I asked.

"Oh, I was just thinking that I wish I had told him that I loved him. I remember holding him. All I could think about was breaking open the bedroom door and attacking Paul. Hurting him badly." Anger filled Chris's voice.

"There's your anger again."

"I know."

"You were feeling protective of David because you love him."

"I wish I had said so. I was just too afraid." There was a long silence that I decided to sit with. He hardly moved in the chair. I tried to sit as quietly as possible. He turned his head and glanced at me and asked, "What happened at graduation?"

"Well, will you settle for a guess?"

"Yeah, anything to make sense of it."

"I'll do my best then. I think many things came together: your father's death, the letter from Jean—that was one nasty letter; Then there was all that happened with David. First, he offered you his love. That brought you, on the one hand, hope, and on the other, dread. The hope that you could realize the love you wanted and also the dread of that very love."

"I don't understand," Chris interrupted.

"So much of your private self is filled with hate and guilt and shame, that the love offered to you puts you into extreme conflict. You want to be loved, but you don't think you deserve it. And of course, you're afraid that once again you will lose it, or imagine you could destroy it. You want David in New York City, but you don't. The fantasy solution is David in a nearby city—physical distance between you seems the way to survive the love you both have. Living together brings fear of loss—loss of very important people like your mother and grandparents.

"Then there was David's rape, his turning his rage on you, which then aligned him with the cacophony of voices in your head—night demons. Interestingly, actions against Derek and the others were not for what was done to you, but for what was done to David. And then finally, there you were at your graduation, feeling so hateful toward yourself, standing before all those people who so greatly admired you. And perhaps you deserved their admiration: you were valedictorian, and their student body president. A great deal of conflict, and you hate conflict.

"Well, my best guess is that in an effort to stop the conflict, your private self went public, 'here I am, the real me,' and then, because your private self became public for the first time, your system went into overload. Also, it is not uncommon for adolescents to experience panic when they 'come out,' especially when they do it so publicly and without a support system. You see, to truly acknowledge the support you have from your mother, grandparents, Father John, and others, would be building a bridge. So your demons undermine any support you might feel. Not internalizing the support that is there for you means that you cannot make use of it.

"I would also guess that at your graduation, all that pain, sadness, fear, anger, joy, exhilaration et cetera, came rushing in and overwhelmed your psyche. This has happened to you in the past, but with the help of your psyche, you found short-term solutions. An example is your salivating instead of crying, your guitar-playing to soothe yourself.

"I'm curious, you said that when you were waiting for your father to come home and take you to the doctor's office you would hum a tune. Do you know what tune it was?"

"I think it was just something that I made up in my head when I was a kid. I've tried to play it on my guitar sometimes, but I never get very far."

"Oh, then you do remember it?"

"Yes, do you want to hear it?"

"Yes."

Chris hummed the melody of a tune that had remained silent in his head for years. It was a fast-paced tune that I thought I had heard before, but I was not sure.

Lies That Bind

"Oh, I expected it to be a lullaby. Okay. Thank you. As I was saying, your psyche was fighting to keep itself in equilibrium. So, both the good and the bad news is that all that had been working for you stopped working."

"What now?"

"Another good question. You've been here for four days. I think it's time for you to leave here and return home. I understand that you will be going to New York and attending college at Columbia University in the fall."

"Yeah," Chris said, feeling his palms sweat.

"I am going to give you the name of a psychoanalytic psychologist that I know in New York. He is someone who trains therapists at the New York University Postdoctoral Program in Psychoanalysis. I know him, and he knows me. I am not sure he will be able to see you, but I trust him to help you find a therapist who can help you. Chris, I've talked to your mother and your grandparents, and it is my very strong recommendation that you be in therapy. Not because you 'cracked up,' to use your words, but because you are young, bright, and have a great future before you. I believe, to make the most of it, you need to be emotionally whole."

"You think I'm sick?"

"No. I believe that there is a possibility that you could learn to tuck your emotions away again and walk through life the way your father did. You don't want to become like your father, do you?"

"What? Of course not."

"Well then, you might think of this as me suggesting various baseball coaches that might help your game. I'm saying you've got great talent, but you need work."

"Okay. Got it," Chris said, with a smile.

I smiled and said, "Chris, your dad dealt with his emotions in a very destructive way. Do you agree?"

"Yeah, I guess."

"Well, I never met your father, but from all that you and your family have said, I believe that he did. I don't know what was going on with him, but the way he dealt with his anxiety over the possibility of your being a gay boy, or as he said, 'a sissy,' was destructive."

"No dad wants a gay kid," Chris insisted.

"Perhaps that's true, but there are different ways of dealing with those feelings. One way, the way he chose to deal with them, was to become extremely sadistic and rejecting. Again, I didn't know him, but his anxiety seemed overdetermined."

"What's that?"

"Excessive. From what your mother said to me, it was all that he saw in you, and that he was relentless. Chris, you were so much more than a boy who was a sissy, or a boy who would grow up to be sexually attracted to men."

Chris nodded.

"I think therapy can help you learn to deal with your emotions, your insights, your fantasies, all that makes up your internal world, in a far more constructive and rewarding way. I believe therapy can help you heal and give you the opportunity to experience intimacy in a loving relationship. As I said, he is someone I know and trust. I don't want you to see just anyone. I've talked to your mother about this, and she agrees.

First, the issue of your sexual orientation. There are some yahoos out there that will look to cure you of being gay. They will see a bright, attractive, strong, athletic young man who has been molested, and decide to make you their new hobby and turn your therapy into their therapy. They will say that they hope your homosexuality is not too deeply embedded in your psyche, so that they can make you heterosexual." Chris smiled and laughed. "What?" I asked.

"I was just thinking of that guy telling David that if he didn't have sex with a guy he could change."

"I know, and that you said it would take forever."

"I tried being straight. Except for all the stuff people say, I like being gay. I loved being with David. Being his boyfriend. Holding his hand. Kissing him, especially kissing him." He hesitated. "Can I ask you something?"

"Sure, but I don't usually answer very personal questions. But, I will answer any question that you might have about what goes on with you or in here between you and me."

"Oh, okay. But only answer honestly. Okay?"

"Chris, I won't lie to you. I promise. And my word is as good as yours."

"Does it gross you out when I say stuff about David and me? You know, about kissing him and making love to him?" He looked at me. I could see the tension and sadness that came with the question.

"No, it does not. Do I seem to be disturbed by it?"

"No." He paused. "Being in therapy sounds a little scary."

I nodded. "I also don't want you to see someone who has decided that you are gay and that you should be proud of it and that's all there is to that.

Lies That Bind

I would hate to see happen to you what has happened to so many gay men and that is, their therapy is turned into someone's political agenda. Your mother and I both agree that you don't need some therapist who is pro- or anti-homosexual practicing a sophisticated form of psychic brainwashing on you. You've been twisted and turned to fit too many people's agendas."

"My mom doesn't want me to be cured?"

"She never suggested anything like that to me. Her concern has not been with your being gay or straight. It has been about your mental health, your emotional well-being.

"Chris, again, I want to say that you've been through a great deal of abuse and betrayal, but that you have your mother and grandparents who have loved you deeply and let you know it. They've been your rudder in what has been one category five hurricane called your emotional life."

"I should just call this doctor when I get to New York?"

"Yes. I've talked to Dr. Lewis Aston. He is the director of the program. I trust him immensely. He is more than eager to be of help. He said, as a favor to me, that he would see you and give you a list of names."

"This all sounds really scary."

"It is a scary process. I am going to give you a number to call if you have any problems in New York. It is Dr. Torrel's phone number here at the hospital. She is familiar with your case and my work. If you're having difficulty, let her know. Give her a number where you can be reached and I will call you as soon as I can. Okay?"

"Why can't you just give me your number?"

"This way will work out best for me."

"Okay. Thank you. I'm sorry. You're being kind," Chris said.

"Why the apology?"

"You're giving me a lot and I..." he shrugged.

"You asked for what you want. Chris, there is no need to apologize for asking for what you need. I can say yes or I can say no. I'm not harmed by your asking. And you're very welcome." He looked at me and nodded. "Now, what was it that you wanted to tell me?"

Chris looked at me blankly for a moment. "Oh yeah. I was thinking about what we talked about. You know, a different metaphor."

"What did you come up with?"

Energy seemed to fill his body. He sat up straight, his eyes came to life, and a smile began to move his face. "Have you ever read Tolkien's *The Lord of the Rings*?"

"Yes, a couple of times."

He smiled and nodded and said, "Maybe this is going to sound off because I haven't had a long time to think about it, but…" he hesitated and took a breath. He looked as if he was trying to reassure himself. "Anyway, Frodo is this happy hobbit; he's adventurous, curious, smart, and living in the Shire. Then Bilbo, his cousin, gives him the Ring. He accepts the Ring without knowing all that comes with it—my father's demands and my molestation. Then Gandalf the Grey tells Frodo that the Ring is the Ring of Power. It's the Ring Sauron the Dark Lord is searching for. Gandalf tells Frodo he must take the Ring and leave the Shire. He has to journey across Middle Earth to Sauron's realm of Mordor and throw the Ring into the Cracks of Doom."

"The journey of the hero, like Odysseus in the Odyssey."

"Yeah, but different," he said. "The Greek heroes were like soldiers, warriors. They were strong, godlike men."

"And they typically went it alone," I added.

"Right. Frodo was given this Ring that is actually a burden he has to carry through Middle Earth. He was an ordinary kind of guy, not a superhero, and he just wants to rid himself of a burden—the Ring."

His face and body became animated as he explained in detail the start of Frodo's journey from the Shire to Mordor. "…he does battle with the Black Riders…"

"The Ringwraiths," I added. He smiled at me, his excitement increased.

"…at Weathertop, and he is wounded. He almost dies, but is healed by Elrond in Rivendell. Then Frodo sets out from Rivendell with his friends across Middle-Earth."

"Who was Elrond?"

"He was half-man and half-elf. He had to choose to be either mortal or immortal. He chose to be immortal, and therefore, when the war is over he must leave Middle Earth. He's supposed to be very wise."

"You know the trilogy well," I said. I knew he had read it several times, but I was surprised at his ability to retain the details.

"So do you," he said. "It's my favorite book. I've read it four times now."

"You touched on something. You were right when you said that Frodo is a different kind of hero. He is an ordinary hobbit and not a warrior. He isn't seeking glory or conquests, but rather to free himself from a burden. And unlike the Greek heroes, he doesn't go it alone. His friends help him on his journey."

"Without them he'd never have made it," he said.

Lies That Bind

"You're right. Actually, you might say that Frodo's strength, his strength of character, allows him to accept the aid of others. He is determined to survive and destroy the Ring, and isn't being heroic about it. Rather, he is being determined, which allows him to use all the resources at his disposal, and in many cases those are the people who are invested in helping him."

I added, "Also, the battle that Frodo is fighting is not just an external battle."

"What do you mean?" he asked.

"It's an internal battle, also. The Ring has a power to seduce him away from his goals. The Ring attacks the heart and the mind of the wearer. Frodo battles internally against its effects."

"Right. Wow, cool," he said, nodding.

I asked, "Do you, like other Tolkien fans, have a favorite quote?"

He smiled and nodded. "Well, it's when Frodo is told about the Ring and its power by Gandalf. Frodo says, 'I wish it need not have happened in my time'. And then Gandalf says, 'So do I, and so do all who live to see such times. But that is not for them to decide. All we have to decide is what to do with the time that is given us'."

"Oh. Nice, not a victim, but a survivor." I said.

"What's yours?" he said, grinning.

I chuckled, "Well, Gandalf sends a letter to Frodo and says, 'All that is gold does not glitter, not all those who wander are lost.'"

Chris smiled, looked at me and began to laugh. "You are a wanderer."

"You are perceptive," I said and smiled. "So, Frodo, where are you in this story?"

He nodded, "Today?" His eyes moved toward the ceiling as he thought about it. "I guess setting out from Rivendell. I guess, almost at the beginning of my journey." Again, he smiled. I watched the healing power of his creative self. "I guess that makes you Elrond, the elfin healer."

"You've noticed my pointy ears?" We both laughed. "I like your metaphor. It's a great idea. The journey of the hero, but the ordinary hero. What made you think of it?"

"I was talking to Carl last night. We've been talking about you. I hope that was okay. I didn't know what to say to him, and we were talking about surviving, and he told me that he likes to read and listen to music to block out his voices. I told him that I do, too. I told him about the trilogy, and what it was about, and then when I went to bed I started thinking about what we had talked about."

"Good job," I said. As quickly as he had become enlivened and energetic he seemed to wilt before me.

"Can I come back here to bring Carl the books, so he can read them while he's here?"

"If you're willing to leave them with the nurse to give to him. You can leave a note for him if you'd like."

"Cool, I'd really like to do that." He seemed to drift away. He became sullen again.

"Where did you go?"

"Gandalf—my grandfather." I nodded. "Is he here?"

"He's waiting to see you." His eyes closed slowly. He began to rub his stomach. "What are you feeling?"

"What? Oh, I don't know," Chris said, staring at the floor. He rubbed the palms of his hands on his pant legs.

"Chris, if you can, try to know."

"Oh Yeah. Scared," Chris said nodding his head.

"Of?" I asked.

"Seeing my grandfather. What he's going to say to me," Chris said as he again wiped his hands on his pant legs.

I could see from the quickness of his breathing that his anxiety level was high. "What are you afraid he'll say?"

"That he's disappointed in me." He swallowed hard.

"And why would he be disappointed in you?"

"For being weak, you know, having to be put in a hospital, because I cracked up."

"Is that all you're worried about?"

"No. I think he's going to be angry with me, or ashamed of me, because I'm gay," Chris said, as tears filled his eyes. He dropped his head and his hair fell forward.

"What are you feeling?"

Chris shook his head and shrugged his shoulders.

"You're in a lot of pain, do you know that?"

Chris shrugged again.

"Each time we've talked I've felt a sadness fill this room like I've seldom experienced. It is so heavy that I've sometimes felt it sitting on my chest. It's not my sadness, Chris. It's yours. I know the weight of the pain you feel is frightening, but my hope is that eventually you will allow yourself to experience it, rather than try to turn away from it." I paused. I wanted to reach over and touch him, to console him. But, of course, I did not. "I know this is going to sound absurd, but there is no path in life without pain. A very wise man once said to me that life is full of surprises, and if you are lucky, some of them will be happy ones. The others you have to learn from." I waited and then added, "I guess that must sound like a lot of crap." I realized that I was lecturing him, but my time with him was growing short, and if he could take one thing I said with him I would feel I had helped him.

"No, not really. I mean when I was on the baseball team I knew that I had to practice and learn and improve my skills and stuff so that I could be ready for whatever happened in a game. I mean, no game is like another, so you have to practice and then just let what happens happen. If you fuck up, you learn from that. I guess you're saying the same thing. The worst thing you can do is not to learn from a mistake."

"Thank you."

"For what?" he asked.

"For listening and taking the time to understand what I am trying to tell you," I said, and then hesitated. "You see, I worry that, especially when it is important to me, like now, I don't make myself clear. I say too much. I ramble, rather than being concise and to the point. It is good to hear that I am being successful in my efforts to both understand you and to be understood by you."

Chris nodded. "Cool. Well, I do understand."

"Now, one more thing. It's about Jack Payden."

"What about him?"

"I reported to the authorities that he molested you. They've started an investigation. The police want to take your statement."

"I figured you had. What do I tell them?"

"Tell them exactly what happened, how it happened and when. Chris, they are not here to judge you. I know these people; they just want you to tell them what happened as best you can remember it. I'll be back to see you after lunch."

"Will I see my mom and my grandfather then?"

"Yes."

"Will you be with me when I see them?"

"Yes. First, I think we'll talk to your grandfather. Then, if there is anything else that needs to be said, we'll spend time with you and your mom."

"Okay." Chris said, looking forlorn, then he looked up at me and smiled.

"Where did you go?" I asked.

"Scared about this afternoon. Then I thought that you reminded me of Father John."

"How so?"

"I'm not sure, but he makes me feel safe and I trust him." He nodded at me and smiled again. "I guess I feel like you care about me, too." He looked away and shook his head no.

"What did you just tell yourself?"

He looked at me, "I…I…" he looked away. "I trusted Jack."

"So I might be like Jack."

"I don't believe that you are like him, really I don't," he said pleadingly.

"But something inside you worried, or warned you." He shrugged. "Chris, from your experience it makes complete sense to me that you would worry. Like Father John said to you, you should withhold your trust. Let people earn it."

"Are you angry at me?"

"Not at all. I know how hard that was for you to say to me. Your sharing that fear with me was a gift, not an assault. I know it took courage on your part, and that it is the first step toward opening the door to that part that can trust. That is the beginning of the process of change, of building those bridges."

Chris shook his head and smiled. "Thank you, Dr. Mitchell."

I smiled. I felt touched, my throat tightened. "Again, Chris, you are very welcome." There was a moment of silence and then I said, "We are going to have to stop. You've got work ahead of you: the police, and then your family this afternoon."

He took a deep breath, wiped his hands on his pants, stood as I stood and offered me his hand to shake. We shook hands. "Nurse Ortiz will come for you when they are ready to speak to you." He nodded and left the room.

Chapter Eighteen

AFTER MY MEETING WITH Chris I went to the lobby where Diane was holding vigil, and informed her that I would discharge Chris late that afternoon. She said David was still giving his statement to the police. As I stood to leave, David entered the lobby.

"How did it go?" Diane asked him.

"Fine. You were right, Doctor Mitchell. They were cool, and they didn't make me feel weird at all." He turned to Diane and said, "I really tried not to cry. But I did. But they were great."

"Good," I said, "I am glad it went well. And David, there is nothing wrong with crying. You were talking about something very painful that happened to you."

"Actually, I feel really good about doing it. I mean, I really do, Dr. Mitchell."

Diane said to me, "David has something he'd like to ask you."

"What is that, David?"

"Well, Mrs. Patrona told me that when Chris gets to New York he's going into therapy. She said that you are from New York and that you thought that Chris had to be careful finding a good therapist. She said that you were going to give him the name of a person you trusted. I was wondering if, I mean, I know I really need therapy too. And, well, I want to get someone who you trust."

"David, I was just going to the cafeteria to get something to drink. Come with me, and I'll tell you what I told Chris. Actually, I have the letter right here with a name and number. I can make a copy and give it to you."

Diane touched my arm and said, "Thank you, Dr. Mitchell."

As we walked toward the cafeteria David talked about his interview with the police. He thought others would eventually come forward. Then we walked through the line and paid for our drinks. As we found a table, David said, "Mrs. Patrona is pretty angry with me."

I was hesitant to respond, other than to nod.

"I guess I can't blame her," he said, frowning.

"She's having to take in a great deal, and all at once," I said.

"I know, Chris in the hospital, finding out he was molested, that he's gay, and about us. We lied," he paused. "I lied to her."

"I think she understands, or will understand," I assured him.

"She said she was hurt and worried when I just disappeared. She said she was getting sick worrying about me. She said she thought I was dead." His mouth twisted.

"Your parents must be worried."

"Maybe my mother is," he shrugged, "but I can't contact them until I'm eighteen, or they could still put me in a hospital. But, I think they are kind of relieved. I don't think they called the police or anything."

I wondered if I should gracefully push for us to leave, but instead I let my curiosity get the better of me. "Why is that?" I asked.

"I guess you know what happened to me in the shower in the gym." I nodded.

* * * * *

When David arrived at his home after storming out of the school gym, his father had not yet arrived. His mother glanced toward him when he entered the kitchen, but said nothing. "Did you know what Dad did?" David asked his mother. He was having a difficult time containing his anger. He was feeling especially betrayed by his mother.

"What are you talking about?" Helen asked, hoping Paul would arrive home soon. Although, she did not agree with what Paul had done, she knew that she could not give comfort to David without becoming the object of Paul's wrath. But in fact, it had never occurred to her to tell David.

"At the Eagle Scouts meeting Monday night. Did you know about what he did?" He knew that she did. In reality, it did not matter. She would never object to anything Paul did or said. She feared him too much.

"Yes, he told me Monday night. I didn't know he was going to tell everyone," Helen added, "but he told me afterward."

"Would it have made a difference if he had told you before?" The tone in David's voice was unusual. Helen turned to him as she heard Paul drive up into the driveway. Her anxiety was obvious. "Why didn't you tell me what he did?"

"He told me not to tell you. And besides, why does it matter?"

"I was attacked at school today," David said, his voice and lips trembling.

"Are you okay?" Helen asked, never looking up from the pot she was scrubbing at the sink.

"No, damn it! How could you not tell me?"

Lies That Bind

"Calm down, David, your dad is home. Don't start anything, please."

David watched through the kitchen window as Paul waited for David's brothers, who were walking toward the house. Paul reached out and hugged them both. The boys smiled as they talked to him. He noticed Paul laughing. David saw his mother watching him watch his father. "Why don't I remember him ever being kind to me? I can't even remember him hugging me. Look at how he enjoys them. Did he ever act like that with me?"

Helen sighed. She looked like she might cry as she glanced back toward David. "David, I just don't know. I always thought he saw something in you that scared him, but I guess I was wrong. When you were very young he delighted in you. But it seemed that at some point he stopped. It seemed like it happened when you started school. You were so bright, so much ahead of other kids your age, so artistically talented. Your grandmother thought your intelligence and talents threatened him. But I don't think it was fear."

"What do you mean?"

"I think it was dislike. I'm not sure he knew what it was until last week. Odd, but I think having it out in the open makes him feel more at peace. David, he really is a good man. Look at him with your brothers. When you are heterosexual he'll hug you, too."

"You know, before Grandma died she told me something."

"What?"

"She told me that she didn't like Dad because of the way he was. She said he was unloving. She told me not to think I was unlovable. Can I ask you something?"

"What?"

"Why did you stop being friends with Julie's mom?"

"What do you mean?"

"When we lived next door to them, I remember that you and Jane were really good friends. Then, it was like you never knew her anymore. Why?"

"Your dad decided that he didn't like her."

"No, I know that. I asked you why you stopped being her friend."

"Your dad said it was best. Why are you asking this now?"

David's face reddened, his lips trembled with anger. "Grandma said that she didn't like Dad. Then she said that she didn't like you or respect you. She said she thought you had no backbone, and that you were pathetic, and that she was ashamed that you were her daughter." Helen blushed and turned away from David. "I told her that she was wrong. I remember she touched my face and kissed me and said, 'You love your mother, and that is good, but just remember what I am saying to you.' Then she said she loved me." David moved away from the window. "It's weird, Mom. I remember that because when she touched me on the face and kissed me it felt wonderful. Why don't you ever kiss me?"

"Your dad is coming in. Enough of this. Don't make this our fault."

Paul entered the kitchen from the garage. He was carrying his jacket and tie in one hand and his briefcase in the other. As he set it all down on the kitchen table, Helen walked over to him and kissed him on the cheek. David glared at them both. It was clear to Paul that Helen was upset. "What is going on here?" Paul asked, looking at David.

"Chris told me what you did Monday night," David growled. His stare was piercing, his voice was filled with contempt.

"I told him to stay away from you." Helen had accidentally placed herself between David and Paul. Paul, gently but with purpose, moved her aside.

"How could you do that? Everyone knows, everyone. I was raped at school, you bastard!" David's heart was pounding.

"Watch your tongue, young man," Paul demanded. "What do you mean, raped?"

"In the shower. After baseball practice." David's eyes welled up. He hated it that his anger manifested itself in tears.

"By whom?" Paul asked, sounding concerned.

"I don't know."

"You weren't raped," Paul said, as he moved back to the kitchen table and opened his briefcase to remove an envelope. "You're a liar, that has already been proven."

David reached into his pants and pulled out the blood soaked toilet paper and yelled, "Does this look like I'm lying?"

"Well, I told them that you were going to change. This is your fault anyway," Paul said, glancing up at David for a brief instant and then back to his briefcase.

"You bastard, I hate you! I can't go back there. I can't go back to school." David was no longer surprised at how little he was able to affect his father.

"That's up to you." Paul shrugged his shoulders.

"I'm not going back. Everyone knows, and they'll all know about this, too."

"That's fine with me. I don't want you in the house any longer than is necessary," Paul said matter-of-factly, as he began to read through some

Lies That Bind

papers. No one said a word as David looked to his mother, who looked away. She had no idea what Paul's intentions were, but she knew not to interfere.

"What does that mean?" David asked calmly, but with growing anxiety.

"I was going to let you graduate, but you can get your GED at Fremont-Calloway."

"What is Fremont-Calloway?"

"It's a hospital in Colorado where they cure people like you," Paul said, never looking up at David. "Here, you can read all about it." Paul handed David the papers that he had been reading, as though they were brochures for a summer holiday.

"What are you talking about?" David did not take the paper from Paul.

"I was going to let you graduate and then send you there, but if you're not going back to Sacred Heart then you can leave right away. I don't want you in this house. I have two other sons to think of." Paul finally looked at David, "I am sorry about what happened to you. I never thought they would be violent. Do you need to see a doctor?"

"What?"

"Are you still bleeding? Do you need me to take you to a doctor?" His tone was calm. He almost seemed at peace with himself.

"What the fuck do you care?"

"Get out of my sight. Go to your room," Paul ordered, as he searched for the key to unlock David's bedroom door. "I'm locking you in. I'll bring you your dinner. You better pack some clothes. That is all you are allowed to take with you. Nothing else," Paul said, as he closed David in his room and then locked the door.

David remained frozen, standing in the middle of his room. He heard Paul talking on the phone. He was making plane reservations for them. "That is for this Saturday, at ten a.m...No, only one round trip. David Jarrett's ticket will be a one-way ticket...Yes, I will be returning on Sunday...Thank you," Paul hung up the phone.

That night, after everyone was asleep, David carefully crawled through his bedroom window. All he took with him was what he could fit into his backpack. His only regret was not saying goodbye to his mother and his brothers, but he decided that no one should know where he was going.

*****

"I didn't want to let anyone know where I've been staying, so if the police ask no one will have to lie. But the police haven't been around asking anyone, as far as I know. I think my dad figures he can save a lot of money and be rid of me."

"Are you going to NYU in September?" I asked.

"Yeah. After my birthday I'm going to get a job here, so I'll have money to fly to New York. I have a trust fund that will pay for most stuff."

His lips tightened. "I asked Mrs. Patrona if she'd let Chris call me." He took a deep breath. "If I should try to get into the dorms or…" He shrugged. "I gave her the phone number where I'm staying. Chris will know where it is when he sees the number. I am hoping that if we can't be roommates, we can at least be friends. I hope he can forgive me for blaming him, and for not calling him and letting him know that I was okay."

I sat quietly, although I wanted to give him some reassurance.

"No matter what happens, I know that I need therapy."

"David, I'm a psychotherapist and I believe very strongly in the process. So, of course, I am going to encourage you to give therapy a try."

"I want to do it."

"Like I said, I'll give you the same referral that I am giving Chris. I'm sure he'll find someone good for you."

"Thank you, Dr. Mitchell."

"Okay, then let's go to the front desk, and I'll make a copy of this for you," I said, removing an envelope from my pocket.

When David and I returned to the lobby, he sat and talked to Diane for a few minutes. He said goodbye to the Dinatos, thanked me, and left the hospital. I talked to Mrs. Patrona and the Dinatos regarding my plan for the last meeting with Chris. We agreed that Mr. Dinato would meet first with Chris and me. I explained that Mrs. Patrona could wait to meet with Chris, or she could begin the discharge process while Mr. Dinato and I met with him. She was anxious to have her son leave.

I explained to Mr. Dinato that I was hoping Chris might allow himself to experience whatever feelings arose during our meeting. I cautioned Mr. Dinato to give him whatever time he needed. He asked me how he would know, and I asked that he watch me so I could help him through the session. I also explained that after lunch I wanted to meet with Chris alone for a while, and then I would come for Mr. Dinato and bring him to the treatment room.

Diane pulled me aside. "Dr. Mitchell, can I speak to you alone for a minute?"

"Should we go to my office?"

Lies That Bind

"If that's okay, yes."

As I closed the door behind us, I asked, "What is it, Mrs. Patrona?"

"I know you can't give advice, but I need to talk to you about something."

"What is it?"

"Is Chris well enough to go to Columbia in September?"

"Yes. I would go as far as to say it will be very good for him. Let him get on with his life. But I do believe he should be in psychotherapy. It will be expensive, but I would recommend twice weekly."

"That's no problem."

"Then what is your concern?"

"Chris and David. I don't know what to do about them. My parents were going to give them both jobs. They were going to find an apartment together and go to college. Of course, when I agreed to this I didn't know what was going on."

"Okay."

"Now I do. David said he's still going to NYU."

"He told me that, too."

"Part of me wants to keep them apart, but I know Chris. And I really do love David. He's a good boy."

"So what is your question?"

"Well, I can help them out by letting their plans materialize. My parents are fine with giving them a place to stay until they find an apartment, and giving them a job so they can earn money. Or I can make it difficult."

"What does your gut say?"

"My gut? My parents are leaving for New York on Friday. I talked to Richard, he said he'd buy David a ticket to get him out of L.A.. Richard is a lawyer and can help him take control of his trust once he's eighteen. I'd like Chris to spend time here, maybe a month, and then I'd fly to New York with him and help them find an apartment in a safe neighborhood."

"You seem to have thought this through. How can I help you?"

"Is Chris emotionally strong enough to handle being gay, having a relationship with David, and being away at college?" She was distressed. She was not only battling with whether Chris was strong enough to go to college, but with her own fears of letting him go, now compounded by his hospitalization. "I don't want him having to be in a hospital again."

"Two things. My guess is that you are going to have a hard time keeping them apart if they decided they want to be together. If you are fighting it…well, that's added pressure. I suggest you talk to Chris and find out what he wants to do about his relationship with David."

"Okay. And the other?"

"Well, your father's advice when Chris moved to L.A. is still good advice. Make sure Chris gets involved in school activities, so that he has a support system, friends, activities that are separate from his relationship with David. And David should do the same. Chris is bright, energetic, outgoing, and athletic. I am sure he can find extracurricular activities."

Diane nodded and gave what sounded like a sigh of relief. "That is helpful. Thank you. You are a saint, Dr. Mitchell. I will talk to Chris. Thank you." She stood. I walked toward the door and opened it for her. "I'm going to ask Richard to buy David a ticket so he can fly to New York with my parents. He can stay with them and work with my father until Chris comes to New York. Also, Richard said he would help David take control of his trust. That boy is like a son to me." I nodded. "Of course, I'm going to talk to Chris about what he thinks is best for him. Thank you," she said, extending her hand.

After lunch, I headed back up to the ward. Chris was waiting in treatment room six for me. It was where we usually held our family therapy sessions.

"How did it go?" I asked him, as I took my seat.

"Okay. They said that they have the names of three other guys who have given or will give statements saying that Jack molested them."

"I know."

"Really? How did this all happen?" Chris was surprised.

"When you told me about your being molested, I filed a report. At first, he denied it. He said you were lying. Then your friend David came in and said that he had also been molested, and that he knew of others, also. This morning, David gave a statement to the police."

"David? David was here?"

"Yes."

"When? Why didn't I see him?"

"Only family members are allowed on the ward."

"When was he here?"

"I talked to David briefly. Mostly about his talking to the police before you talked to them. I also talked to him about getting himself into treatment. But I at no time talked about you, your being here, or anything you've talked about. I was very clear with him about that from the start, and he understood."

Lies That Bind

"No, it's fine with me that you talked to him. Really. I just wish I had."

"I want to be clear that my concerns about confidentiality are with you and no one else."

"I understand. I'm okay with you talking to him."

"He wouldn't tell me or anyone else where he was staying, but he did tell me that his father was trying to have him committed to some hospital. David's been hiding out, but he was able to finish at Sacred Heart, and take his finals. He said he was waiting for his eighteenth birthday to come out of hiding, but then he heard what had happened to you at graduation, and called your mother. She told him about Jack. David told her that he had been molested too. I guess that was on Saturday. David told his friends Julie and Peter all that was going on, and that Jack was denying it all. Well, I guess that's when Peter told David and Julie that Jack had also molested him. On Sunday, David came with your family to the hospital. Today he gave his statement. I don't think he wants anyone to know where he is, just in case the police should ask."

Chris nodded, "In case his dad wanted to find him, I guess," Chris sighed. "I wish I'd seen him."

"Your friend Peter Cartola also gave a statement. Actually, he's supposed to go down to the D.A.'s office sometime today to give a statement."

"Peter was molested, too!" He shook his head and said, "Damn. I would have never thought that Peter could be molested."

"Yes, he was. They think that Jack molested several other boys also. They will be interviewing most of the boys in his present and past troops."

"Oh God, I should have told someone."

"You did, Chris. You told me."

"But before. I should have told before."

"You go to that place quickly, don't you? You did the best you could, Chris. He won't molest anyone else because you told me what happened to you. You did it when it was the right time for you."

"Damn, I had no idea that Peter had been molested. I knew that David had been and I figured Derek, too, but not Peter," Chris said, shaking his head.

"Peter said the same about you. Chris, you have a lot of work to do in therapy. Like I said, I talked to your mother and grandparents at great length. Clearly, they're concerned and want to help, but you are going to have to do the work. If you continue to bury all your feelings, and deal with situations by becoming either angry or numb, all your relationships will suffer. It sounds as though your father's way of dealing with people was either intimidation or withdrawal from intimacy."

"I'm not like my father."

"No, you're not, but he lives inside of you, and so do your mother and grandparents." He sat staring into space, not moving, not even blinking his eyes. "Chris, we can't help who our parents are, but we can do something about who *we* are. You're going to have to learn to feel a full range of emotions, and how to communicate them to others."

"You mean like with David?"

"Relationships, like with David or any relationship that is more than superficial."

"I understand. Really, I do," Chris said, looking away.

"What are you feeling?"

"I don't know. No, I mean, well, scared and sad, I guess."

"Tell me, if you can."

"I'm happy that he graduated and stuff. But I'm sad that I didn't see him. I thought he had run away. He has an aunt or cousin up north someplace, and I thought maybe he went there. But he was here all the time, and I guess he didn't want me to know. I guess he's really angry with me." He paused and shook his head. "I guess that's really selfish. I mean it's better that he was safe. I can't blame him, I guess."

"No, it would be very hard for you to blame him. You'd want to apologize to him."

"Yeah, and maybe ask him to give me another chance."

"You said you felt scared, too."

"My mom, my grandparents," Chris sighed. "I mean, I know they love me. But I know in their hearts they're really disappointed. They'll say that they love me, but they'll be…" Chris stopped. "Actually, my mom will say what's on her mind, she always does. But, my granddad, he'll be quiet. He'll be cold."

"Like your father?"

"Well, not angry. He won't say stuff, but he'll think it. It will be in his heart."

"Your grandfather lies to you."

"What?" He turned and stared at me as though I were a fool. I wondered if everyone loses the ability to be so facially expressive when they become adults. In my case, I had never allowed myself the luxury of silently voicing my outrage. I had chosen to play the roll of the perfect son, in the perfect home, with the perfect parents.

Lies That Bind

"What didn't you understand?"
"No, he doesn't lie," he said, adamantly.
"But he will withhold the truth from you?"
"I guess," Chris said with a shrug.
"He's done this to you before."
"No, but…"
"But your being gay makes it all different."
"I guess."
"So you don't trust him."
"What? No, I trust him," Chris said again emphatically.
"I see, so you're in conflict. On the one hand, you trust him to tell you what he feels, but on the other hand, you think he'll withhold the truth of his feelings. It's different with your mother, she'll just straight out reject you. Is that it?" I found myself thinking about the future; thinking about what an interesting, challenging, exciting, and rewarding experience it would be for a good therapist to work with this bright, complex, conflicted, and sensitive young man.

"Yeah, I guess."
"Are you wanting them to be disappointed?"
"Of course not. Why would I want that?" He gave me a look that I had not seen before—the sarcastic smirk.
"Well, I don't know, but you've got it all scripted out that way, so I was wondering if perhaps you wanted him to be disappointed." He again gave me the look. He shook his head, tightened his brow, and twisted his mouth as if to say "whatever." "Is this where you say 'whatever' to me?"

Chris laughed. He nodded and said, "I was thinking it, but I decided not to say it."

"I see. Your face shouted it," I said, smiling.

He nodded and asked, "But really, why would I want that?"

"I don't know. But you've got it set up so that that's the only outcome. Your mother is going to be honest with you and tell you she's disappointed. Your grandfather will withhold the truth from you." I waited for a response, but none came. "If you're right, and you know how they will respond, then I must admit I'm confused as to why you're anxious. You know their hearts. You know how they feel. The only thing that remains is to hear your mother say it and to see whether your grandfather will tell you the truth of his feelings or withhold them from you."

"I guess."

"So you're both very powerful and all-knowing?" I waited. "I wonder if your fear is about *not* knowing, and about how you'll feel hearing what they have to say to you. I wonder if you're predicting the worst outcome so as to quiet your anxiety. I mean, you know how to deal with rejection."

"So you're saying that maybe I don't know how he really feels," Chris said, looking more agitated.

"I am saying that it's easier for you to predict the worst you can imagine than it is for you to suffer the anxiety of being open to whatever might happen." Again, he withdrew. "What's going on?"

"I'm feeling weird."

"Tell me."

"My stomach is queasy. My hands are cold, but I'm sweating, too. I feel like I can't take a deep breath. I feel like I'm going to jump out of my skin."

"Sounds like anxiety." I could see his agitation. "Good, that sounds appropriate. I'd be anxious if I were you, too," I said pointedly.

"Good? It doesn't feel good," he barked.

"No, it doesn't. But you can understand why you're anxious, can't you? Your grandfather is very important to you. You're questioning his feelings for you and his willingness to be honest with you."

"Okay."

"Shall I get your grandfather?"

His eyes welled with tears. "I guess," Chris said, taking a deep breath. "Yes."

I walked down the hall of the hospital ward, unlocked the door, and greeted Mr. Dinato, who was sitting in the waiting room. "Mr. Dinato, please remember what we talked about. I know it will be difficult for you to sit and see Chris struggle, but it's important that he start learning to experience and tolerate his feelings, whatever they are. Before you leave today, I promise you that you will have the opportunity to say all that you want to say to him. But first, give him time to search out his feelings."

"Okay, Doctor Mitchell. All I want to say is that I love him, and I want to help him."

"I know you do, and believe me, he knows that also."

Mr. Dinato and I entered the room. I sat across from Chris. Anthony sat in a chair next to him. "What's happening, Chris?" I asked. Chris sat looking at the floor and shaking his head. "I know this is very difficult for you," I said to Chris.

Lies That Bind

"I feel like I'm going to throw up," Chris said, as sweat gathered on his upper lip.

I slid a waste paper can over toward Chris and asked, "Are you feeling like saliva will start to pour out of your mouth?"

Chris shrugged and swallowed hard. He wiped the sweat from his forehead.

"Chris, try to stay in your body and let it do what it wants. If you need to throw up, then throw up. If saliva runs from your mouth, that's okay, too." Chris sat and continued to stare at the floor. Anthony looked at me. I continued to stare at Chris. Chris shook his head.

"No, you don't need to throw up, or no, you won't let yourself throw up?"

"I don't need to," Chris said, wrapping his arms around his waist.

I looked at Anthony. He was clearly distressed. Other than at the graduation, I imagined it had been a long time since he had seen Chris being anything but self-assured and in control. Right now, Chris looked nearly overwhelmed.

"Chris, can you look at your grandfather and tell him what's going on with you right now? Can you tell him what your concerns are?"

Chris made a moaning sound. His breath quivered as he inhaled deeply. Anthony looked over at me. I raised my hand slightly, signaling Anthony not to say anything. Chris continued to stare at the floor. "Grandpa, I know you're disappointed in me," Chris hesitated. I again signaled Anthony not to respond. "I know in your heart that you're disappointed and that you won't say so," Chris said, his voice breaking. With his arms wrapped around his waist, he started rocking in his chair. I imagined him as a child being held and rocked by Anthony.

"How does the thought of your grandfather being disappointed in you make you feel?"

Chris shrugged as he continued to rock and stare at the same spot on the floor. "Sad."

"Do you want your grandfather to be honest with you?" I asked Chris.

"Yes."

"Can you look at him and tell him that?"

Chris looked up and saw that Anthony had tears in his eyes. "Grandpa, I love you," Chris said, bursting into tears. He threw both his hands up and covered his face as he rocked back and forth in his chair. Then he pulled his knees up to his chest and buried his face in his legs. His crying was almost violent. Anthony moved to reach out to his grandson, but I cautioned him.

My eyes filled with tears as I watched Chris give in to his pain. Anthony wiped tears from his eyes. Chris sobbed loudly. I took a deep breath and asked, "Mr. Dinato, can you tell Chris how you feel?"

"Sonny, I love you. *Carissimo mio*," Anthony said. "I am not disappointed. I am always so proud of you!" Anthony said, as tears began to roll down his cheeks. "My pride sometimes feels like it will break my chest, it is so much." Anthony paused. Tears dropped from his eyes, as they did from mine. "I am sad, though," Anthony confessed.

"Why, Grandpa?" Chris asked through his sobs, looking up at Anthony. He looked relieved when he saw Anthony's tears. His hands fell from his face.

"It is my fault. I should have let you know more that I loved you and that I was proud of you. If you didn't know that I love you and would always love you, then I did you wrong, and you must be disappointed in me."

"No, Grandpa. You always let me know," Chris said, shaking his head. He was beginning to feel like all that made sense to him was being made nonsense.

"But then, why would you think I would be disappointed in you, that I would be mad at you and not love you anymore?" Anthony's love and concern were clearly expressed in his tone of voice. His pain was obvious.

Chris wept and continued to shake his head. Tears streamed down his cheeks and dropped off his chin. "Chris, try to answer your grandfather if you can."

"Because I'm gay." Chris's voice trembled through his sobs.

"Because that nice boy David is your boyfriend?"

"Yes—was my boyfriend. He hates me now. Grandpa, I was a coward. I didn't do what I should have done to help him." Chris clenched his fists as the disgust he was feeling for himself began to surface.

I raised my hand and signaled Anthony not to speak. "You're really angry at yourself for failing David, aren't you?" I asked.

"Yes. Damn, I hate myself!" he shouted.

"That's how you know that David hates you, too?" I asked.

"He said he did."

"He also said he loved you," I reminded Chris.

Chris shrugged.

Again Anthony began to speak, and again I held up my hand, cautioning him. "Are you sure he hates you?" I asked. "Do you think he could have said that in anger and fear?"

"I guess so," Chris said, even though he continued shaking his head.

Lies That Bind

"When he said what he did to you, out of anger and fear, did you stop loving him?" I knew my questions were challenges to long-held thought processes.

"No, not at all. But I really fucked up that day." He kept shaking his head. His voice was sounding impatient now.

"I see, so his words didn't destroy you. His words aren't as powerful as yours."

"I'm confused," he said with irritation.

"I know you are." He glanced up at me and glared.

"I failed David." Chris said and then turned to Anthony and said, "I tried to be a good friend, like you say, but I failed."

"Like your grandfather failed you?" I asked.

"What? No. What do you mean? He didn't fail me," Chris said emphatically.

Anthony nodded, and then taking his cue from me, he said, "Chris, look at all your father did to you and I stood by. Your mother knew best, but I stopped her from leaving him. Then you were molested, and I wasn't there to protect you. Then you worry that I will not love you. I must have failed you."

"No. You did everything you could do, Grandpa," Chris yelled. "And it wasn't your fault that I was molested. It just happened."

I said, "You don't believe your grandfather is to blame for everything that happened to you?"

"No, of course not."

"But he feels like he should have done more. Like you're feeling that you should have done more for David."

"That's different. I should have told David I loved him, and I should have told him what his father had done. It's different. I don't know," Chris said crying, "I'm so confused."

"Right now, I think confusion is good," I said. "Right now, you might think of confusion as a good friend, Chris."

"Why do you say shit like that?" Chris yelled angrily.

Anthony seemed to want to interrupt, but I stopped him. "You're angry with me, Chris?"

"How can you say that being confused is good? That's crap!" He paused, stared down at his hands, and then shook his head. "I am sorry. I didn't mean that." His anxieties about the destructive power of his anger were quick to follow.

"It's okay to be angry with me, Chris. I'm still here and I'm okay. What crap am I saying?"

"How is confusion good?" he asked.

I could understand his disbelief and discomfort with the idea that being confused was at all constructive. "Let me say that in order to undo what has been done, we might first have to make a mess of things. That mess will feel like confusion. Okay? We've got to get those demons out of their caves, into the sunlight." He nodded. "Chris, it isn't going to be pretty."

"Okay. I guess. But I just know I did something wrong. I must have."

"You must have, because David suffered the cruelty of his father and his teammates."

"I feel like I should have been able to stop it from happening."

"I know you do. It seems to me that you did all you could do at the time. If you had known what was going to happen, my guess is that you would have done things differently. At the time you did the best you could. Just like your grandfather." I thought about further confounding him by suggesting that, in his world, where people could save others from suffering, he would have to be blaming his grandfather for not saving him. Or that the other alternative was that he was the only person in his world. But I decided this was probably a bit premature.

After a moment of silence, Anthony looked at me. I nodded. Anthony said, "Sonny, we all do things that when we look back we wish we could do them over. There are many things I would have done over." Chris nodded and shrugged, but again was still focused on the floor.

"Chris, what are you thinking about?" I asked.

"I just keep wondering if you're really disappointed in me for being gay," Chris said, glancing toward Anthony.

"I am not disappointed that you are gay. I love you. It breaks my heart that you don't know that."

Chris again looked to the floor and shook his head. "You go to church every Sunday. I know what the church says."

"I do go to church on Sunday," Anthony said, reaching over and touching Chris's arm. "I go so that I remember that Jesus loves those who love, and judges those who judge, and turns his back on those who turn from him. I go to church and ask forgiveness for all the mistakes I've made and the pain I've caused people I love." Chris continued shaking his head. "You think that I am lying?" Anthony asked. Chris shrugged and wiped tears from his eyes. "Do you think that I love all my brothers and sisters?"

Lies That Bind

"Yes, of course."

"All of them?"

"Yes, sure," Chris said, looking up at Anthony.

"How about Uncle Mike? Do you think I love him?"

"Uncle Mike? Sure, probably the most of all of them," Chris stared at Anthony.

"Uncle Mike is gay?" Chris asked with surprise.

"Yes. And your cousin Tony is gay, too."

"Tony who works in your store?"

"Yes, my godson. Do you think I love him?"

"Yes," Chris said, taking a calming breath. His mouth remained open.

"Well, I love you more. Your grandmother and I talked about you and David months ago. She said that she thought you two might be gay. You know, when you asked if you both could live with us for the summer and work with me." Chris glanced up at Anthony. "Sonny, you are my blood. I love you, your mother loves you, and your grandmother loves you. If she heard you today, she'd smack you on the side of your head and say, 'What are you, stupid?'"

Chris suddenly looked downcast.

I said, "Chris, you seemed to be engaged in all that you and your grandfather were saying, taking in what he said, and now you've quickly turned inward again. What happened?" Chris shrugged and shook his head again. "Chris, try to stay with what's happening to you if you can. You were looking involved until your grandfather mentioned your grandmother, and then you withdrew."

Chris nodded his head, and then he sighed and shrugged again. "I guess I thought she would disapprove." I held up my hand to prevent Anthony from saying something.

"It happened that quickly. Are you still thinking your grandfather disapproves?"

Chris shrugged and then said, "No, but he has family who are gay."

"So you are back thinking you'll be rejected by those who love you."

Chris pushed the hair from his face and asked, "I guess."

"I see." He bent forward, leaning his elbows on his knees. He ran his hands through his hair and shook his head. I asked, "Is that how you know your grandmother?"

He turned his head sideways to look at me. "What do you mean?"

"Is she harsh, rejecting, critical, or judgmental? Is that how you experience her?"

He stared at me.

"I am asking you to step back and look at who your grandmother is, who she is in relationship to you."

He leaned back in his chair and exhaled loudly. Mr. Dinato stared at him.

"I know in that picture she doesn't know you're gay, but who is she in that picture?" He didn't respond, he seemed to be getting annoyed, he continued to shake his head. I could almost hear the voices arguing in his head, screaming at him. "Chris." He suddenly focused on me as though I had just appeared. "How does she see you and respond to you?" His chin began to tremble.

Anthony said, "*Carissimo mio*, she adores you."

Chris shook his head and burst into tears. The pain of allowing in the love that his family felt for him was surely exquisite. The work he had been doing to defend against it must have been exhausting. Letting it in had to be exhilarating, releasing a flood of emotions; unrealized pain.

"Chris, can you speak?"

He opened his mouth to speak, but sobbed instead. He wiped tears from his chin. He took a tissue, blew his nose, and sighed. His chest quaked. He shook his head, "I don't know how to describe it. I mean I believe this, and now I don't understand why I didn't know. I guess my head sees things in two ways. I know my grandparents love me," again his lips trembled. He paused, "but then something takes over. Something says something different. There's like a wall there."

I said, "That wall keeps their love out, and keeps you from being able to express the love inside of you."

He nodded.

"Chris, it took years to build that wall, and psychotherapy is the best way I know of to dismantle it."

He nodded. I looked at Anthony, and noticed tears on his cheeks. My throat tightened. I envied Chris his grandfather's love. I also appreciated it.

"Chris," I said, "do you have a sense of how quickly you see yourself as doing harm to others and assume they have turned against you?" I asked. "Do you understand how alive that part of you is, and the self-hate it holds for you? It's as though it were your closest companion. And if you don't allow other parts of you to breathe, it will be your only companion."

Chris nodded and began to cry. "I don't understand."

I asked, "What don't you understand?"

"I thought people would never want to talk to me again. I was sure of it. I thought David went away because of me."

Lies That Bind

Anthony said, "He went away because of his father."

I said, "Yes, David was angry, Chris. And yes, he struck out at you. Probably because he knew he could and that you would still care about him. And yes, he withdrew from you, just like your father did." Chris looked at me; he was still crying. "But David is not your father. David cares about you, and, remarkably after all he's been through in his life, he's fighting his demons and you are not one of them. In fact, I would guess you're part of his strength. Do you understand?"

"I think so."

"I don't know how it is that he found a place for you, with all the neglect and abuse he's experienced. All I can figure is that it was through the love of his grandparents. I think he saw the bond you have with your grandparents and recognized a place of safety where he could find love. But how it happened isn't important right now. What's important is that it did happen.

"Chris, we are going to have to stop soon. Here is the letter with instructions for you on how to get in touch with the person I talked to you about. You are very fortunate to have a family who loves you as much as they do. Not everyone who is gay is as fortunate as you—David is a good example of that.

"I'm going to go to the office and sign your release papers now. I'll leave you here to talk to your grandfather. If your mother is done, I'll bring her in to see you. But before I go, would you do something for me, Chris?"

"Sure."

"Would you hum for your grandfather the tune you hummed for me before? Mr. Dinato, see if you know this tune."

Chris hummed.

"Oh yes, sure, that's an old Italian song."

"And how would Chris know that tune?"

"I used to sing it to him when he was a baby, and he would get so excited when I would hold him and sing it. He would kick his feet and laugh and wave his hands. He was such a happy and beautiful baby. Now he is a beautiful young man," Anthony said, as he pinched Chris's cheek. "Doctor, let me show you his baby picture. I carry it here with me all the time," Anthony said with obvious pride, as he pulled out his wallet. "Look at those eyes. They're so big! He gets them from me. They say when I was a baby I had really big eyes, too."

I looked at the picture, "You're right, Mr. Dinato, he was a beautiful boy. Any reasonable man would have been proud to have him as a son,"

I said, as I nodded at Chris. I noticed that not only did tears fill his eyes again, but now they freely streamed down his cheeks. "Chris, good luck," I said, as I stood. Chris stood, wiping his eyes. Anthony also rose. They both shook my hand.

"Thank you, Doctor," Chris said.

"Yes, thank you," Anthony said.

I smiled and waved to both of them as I walked out of the room. Before the door closed behind me, I stuck my head back in and said, "Chris, I see your mother and your grandmother. I'll let them in and bring them to the room."

When I returned with the two women, Diane threw her arms around her son. Again Chris sobbed. Diane cried silently as she stroked his head. Anthony nodded to me. Diane released Chris as he moved toward his grandmother. They embraced. "*Peschadelle*, kiss your grandma," she said. He kissed her on the cheek, then they hugged again. Diane reached over and gently wiped the tears from Chris's face. I decided that whatever they had to say to each other could be said while I signed Chris's discharge papers. As I left the room I heard Diane say, "How could you ever imagine that I'd hate you? Chris, you are my heart."

"Dr. Mitchell?" Nurse Ortiz called out. "Carl said that you would be seeing him this afternoon."

"Yes, I'll see him at three."

"It's almost that now."

"Room three," I said, as I continued to sign the appropriate papers in Chris's chart. "The Bellesanos will be ready to leave soon. All the paper work is in order. So when they're ready, could you please escort them off the ward?" I asked, as I looked for Carl's chart.

"Sure, I'd be happy to. He seems like a nice kid, very polite and well mannered," she said. I nodded and smiled. "A handsome boy, too," she added.

"I have a meeting with Dr. Torrel at four. Can you have Mr. Bellesano's chart ready?"

"Yes, Doctor," Nurse Ortiz said.

As I walked down the hall, I saw Chris leaning into treatment room three. He was shaking Carl's hands. Then they gave each other a hug. I noticed that Chris's shirt was wet—sweat on the back, tears on the front.

"Hang in there, dude," Chris was saying. "Dr. Mitchell is cool. He'll help you straighten things out. He helped me a lot." As he turned to leave the room, he noticed me standing there, and smiled. "I like Carl. He's going to be okay, right?"

Lies That Bind

I didn't answer, but I smiled and nodded and said, "Make that call when you get settled in the City." We smiled at each other. "Okay?"

"My mother said David gave her his phone number and that he's going to NYU, and that he wants to talk to me about living together. I know where he's staying," he said, smiling. "I know the phone number." His excitement warmed me.

"Thank you again, Dr. Mitchell. I promise I'll make that call."

"And when you make a promise..." We smiled at each other.

"Dr. Mitchell, can I hug you?" he asked. I nodded and opened my arms, and we hugged. He laid his head gently on my shoulder and sighed. "Thank you," he whispered. I could feel the power of his arms in the gentleness of his embrace and the strength of his character in the honesty of his appreciation. It was hard not to hope that I would see him again.

I watched as Chris joined his mother, Anthony, and Josephine while Nurse Ortiz unlocked the door. Again, Chris turned, pushed the hair from his eyes, gave me the full force of his smile, and waved.

I looked toward Carl as I stepped into treatment room four. I was not at all surprised that he and Chris had become friends.

"Hi, Carl," I said as the door closed behind me.

"Hi, Dr. Mitchell."